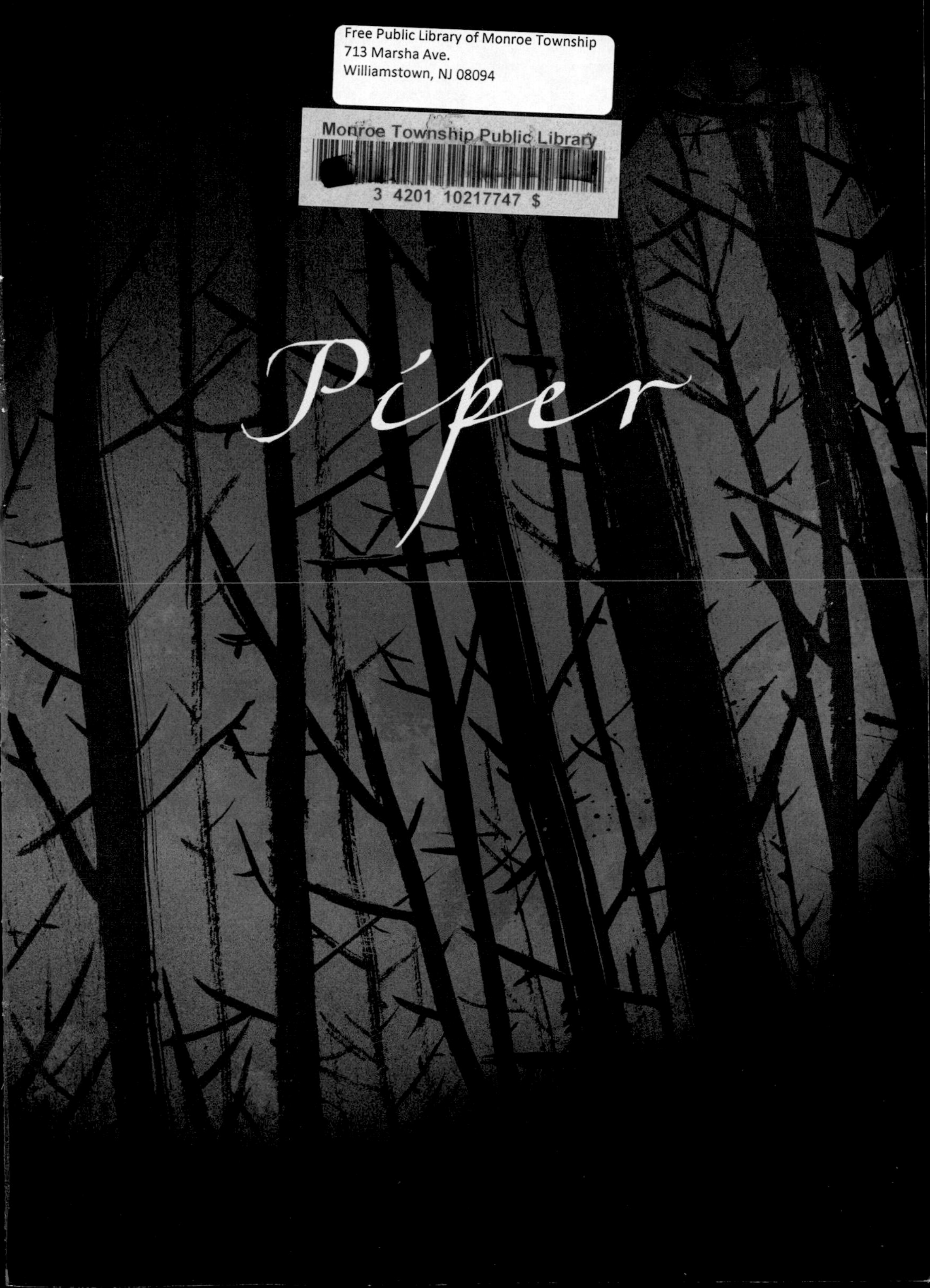
Piper

JAY ASHER & JESSICA FREEBURG

Piper

ILLUSTRATED BY JEFF STOKELY

INK ASSISTANCE BY GIDEON KENDALL
COLORS BY TRIONA FARRELL
LETTERING BY ED DUKESHIRE

RAZORBILL

An Imprint of Penguin Random House

RAZORBILL®

An Imprint of Penguin Random House
Penguin.com

RAZORBILL & colophon is a registered trademark of Penguin Random House LLC.

First published in the United States of America by Razorbill,
an imprint of Penguin Random House LLC, 2017

Text copyright © 2017 Jay Asher and Jessica Freeburg
Illustration copyright © 2017 Jefferson Clap

ISBN: 9780448493664

Printed in Canada

3 5 7 9 10 8 6 4 2

To:

Landon, Logan, Ella, and Brielle Freeburg

&

JoanMarie and Isaiah Asher

Seeking History in a Legend

The Pied Piper legend has been told for centuries. Through repeated tellings and adjustments, it has maintained certain questions and confusions.

As authors, our previous books touched on spooky subjects, unintended consequences, and flawed people brought together because of their flaws. All of these—our fascinations—are found in this medieval legend from a German village.

Researching earliest mentions of the Piper, we found sources quoting the first words in Hameln's town records, written in the *Chronica ecclesiae Hamelensis* of AD 1384:

"It is 100 years since our children left."

The lack of details felt eerie. Where did the children go? Why did they leave? It seemed as if Hameln was trying to forget.

Hameln archivists now deny that the above town record exists. But there is the *Catena Aurea*, written fifty years later, which includes a story with interesting specifics:

"…a very unusual, strange story, which happened in the town of Hameln…"

"…in the year 1284. A young man, beautiful and very well-dressed, so that all who saw him were astonished whether by his form or clothing…"

"…began to whistle through the whole city. And all the children who heard his pipe, almost 130 of them, followed him…"

"They vanished and went away…"

"…the mother of deacon Johann von Lude saw the children depart."

Later versions follow a pattern of adding history back into the story, as well as fiction. We learn of the Piper ridding Hameln of rats, but not why town leaders refused to pay what they'd agreed. And how did the Piper know what musical notes to play? Who was he? In his time there, *did* he connect with any villagers? If so, were they outcasts like him? Were there consequences to these relationships? Is that why we know as much—or as little—as we do?

Something happened in Hameln!

And we've waited over seven hundreds years to find out what.

JAY ASHER & JESSICA FREEBURG

Piper

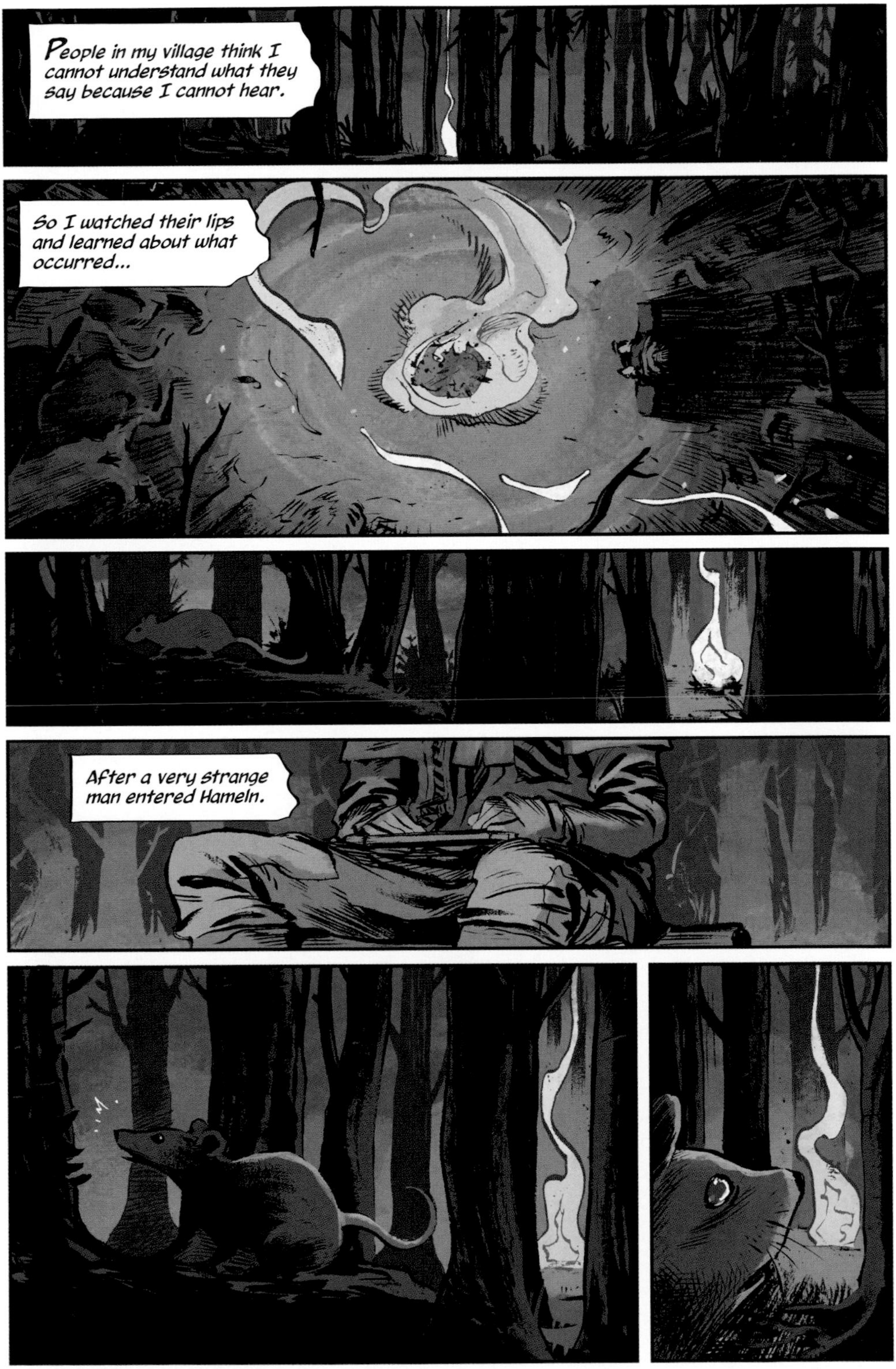
People in my village think I cannot understand what they say because I cannot hear.
So I watched their lips and learned about what occurred...
After a very strange man entered Hameln.

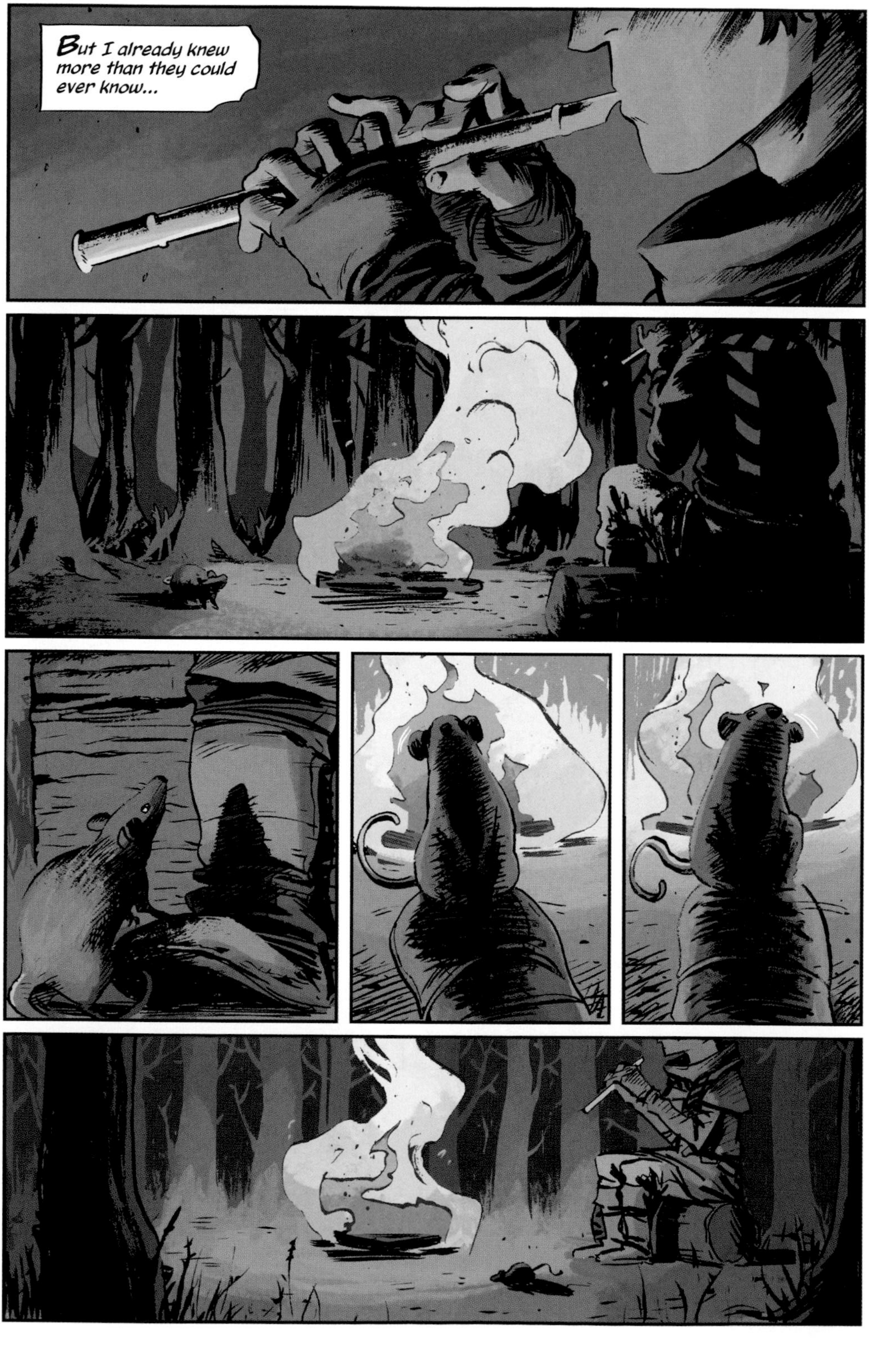
But I already knew more than they could ever know...

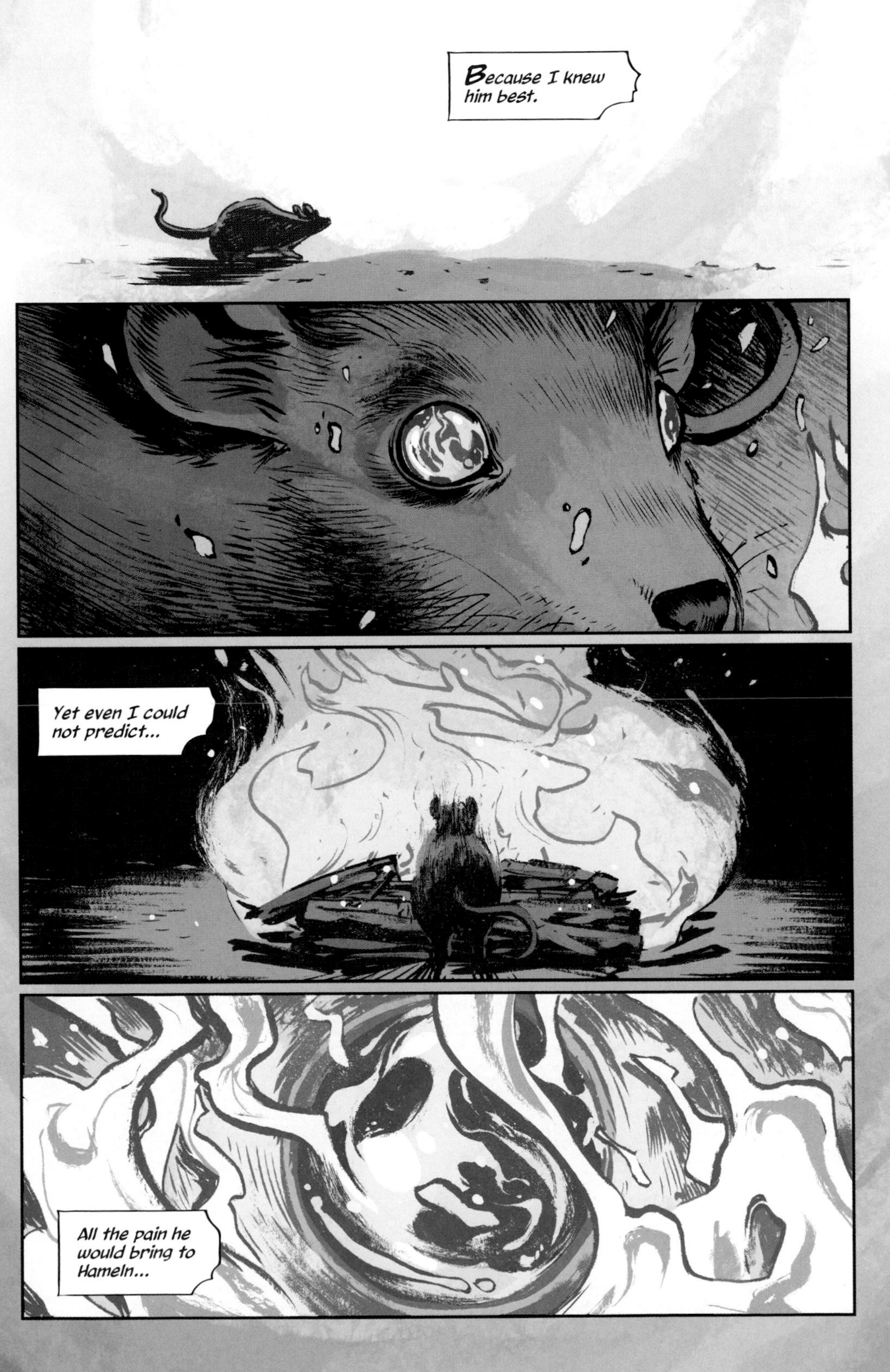
Because I knew him best.
Yet even I could not predict...
All the pain he would bring to Hameln...

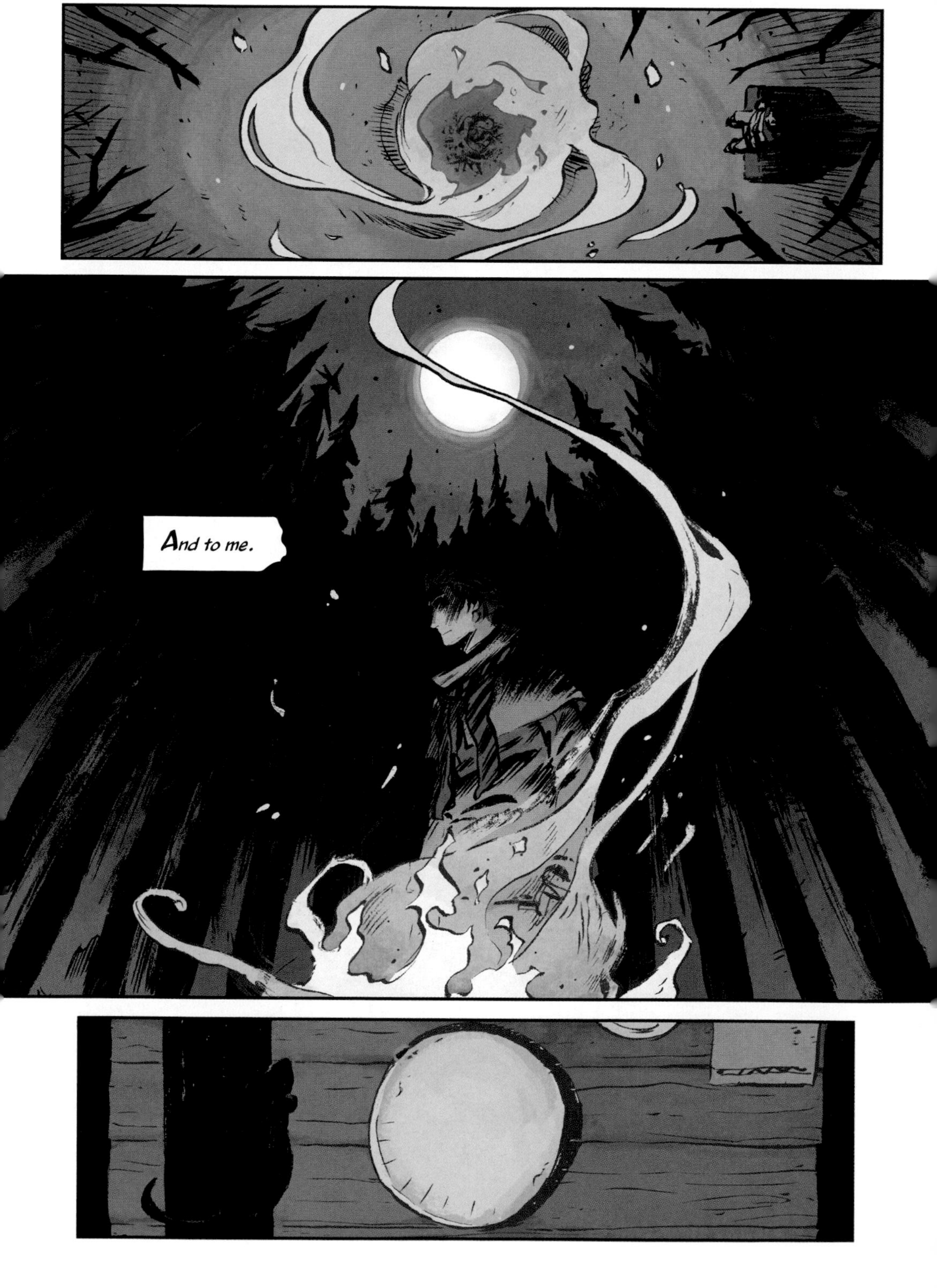
And to me.

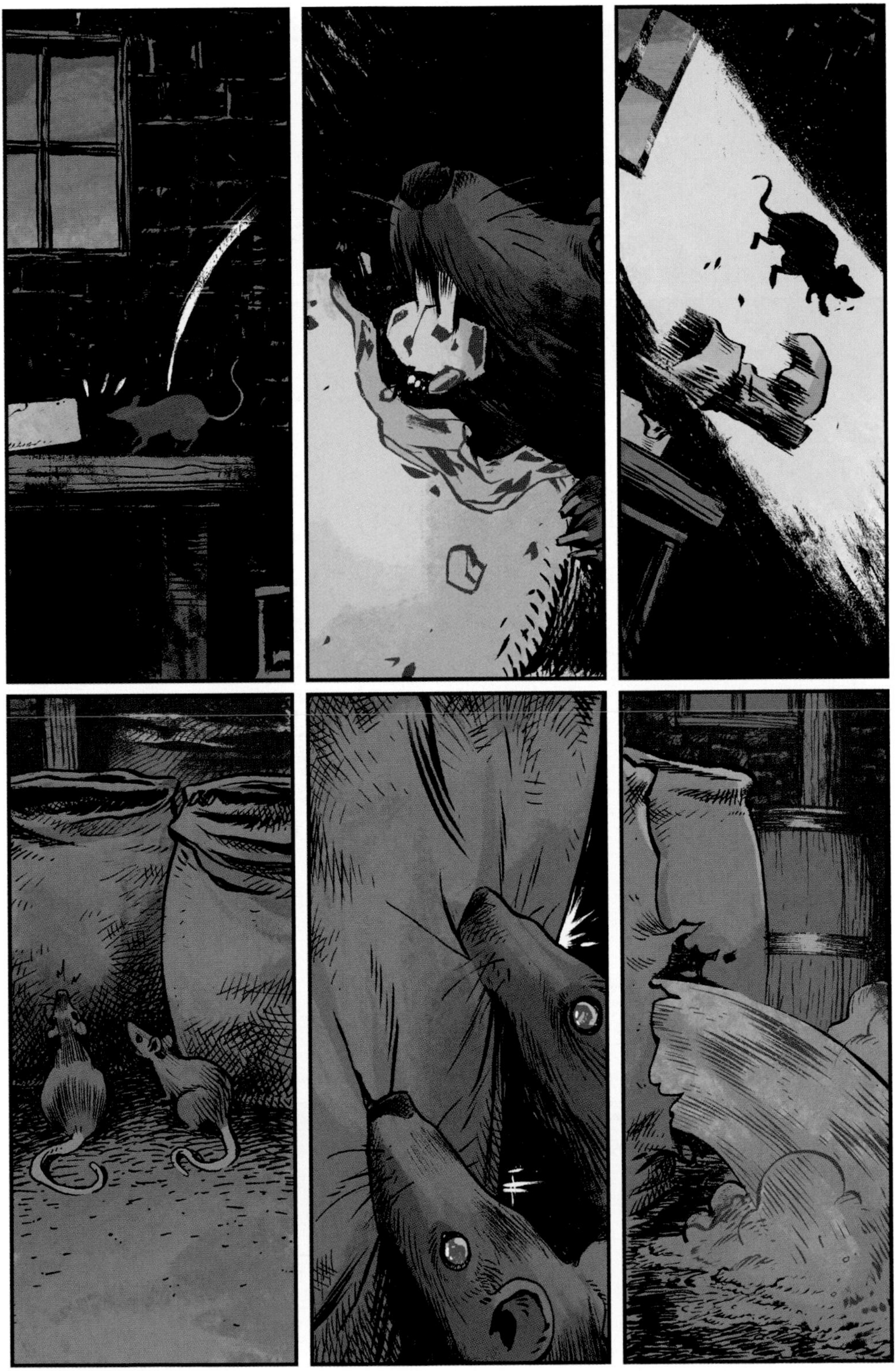

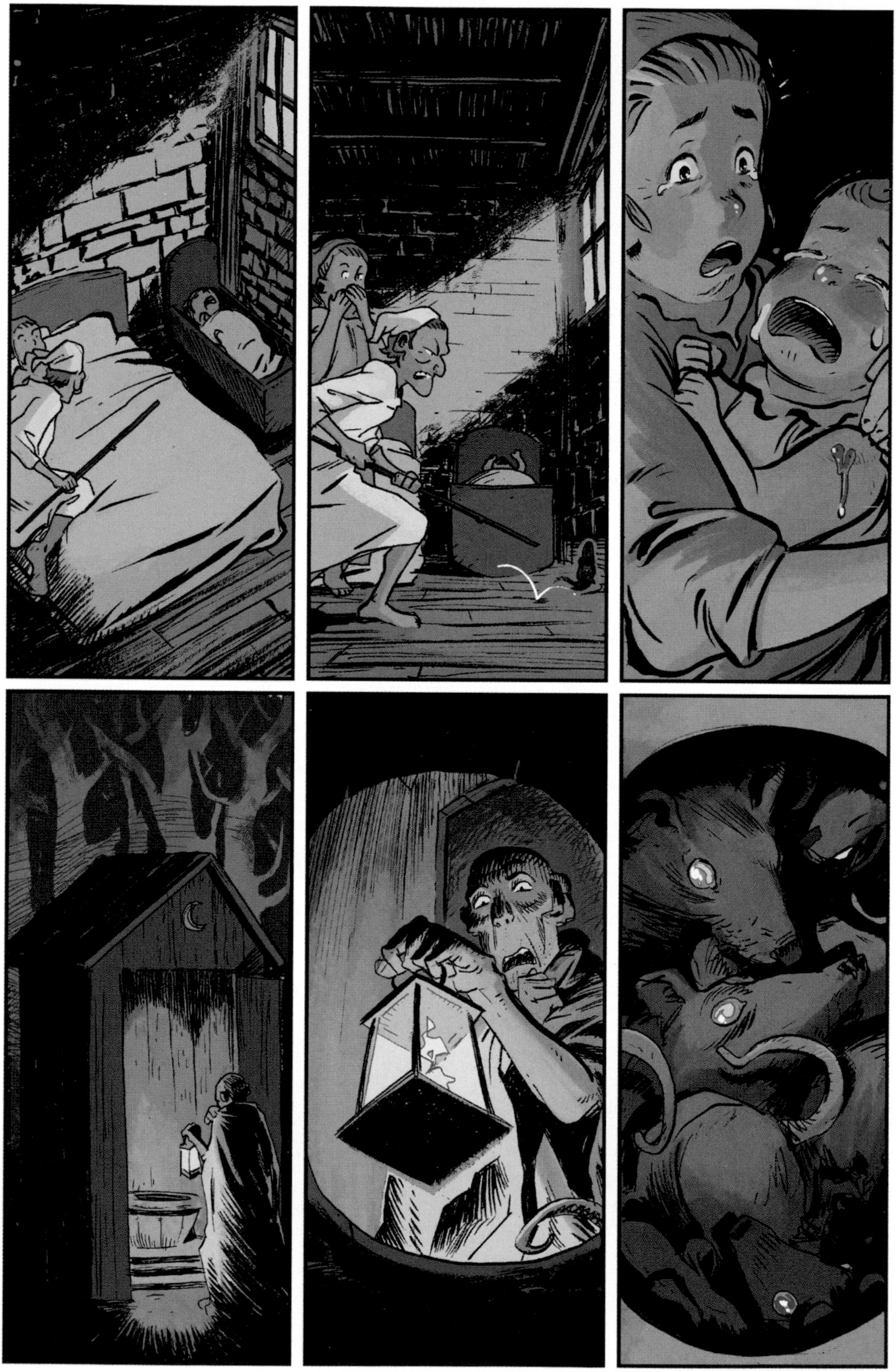

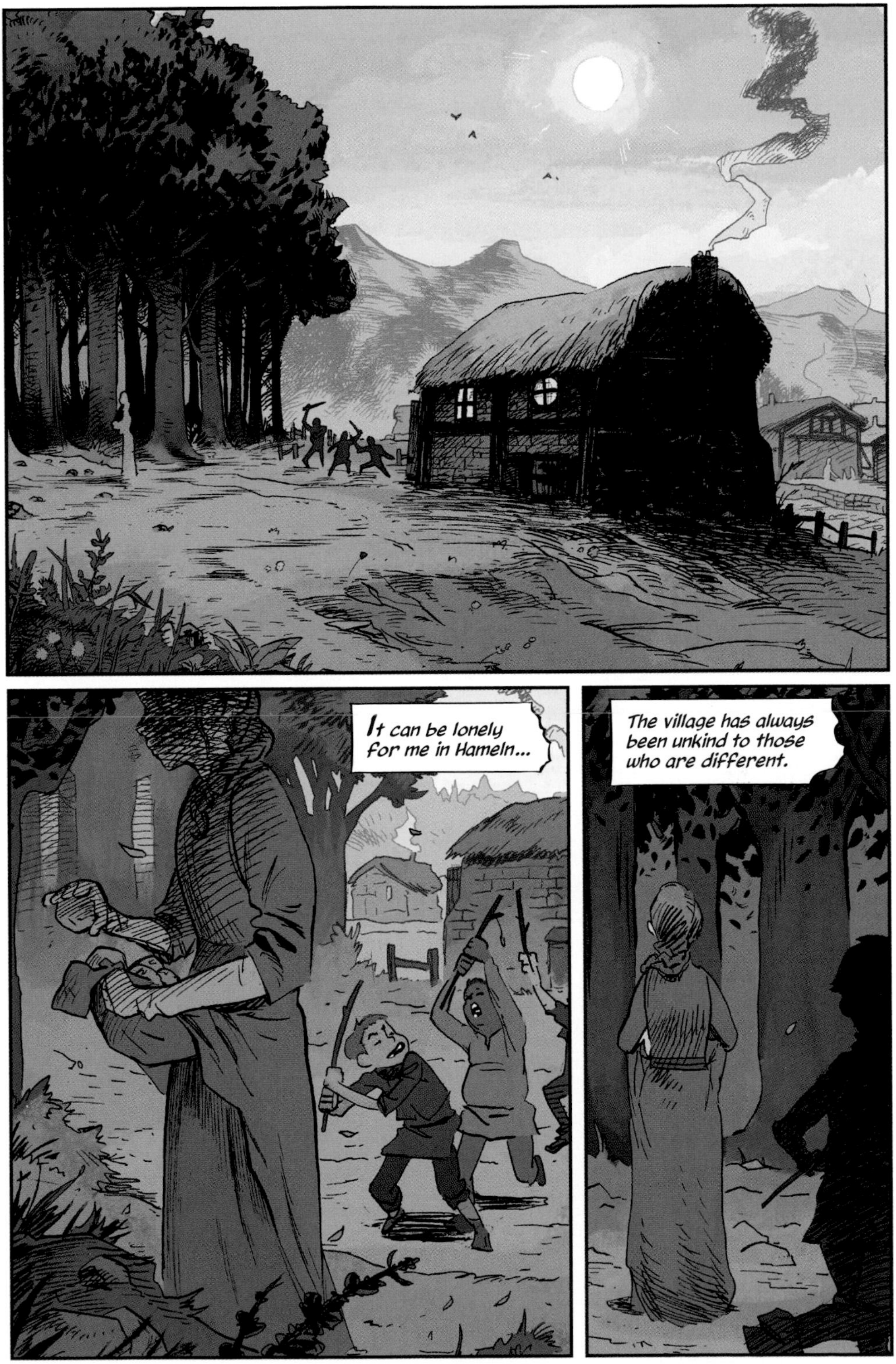
It can be lonely for me in Hameln...
The village has always been unkind to those who are different.

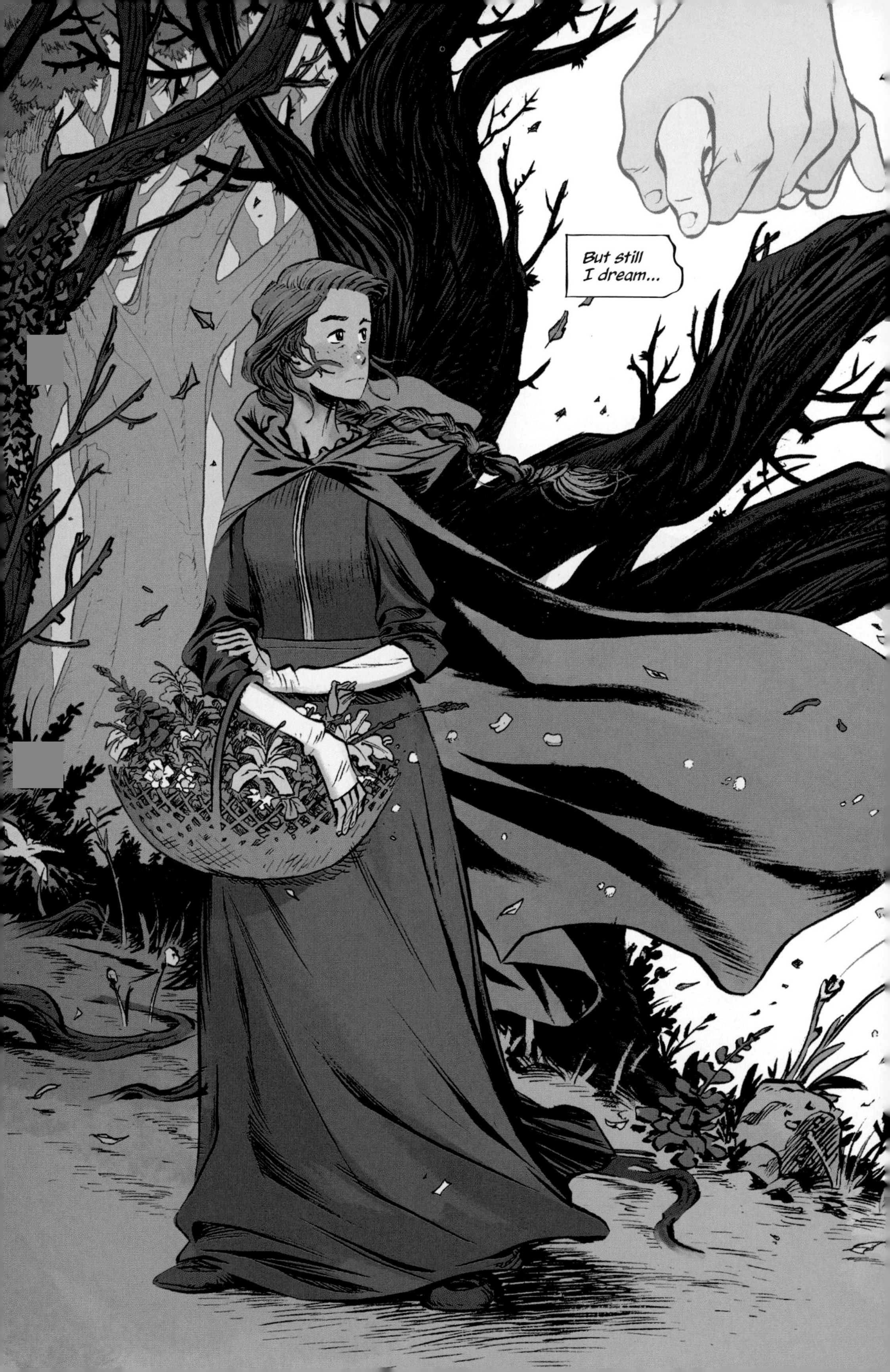
But still I dream...

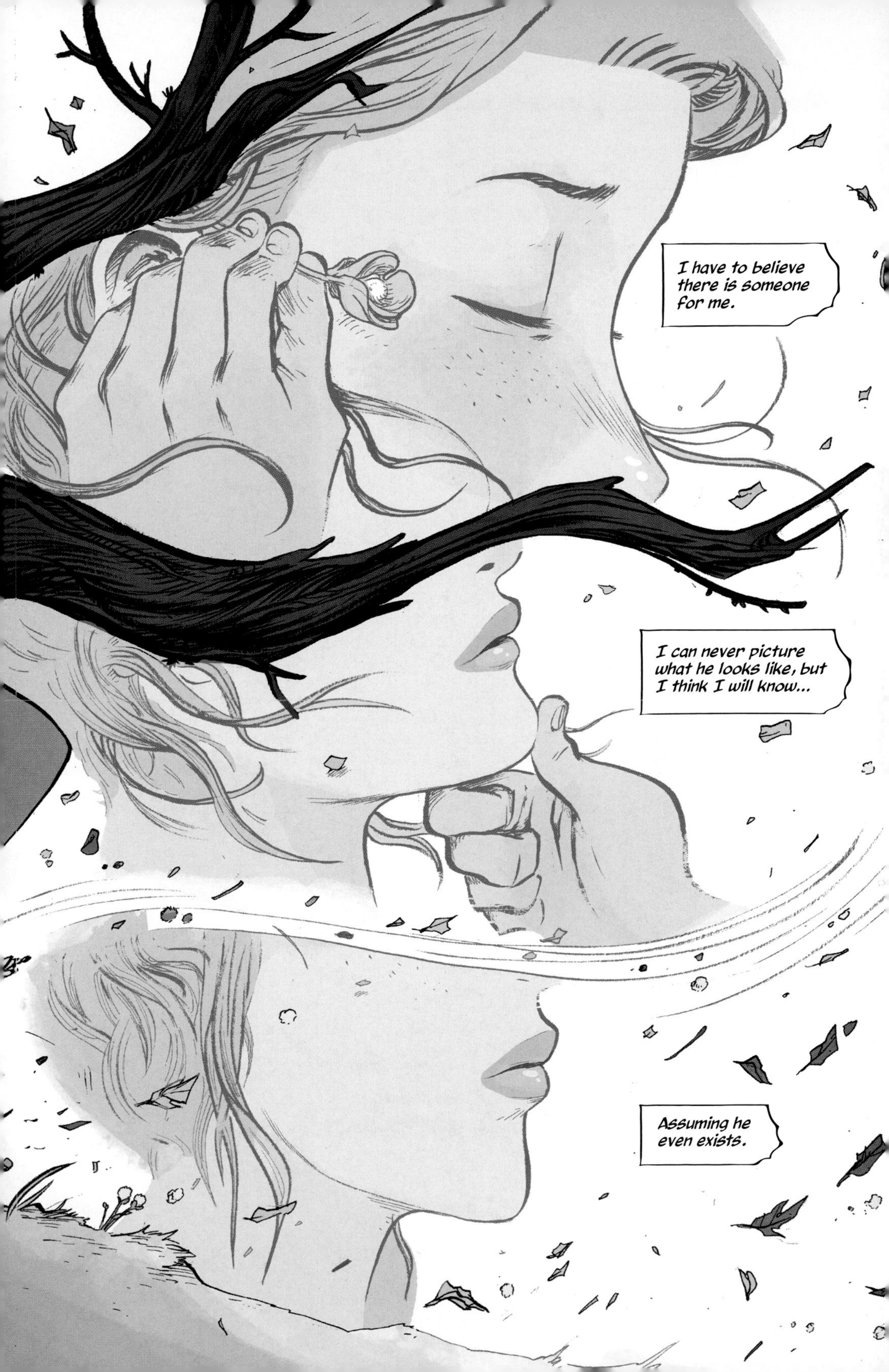
I have to believe there is someone for me.
I can never picture what he looks like, but I think I will know...
Assuming he even exists.

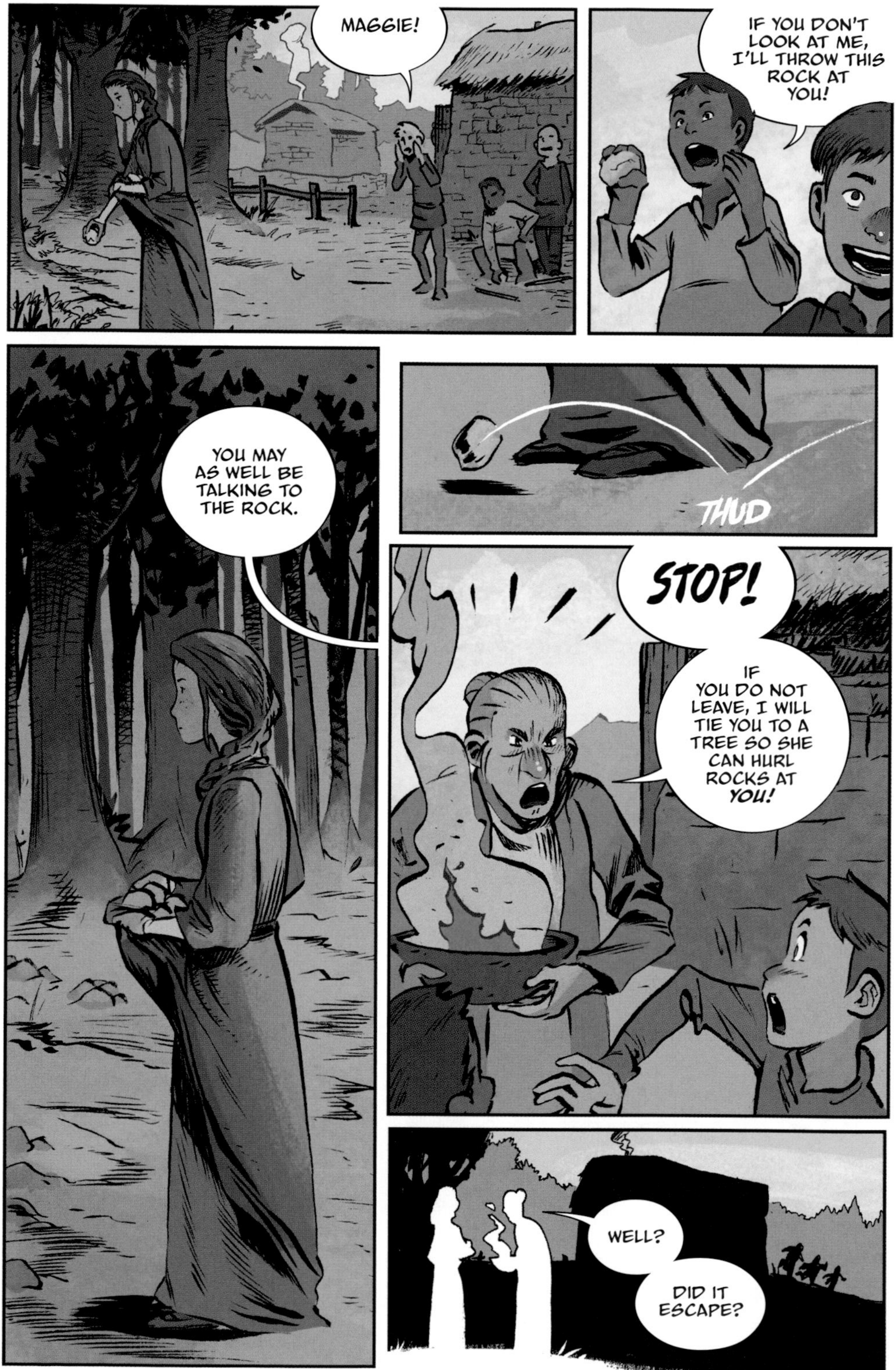
MAGGIE!
IF YOU DON'T LOOK AT ME, I'LL THROW THIS ROCK AT YOU!
YOU MAY AS WELL BE TALKING TO THE ROCK.
THUD
STOP!
IF YOU DO NOT LEAVE, I WILL TIE YOU TO A TREE SO SHE CAN HURL ROCKS AT YOU!
WELL?
DID IT ESCAPE?

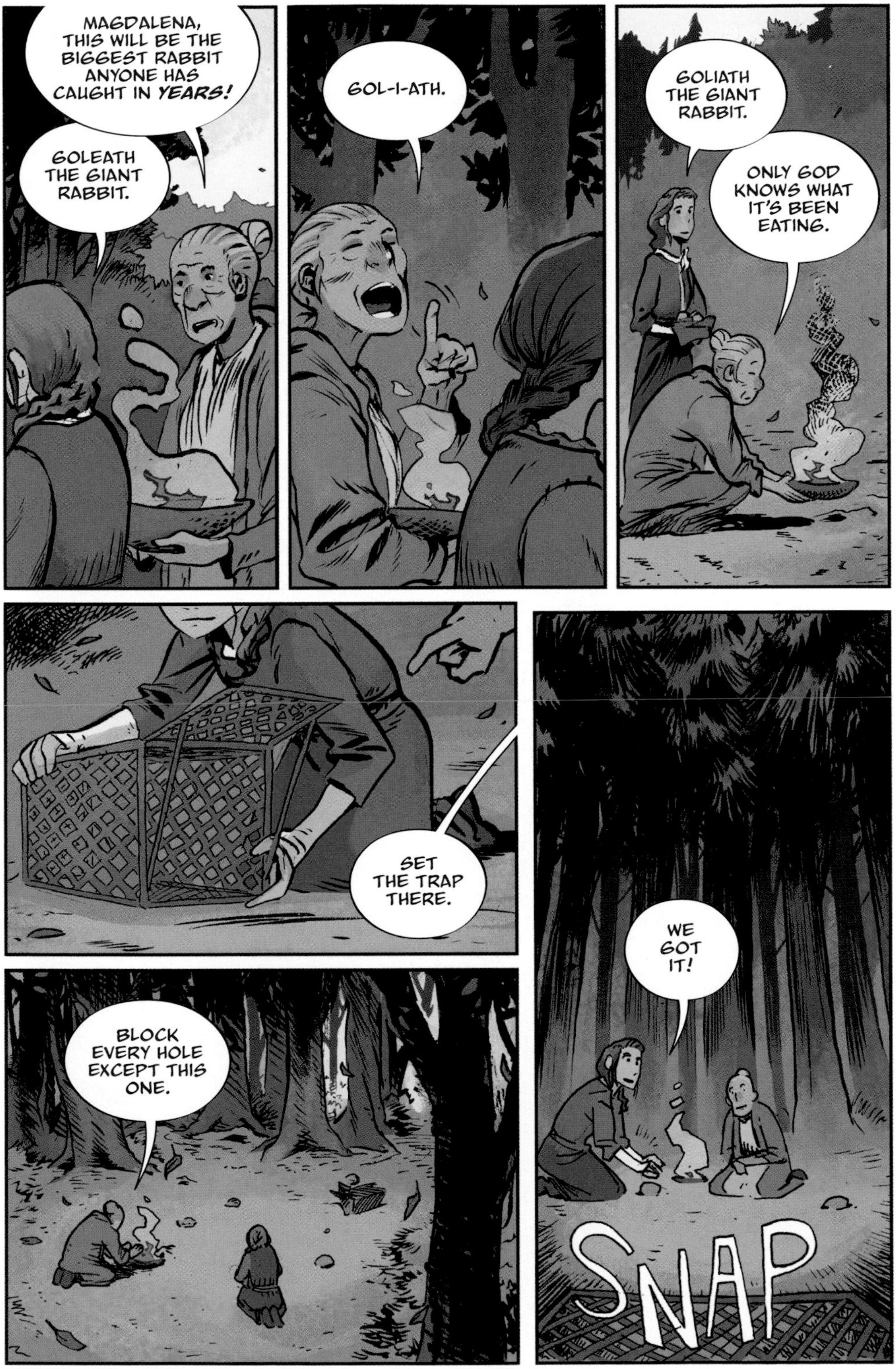
MAGDALENA, THIS WILL BE THE BIGGEST RABBIT ANYONE HAS CAUGHT IN *YEARS!*
GOLEATH THE GIANT RABBIT.
GOL-I-ATH.
GOLIATH THE GIANT RABBIT.
ONLY GOD KNOWS WHAT IT'S BEEN EATING.
SET THE TRAP THERE.
BLOCK EVERY HOLE EXCEPT THIS ONE.
WE GOT IT!
SNAP

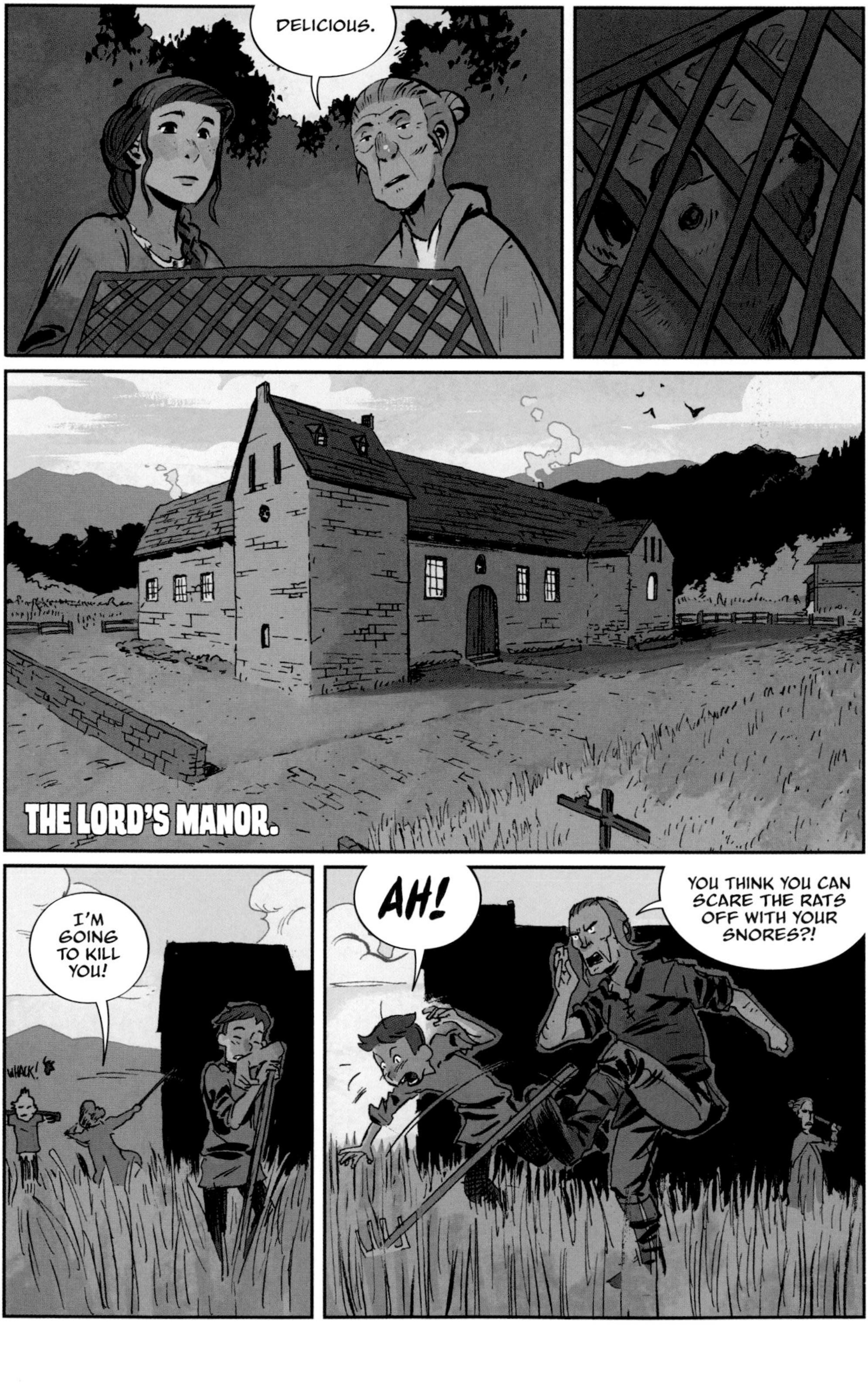
DELICIOUS.
THE LORD'S MANOR.
I'M GOING TO KILL YOU!
WHACK!
AH!
YOU THINK YOU CAN SCARE THE RATS OFF WITH YOUR SNORES?!

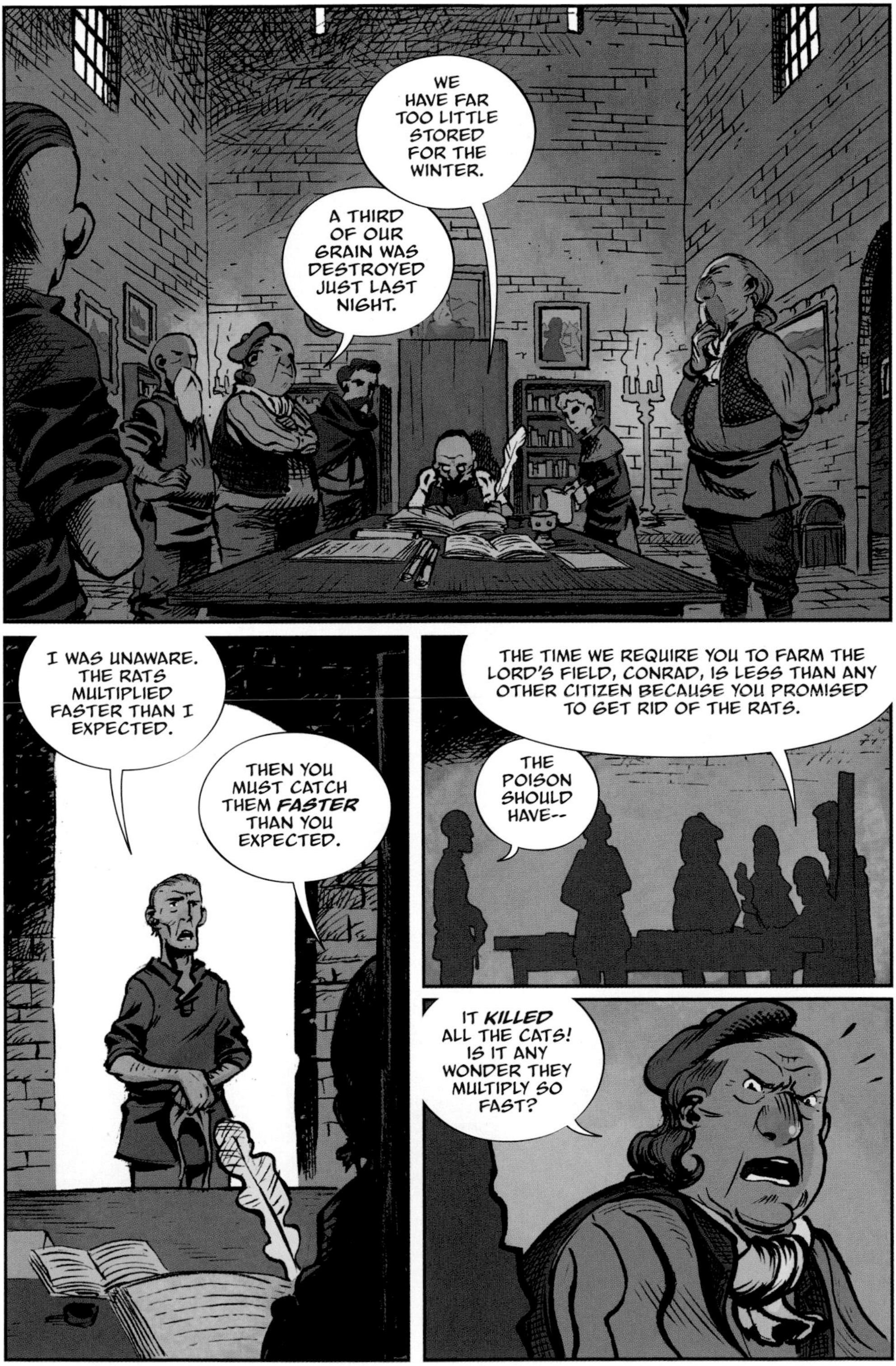
WE HAVE FAR TOO LITTLE STORED FOR THE WINTER.
A THIRD OF OUR GRAIN WAS DESTROYED JUST LAST NIGHT.
I WAS UNAWARE. THE RATS MULTIPLIED FASTER THAN I EXPECTED.
THEN YOU MUST CATCH THEM *FASTER* THAN YOU EXPECTED.
THE TIME WE REQUIRE YOU TO FARM THE LORD'S FIELD, CONRAD, IS LESS THAN ANY OTHER CITIZEN BECAUSE YOU PROMISED TO GET RID OF THE RATS.
THE POISON SHOULD HAVE--
IT ***KILLED*** ALL THE CATS! IS IT ANY WONDER THEY MULTIPLY SO FAST?

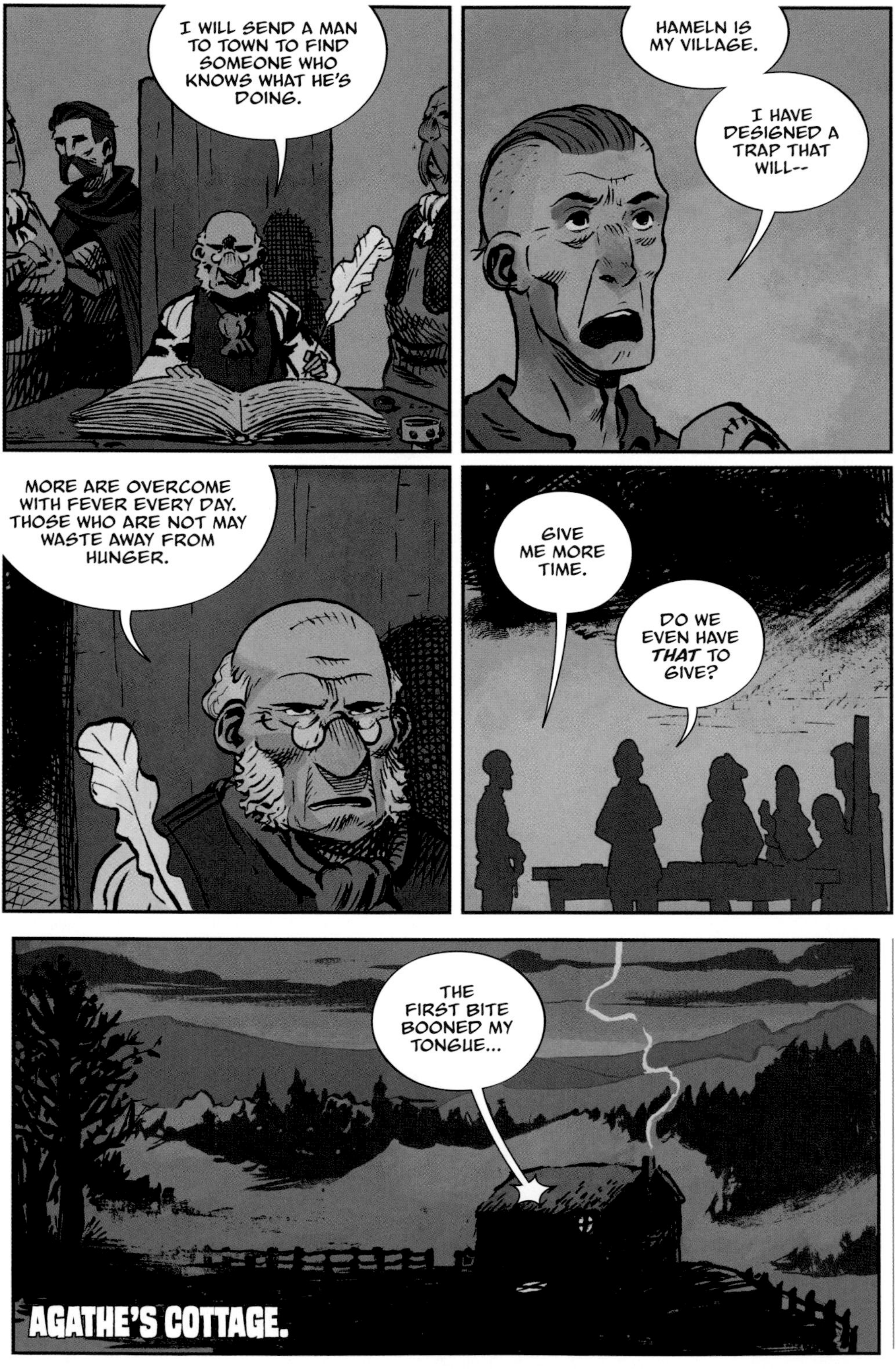
I WILL SEND A MAN TO TOWN TO FIND SOMEONE WHO KNOWS WHAT HE'S DOING.
HAMELN IS MY VILLAGE.
I HAVE DESIGNED A TRAP THAT WILL--
MORE ARE OVERCOME WITH FEVER EVERY DAY. THOSE WHO ARE NOT MAY WASTE AWAY FROM HUNGER.
GIVE ME MORE TIME.
DO WE EVEN HAVE *THAT* TO GIVE?
THE FIRST BITE BOONED MY TONGUE...
AGATHE'S COTTAGE.

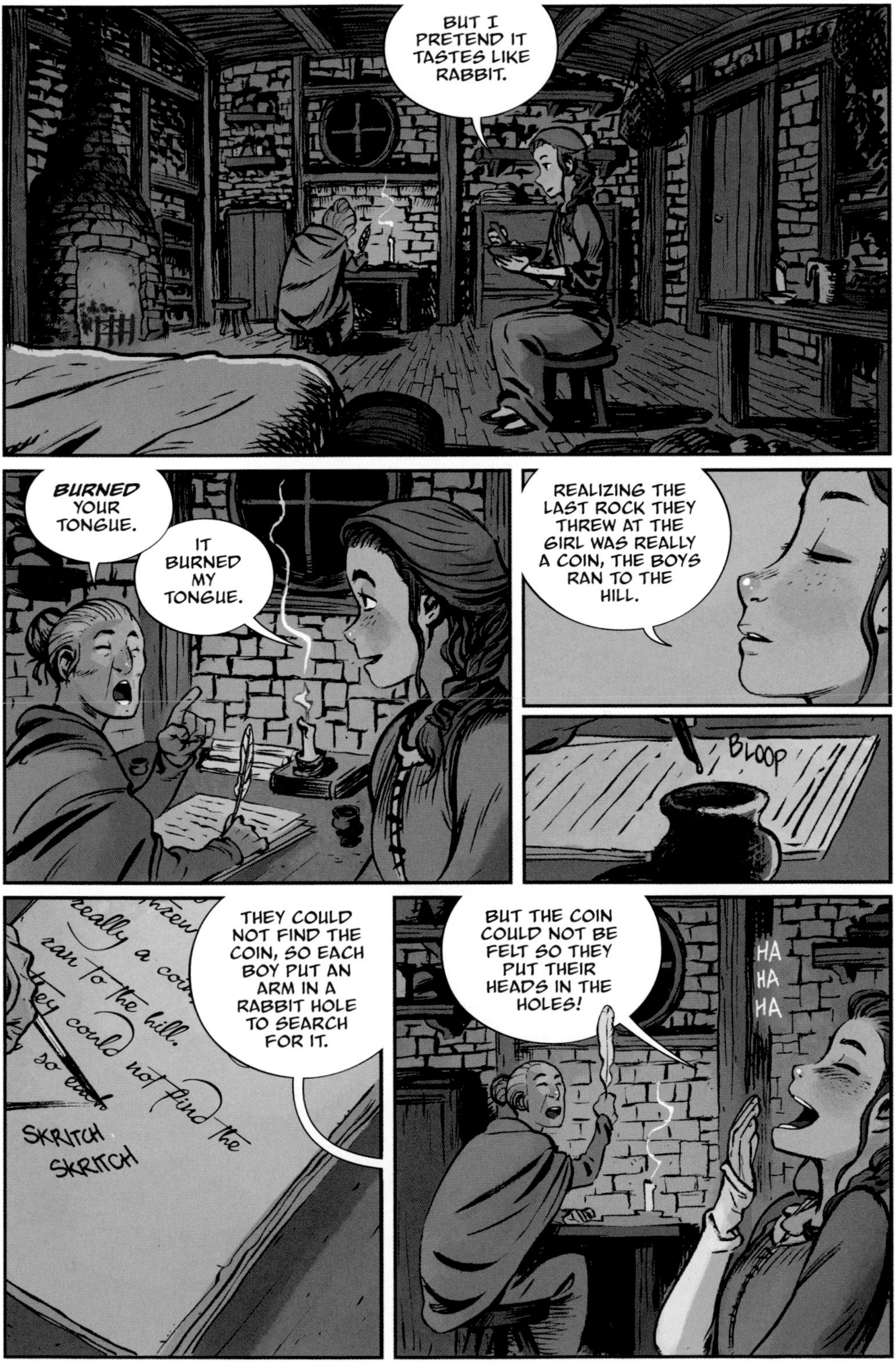

BUT I PRETEND IT TASTES LIKE RABBIT.
BURNED YOUR TONGUE.
IT BURNED MY TONGUE.
REALIZING THE LAST ROCK THEY THREW AT THE GIRL WAS REALLY A COIN, THE BOYS RAN TO THE HILL.
BLOOP
ran to the hill.
they could not find the
SKRITCH SKRITCH
THEY COULD NOT FIND THE COIN, SO EACH BOY PUT AN ARM IN A RABBIT HOLE TO SEARCH FOR IT.
BUT THE COIN COULD NOT BE FELT SO THEY PUT THEIR HEADS IN THE HOLES!
HA HA HA

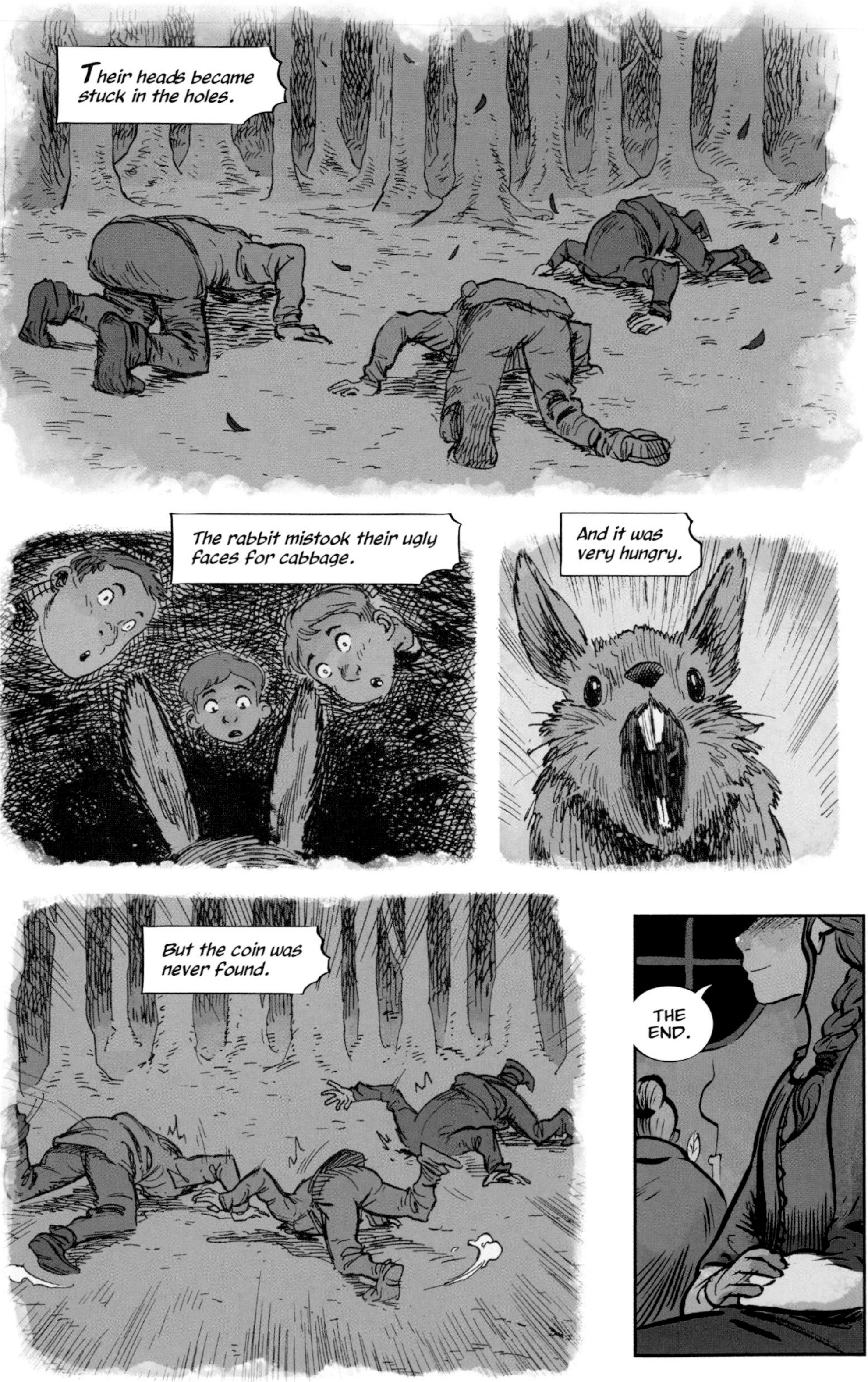
Their heads became stuck in the holes.
The rabbit mistook their ugly faces for cabbage.
And it was very hungry.
But the coin was never found.
THE END.

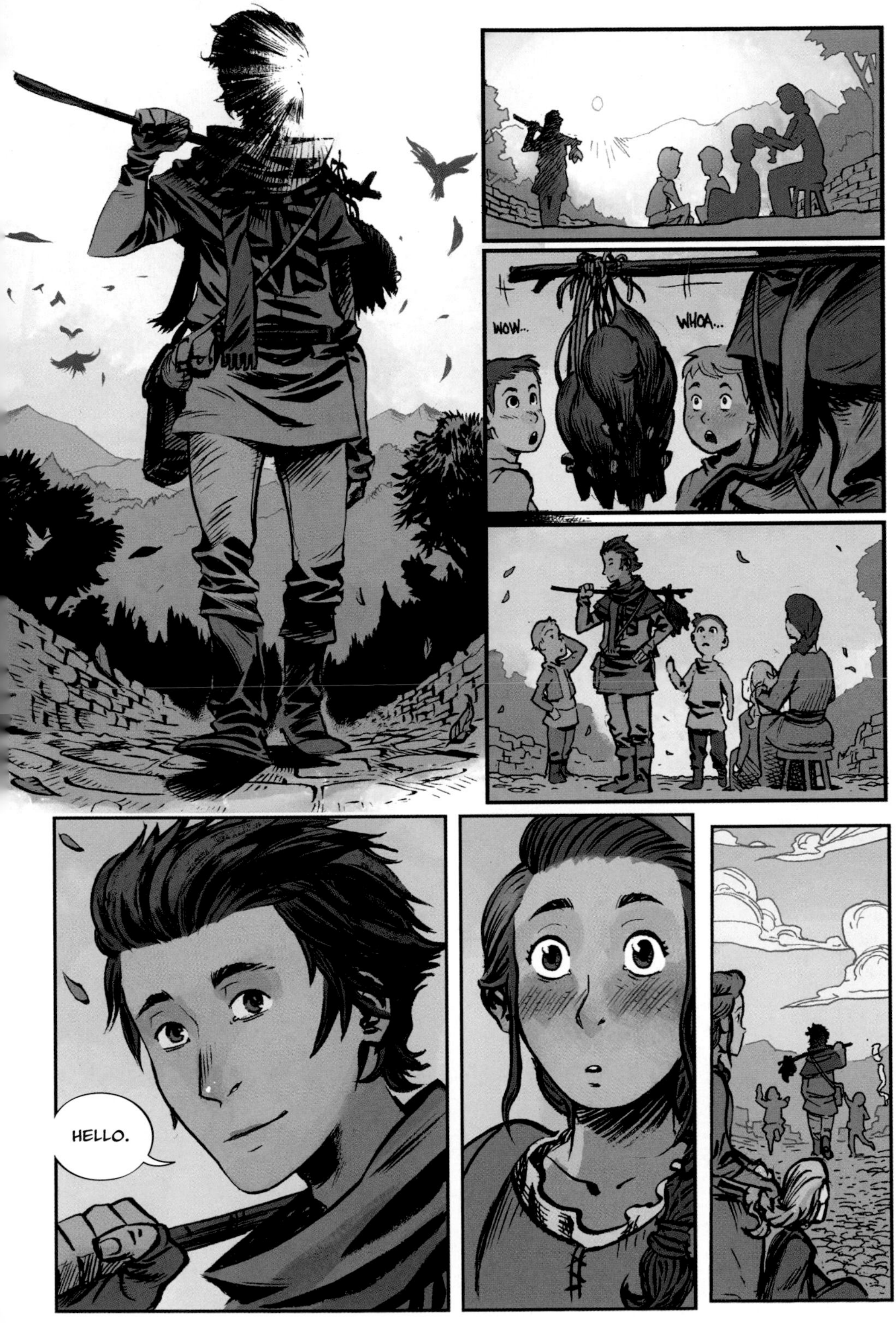
WOW...
WHOA...
HELLO.

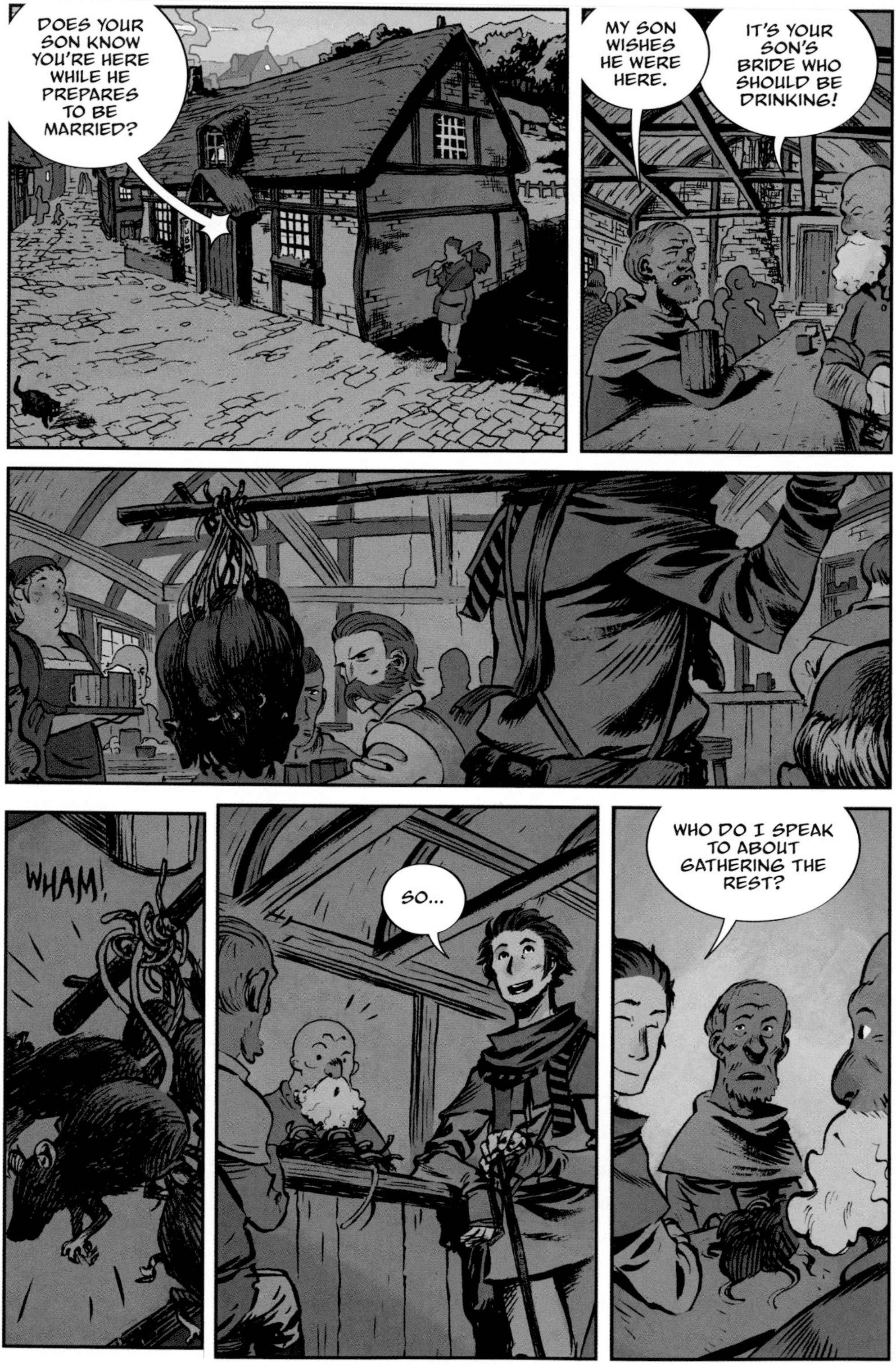
DOES YOUR SON KNOW YOU'RE HERE WHILE HE PREPARES TO BE MARRIED?
MY SON WISHES HE WERE HERE.
IT'S YOUR SON'S BRIDE WHO SHOULD BE DRINKING!
WHAM!
SO...
WHO DO I SPEAK TO ABOUT GATHERING THE REST?

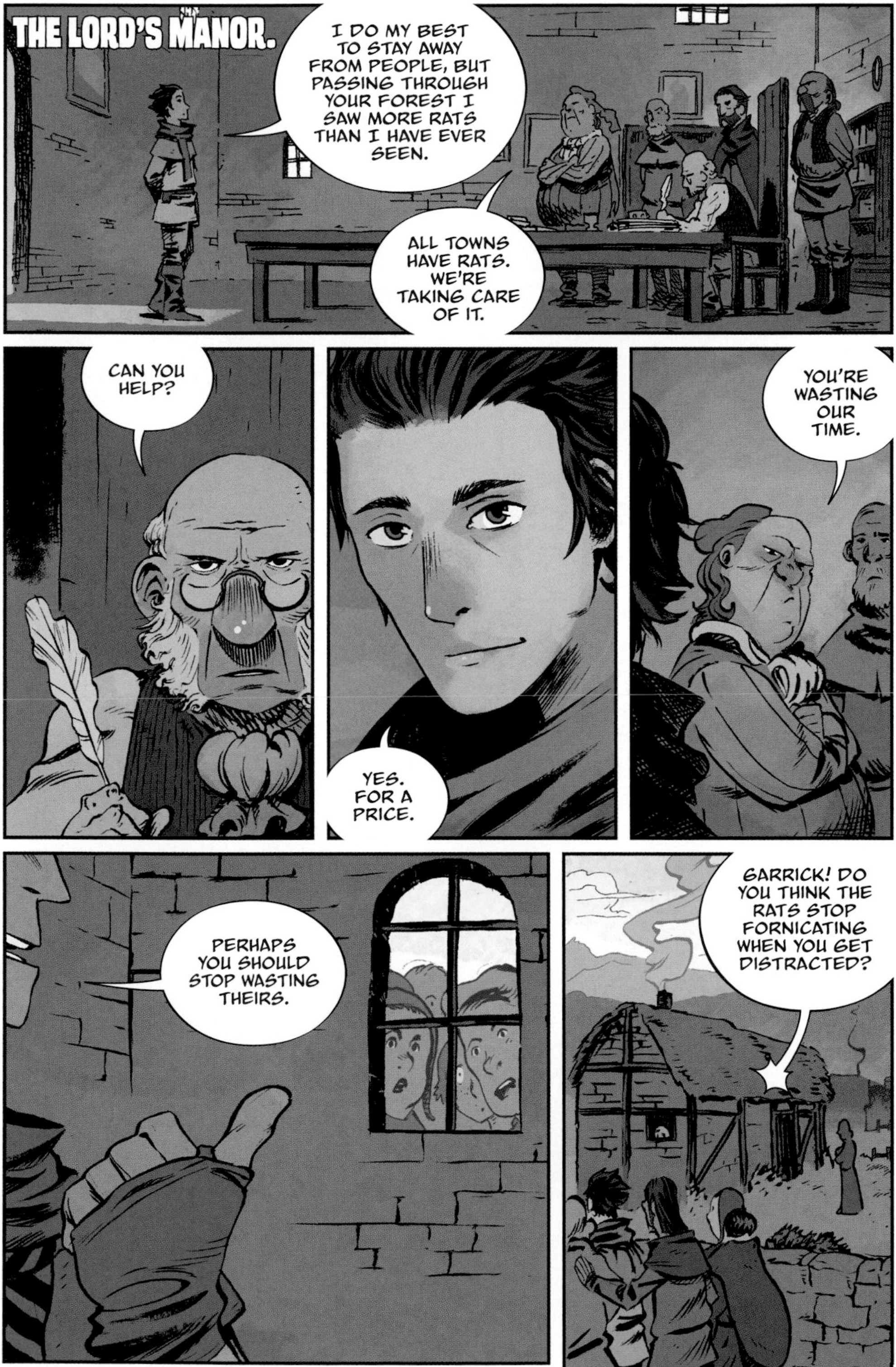
THE LORD'S MANOR.
I DO MY BEST TO STAY AWAY FROM PEOPLE, BUT PASSING THROUGH YOUR FOREST I SAW MORE RATS THAN I HAVE EVER SEEN.
ALL TOWNS HAVE RATS. WE'RE TAKING CARE OF IT.
CAN YOU HELP?
YES. FOR A PRICE.
YOU'RE WASTING OUR TIME.
PERHAPS YOU SHOULD STOP WASTING THEIRS.
GARRICK! DO YOU THINK THE RATS STOP FORNICATING WHEN YOU GET DISTRACTED?

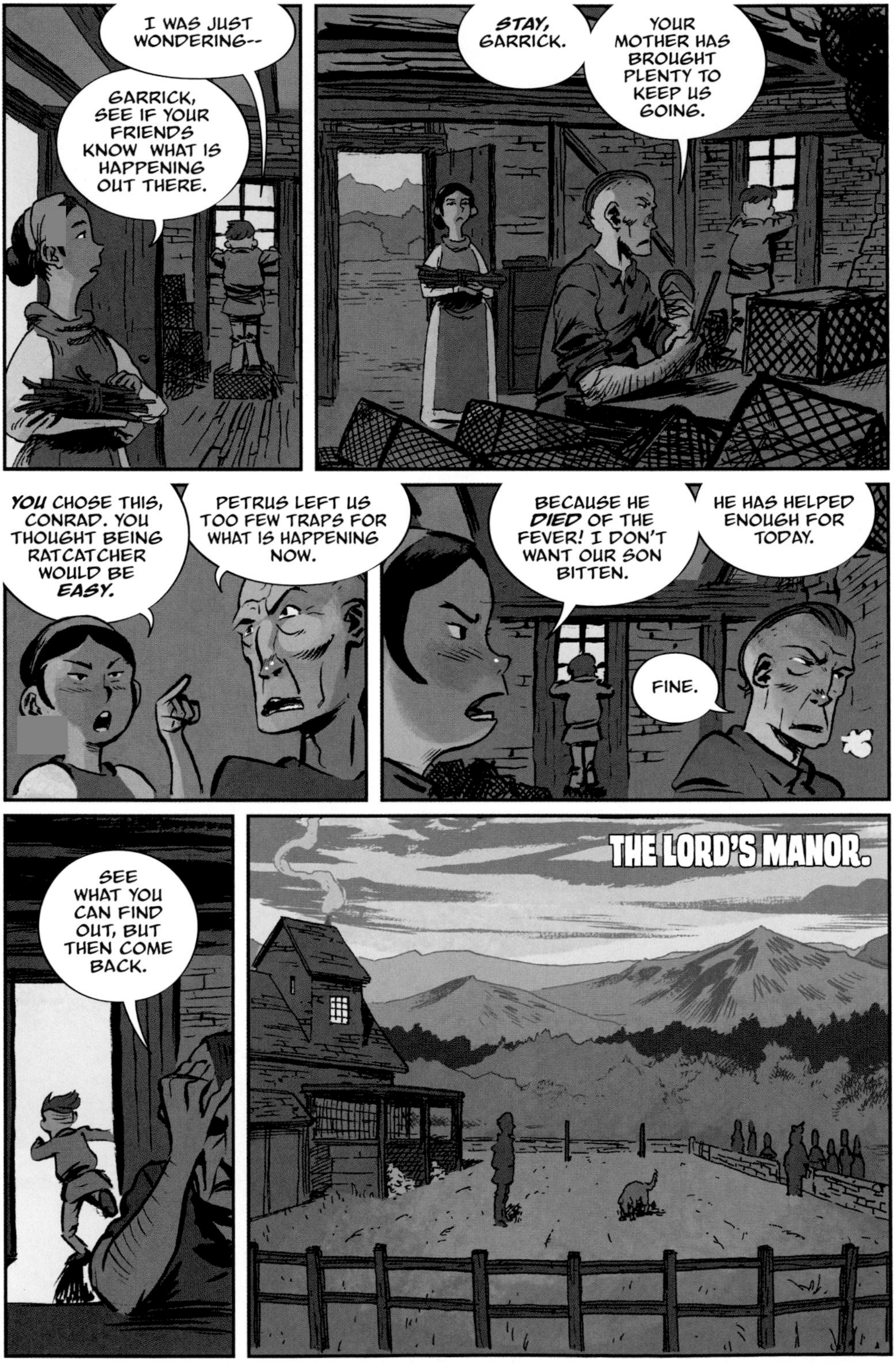
I WAS JUST WONDERING--
GARRICK, SEE IF YOUR FRIENDS KNOW WHAT IS HAPPENING OUT THERE.
STAY, GARRICK.
YOUR MOTHER HAS BROUGHT PLENTY TO KEEP US GOING.
YOU CHOSE THIS, CONRAD. YOU THOUGHT BEING RATCATCHER WOULD BE EASY.
PETRUS LEFT US TOO FEW TRAPS FOR WHAT IS HAPPENING NOW.
BECAUSE HE DIED OF THE FEVER! I DON'T WANT OUR SON BITTEN.
HE HAS HELPED ENOUGH FOR TODAY.
FINE.
SEE WHAT YOU CAN FIND OUT, BUT THEN COME BACK.
THE LORD'S MANOR.

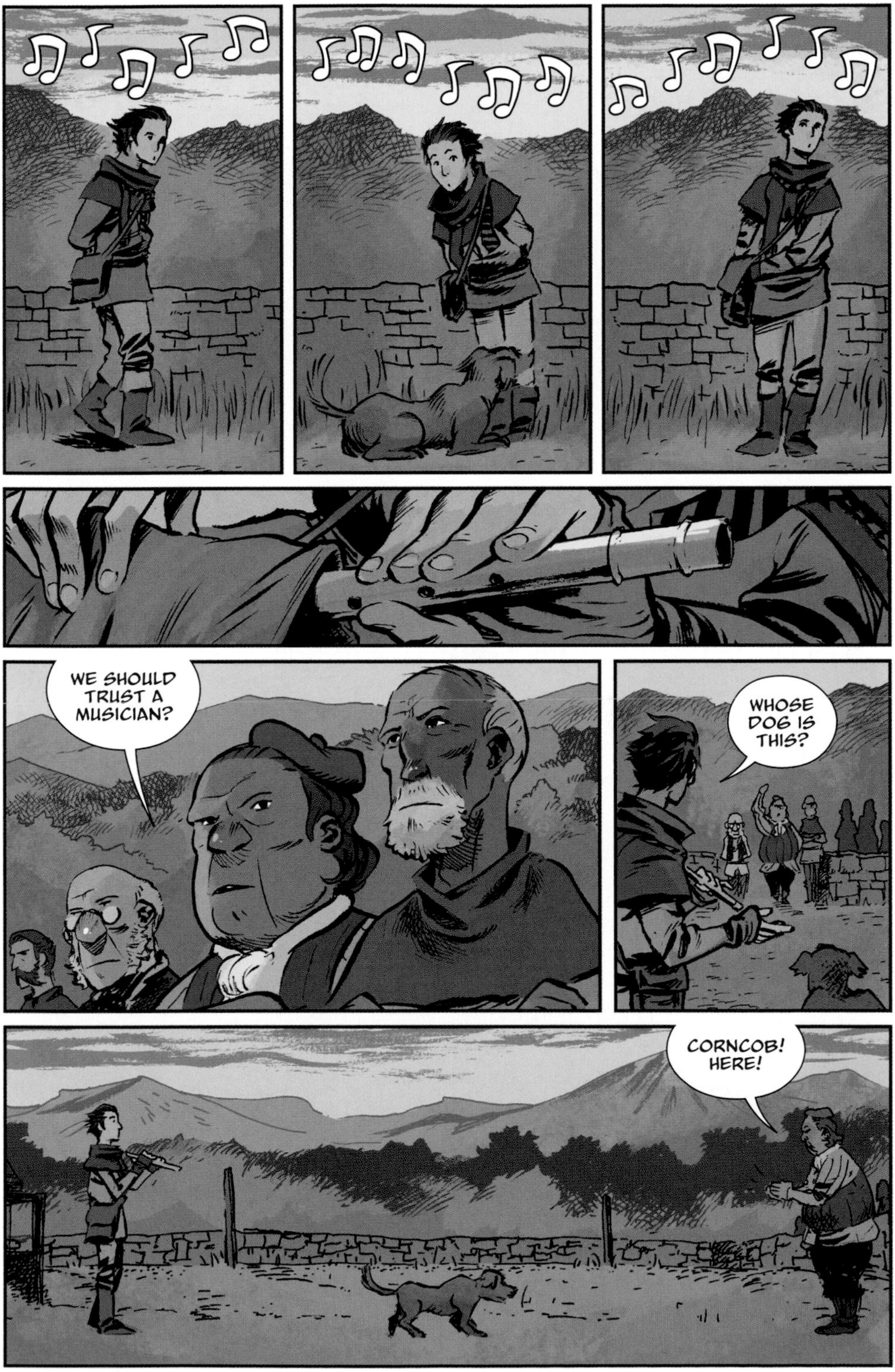
WE SHOULD TRUST A MUSICIAN?
WHOSE DOG IS THIS?
CORNCOB! HERE!

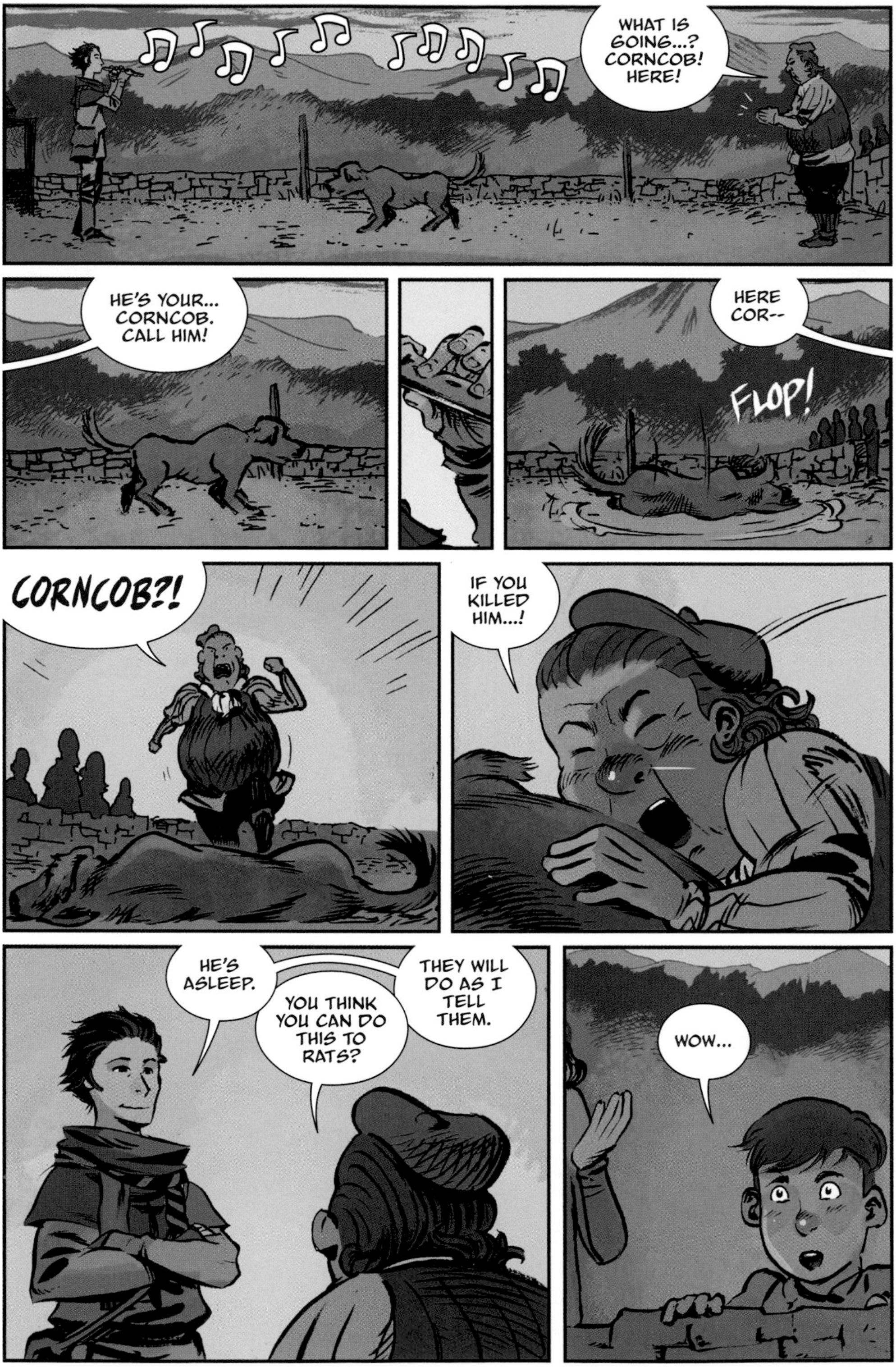
WHAT IS GOING...? CORNCOB! HERE!
HE'S YOUR... CORNCOB. CALL HIM!
HERE COR--
FLOP!
CORNCOB?!
IF YOU KILLED HIM...!
HE'S ASLEEP.
YOU THINK YOU CAN DO THIS TO RATS?
THEY WILL DO AS I TELL THEM.
WOW...

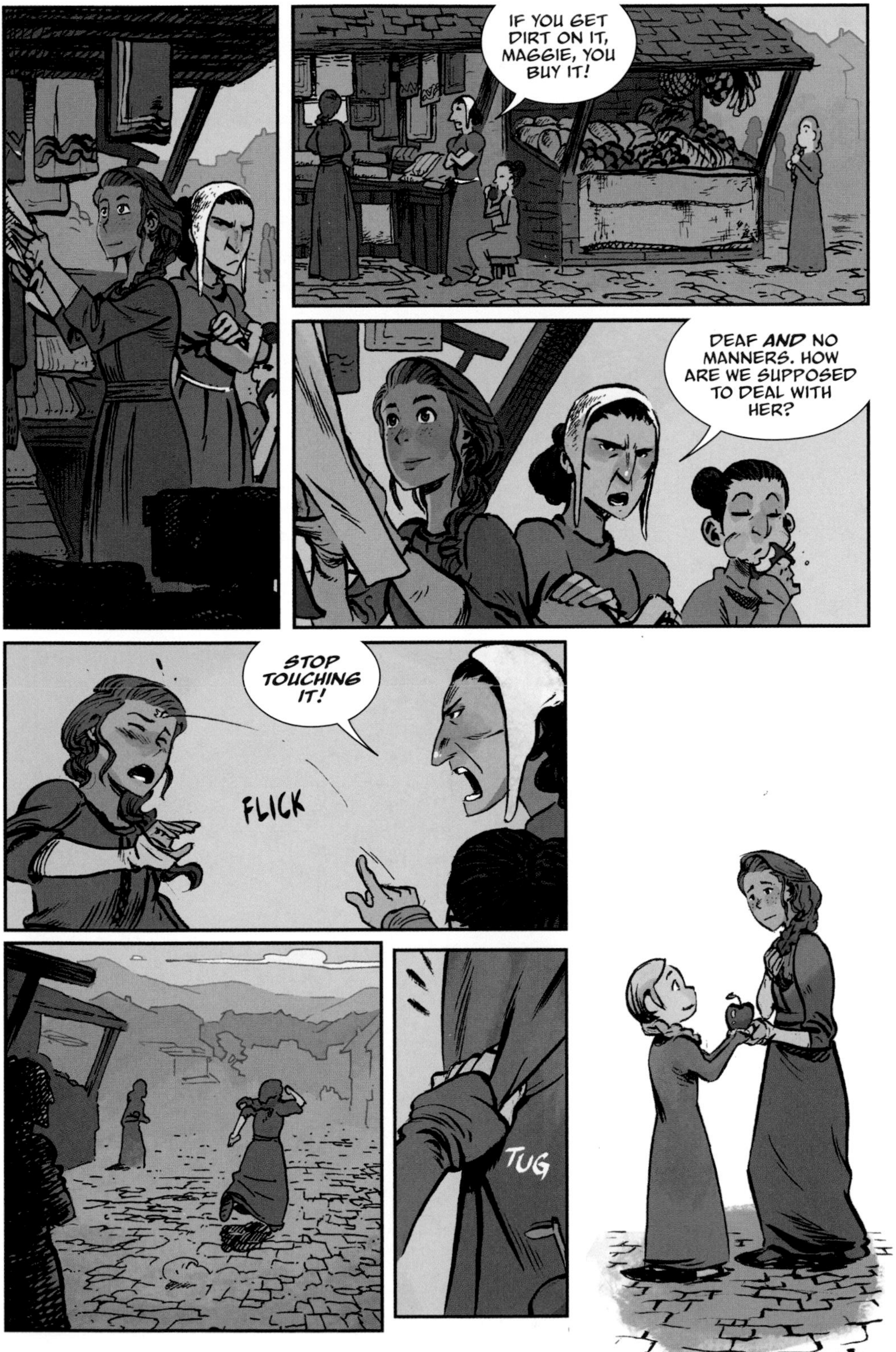
IF YOU GET DIRT ON IT, MAGGIE, YOU BUY IT!
DEAF AND NO MANNERS. HOW ARE WE SUPPOSED TO DEAL WITH HER?
STOP TOUCHING IT!
FLICK
TUG

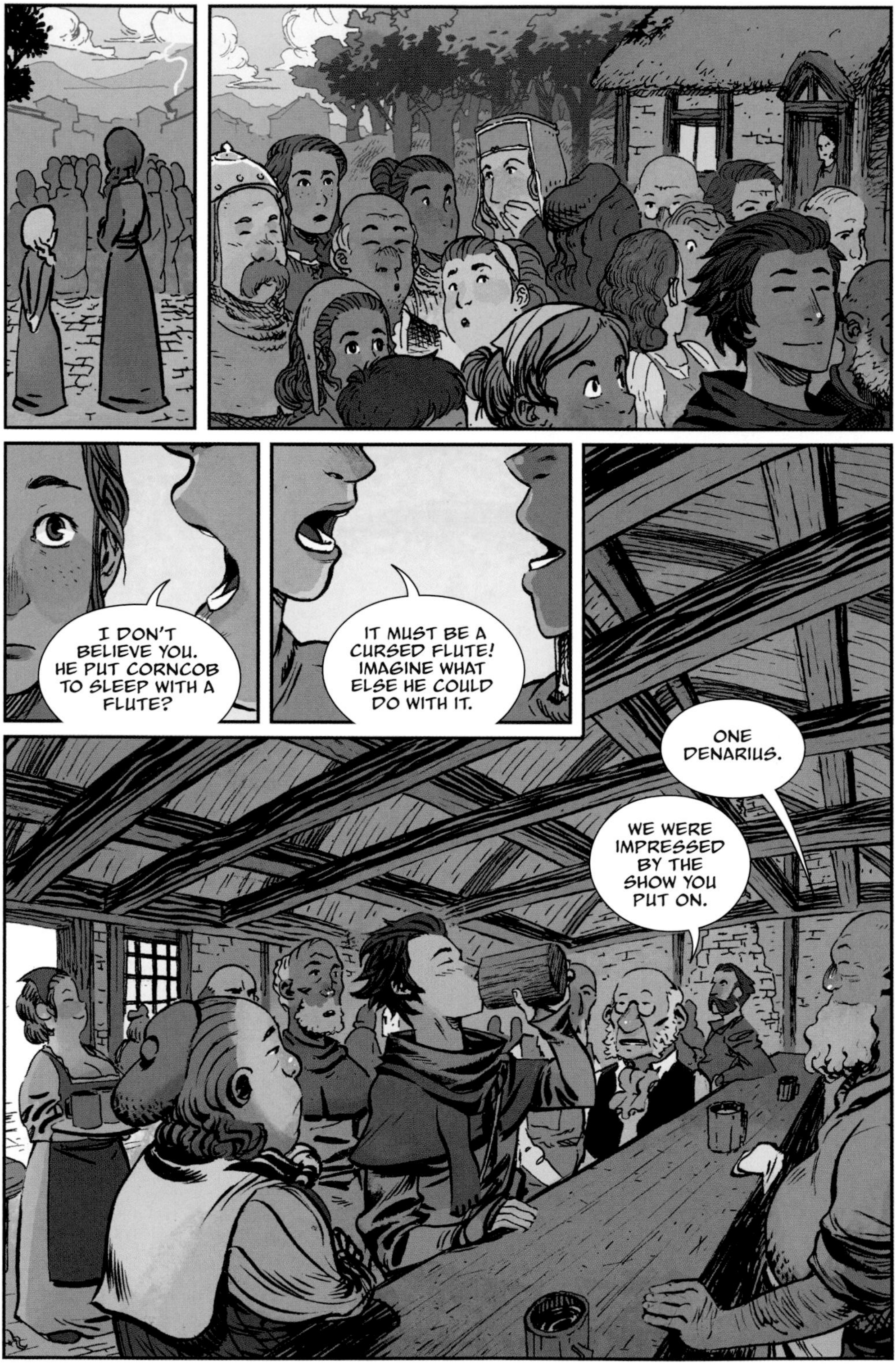
I DON'T BELIEVE YOU. HE PUT CORNCOB TO SLEEP WITH A FLUTE?
IT MUST BE A CURSED FLUTE! IMAGINE WHAT ELSE HE COULD DO WITH IT.
ONE DENARIUS.
WE WERE IMPRESSED BY THE SHOW YOU PUT ON.

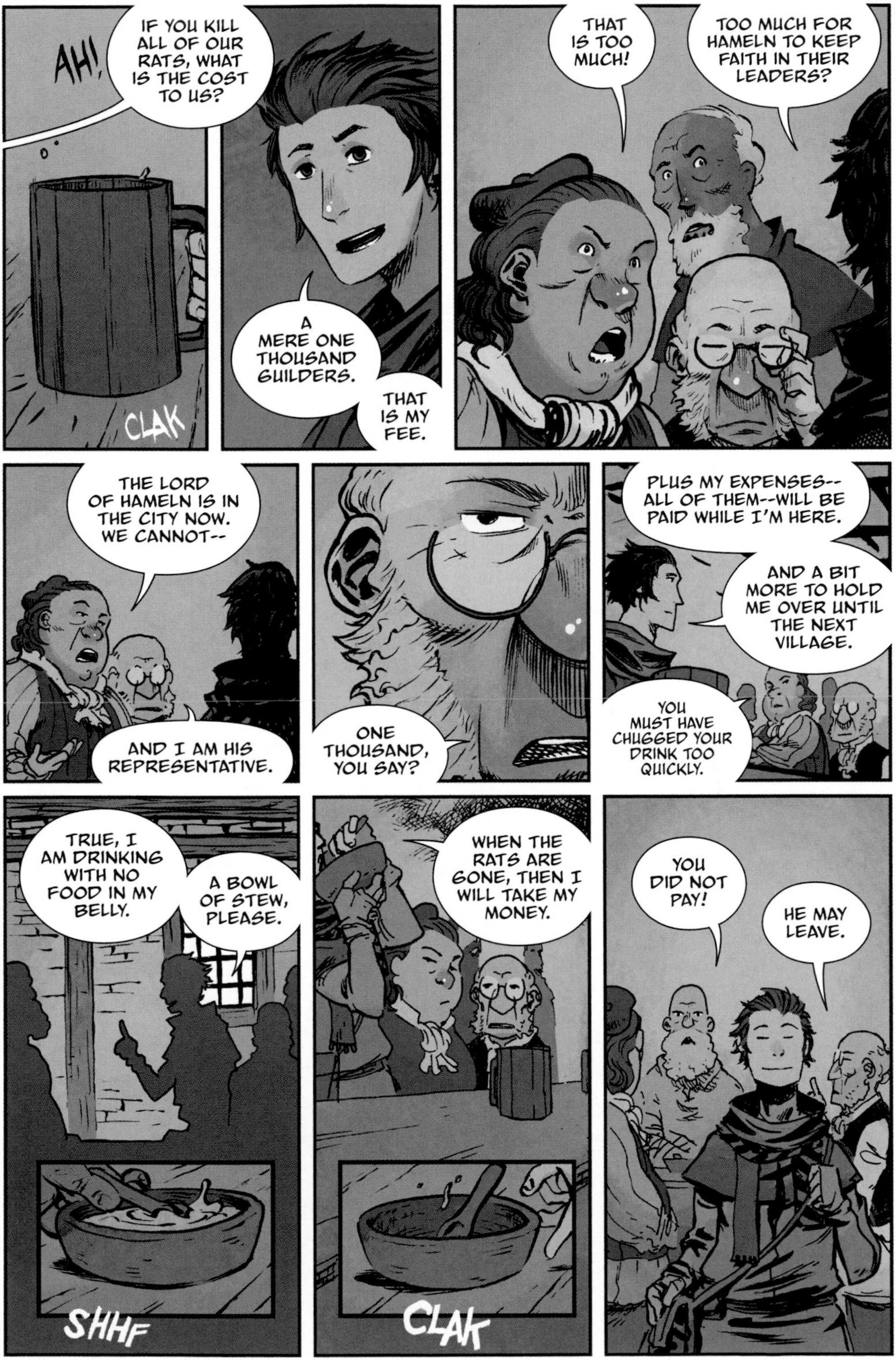
AH!
IF YOU KILL ALL OF OUR RATS, WHAT IS THE COST TO US?
CLAK
A MERE ONE THOUSAND GUILDERS.
THAT IS MY FEE.
THAT IS TOO MUCH!
TOO MUCH FOR HAMELN TO KEEP FAITH IN THEIR LEADERS?
THE LORD OF HAMELN IS IN THE CITY NOW. WE CANNOT--
AND I AM HIS REPRESENTATIVE.
ONE THOUSAND, YOU SAY?
PLUS MY EXPENSES--ALL OF THEM--WILL BE PAID WHILE I'M HERE.
AND A BIT MORE TO HOLD ME OVER UNTIL THE NEXT VILLAGE.
YOU MUST HAVE CHUGGED YOUR DRINK TOO QUICKLY.
TRUE, I AM DRINKING WITH NO FOOD IN MY BELLY.
A BOWL OF STEW, PLEASE.
SHHF
WHEN THE RATS ARE GONE, THEN I WILL TAKE MY MONEY.
CLAK
YOU DID NOT PAY!
HE MAY LEAVE.

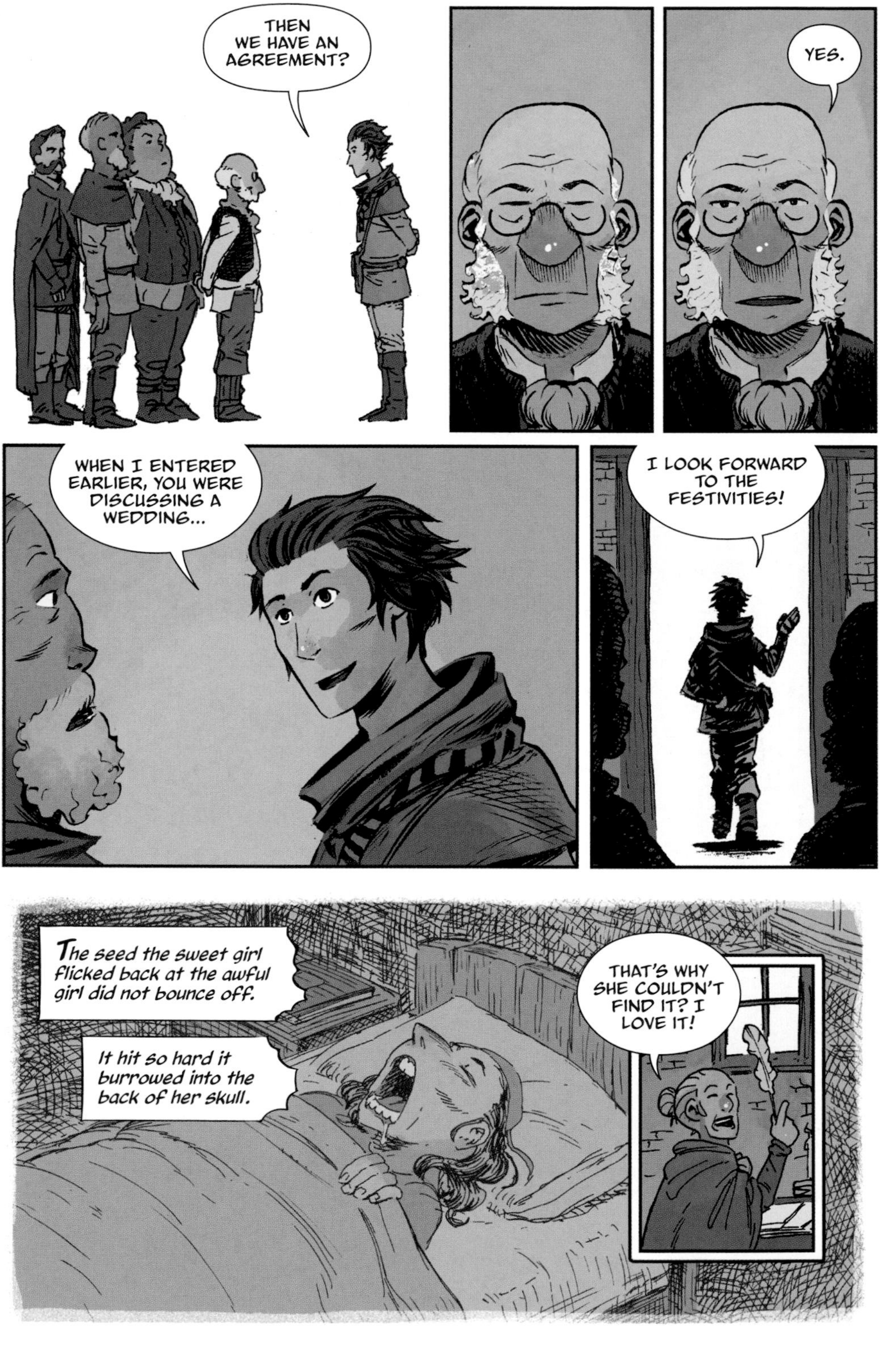
THEN WE HAVE AN AGREEMENT?
YES.
WHEN I ENTERED EARLIER, YOU WERE DISCUSSING A WEDDING...
I LOOK FORWARD TO THE FESTIVITIES!
The seed the sweet girl flicked back at the awful girl did not bounce off.
It hit so hard it burrowed into the back of her skull.
THAT'S WHY SHE COULDN'T FIND IT? I LOVE IT!

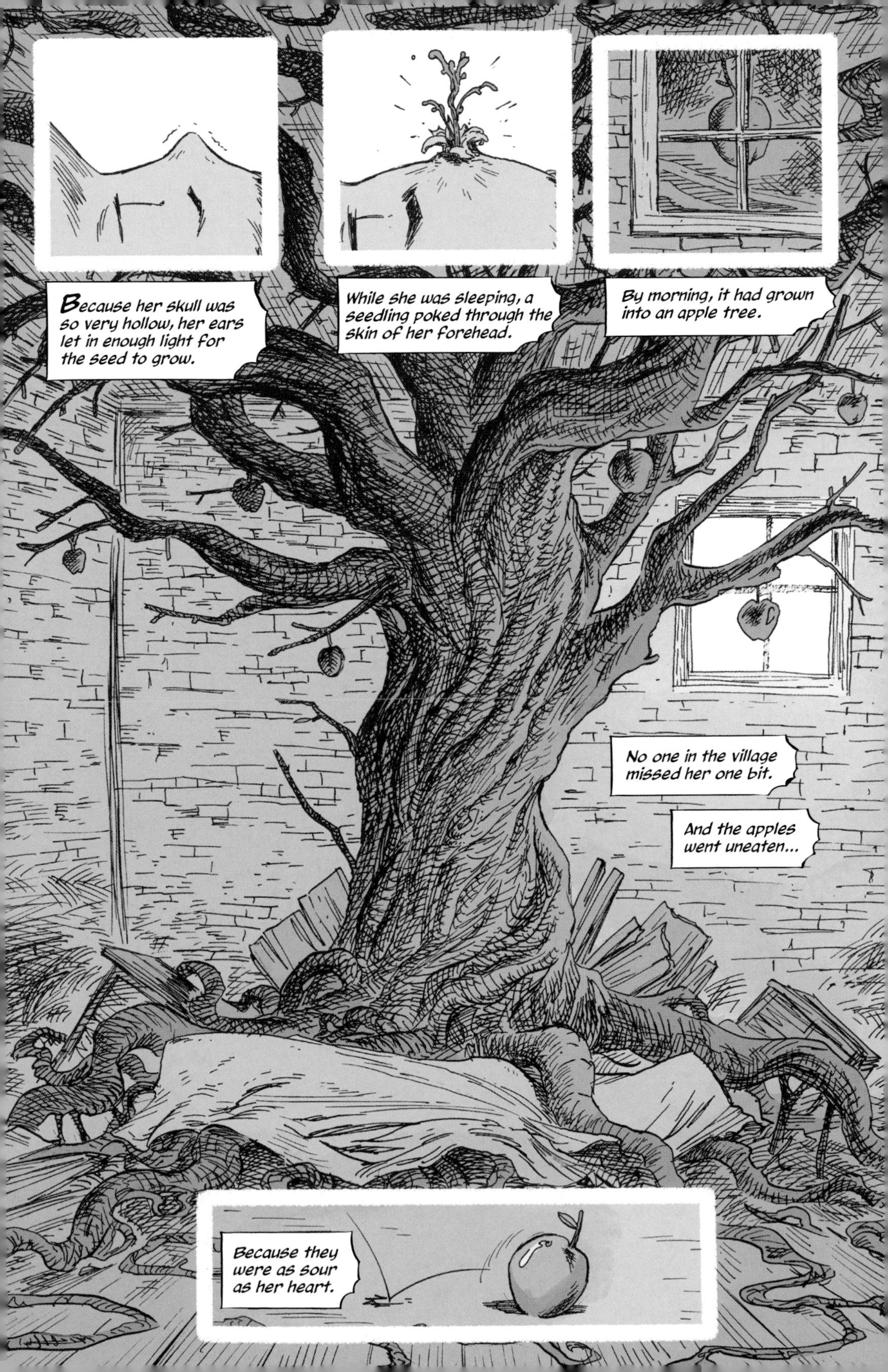
Because her skull was so very hollow, her ears let in enough light for the seed to grow.
While she was sleeping, a seedling poked through the skin of her forehead.
By morning, it had grown into an apple tree.
No one in the village missed her one bit.
And the apples went uneaten...
Because they were as sour as her heart.

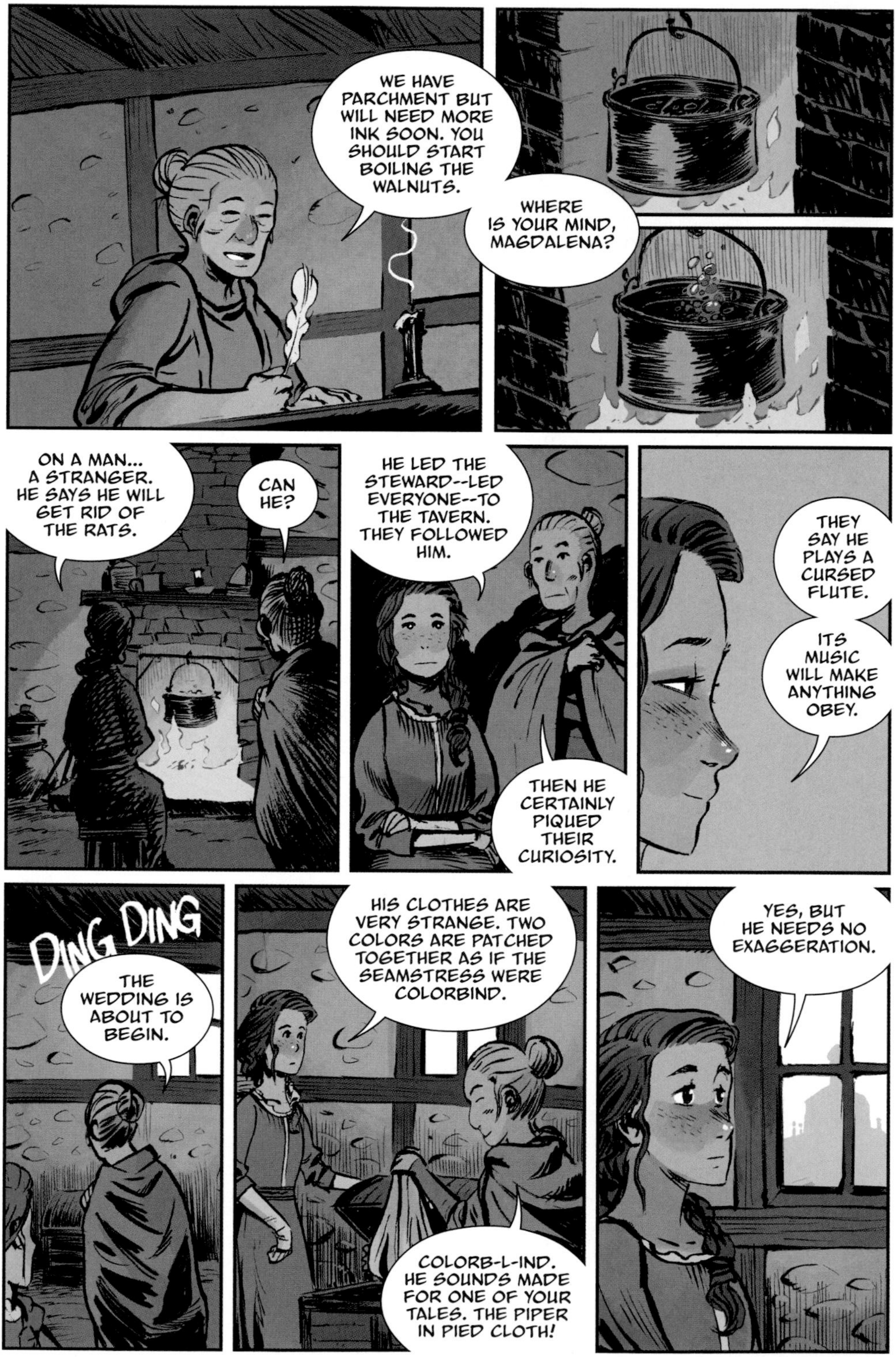
WE HAVE PARCHMENT BUT WILL NEED MORE INK SOON. YOU SHOULD START BOILING THE WALNUTS.
WHERE IS YOUR MIND, MAGDALENA?
ON A MAN... A STRANGER. HE SAYS HE WILL GET RID OF THE RATS.
CAN HE?
HE LED THE STEWARD--LED EVERYONE--TO THE TAVERN. THEY FOLLOWED HIM.
THEN HE CERTAINLY PIQUED THEIR CURIOSITY.
THEY SAY HE PLAYS A CURSED FLUTE.
ITS MUSIC WILL MAKE ANYTHING OBEY.
DING DING
THE WEDDING IS ABOUT TO BEGIN.
HIS CLOTHES ARE VERY STRANGE. TWO COLORS ARE PATCHED TOGETHER AS IF THE SEAMSTRESS WERE COLORBIND.
COLORB-L-IND. HE SOUNDS MADE FOR ONE OF YOUR TALES. THE PIPER IN PIED CLOTH!
YES, BUT HE NEEDS NO EXAGGERATION.

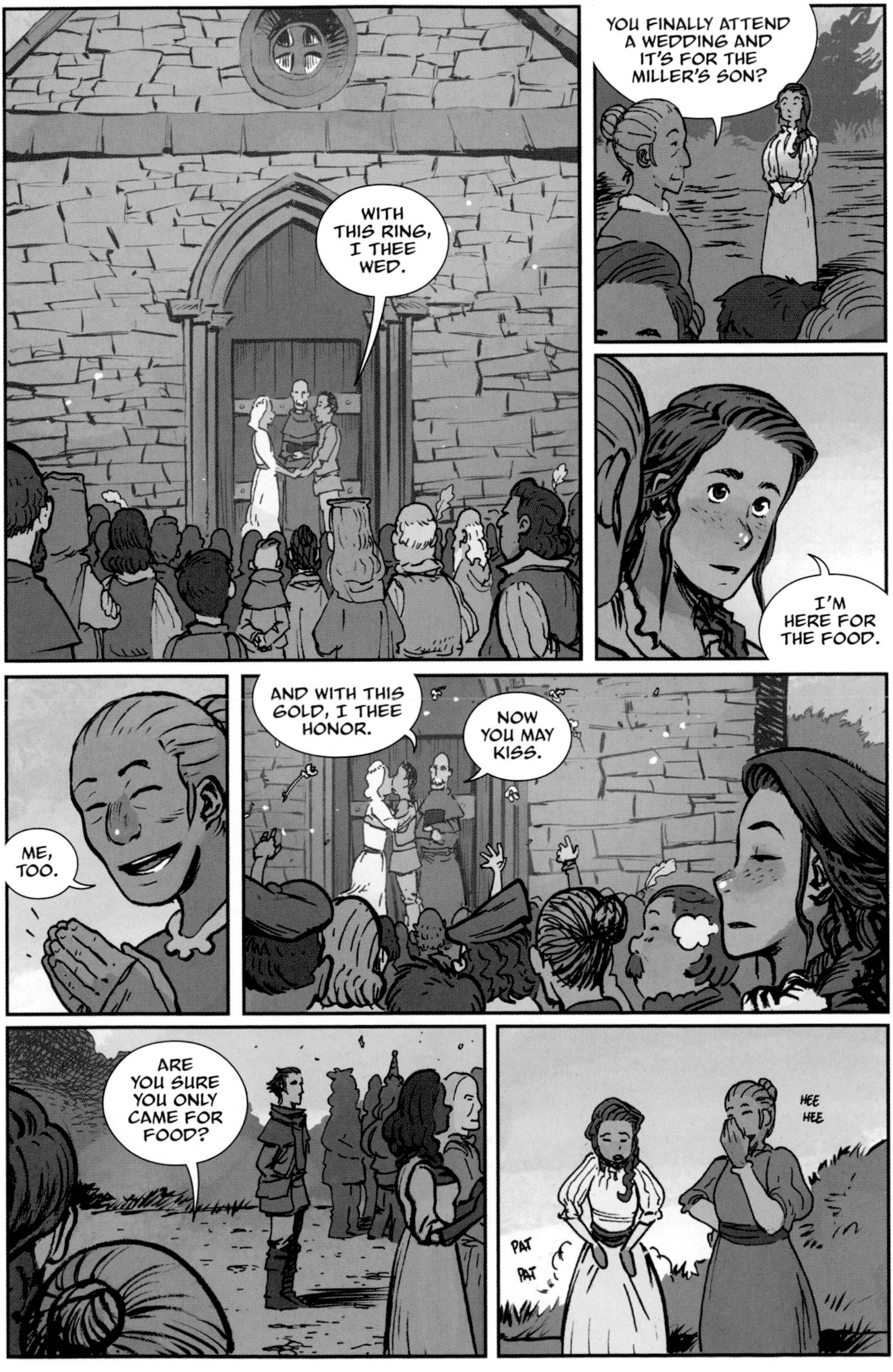
WITH THIS RING, I THEE WED.
YOU FINALLY ATTEND A WEDDING AND IT'S FOR THE MILLER'S SON?
I'M HERE FOR THE FOOD.
ME, TOO.
AND WITH THIS GOLD, I THEE HONOR.
NOW YOU MAY KISS.
ARE YOU SURE YOU ONLY CAME FOR FOOD?
HEE HEE
PAT PAT

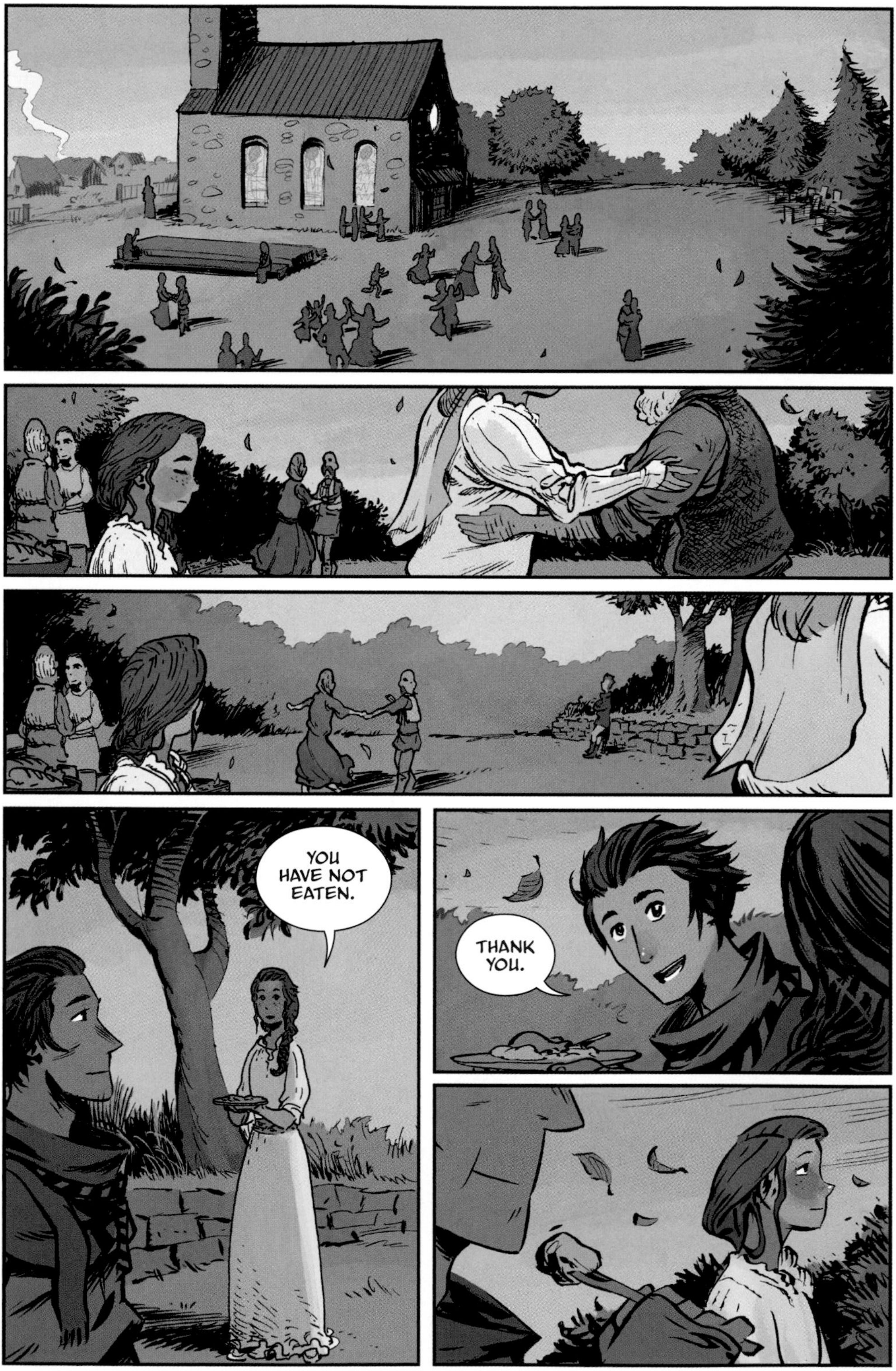
YOU HAVE NOT EATEN.
THANK YOU.

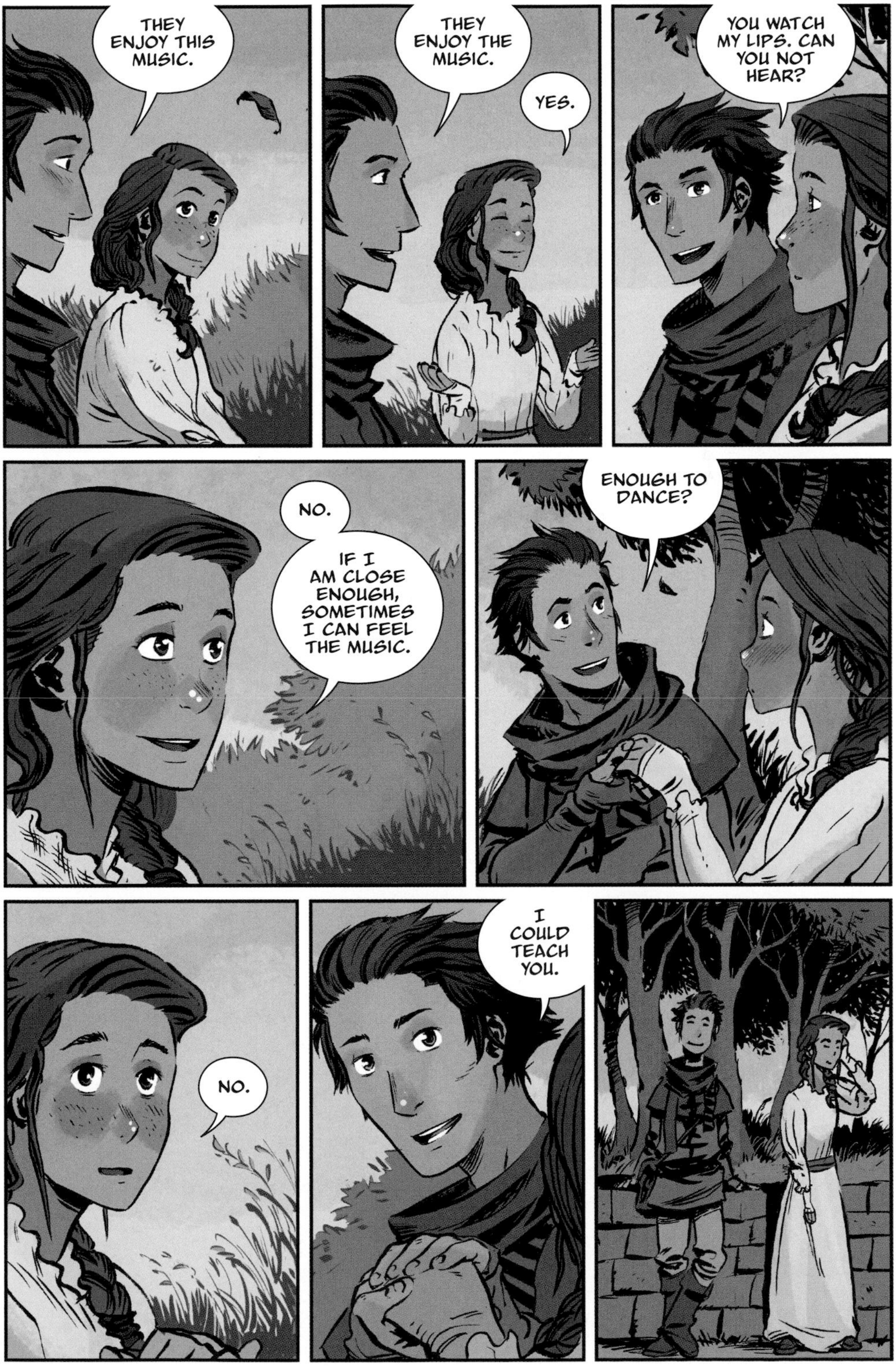
THEY ENJOY THIS MUSIC.
THEY ENJOY THE MUSIC.
YES.
YOU WATCH MY LIPS. CAN YOU NOT HEAR?
NO.
IF I AM CLOSE ENOUGH, SOMETIMES I CAN FEEL THE MUSIC.
ENOUGH TO DANCE?
NO.
I COULD TEACH YOU.

I LIKE YOUR CHURCH. I'VE NEVER HEARD ORGAN MUSIC SO PURE AND FULL. OR, FOR A VILLAGE THIS SIZE, SEEN WINDOWS SO RICH WITH COLOR.

THAT IMAGE INSPIRES ME.

THE LAMB LOOKS RIGHT AT US.

BECAUSE THE LAMB IS US.

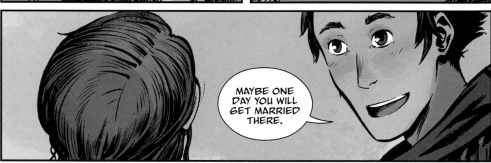

MAYBE ONE DAY YOU WILL GET MARRIED THERE.

I'LL TELL THEM TO STOP DANCING ON THE GRAVES.

I WOULD THINK THOSE WHO HAVE PASSED WOULD BE PLEASED BY THE JOY OF THE LIVING.

CLAP CLAP

BUT IT'S SACRED GROUND, FATHER!

BENEATH A SACRED CELEBRATION. THE LORD KNOWS THEY DESERVE ONE EVENING OF MERRIMENT.

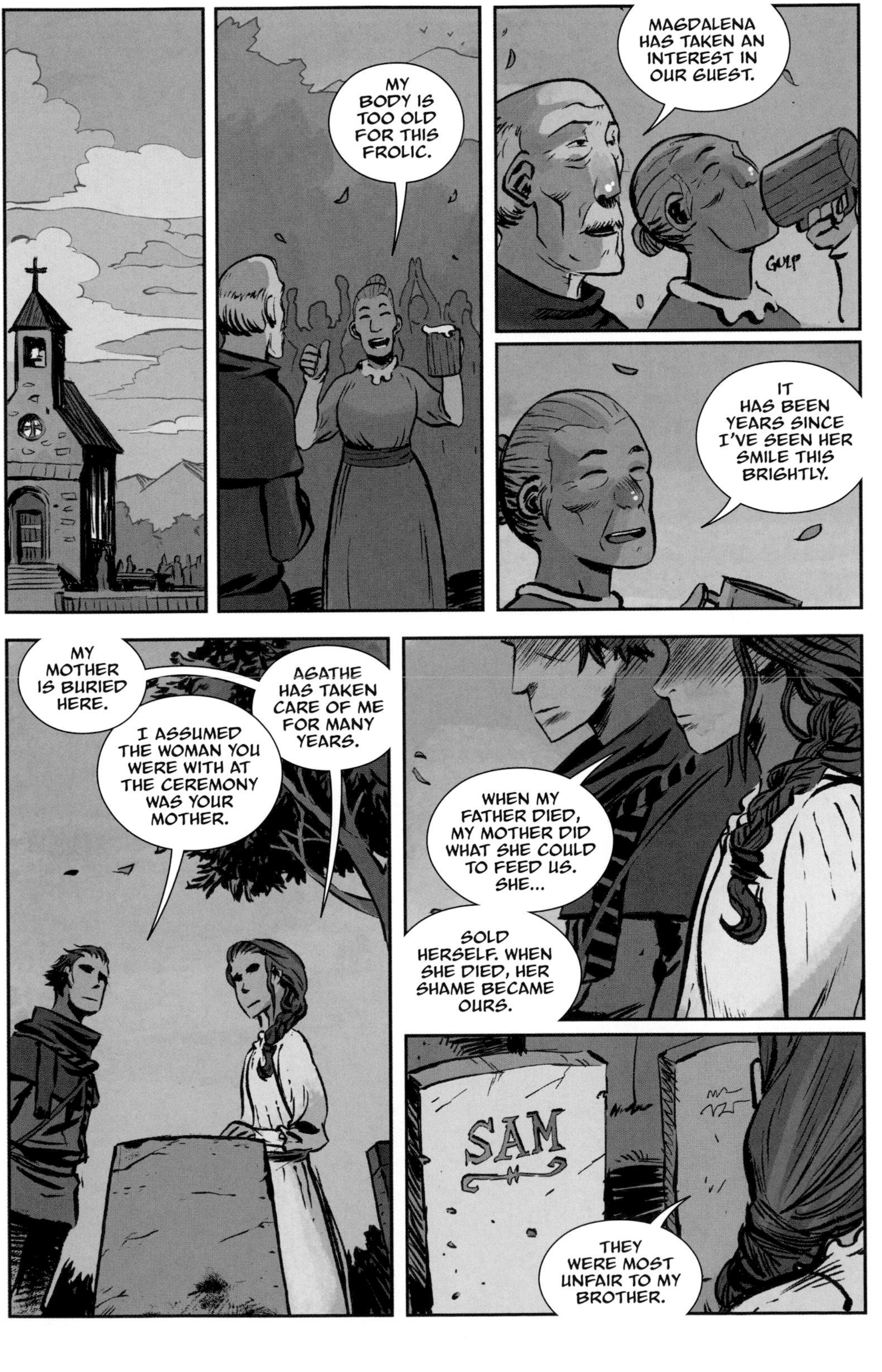
MY BODY IS TOO OLD FOR THIS FROLIC.
MAGDALENA HAS TAKEN AN INTEREST IN OUR GUEST.
GULP
IT HAS BEEN YEARS SINCE I'VE SEEN HER SMILE THIS BRIGHTLY.
MY MOTHER IS BURIED HERE.
I ASSUMED THE WOMAN YOU WERE WITH AT THE CEREMONY WAS YOUR MOTHER.
AGATHE HAS TAKEN CARE OF ME FOR MANY YEARS.
WHEN MY FATHER DIED, MY MOTHER DID WHAT SHE COULD TO FEED US. SHE...
SOLD HERSELF. WHEN SHE DIED, HER SHAME BECAME OURS.
SAM
THEY WERE MOST UNFAIR TO MY BROTHER.

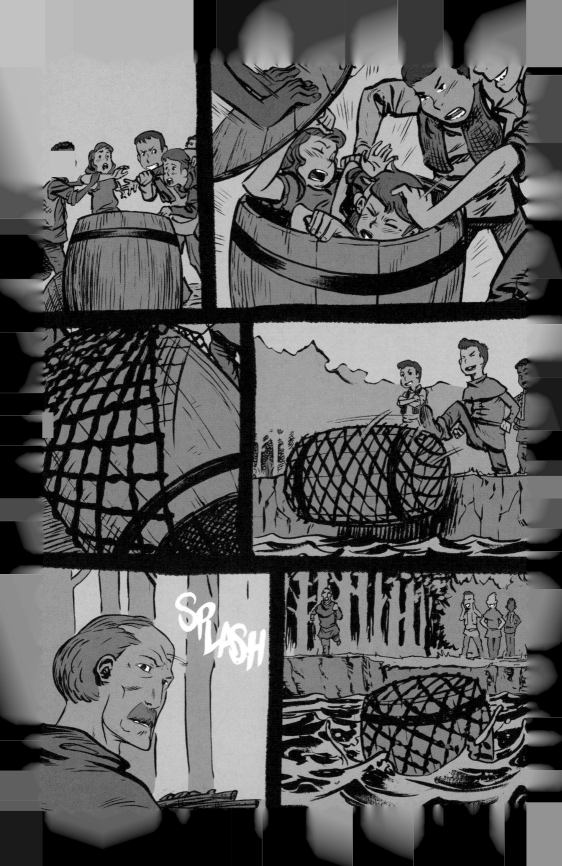

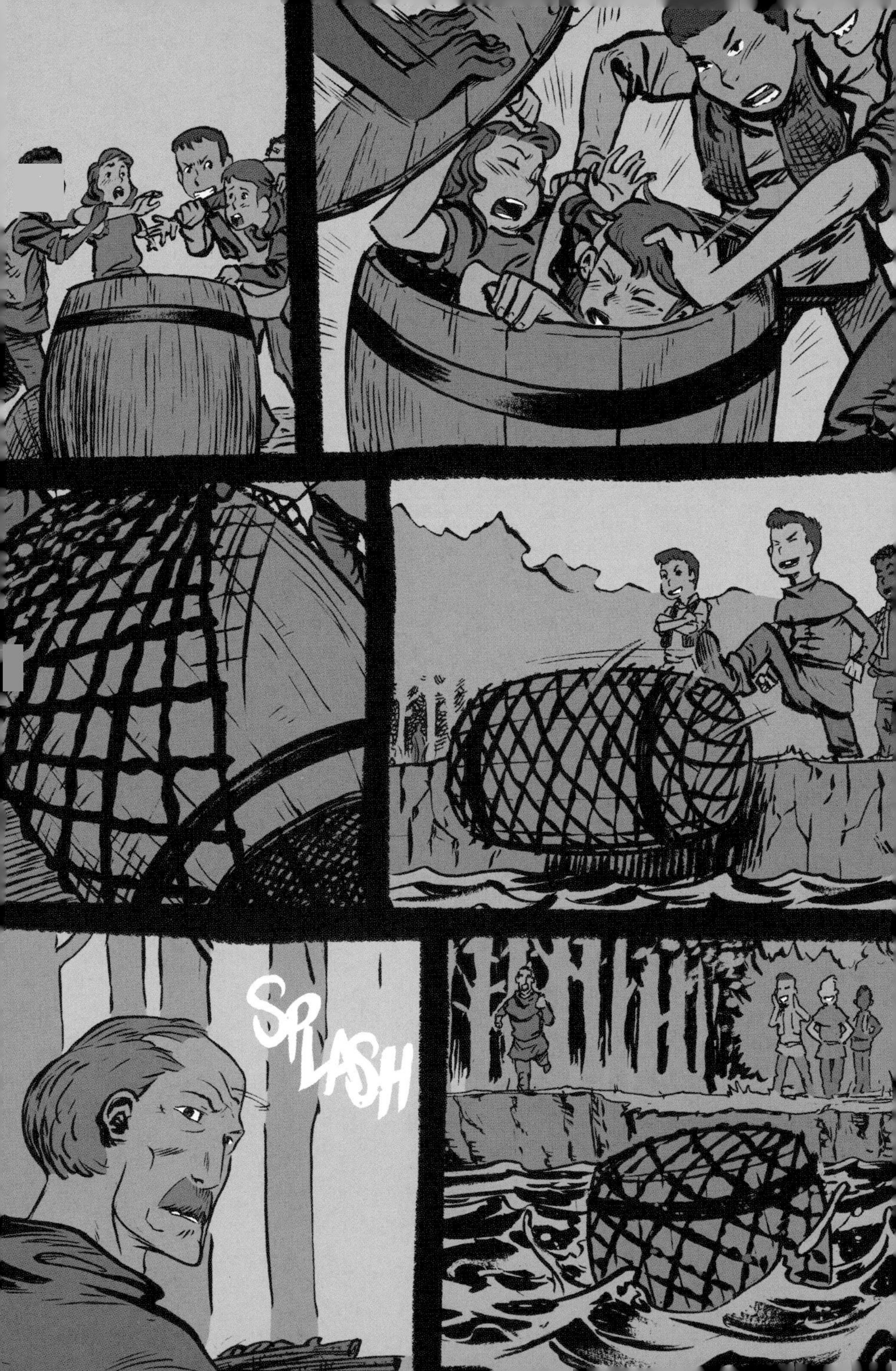
SPLASH

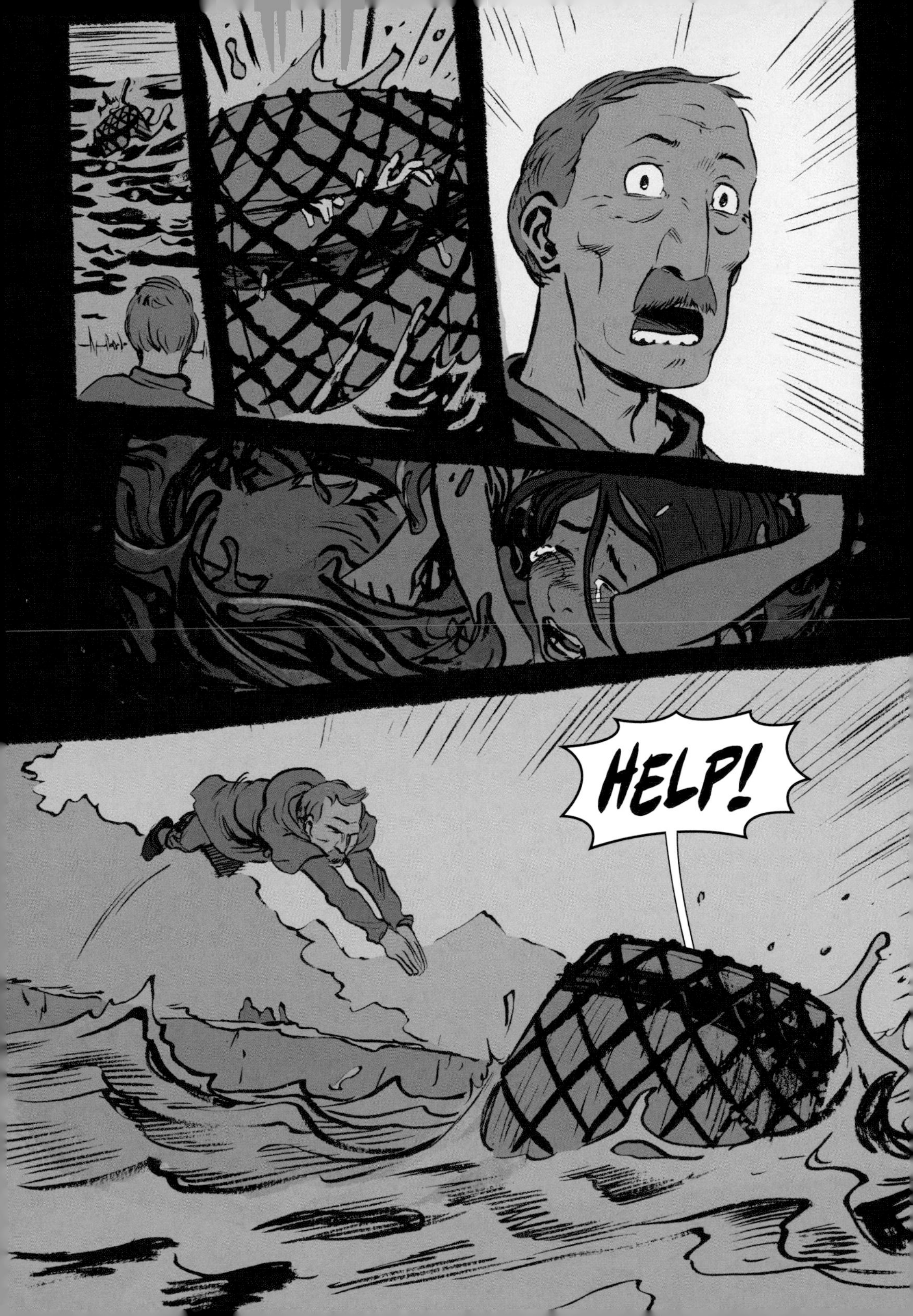
HELP!

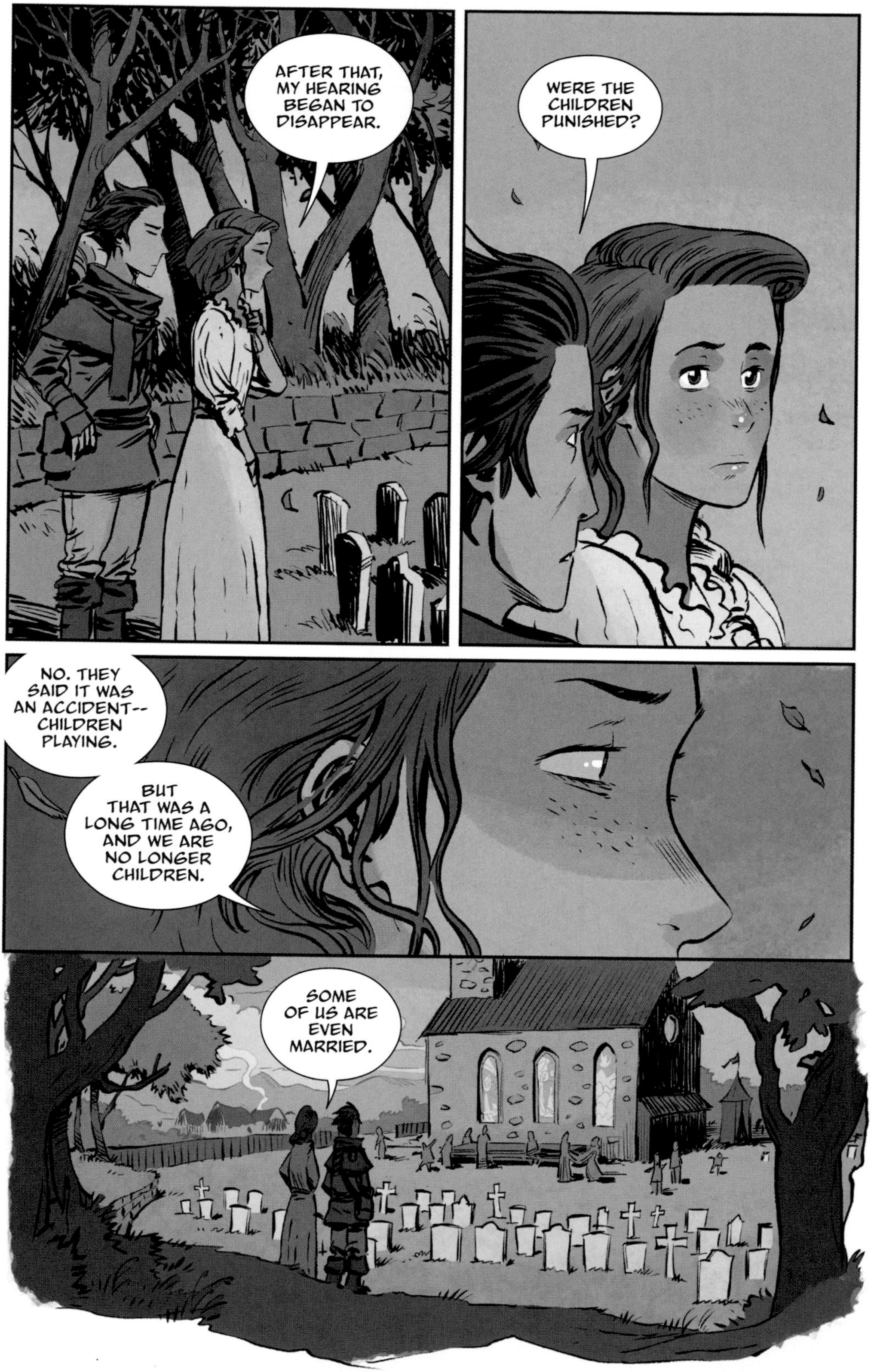
AFTER THAT, MY HEARING BEGAN TO DISAPPEAR.
WERE THE CHILDREN PUNISHED?
NO. THEY SAID IT WAS AN ACCIDENT--CHILDREN PLAYING.
BUT THAT WAS A LONG TIME AGO, AND WE ARE NO LONGER CHILDREN.
SOME OF US ARE EVEN MARRIED.

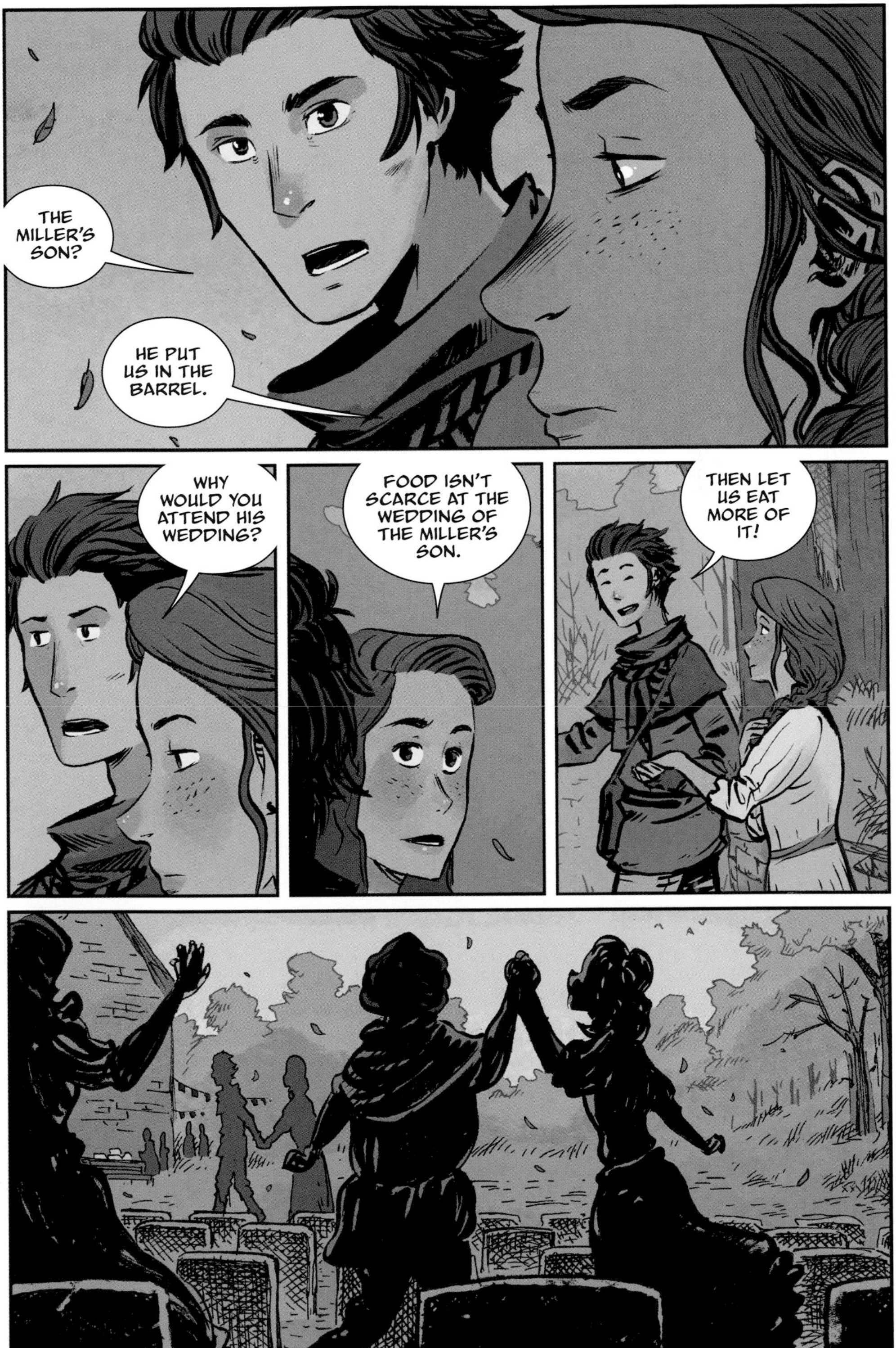
THE MILLER'S SON?
HE PUT US IN THE BARREL.
WHY WOULD YOU ATTEND HIS WEDDING?
FOOD ISN'T SCARCE AT THE WEDDING OF THE MILLER'S SON.
THEN LET US EAT MORE OF IT!

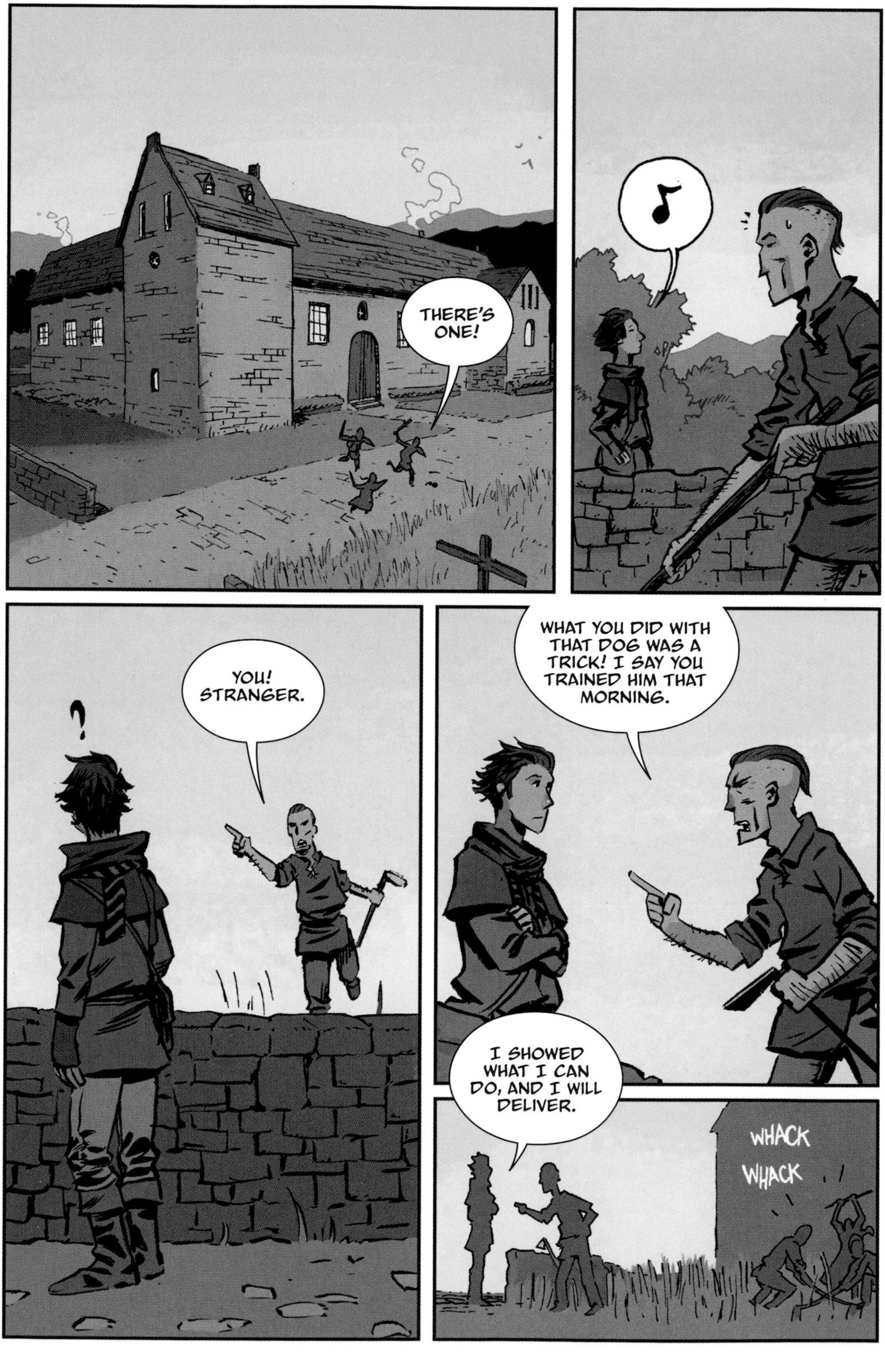
THERE'S ONE!
♪
YOU! STRANGER.
?
WHAT YOU DID WITH THAT DOG WAS A TRICK! I SAY YOU TRAINED HIM THAT MORNING.
I SHOWED WHAT I CAN DO, AND I WILL DELIVER.
WHACK
WHACK

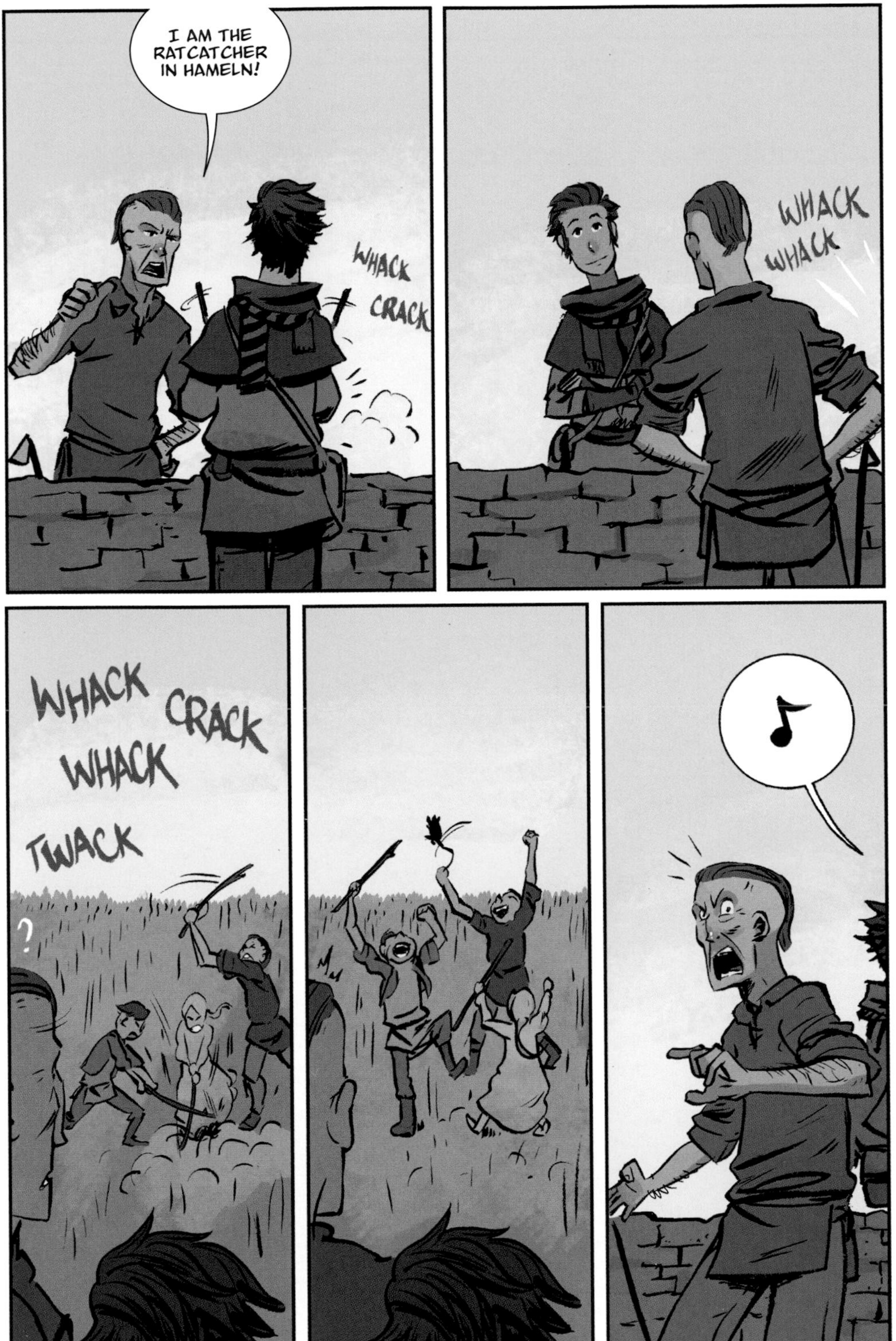
I AM THE RATCATCHER IN HAMELN!
WHACK
CRACK
WHACK
WHACK
WHACK
CRACK
WHACK
TWACK
?
♪

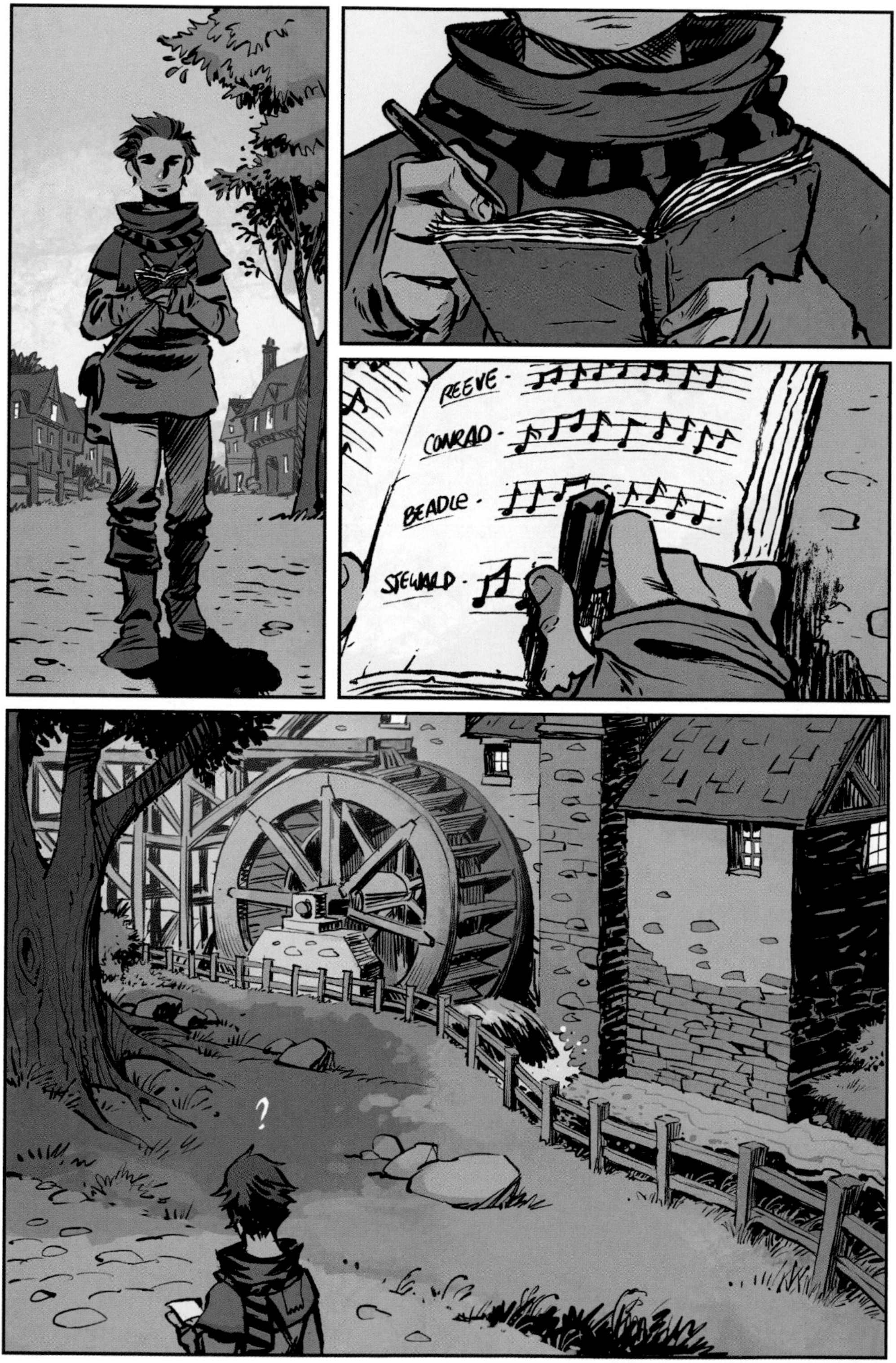

REEVE
CONRAD
BEADLE
STEWARD
?

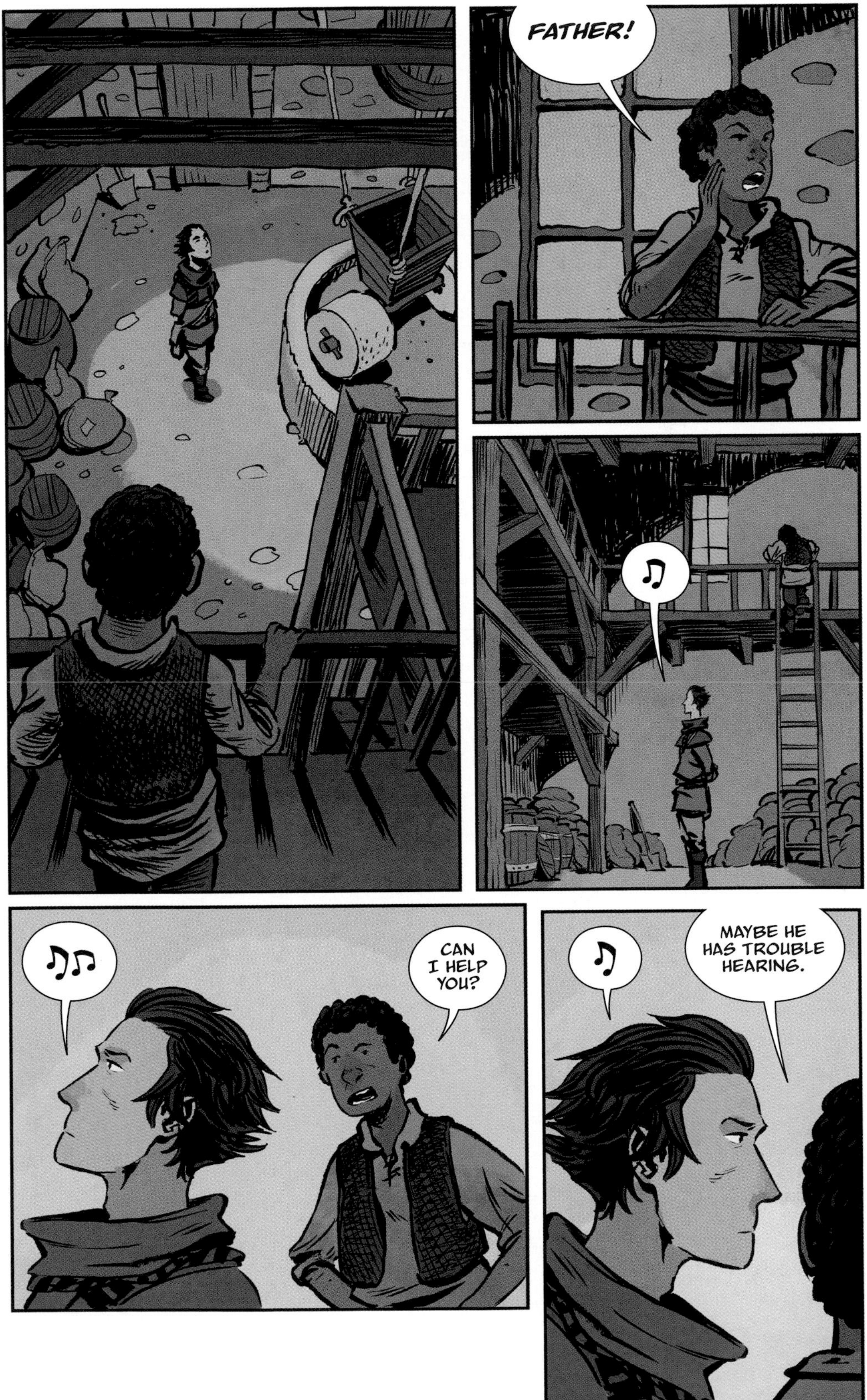
FATHER!
♫
♫♫
CAN I HELP YOU?
♪
MAYBE HE HAS TROUBLE HEARING.

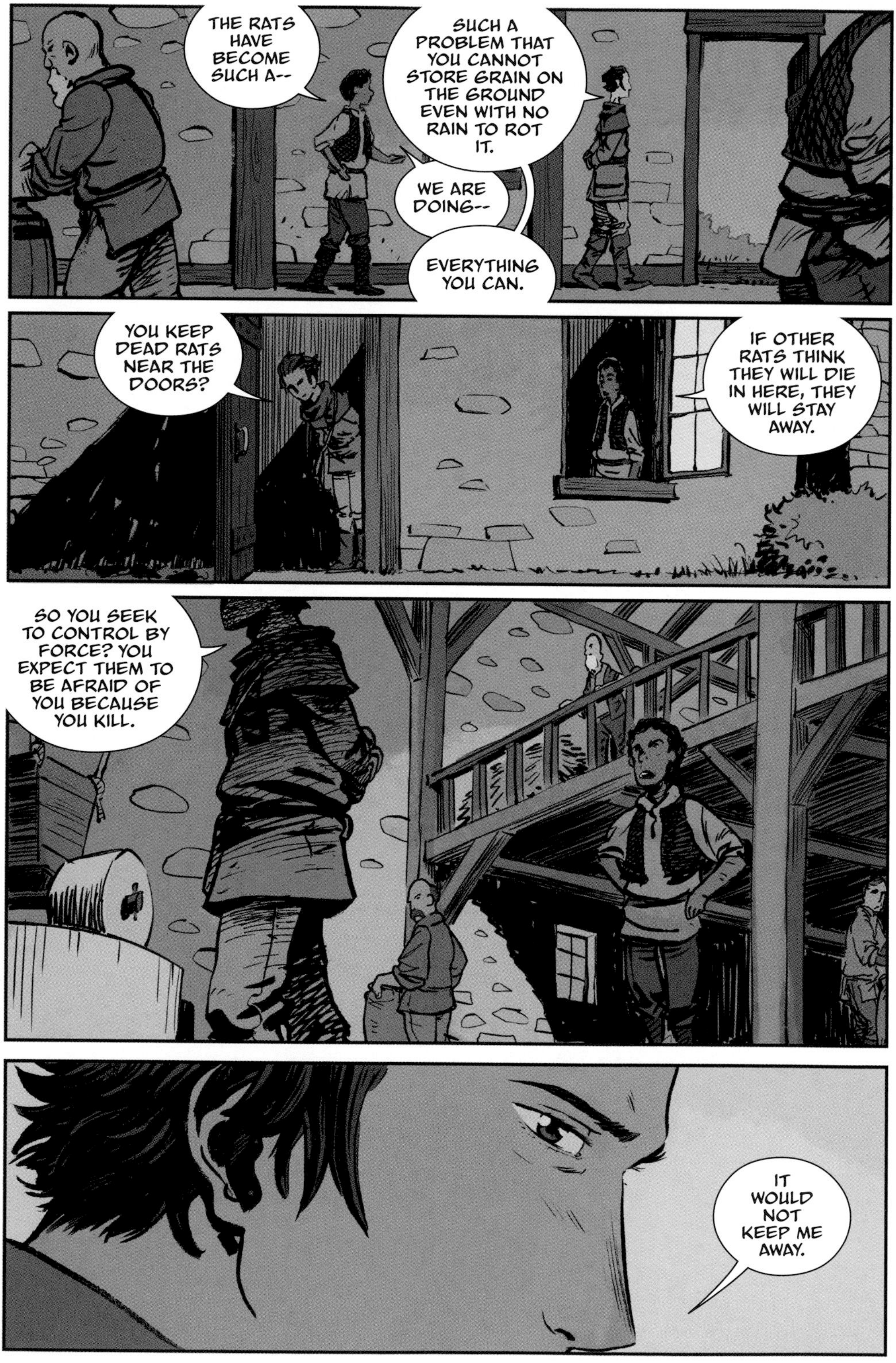
THE RATS HAVE BECOME SUCH A--
SUCH A PROBLEM THAT YOU CANNOT STORE GRAIN ON THE GROUND EVEN WITH NO RAIN TO ROT IT.
WE ARE DOING--
EVERYTHING YOU CAN.
YOU KEEP DEAD RATS NEAR THE DOORS?
IF OTHER RATS THINK THEY WILL DIE IN HERE, THEY WILL STAY AWAY.
SO YOU SEEK TO CONTROL BY FORCE? YOU EXPECT THEM TO BE AFRAID OF YOU BECAUSE YOU KILL.
IT WOULD NOT KEEP ME AWAY.

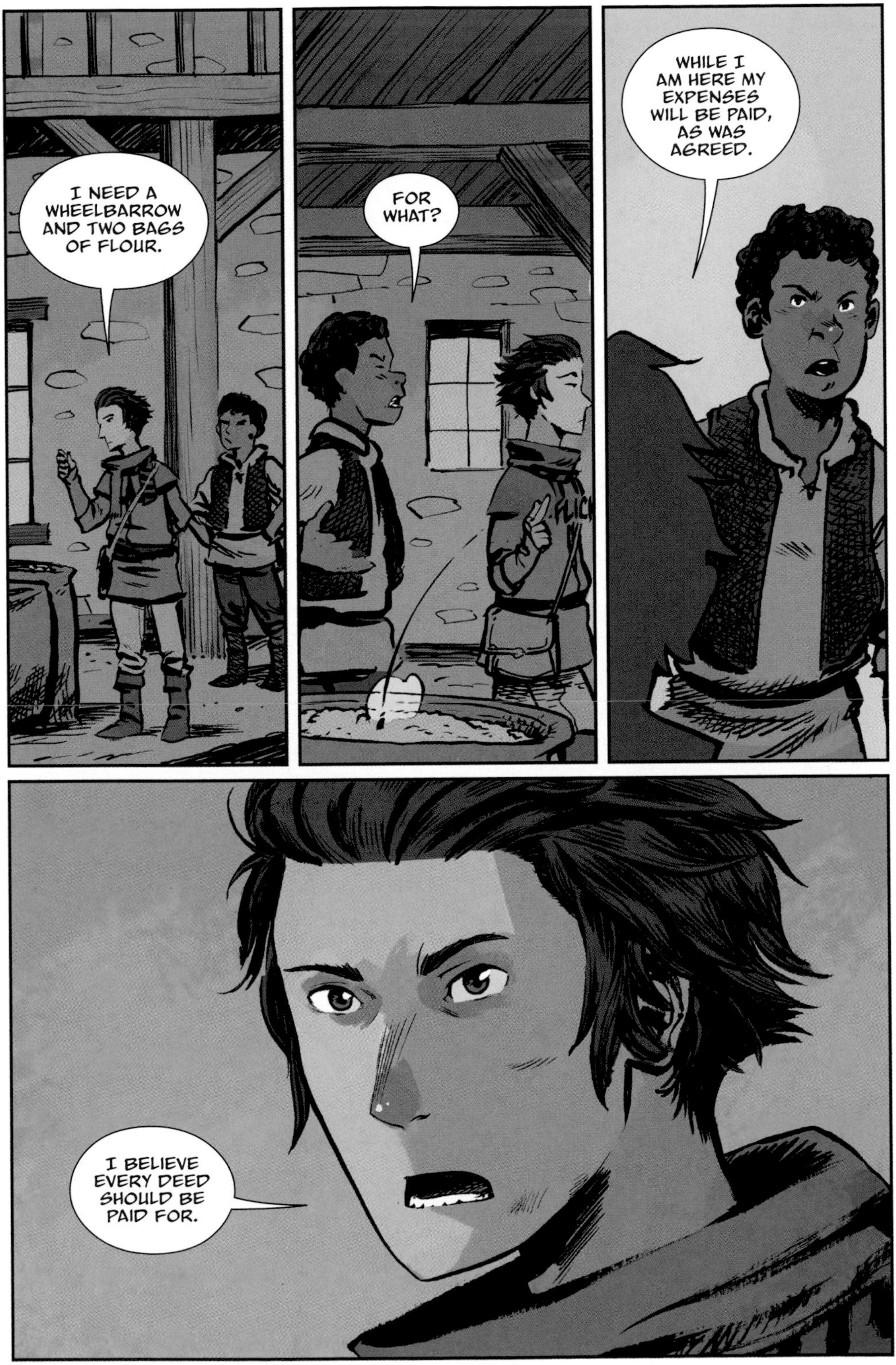
I NEED A WHEELBARROW AND TWO BAGS OF FLOUR.
FOR WHAT?
FLICK
WHILE I AM HERE MY EXPENSES WILL BE PAID, AS WAS AGREED.
I BELIEVE EVERY DEED SHOULD BE PAID FOR.

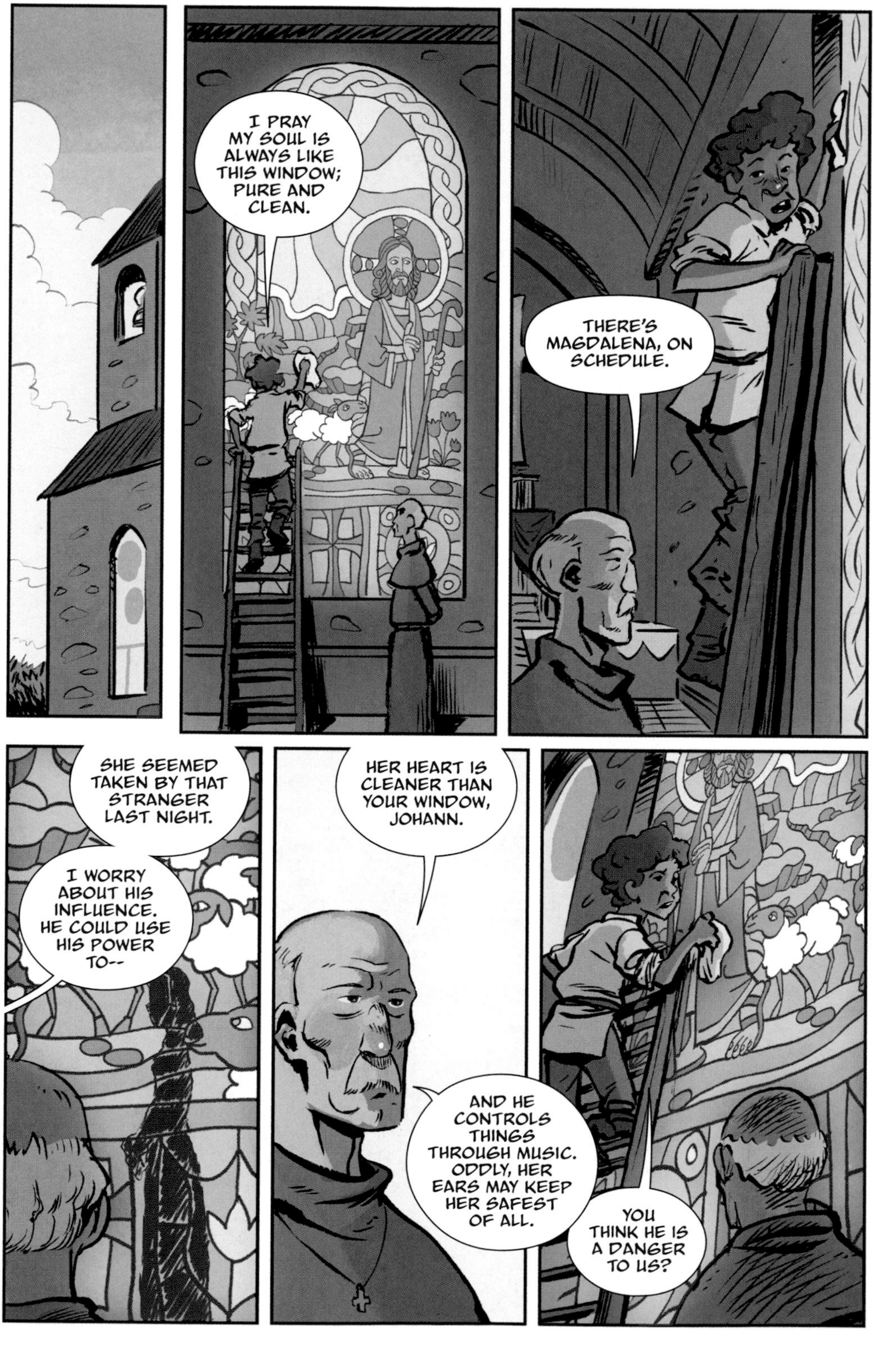
I PRAY MY SOUL IS ALWAYS LIKE THIS WINDOW; PURE AND CLEAN.
THERE'S MAGDALENA, ON SCHEDULE.
SHE SEEMED TAKEN BY THAT STRANGER LAST NIGHT.
I WORRY ABOUT HIS INFLUENCE. HE COULD USE HIS POWER TO--
HER HEART IS CLEANER THAN YOUR WINDOW, JOHANN.
AND HE CONTROLS THINGS THROUGH MUSIC. ODDLY, HER EARS MAY KEEP HER SAFEST OF ALL.
YOU THINK HE IS A DANGER TO US?

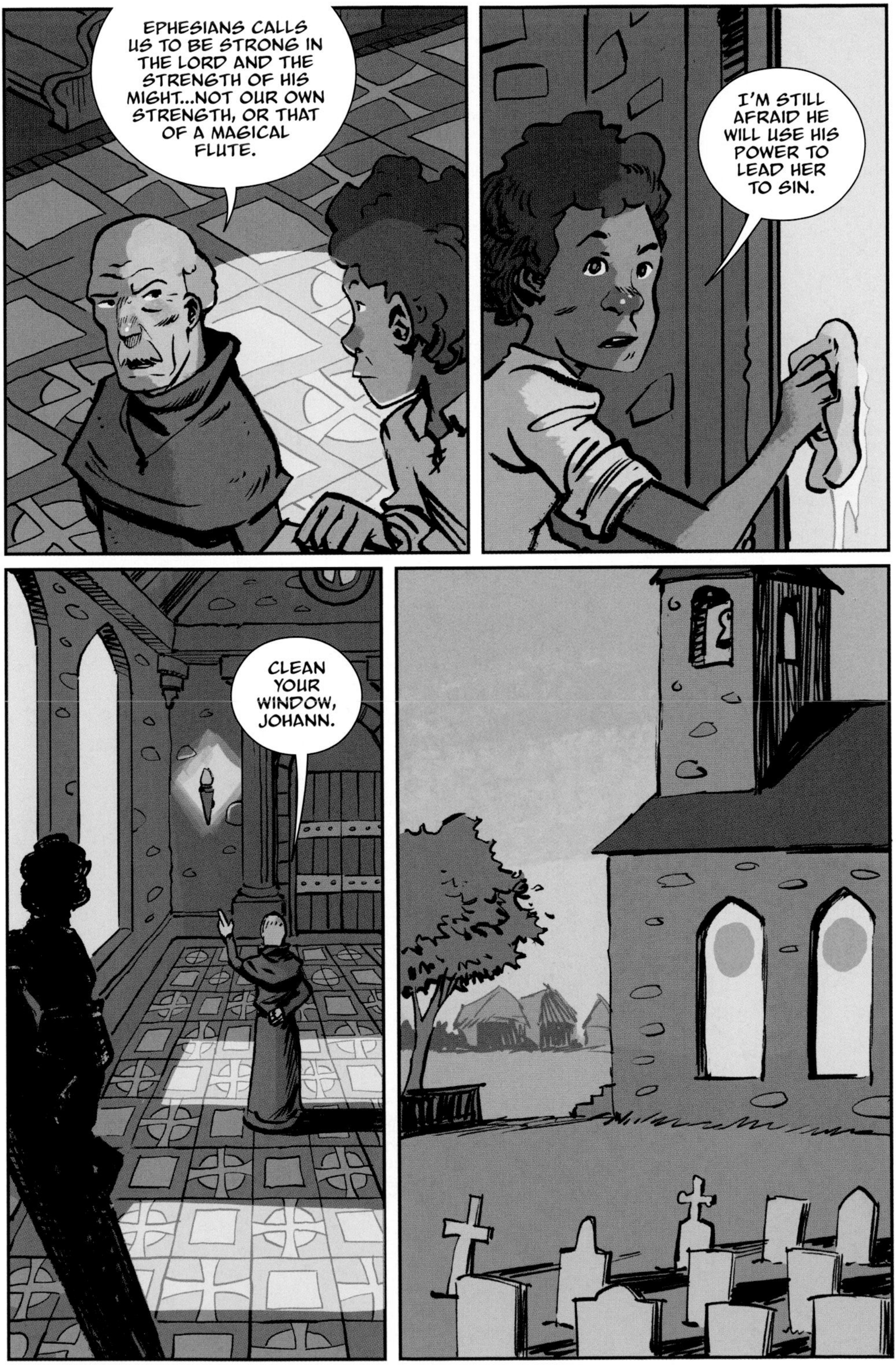
EPHESIANS CALLS US TO BE STRONG IN THE LORD AND THE STRENGTH OF HIS MIGHT...NOT OUR OWN STRENGTH, OR THAT OF A MAGICAL FLUTE.
I'M STILL AFRAID HE WILL USE HIS POWER TO LEAD HER TO SIN.
CLEAN YOUR WINDOW, JOHANN.

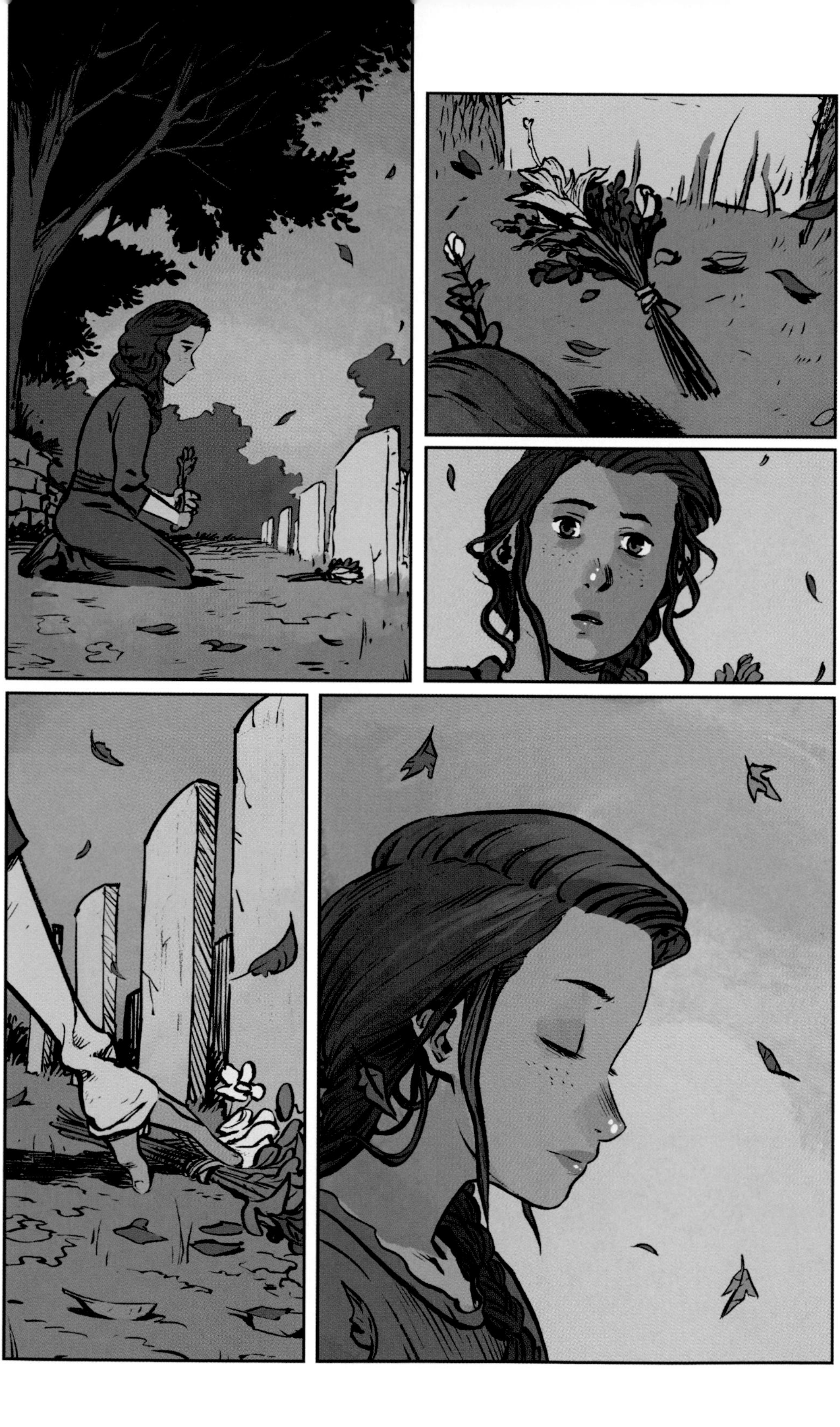

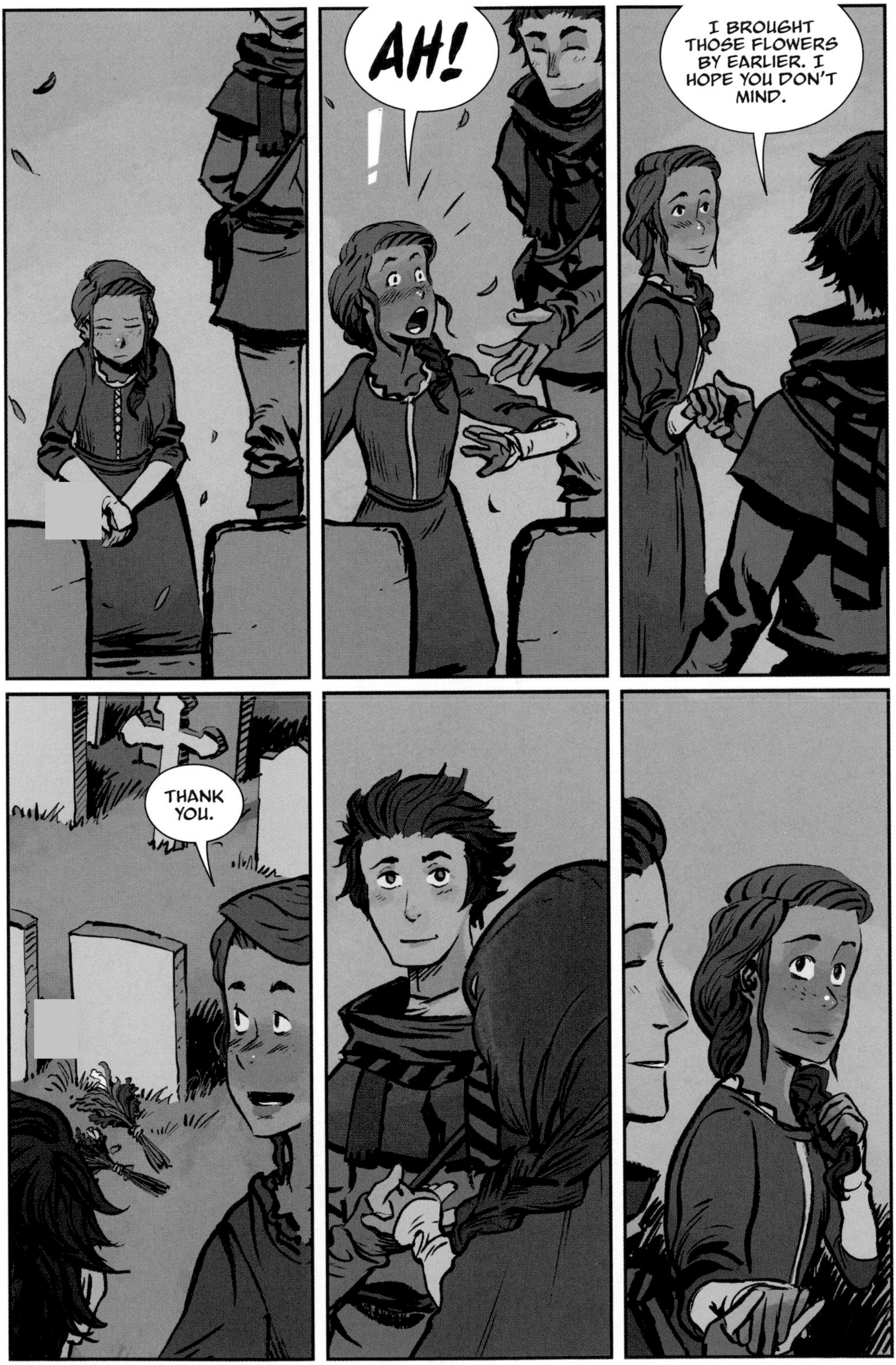
AH!
!
I BROUGHT THOSE FLOWERS BY EARLIER. I HOPE YOU DON'T MIND.
THANK YOU.

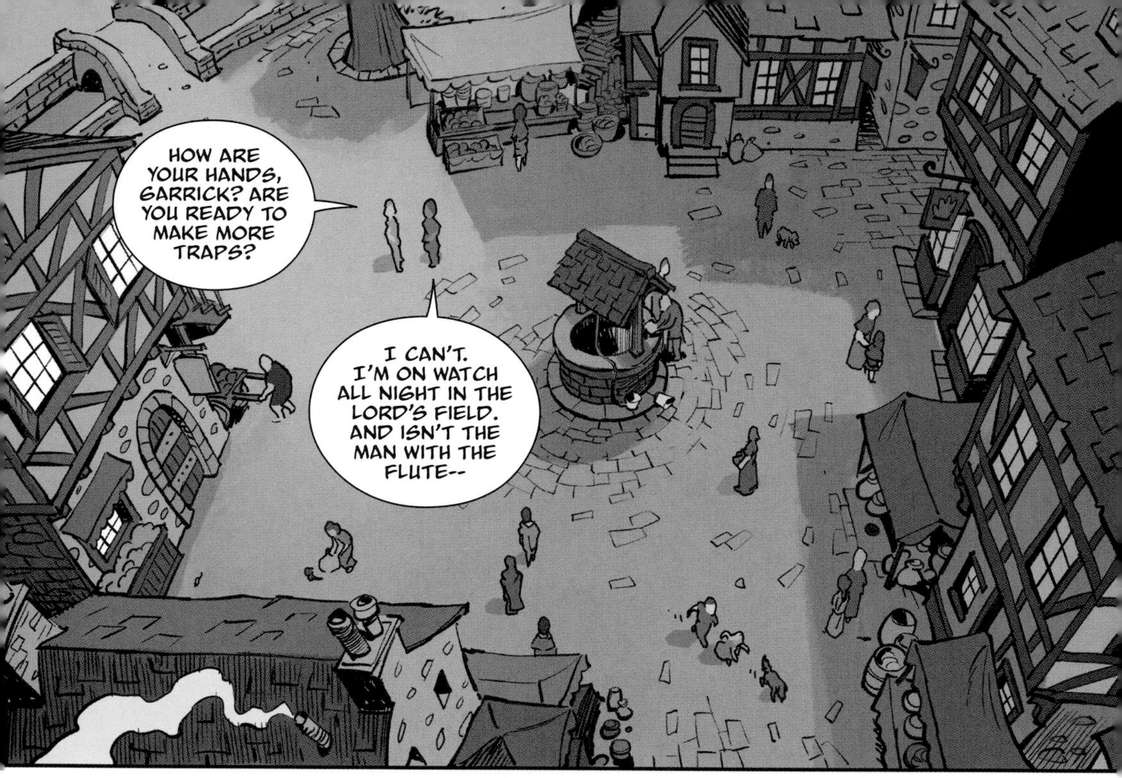
HOW ARE YOUR HANDS, GARRICK? ARE YOU READY TO MAKE MORE TRAPS?
I CAN'T. I'M ON WATCH ALL NIGHT IN THE LORD'S FIELD. AND ISN'T THE MAN WITH THE FLUTE--

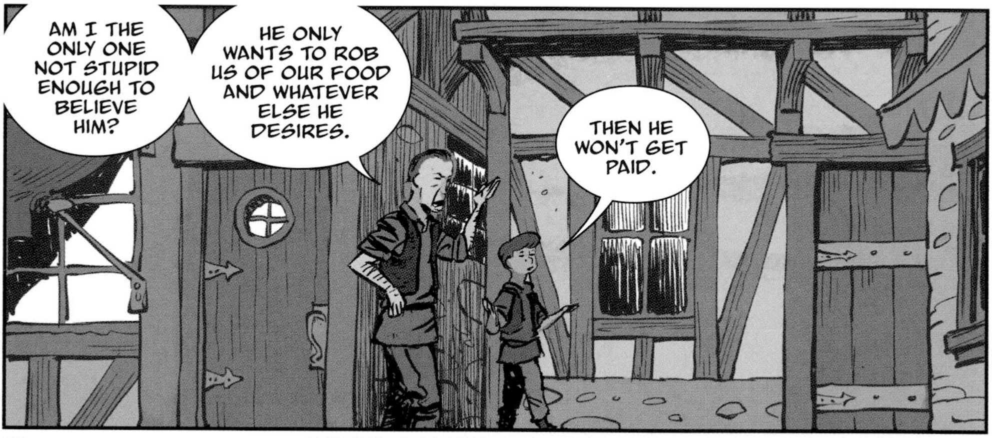
AM I THE ONLY ONE NOT STUPID ENOUGH TO BELIEVE HIM?
HE ONLY WANTS TO ROB US OF OUR FOOD AND WHATEVER ELSE HE DESIRES.
THEN HE WON'T GET PAID.

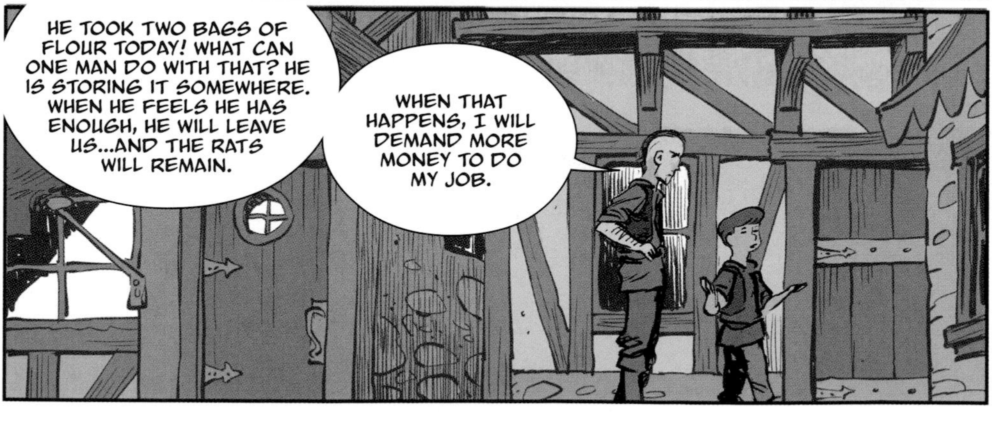
HE TOOK TWO BAGS OF FLOUR TODAY! WHAT CAN ONE MAN DO WITH THAT? HE IS STORING IT SOMEWHERE. WHEN HE FEELS HE HAS ENOUGH, HE WILL LEAVE US...AND THE RATS WILL REMAIN.
WHEN THAT HAPPENS, I WILL DEMAND MORE MONEY TO DO MY JOB.

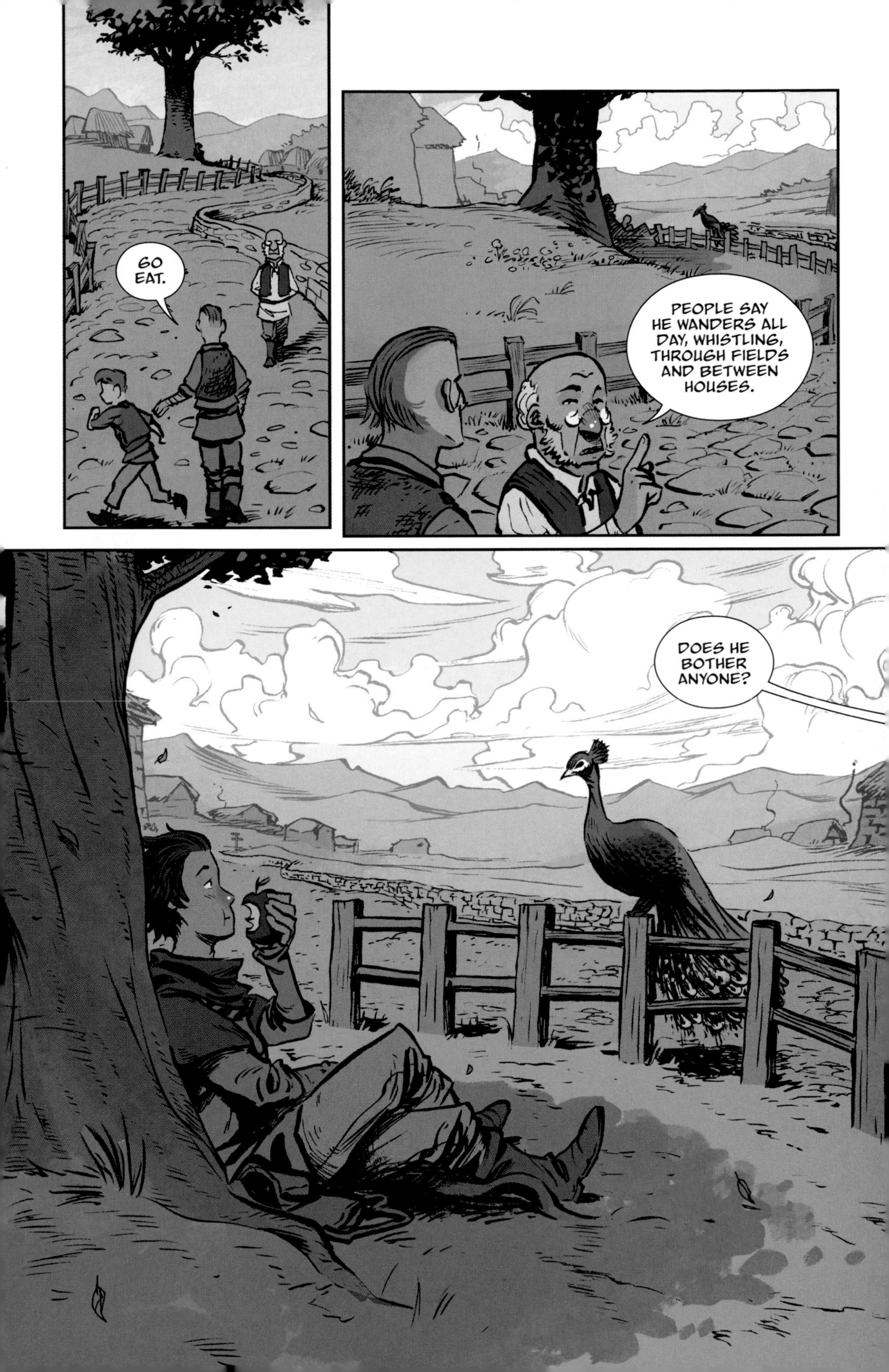
GO EAT.
PEOPLE SAY HE WANDERS ALL DAY, WHISTLING, THROUGH FIELDS AND BETWEEN HOUSES.
DOES HE BOTHER ANYONE?

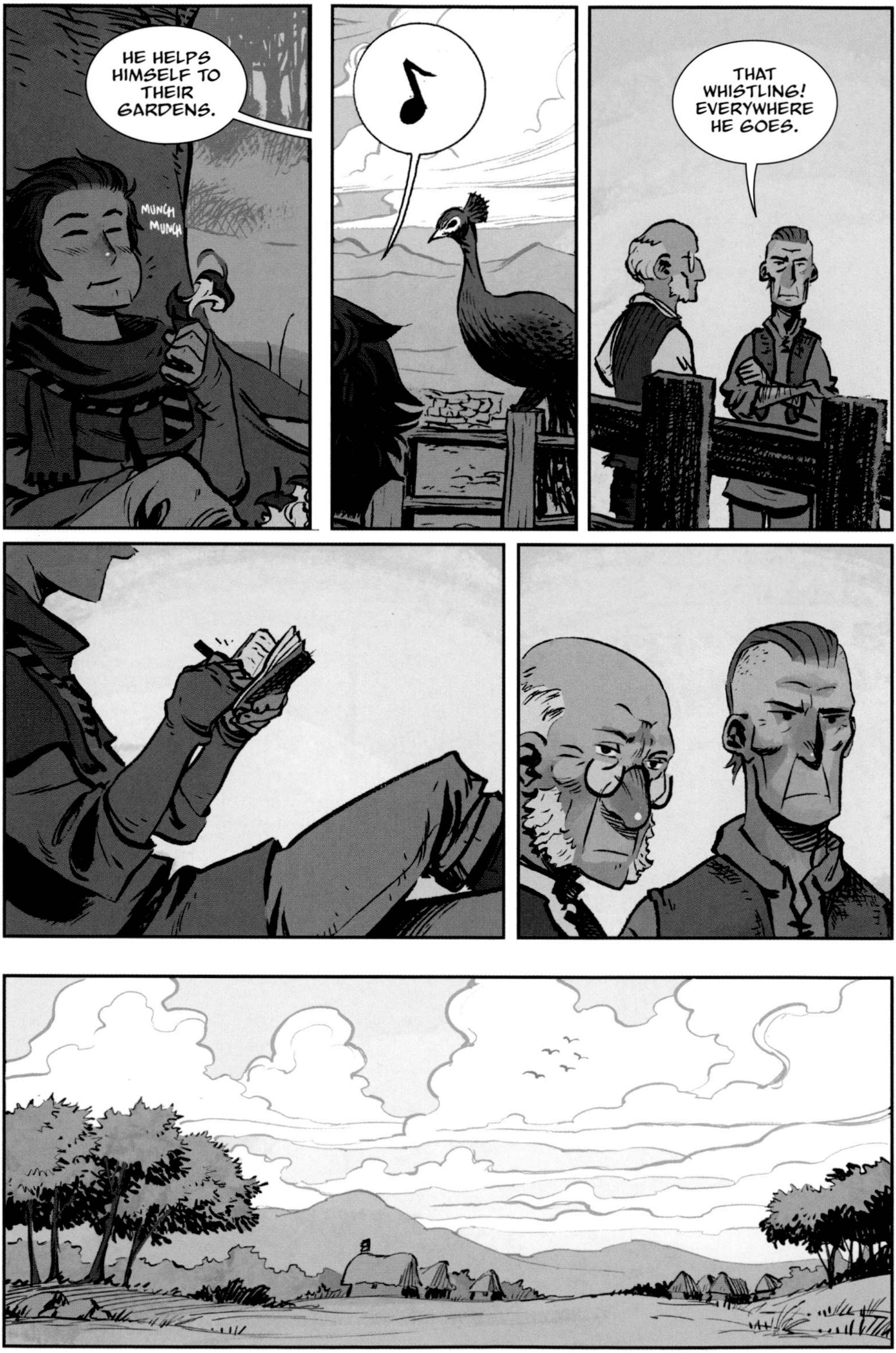
HE HELPS HIMSELF TO THEIR GARDENS.
MUNCH MUNCH
♪
THAT WHISTLING! EVERYWHERE HE GOES.

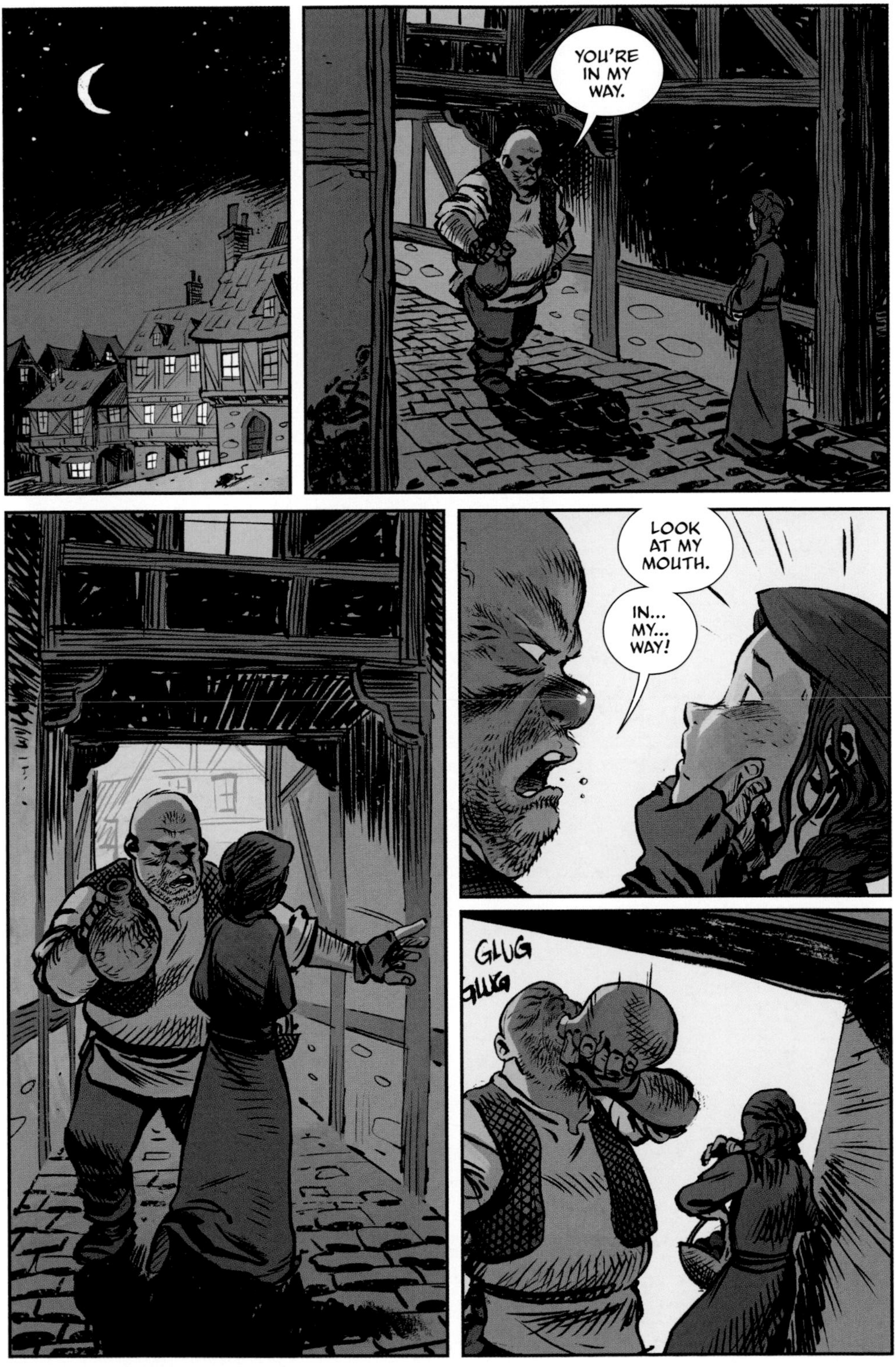
YOU'RE IN MY WAY.
LOOK AT MY MOUTH.
IN... MY... WAY!
GLUG
GLUG

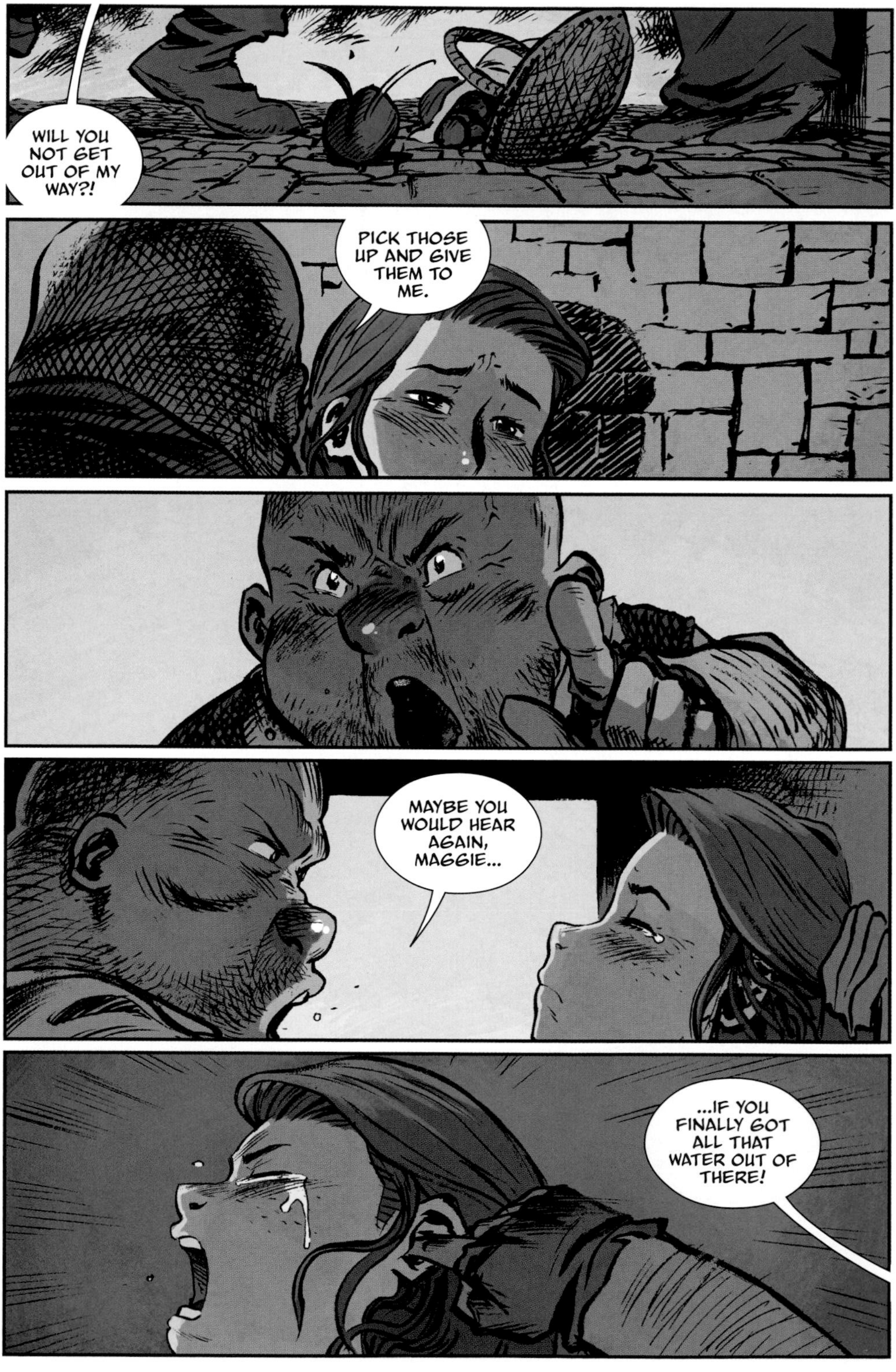
WILL YOU NOT GET OUT OF MY WAY?!
PICK THOSE UP AND GIVE THEM TO ME.
MAYBE YOU WOULD HEAR AGAIN, MAGGIE...
...IF YOU FINALLY GOT ALL THAT WATER OUT OF THERE!

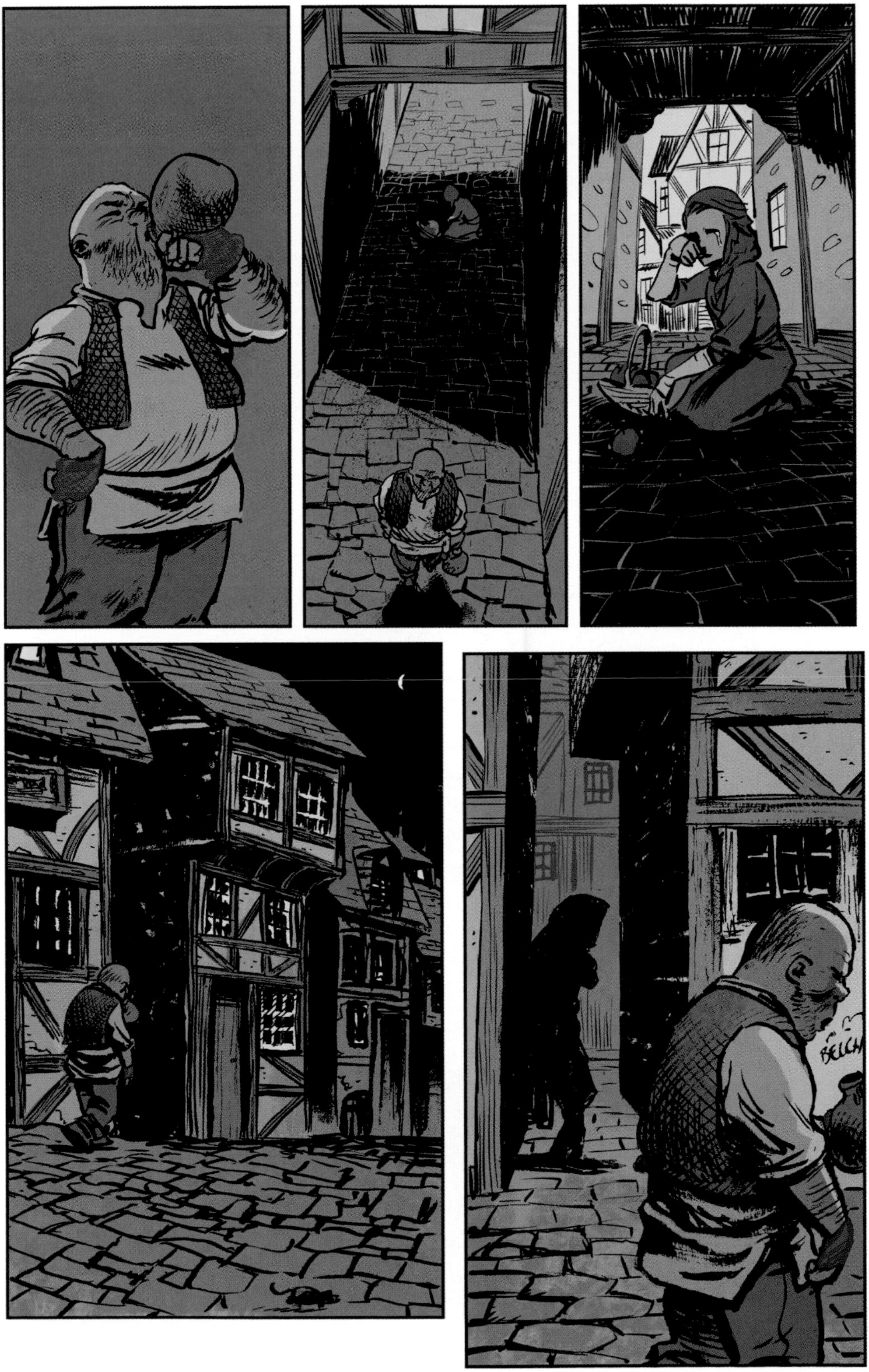
BELCH

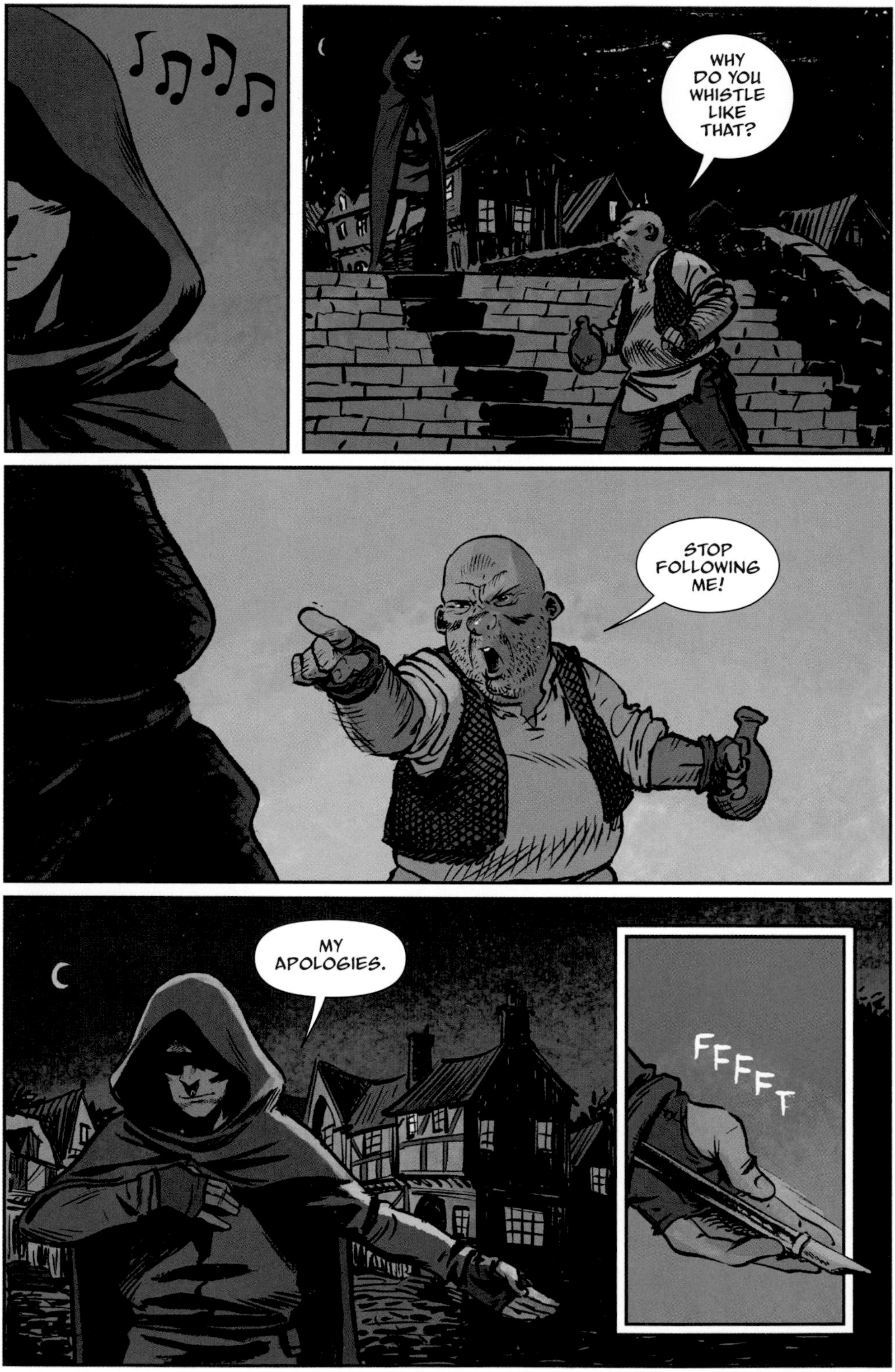
WHY DO YOU WHISTLE LIKE THAT?
STOP FOLLOWING ME!
MY APOLOGIES.
FFFFT

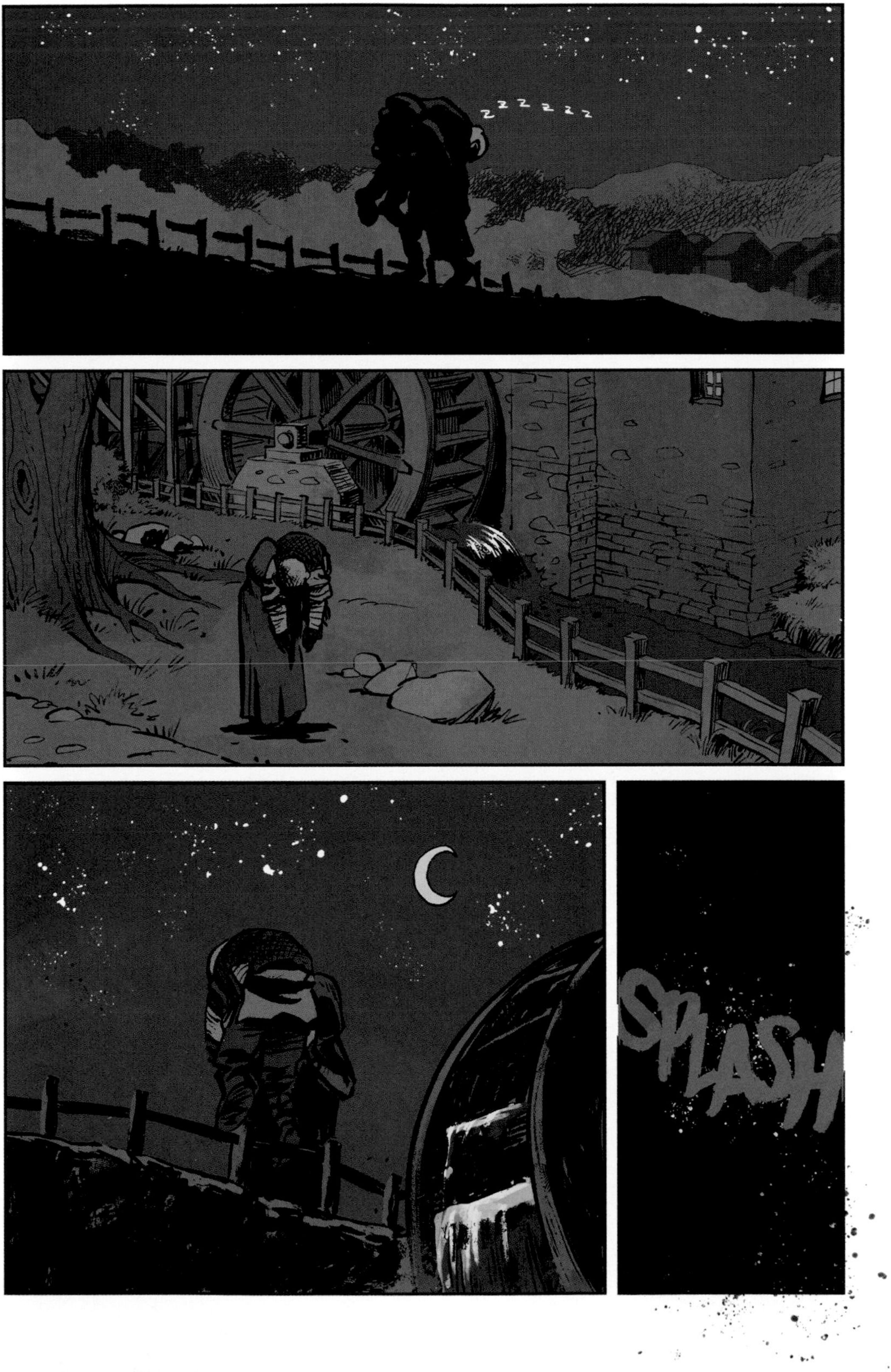
ZZZZZZZ
SPLASH

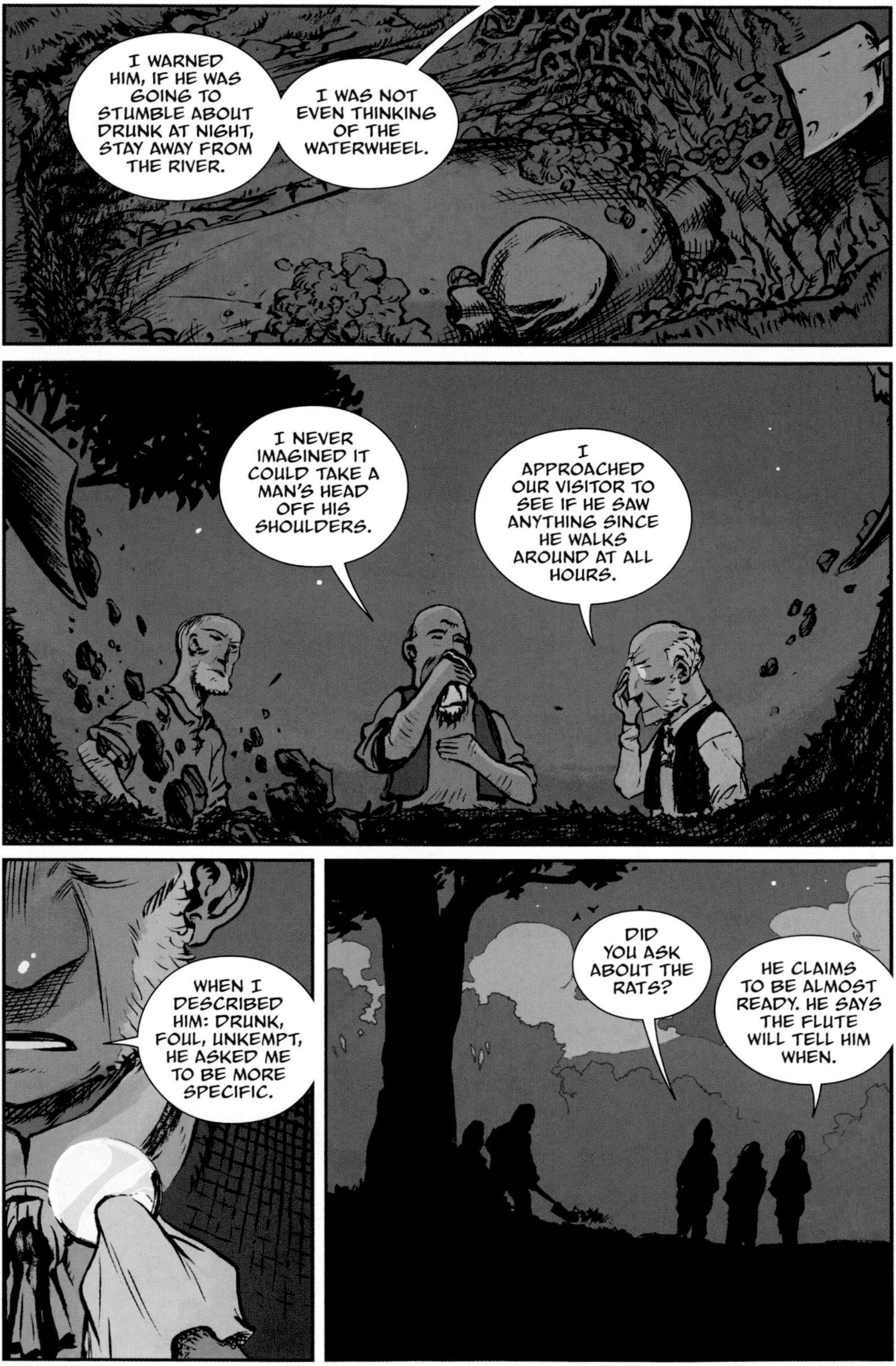
I WARNED HIM, IF HE WAS GOING TO STUMBLE ABOUT DRUNK AT NIGHT, STAY AWAY FROM THE RIVER.
I WAS NOT EVEN THINKING OF THE WATERWHEEL.
I NEVER IMAGINED IT COULD TAKE A MAN'S HEAD OFF HIS SHOULDERS.
I APPROACHED OUR VISITOR TO SEE IF HE SAW ANYTHING SINCE HE WALKS AROUND AT ALL HOURS.
WHEN I DESCRIBED HIM: DRUNK, FOUL, UNKEMPT, HE ASKED ME TO BE MORE SPECIFIC.
DID YOU ASK ABOUT THE RATS?
HE CLAIMS TO BE ALMOST READY. HE SAYS THE FLUTE WILL TELL HIM WHEN.

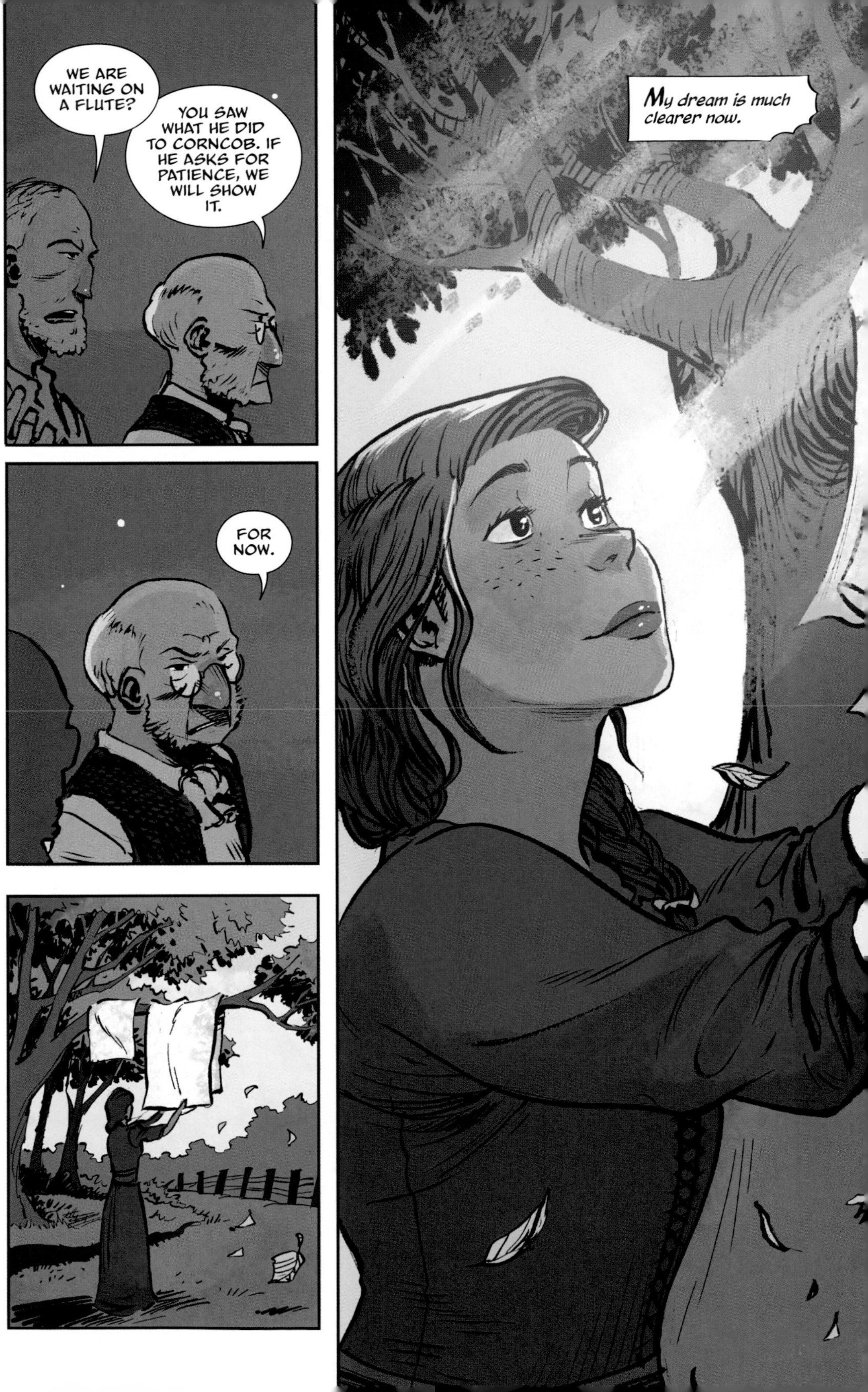
WE ARE WAITING ON A FLUTE?
YOU SAW WHAT HE DID TO CORNCOB. IF HE ASKS FOR PATIENCE, WE WILL SHOW IT.
FOR NOW.
My dream is much clearer now.

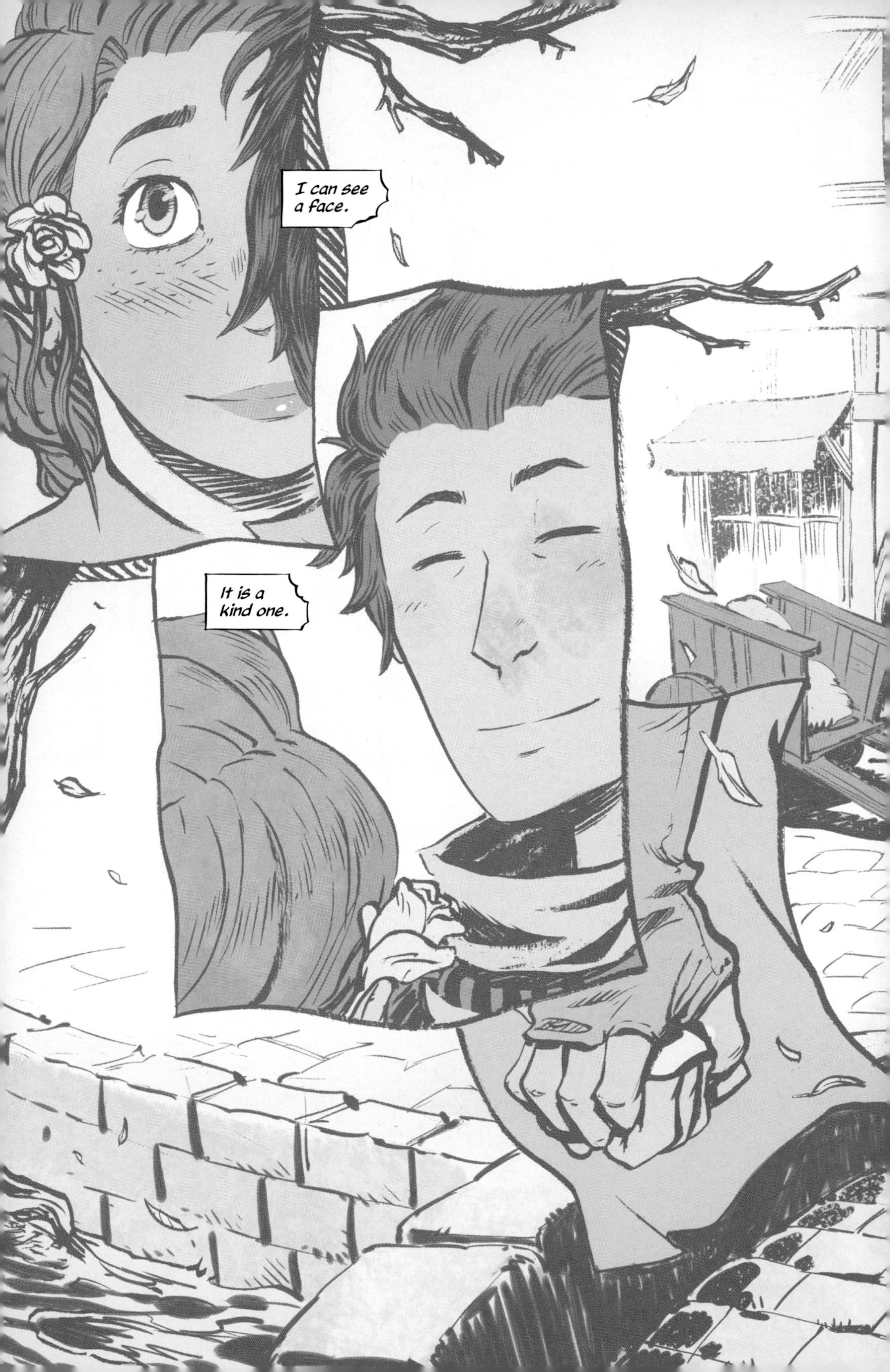
I can see a face.
It is a kind one.

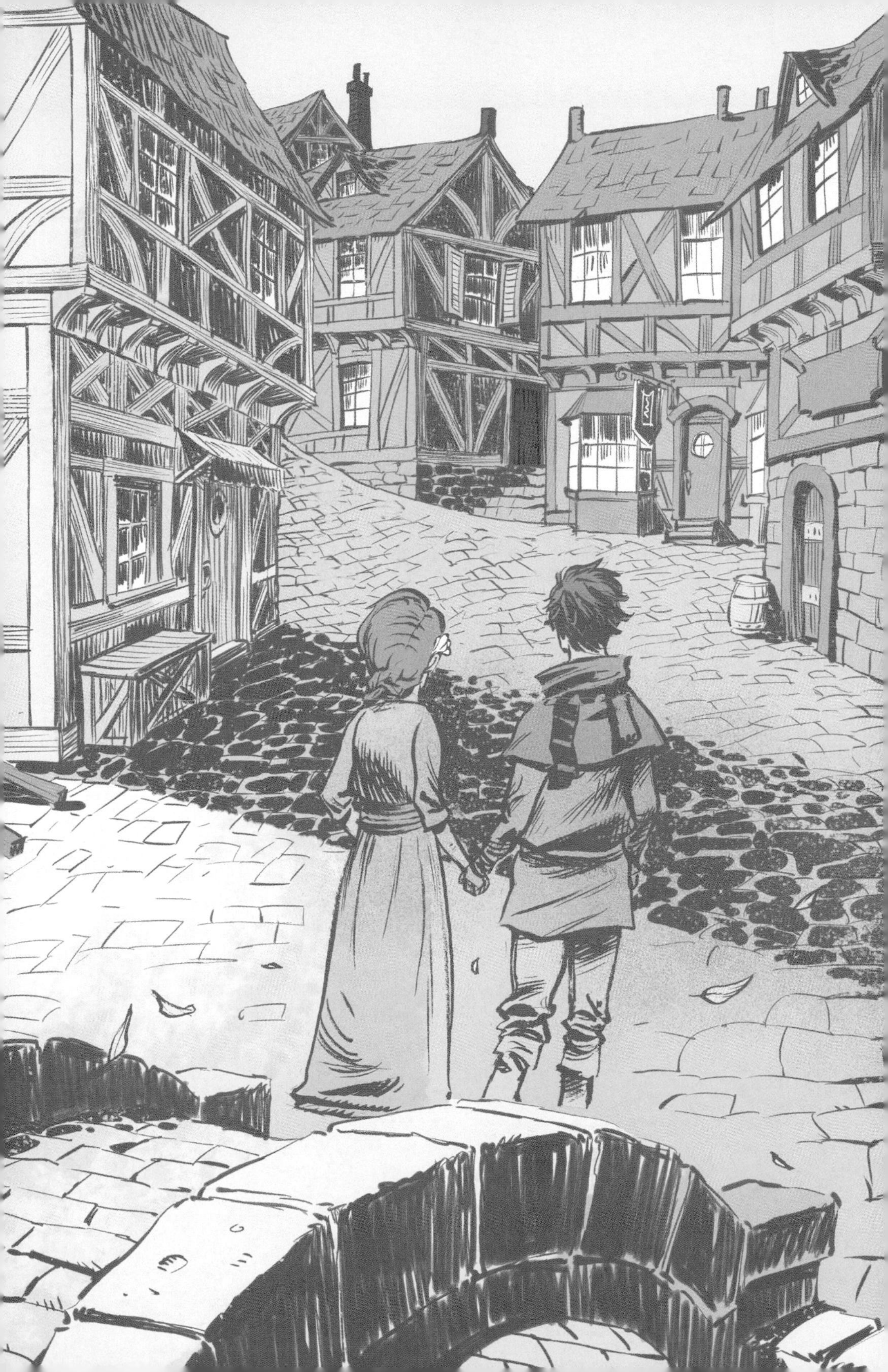

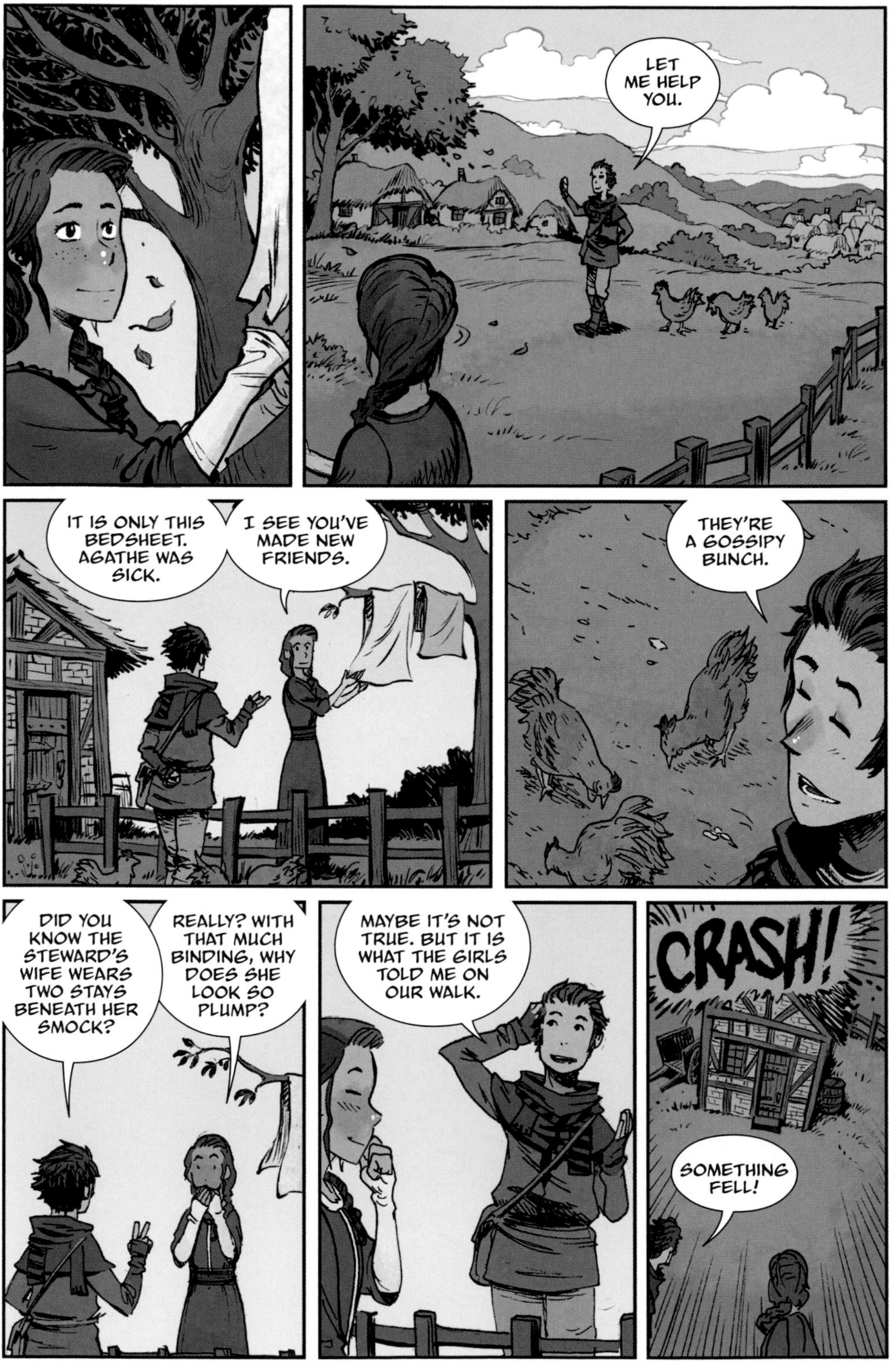
LET ME HELP YOU.
IT IS ONLY THIS BEDSHEET. AGATHE WAS SICK.
I SEE YOU'VE MADE NEW FRIENDS.
THEY'RE A GOSSIPY BUNCH.
DID YOU KNOW THE STEWARD'S WIFE WEARS TWO STAYS BENEATH HER SMOCK?
REALLY? WITH THAT MUCH BINDING, WHY DOES SHE LOOK SO PLUMP?
MAYBE IT'S NOT TRUE. BUT IT IS WHAT THE GIRLS TOLD ME ON OUR WALK.
CRASH!
SOMETHING FELL!

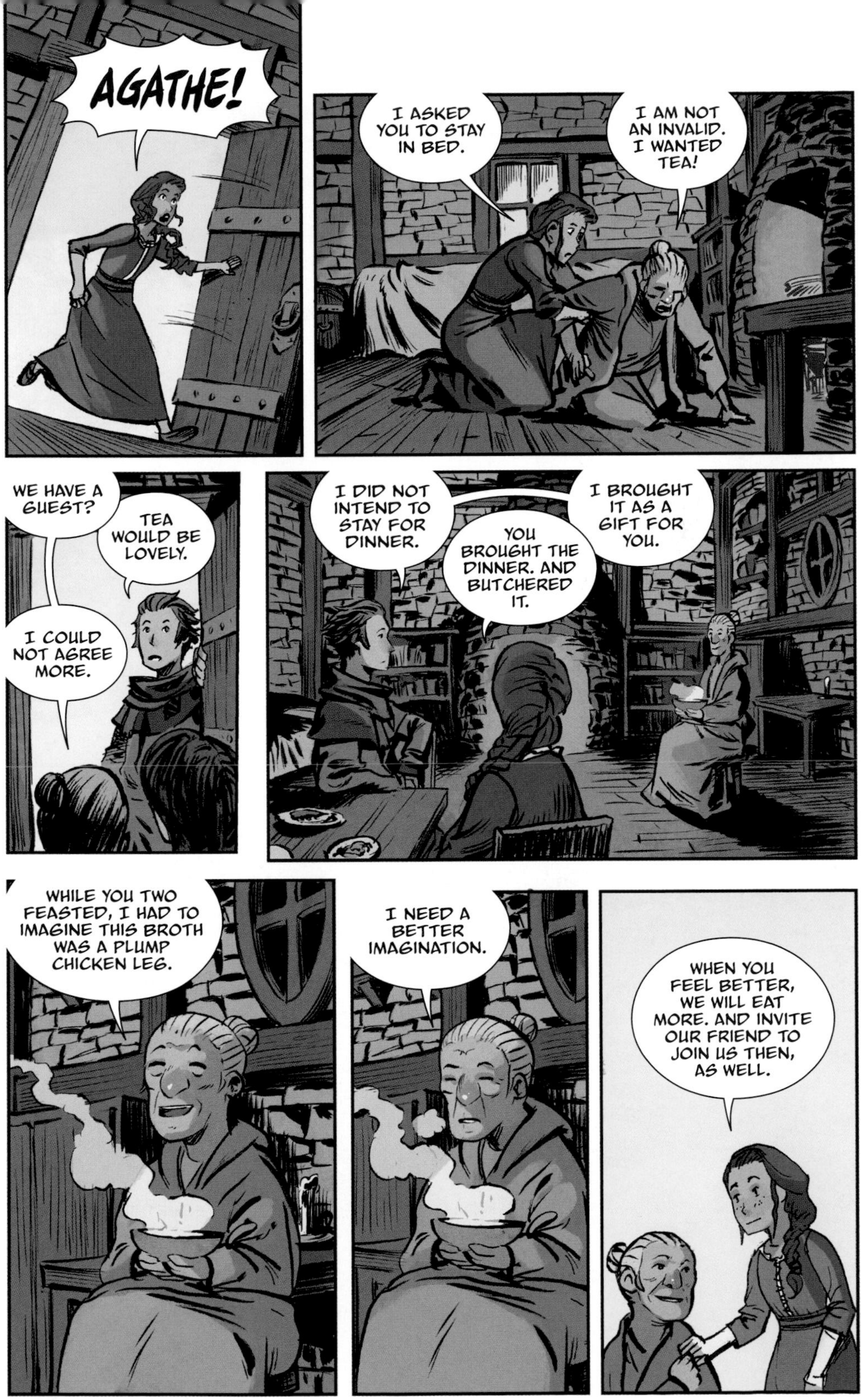
AGATHE!
I ASKED YOU TO STAY IN BED.
I AM NOT AN INVALID. I WANTED TEA!
WE HAVE A GUEST?
TEA WOULD BE LOVELY.
I COULD NOT AGREE MORE.
I DID NOT INTEND TO STAY FOR DINNER.
I BROUGHT IT AS A GIFT FOR YOU.
YOU BROUGHT THE DINNER. AND BUTCHERED IT.
WHILE YOU TWO FEASTED, I HAD TO IMAGINE THIS BROTH WAS A PLUMP CHICKEN LEG.
I NEED A BETTER IMAGINATION.
WHEN YOU FEEL BETTER, WE WILL EAT MORE. AND INVITE OUR FRIEND TO JOIN US THEN, AS WELL.

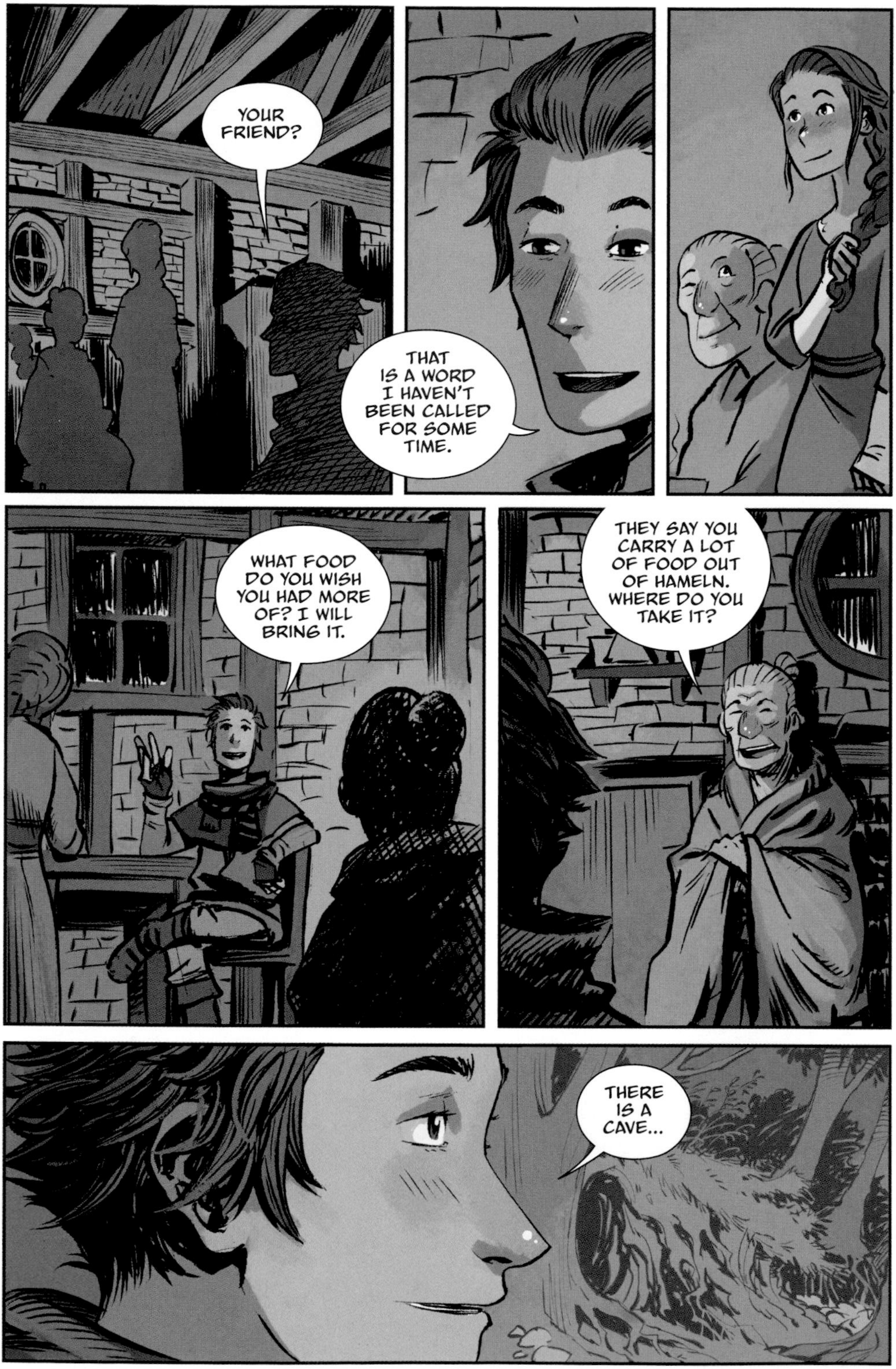
YOUR FRIEND?
THAT IS A WORD I HAVEN'T BEEN CALLED FOR SOME TIME.
WHAT FOOD DO YOU WISH YOU HAD MORE OF? I WILL BRING IT.
THEY SAY YOU CARRY A LOT OF FOOD OUT OF HAMELN. WHERE DO YOU TAKE IT?
THERE IS A CAVE...

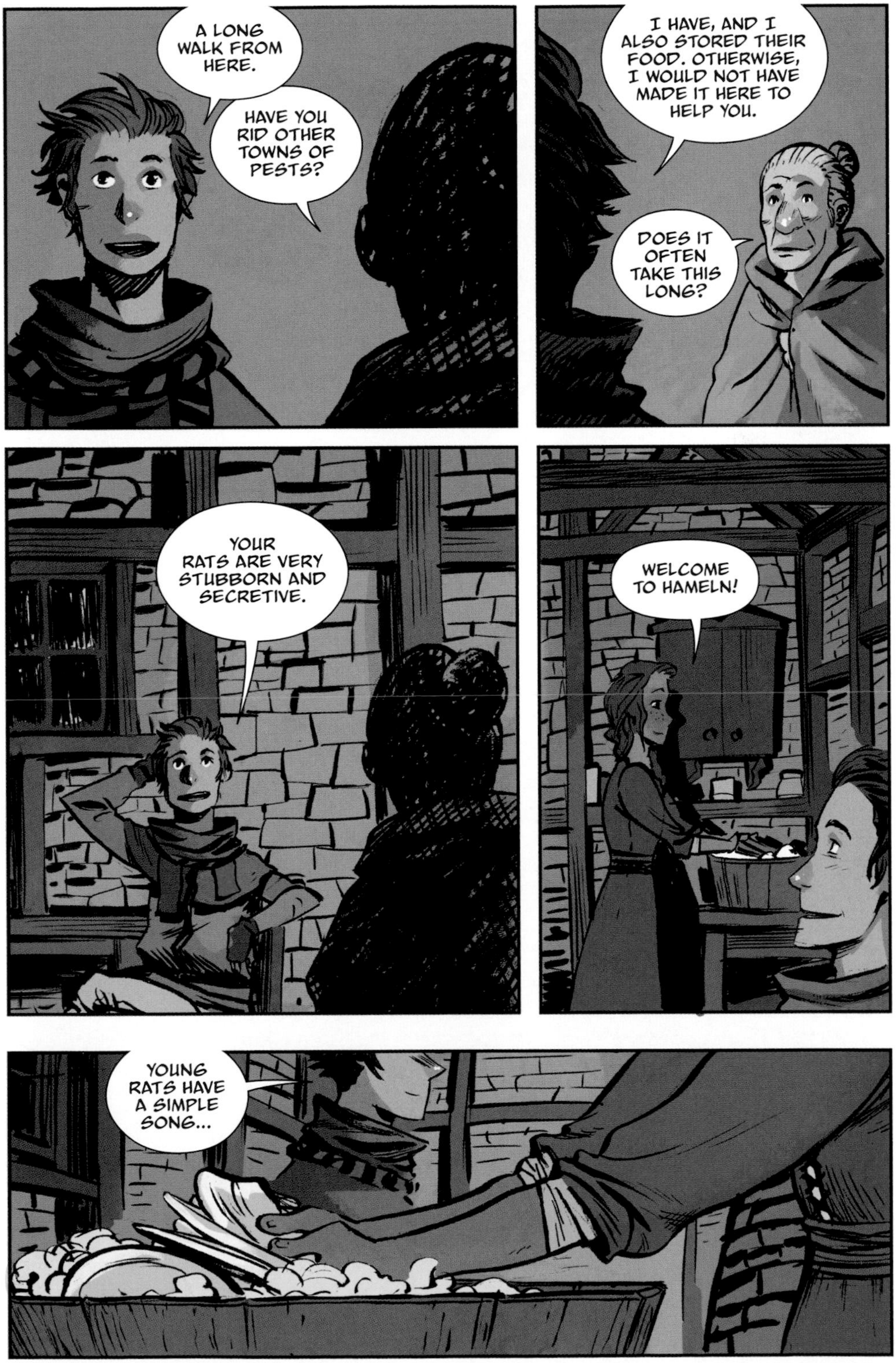
A LONG WALK FROM HERE.
HAVE YOU RID OTHER TOWNS OF PESTS?
I HAVE, AND I ALSO STORED THEIR FOOD. OTHERWISE, I WOULD NOT HAVE MADE IT HERE TO HELP YOU.
DOES IT OFTEN TAKE THIS LONG?
YOUR RATS ARE VERY STUBBORN AND SECRETIVE.
WELCOME TO HAMELN!
YOUNG RATS HAVE A SIMPLE SONG...

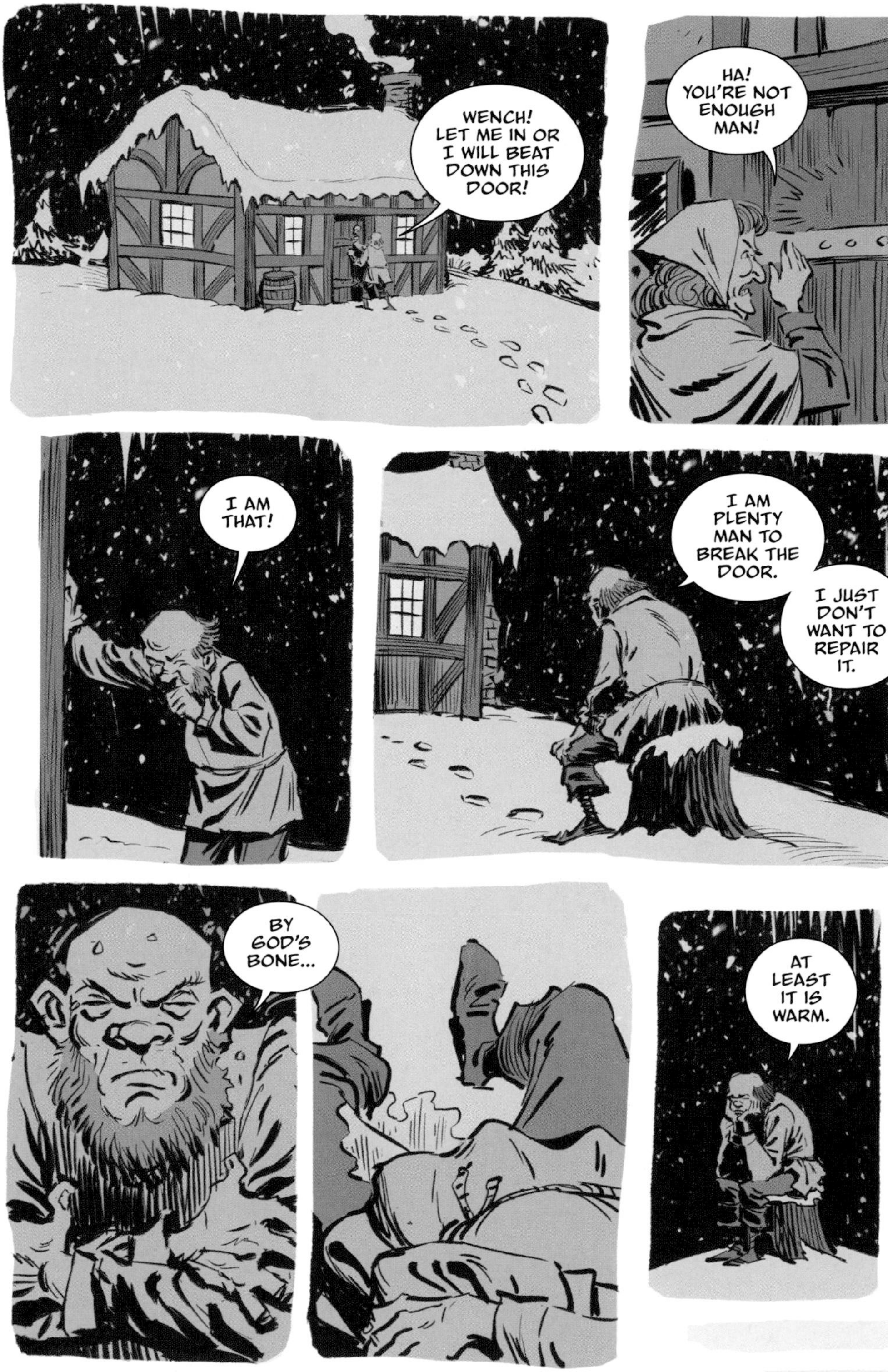
WENCH! LET ME IN OR I WILL BEAT DOWN THIS DOOR!
HA! YOU'RE NOT ENOUGH MAN!
I AM THAT!
I AM PLENTY MAN TO BREAK THE DOOR.
I JUST DON'T WANT TO REPAIR IT.
BY GOD'S BONE...
AT LEAST IT IS WARM.

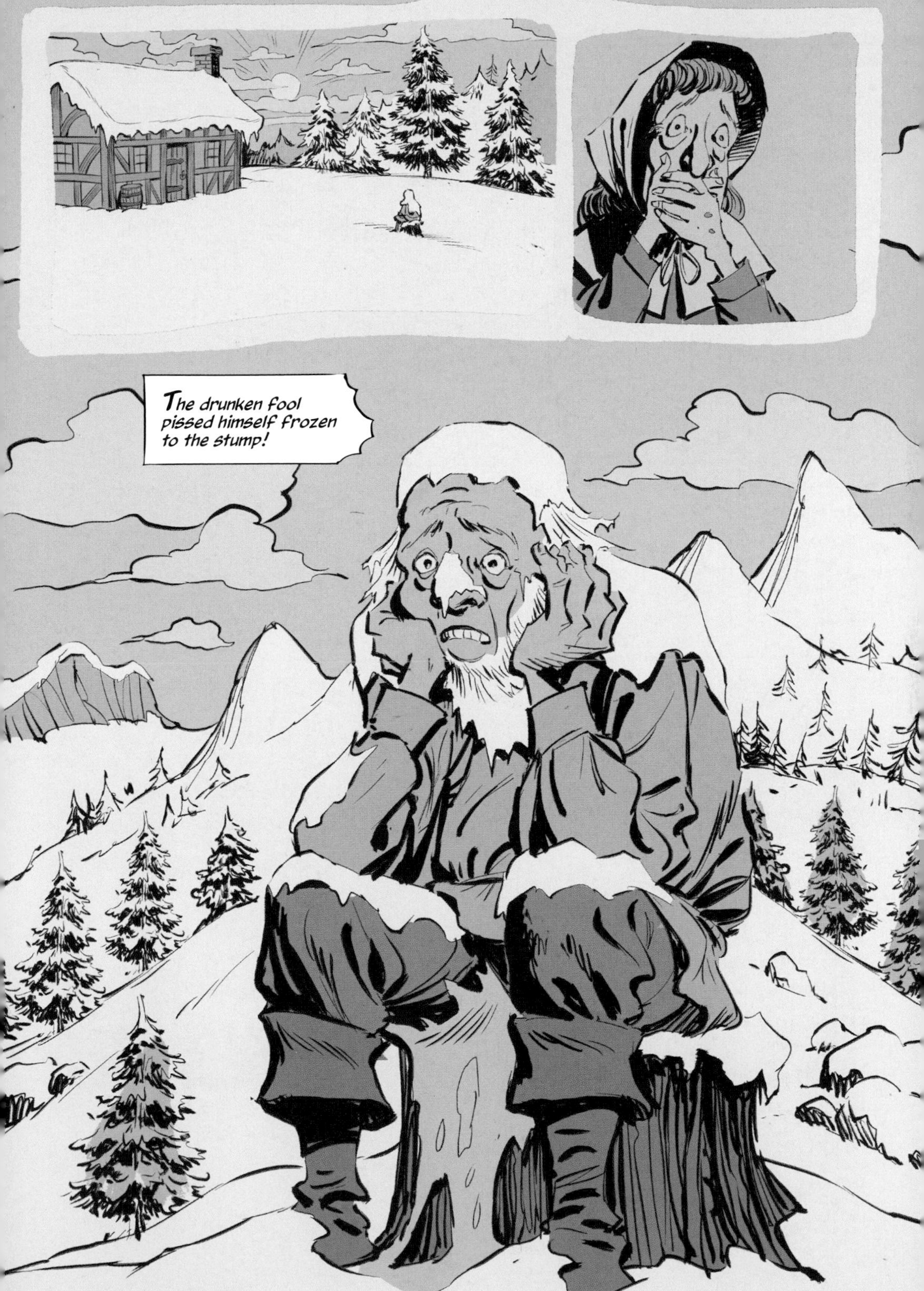
The drunken fool pissed himself frozen to the stump!

HAHAHA
AH AH
AHA HA
AHH

SHE IS TAKEN BY YOU.

WHEN THE RATS ARE GONE, I MUST LEAVE.

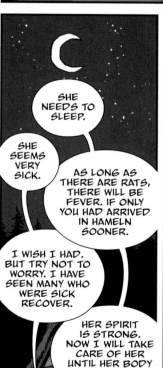

SHE NEEDS TO SLEEP.

SHE SEEMS VERY SICK.

AS LONG AS THERE ARE RATS, THERE WILL BE FEVER. IF ONLY YOU HAD ARRIVED IN HAMELN SOONER.

I WISH I HAD. BUT TRY NOT TO WORRY. I HAVE SEEN MANY WHO WERE SICK RECOVER.

HER SPIRIT IS STRONG. NOW I WILL TAKE CARE OF HER UNTIL HER BODY IS STRONG, AS WELL.

MAGDALENA, I CAN'T REMEMBER THE LAST TIME I DIDN'T WANT TO BE BY MYSELF ALL NIGHT.

WHEN WILL YOUR TASK HERE BE DONE?

I WILL START GETTING READY TONIGHT.

WOULD YOU HELP ME?

I SHOULD NOT LEAVE AGATHE.

IT WILL ONLY TAKE ONE HOUR.

IT WILL TAKE ONE HOUR.

BUT HOW DO YOU DO IT?

IT WAS TAUGHT TO ME BY MY FATHER. ONCE I LEARN ITS SONG, I CAN MAKE A CREATURE DO ONE OF TWO THINGS: SLEEP OR FOLLOW.

EVEN PEOPLE?

YES.

BUT TO CONTROL MANY CREATURES AT ONCE, LIKE WITH YOUR RATS, I MUST FIND A COMMON SONG.

HAVE YOU LEARNED THEIR SONG YET?

ALMOST.

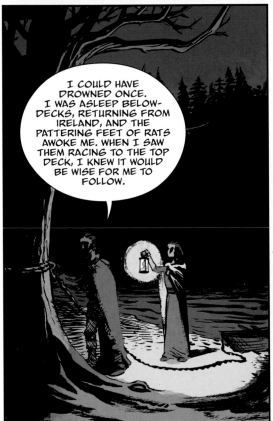

I COULD HAVE DROWNED ONCE. I WAS ASLEEP BELOW-DECKS, RETURNING FROM IRELAND, AND THE PATTERING FEET OF RATS AWOKE ME. WHEN I SAW THEM RACING TO THE TOP DECK, I KNEW IT WOULD BE WISE FOR ME TO FOLLOW.

THAT IS THE ONLY TIME IT IS WISE TO FOLLOW A RAT.

DO YOU ENJOY LIVING IN THE WOODS?

I AM COMFORTABLE HERE.

BECAUSE THERE ARE NOT A LOT OF PEOPLE?

BECAUSE A LOT OF PEOPLE THINK THIS IS WHERE I BELONG.

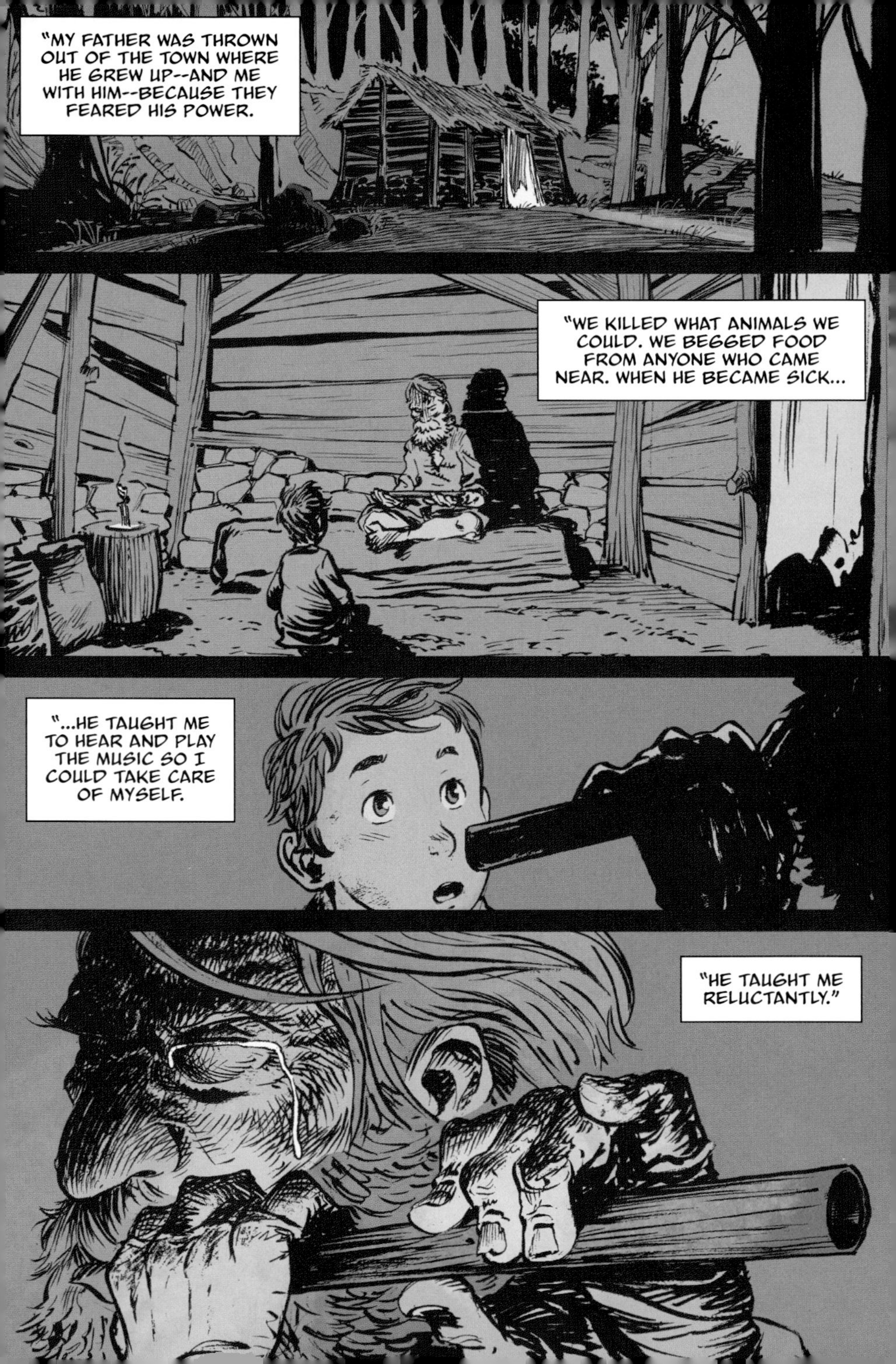
"MY FATHER WAS THROWN OUT OF THE TOWN WHERE HE GREW UP--AND ME WITH HIM--BECAUSE THEY FEARED HIS POWER.
"WE KILLED WHAT ANIMALS WE COULD. WE BEGGED FOOD FROM ANYONE WHO CAME NEAR. WHEN HE BECAME SICK...
"...HE TAUGHT ME TO HEAR AND PLAY THE MUSIC SO I COULD TAKE CARE OF MYSELF.
"HE TAUGHT ME RELUCTANTLY."

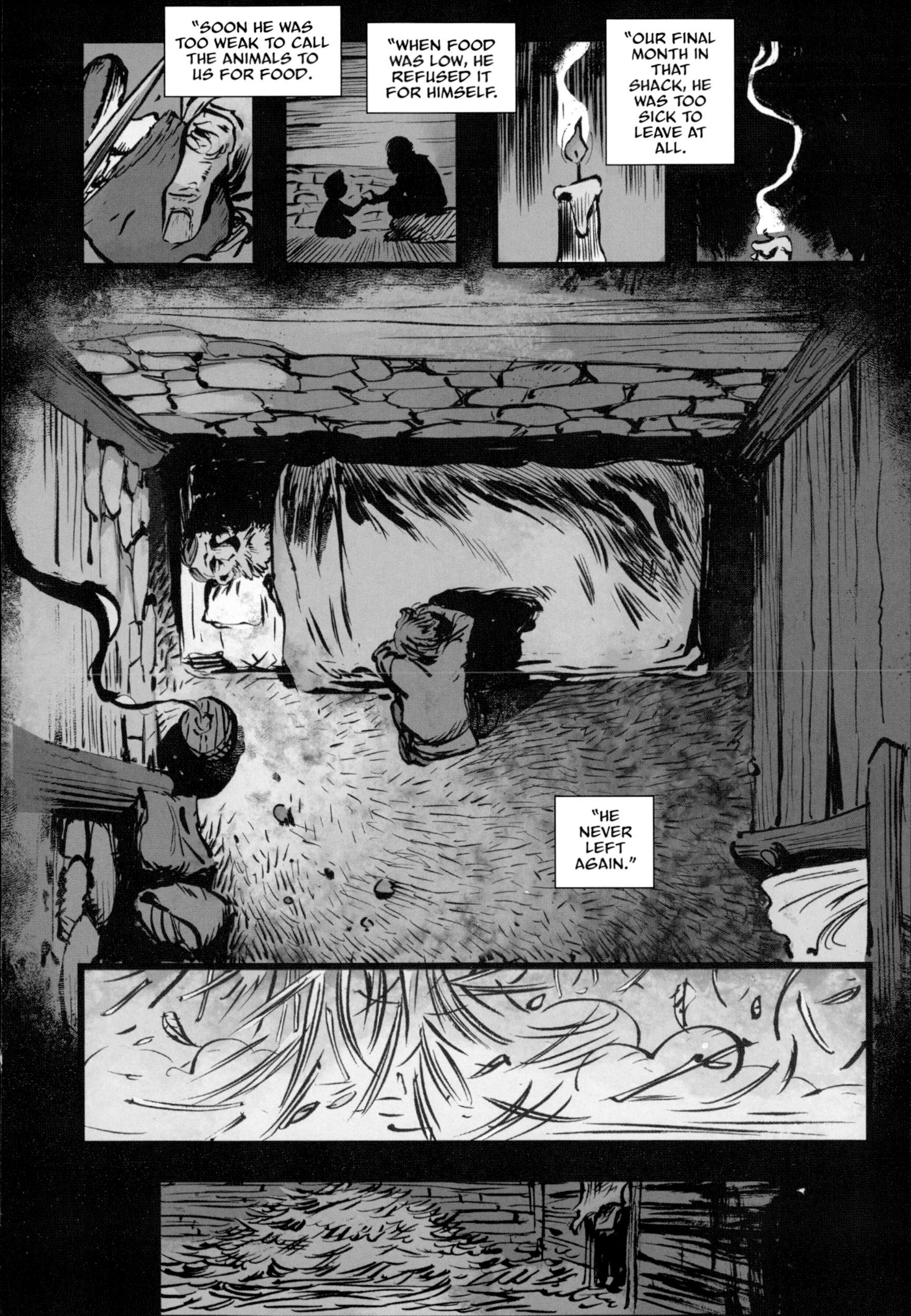
"SOON HE WAS TOO WEAK TO CALL THE ANIMALS TO US FOR FOOD.
"WHEN FOOD WAS LOW, HE REFUSED IT FOR HIMSELF.
"OUR FINAL MONTH IN THAT SHACK, HE WAS TOO SICK TO LEAVE AT ALL.
"HE NEVER LEFT AGAIN."

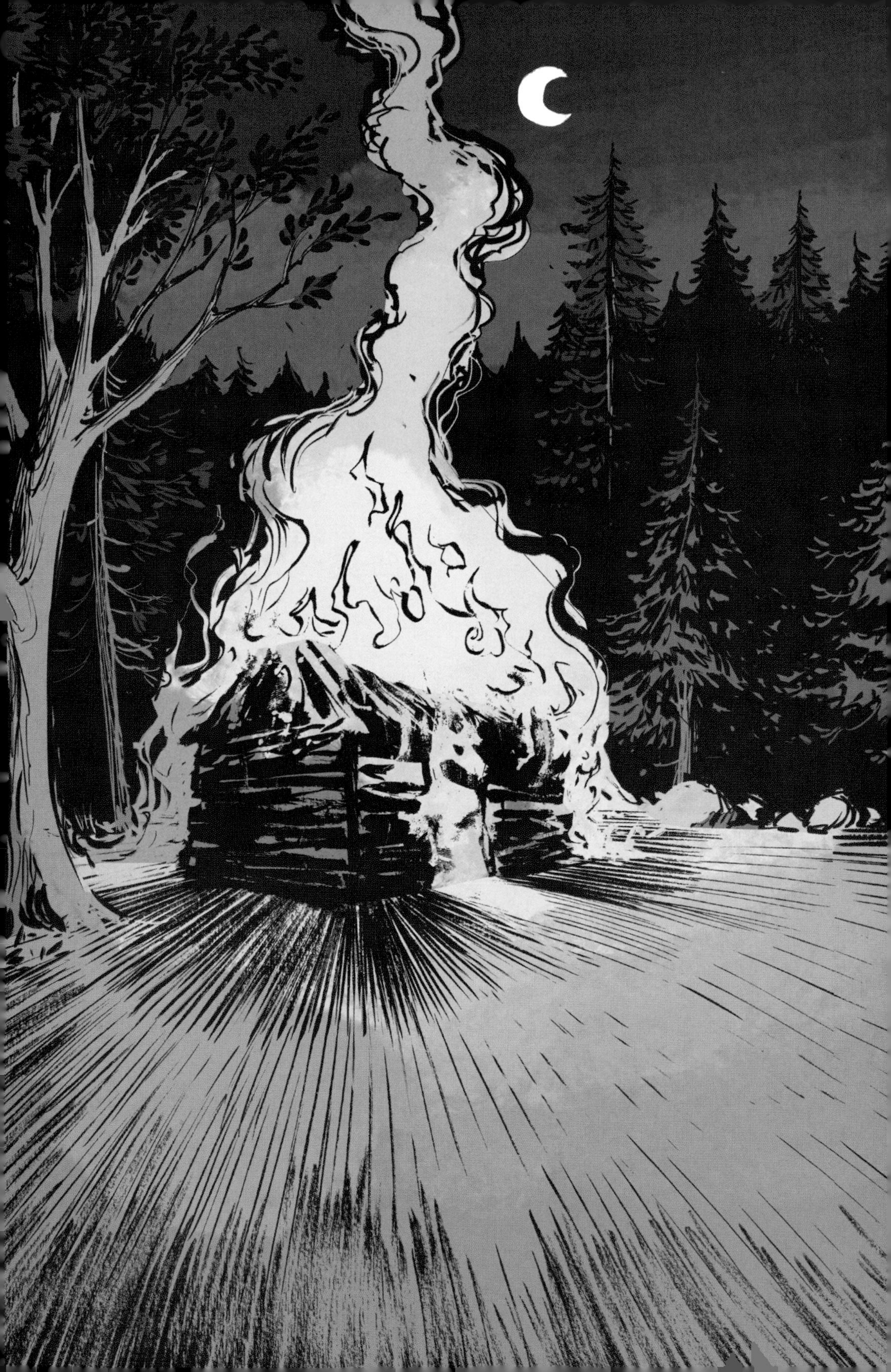

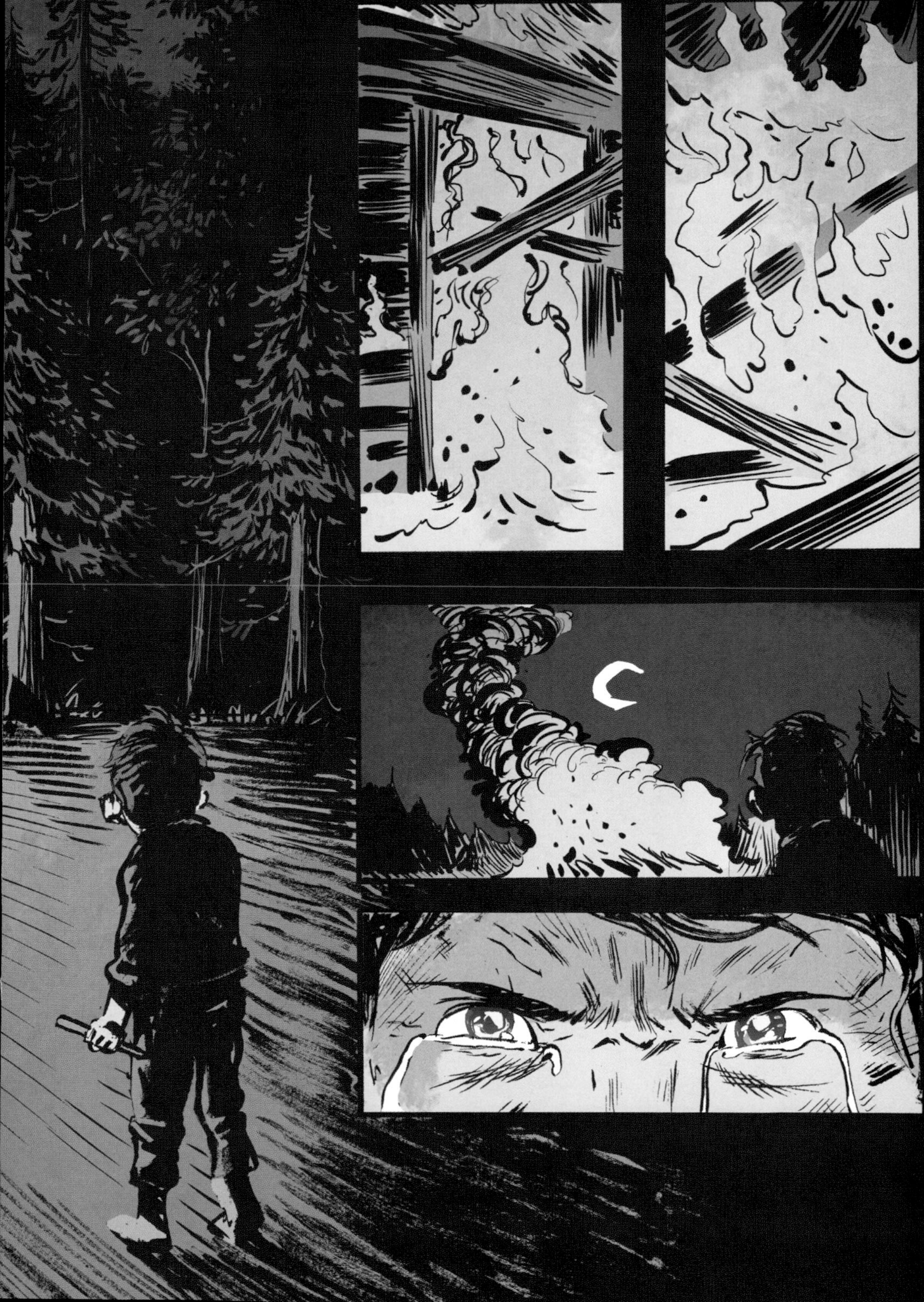

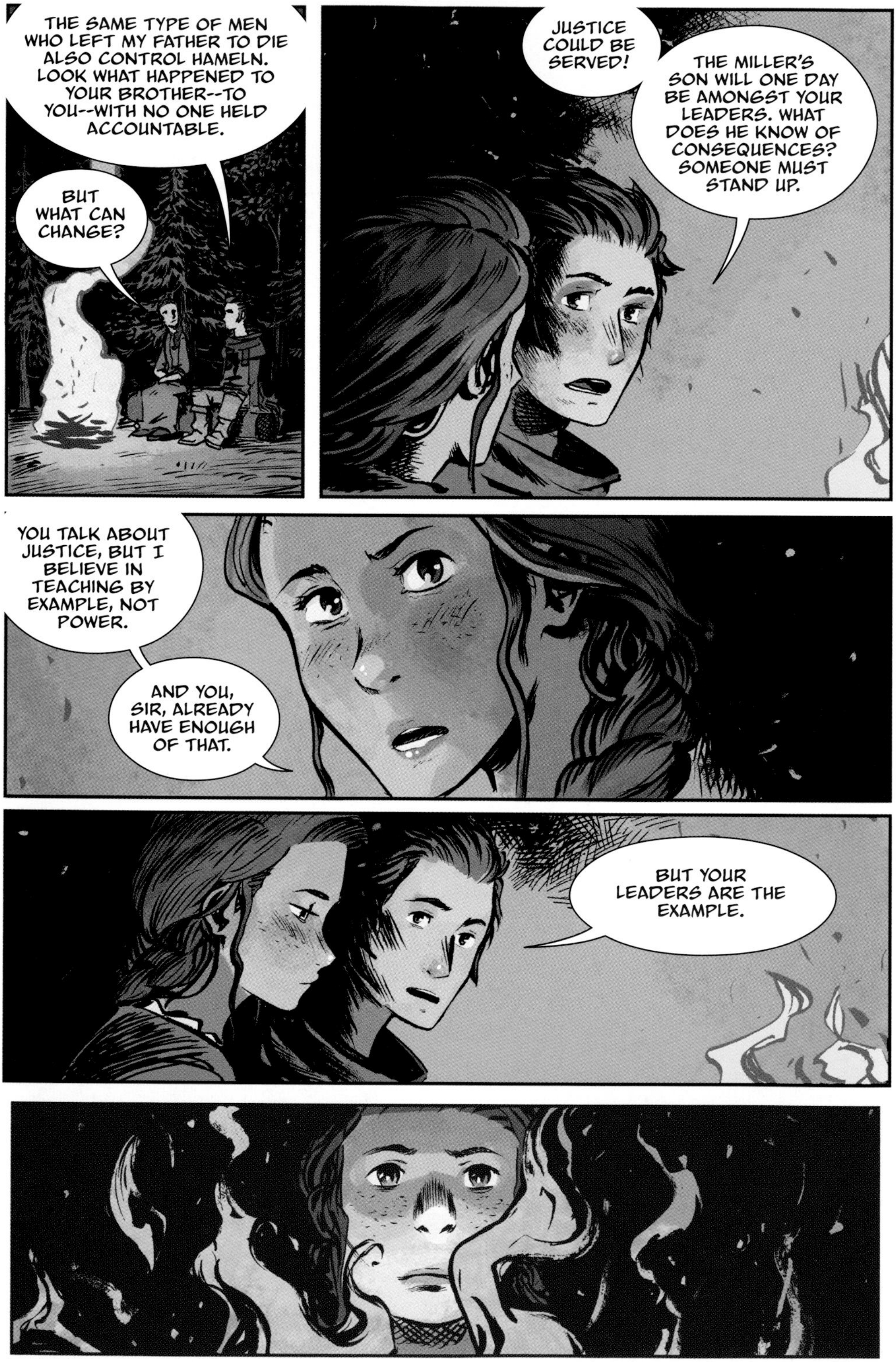
THE SAME TYPE OF MEN WHO LEFT MY FATHER TO DIE ALSO CONTROL HAMELN. LOOK WHAT HAPPENED TO YOUR BROTHER--TO YOU--WITH NO ONE HELD ACCOUNTABLE.
BUT WHAT CAN CHANGE?
JUSTICE COULD BE SERVED!
THE MILLER'S SON WILL ONE DAY BE AMONGST YOUR LEADERS. WHAT DOES HE KNOW OF CONSEQUENCES? SOMEONE MUST STAND UP.
YOU TALK ABOUT JUSTICE, BUT I BELIEVE IN TEACHING BY EXAMPLE, NOT POWER.
AND YOU, SIR, ALREADY HAVE ENOUGH OF THAT.
BUT YOUR LEADERS ARE THE EXAMPLE.

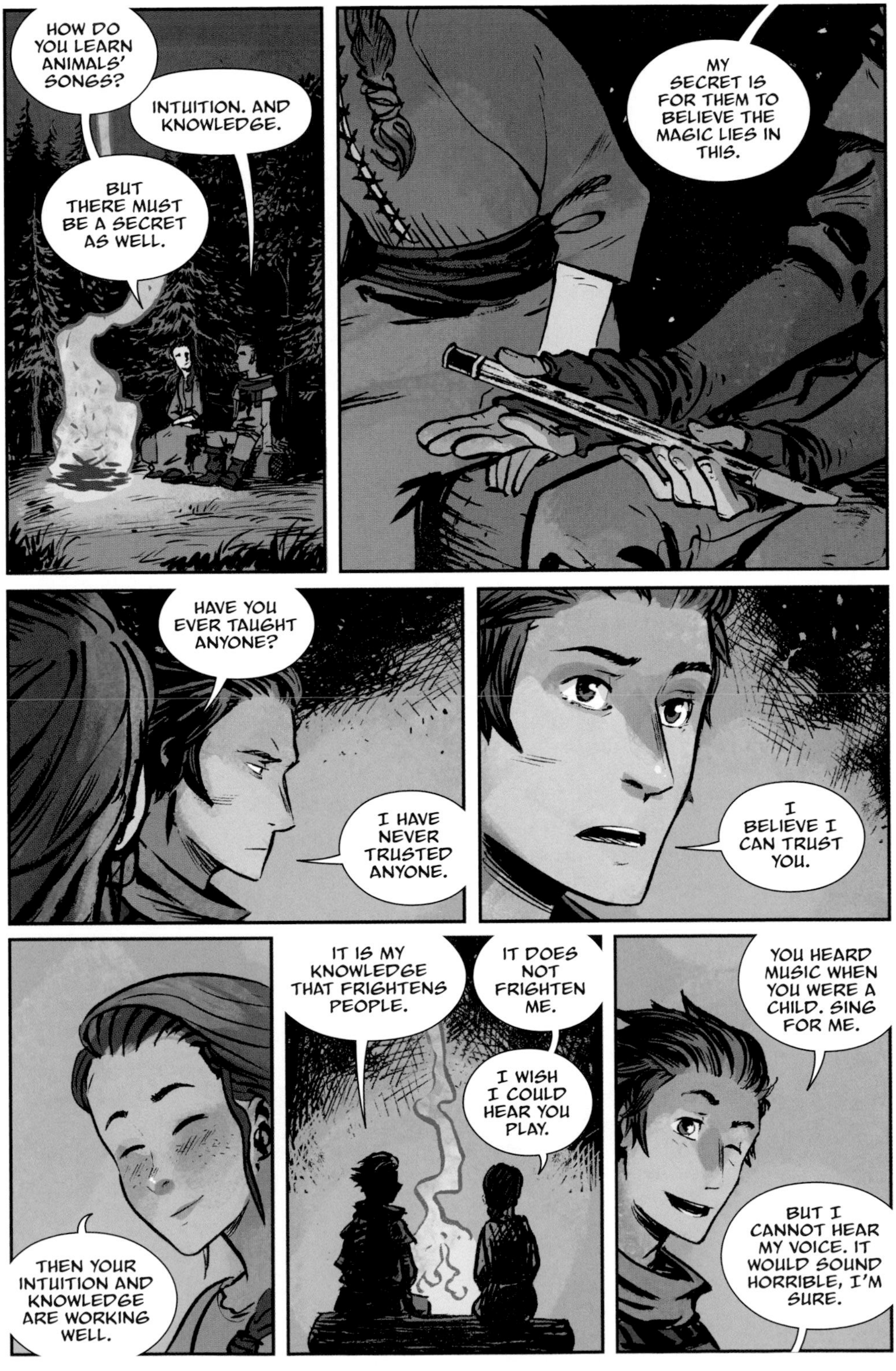

HOW DO YOU LEARN ANIMALS' SONGS?
INTUITION. AND KNOWLEDGE.
BUT THERE MUST BE A SECRET AS WELL.
MY SECRET IS FOR THEM TO BELIEVE THE MAGIC LIES IN THIS.
HAVE YOU EVER TAUGHT ANYONE?
I HAVE NEVER TRUSTED ANYONE.
I BELIEVE I CAN TRUST YOU.
THEN YOUR INTUITION AND KNOWLEDGE ARE WORKING WELL.
IT IS MY KNOWLEDGE THAT FRIGHTENS PEOPLE.
IT DOES NOT FRIGHTEN ME.
I WISH I COULD HEAR YOU PLAY.
YOU HEARD MUSIC WHEN YOU WERE A CHILD. SING FOR ME.
BUT I CANNOT HEAR MY VOICE. IT WOULD SOUND HORRIBLE, I'M SURE.

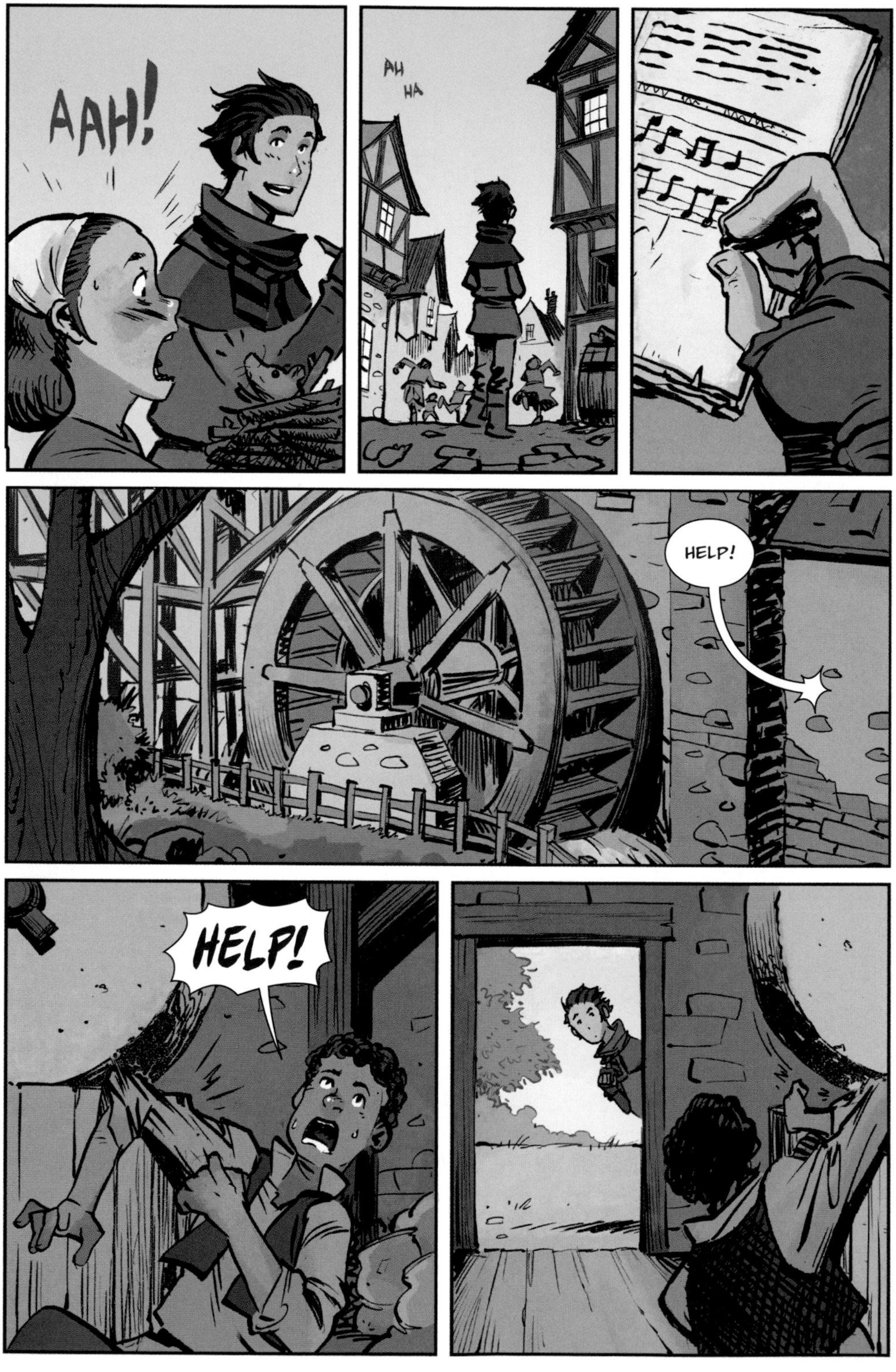
AAH!
AH
HA
HELP!
HELP!

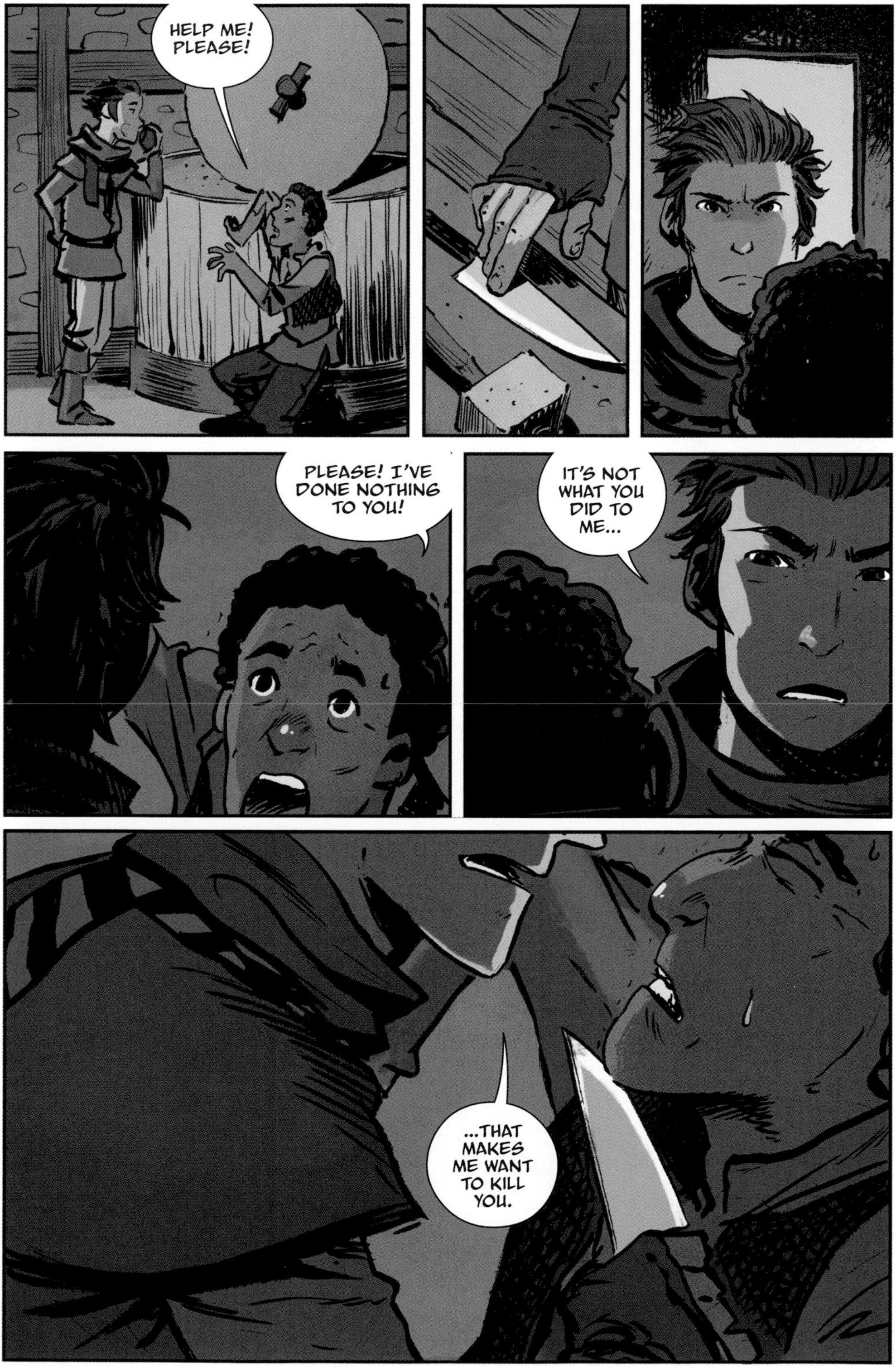
HELP ME! PLEASE!
PLEASE! I'VE DONE NOTHING TO YOU!
IT'S NOT WHAT YOU DID TO ME...
...THAT MAKES ME WANT TO KILL YOU.

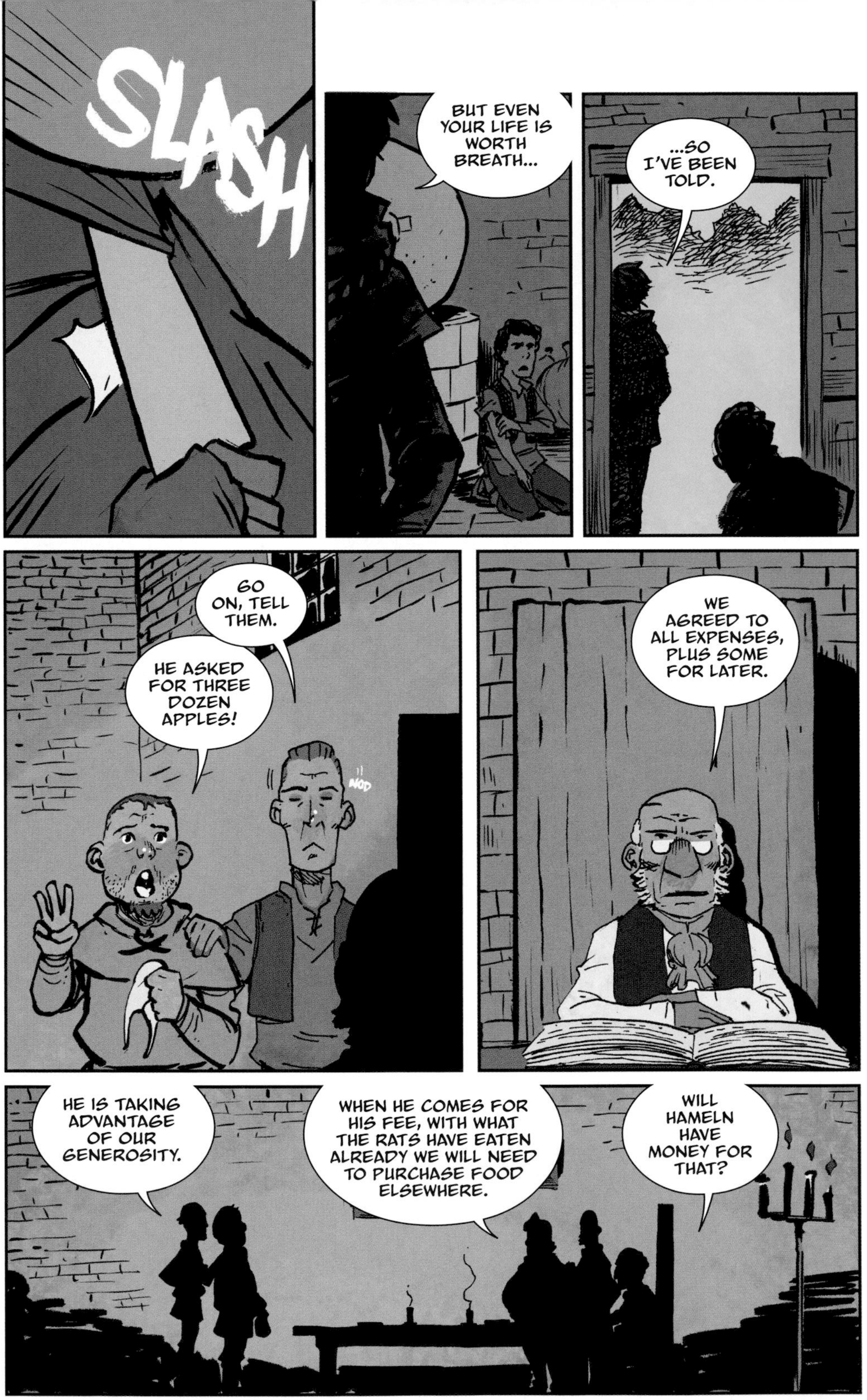
SLASH
BUT EVEN YOUR LIFE IS WORTH BREATH...
...SO I'VE BEEN TOLD.
GO ON, TELL THEM.
HE ASKED FOR THREE DOZEN APPLES!
NOD
WE AGREED TO ALL EXPENSES, PLUS SOME FOR LATER.
HE IS TAKING ADVANTAGE OF OUR GENEROSITY.
WHEN HE COMES FOR HIS FEE, WITH WHAT THE RATS HAVE EATEN ALREADY WE WILL NEED TO PURCHASE FOOD ELSEWHERE.
WILL HAMELN HAVE MONEY FOR THAT?

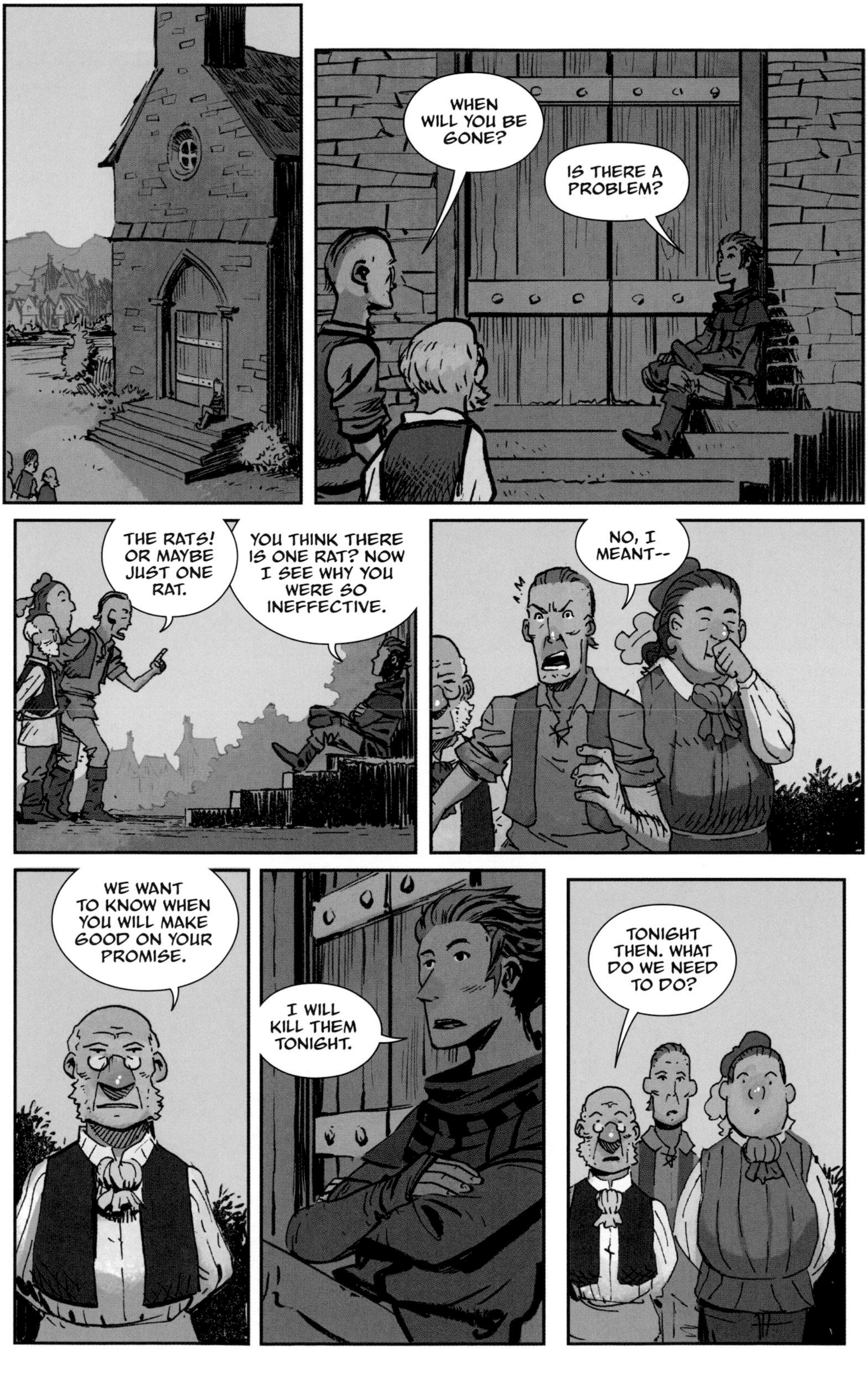
WHEN WILL YOU BE GONE?
IS THERE A PROBLEM?
THE RATS! OR MAYBE JUST ONE RAT.
YOU THINK THERE IS ONE RAT? NOW I SEE WHY YOU WERE SO INEFFECTIVE.
NO, I MEANT--
WE WANT TO KNOW WHEN YOU WILL MAKE GOOD ON YOUR PROMISE.
I WILL KILL THEM TONIGHT.
TONIGHT THEN. WHAT DO WE NEED TO DO?

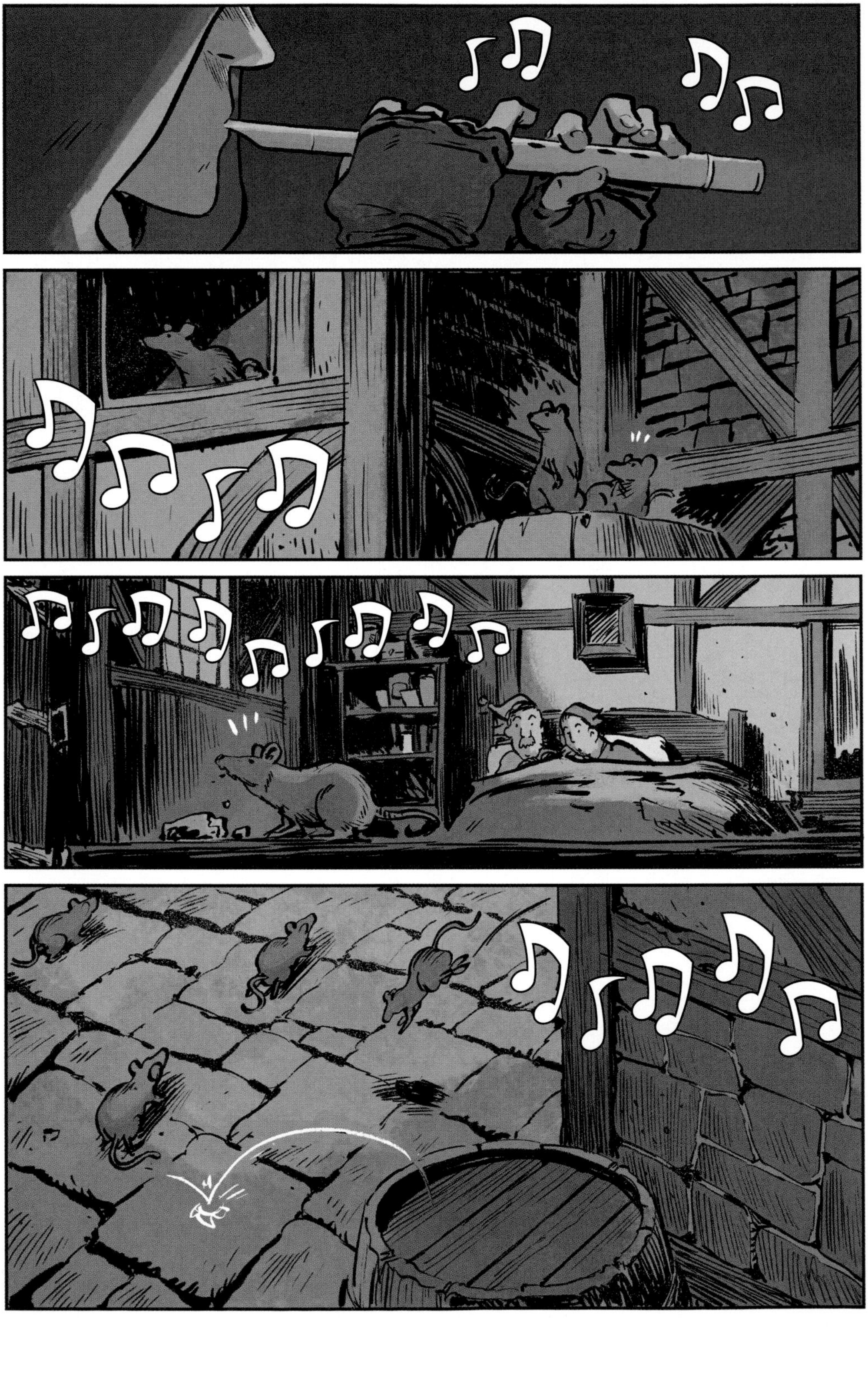

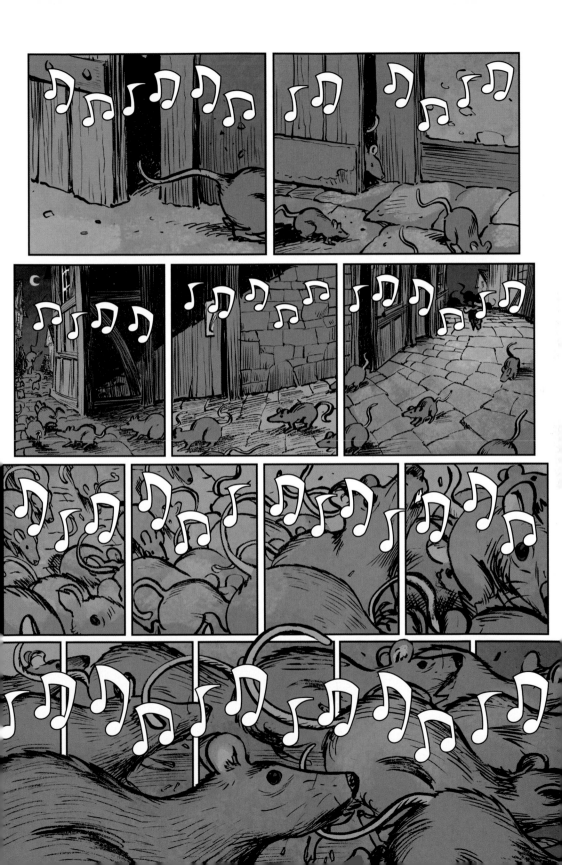

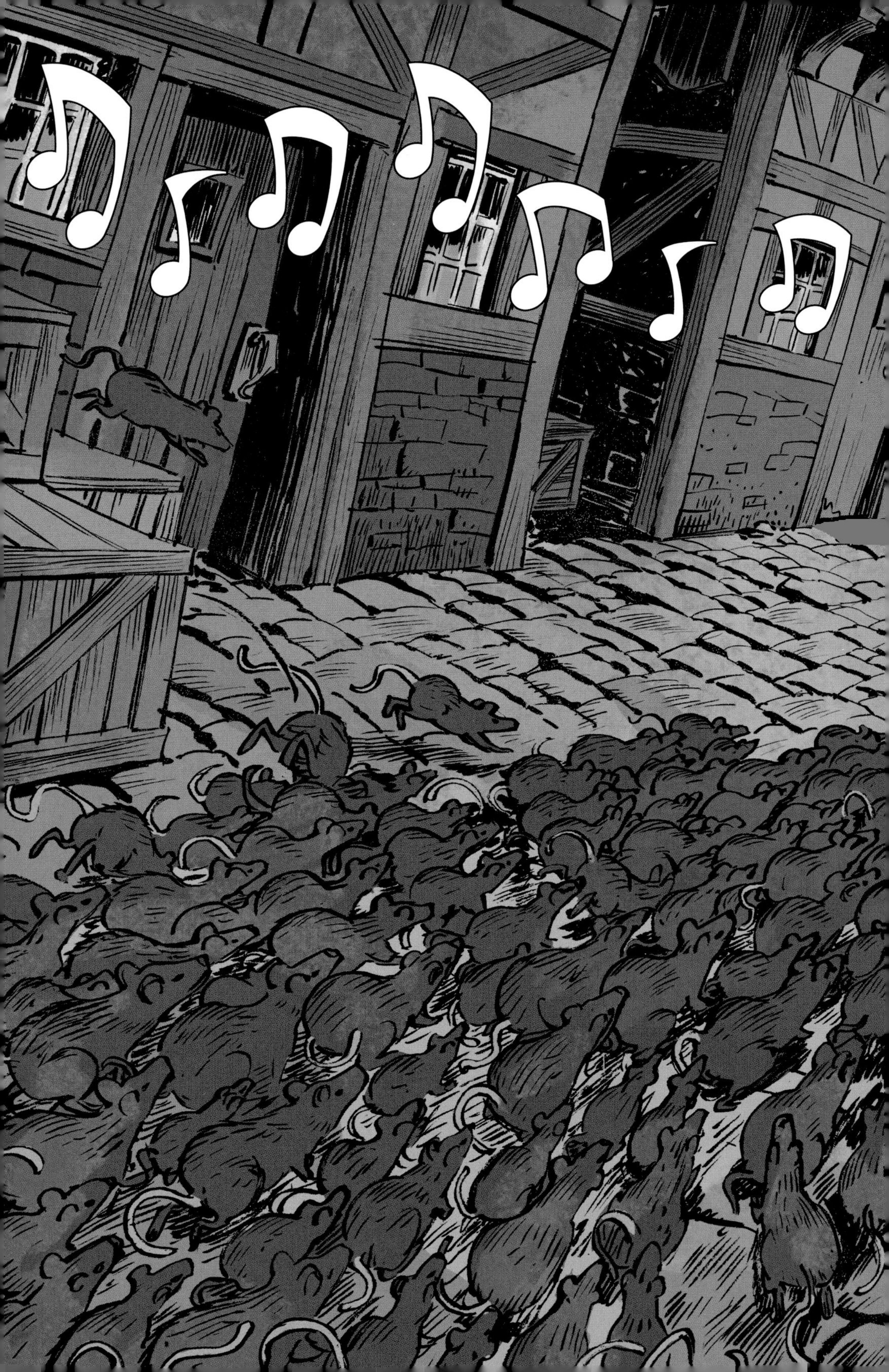

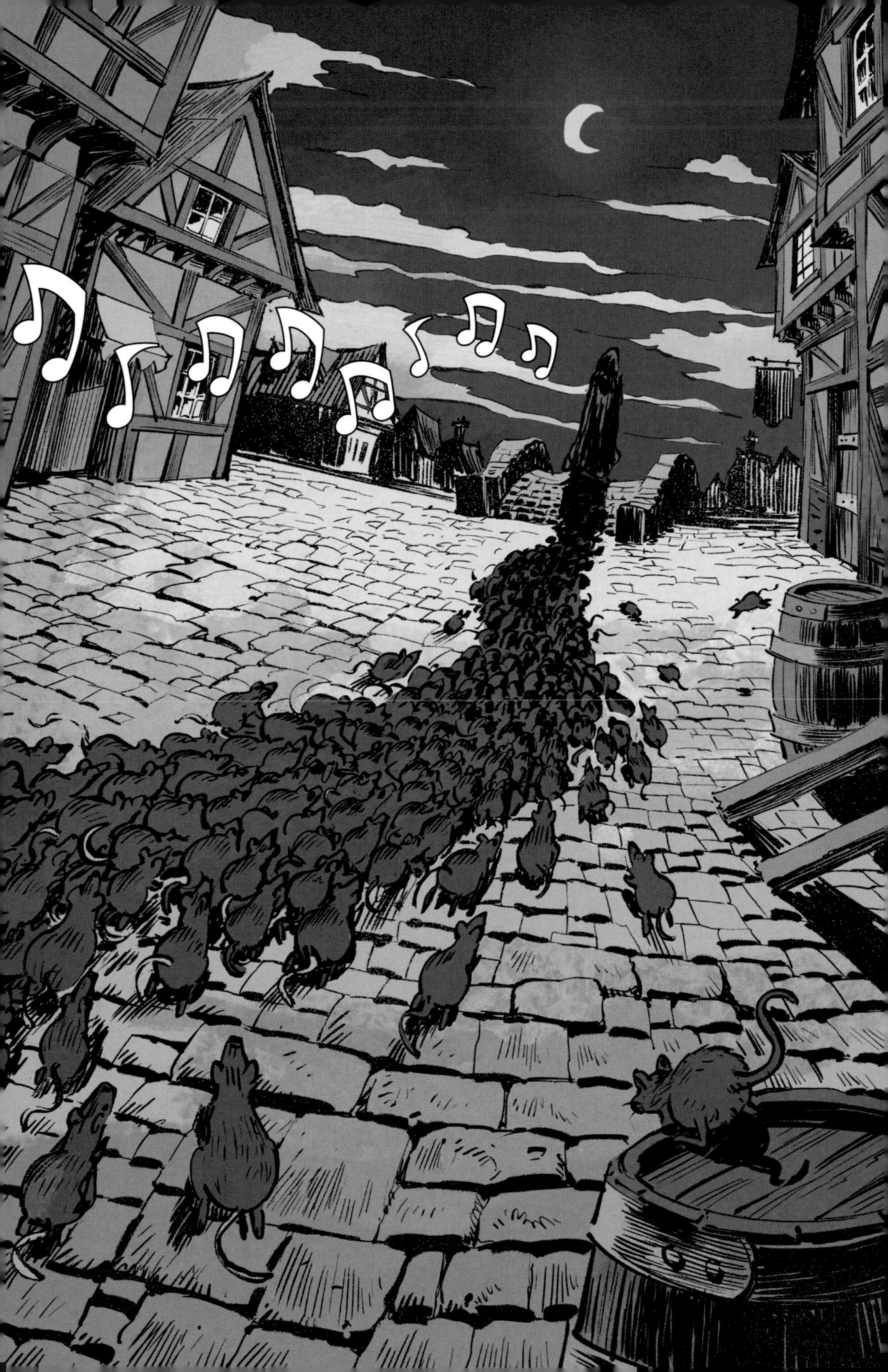

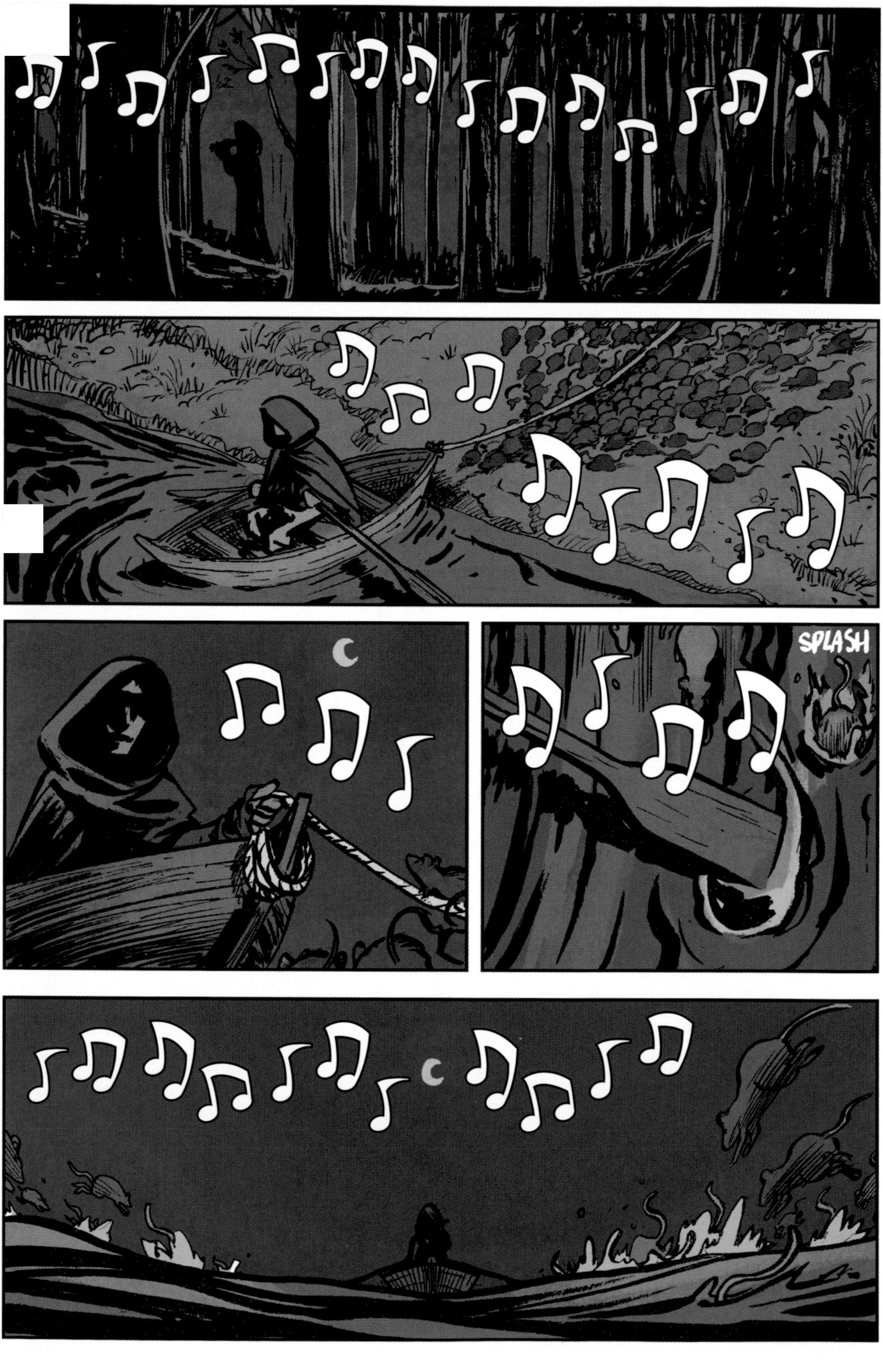
SPLASH

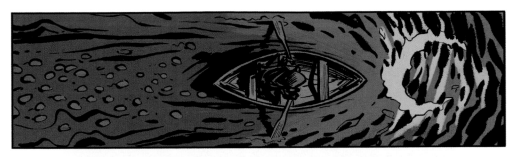

EVERYONE WAS SUPPOSED TO STAY INSIDE.

BUT IT APPEARS YOUR WORK IS DONE.

YOU ARE THE HERO OF HAMELN.

YOU SAID EVERY CREATURE HAS A SONG.

DO YOU KNOW MINE?

YES.

PLAY IT FOR ME.

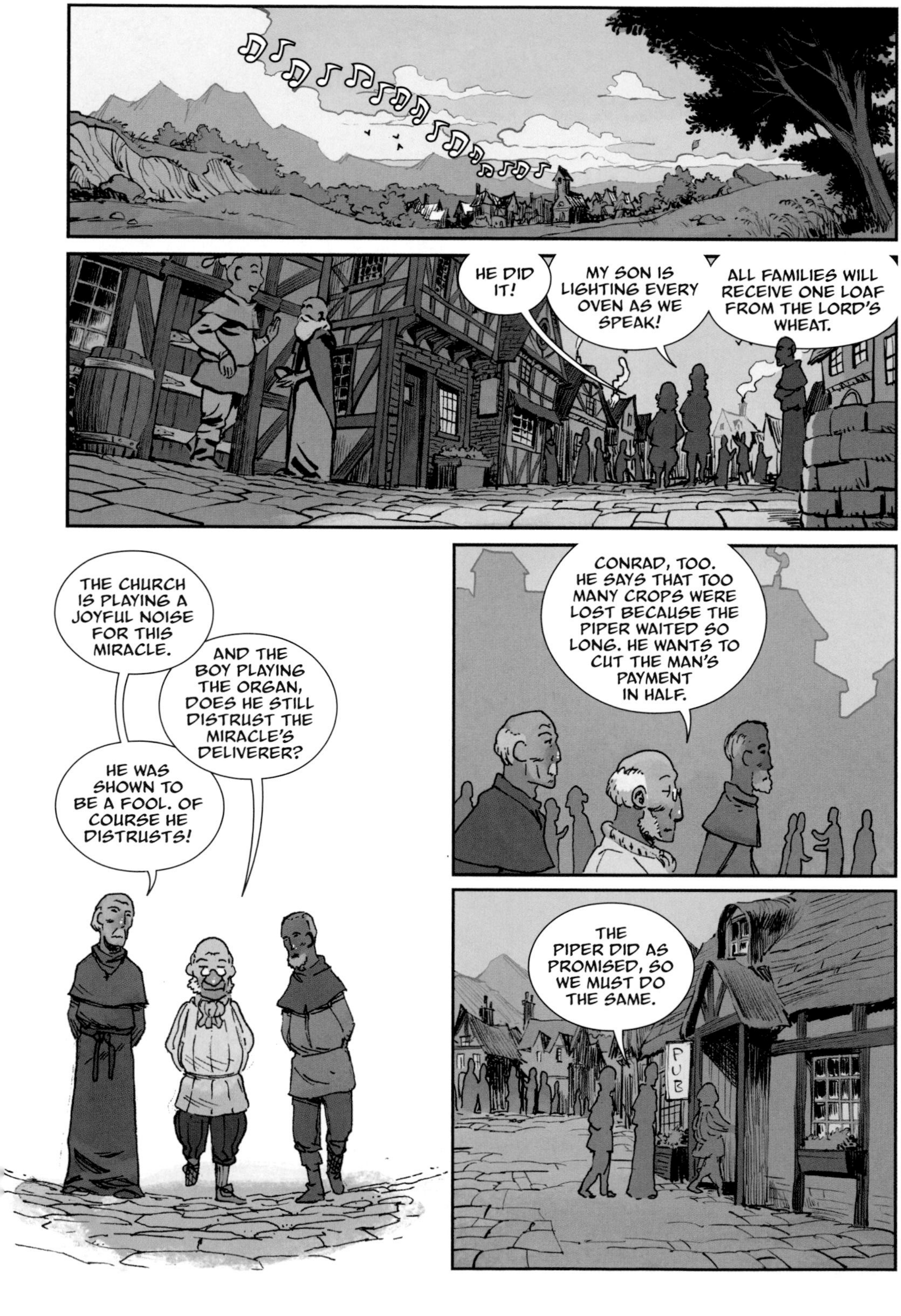
HE DID IT!
MY SON IS LIGHTING EVERY OVEN AS WE SPEAK!
ALL FAMILIES WILL RECEIVE ONE LOAF FROM THE LORD'S WHEAT.
THE CHURCH IS PLAYING A JOYFUL NOISE FOR THIS MIRACLE.
AND THE BOY PLAYING THE ORGAN, DOES HE STILL DISTRUST THE MIRACLE'S DELIVERER?
HE WAS SHOWN TO BE A FOOL. OF COURSE HE DISTRUSTS!
CONRAD, TOO. HE SAYS THAT TOO MANY CROPS WERE LOST BECAUSE THE PIPER WAITED SO LONG. HE WANTS TO CUT THE MAN'S PAYMENT IN HALF.
THE PIPER DID AS PROMISED, SO WE MUST DO THE SAME.
PUB

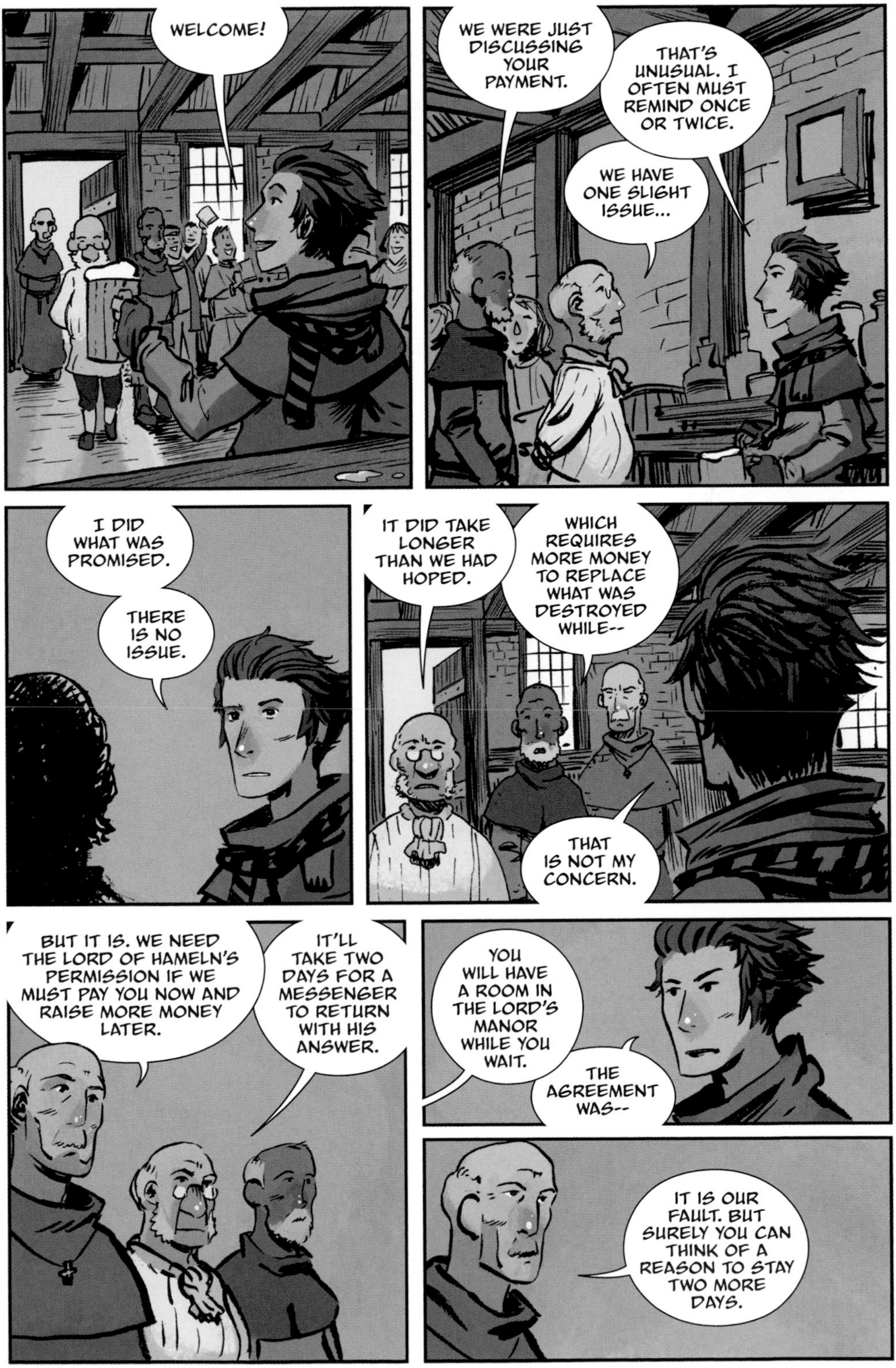
WELCOME!
WE WERE JUST DISCUSSING YOUR PAYMENT.
THAT'S UNUSUAL. I OFTEN MUST REMIND ONCE OR TWICE.
WE HAVE ONE SLIGHT ISSUE...
I DID WHAT WAS PROMISED.
THERE IS NO ISSUE.
IT DID TAKE LONGER THAN WE HAD HOPED.
WHICH REQUIRES MORE MONEY TO REPLACE WHAT WAS DESTROYED WHILE--
THAT IS NOT MY CONCERN.
BUT IT IS. WE NEED THE LORD OF HAMELN'S PERMISSION IF WE MUST PAY YOU NOW AND RAISE MORE MONEY LATER.
IT'LL TAKE TWO DAYS FOR A MESSENGER TO RETURN WITH HIS ANSWER.
YOU WILL HAVE A ROOM IN THE LORD'S MANOR WHILE YOU WAIT.
THE AGREEMENT WAS--
IT IS OUR FAULT. BUT SURELY YOU CAN THINK OF A REASON TO STAY TWO MORE DAYS.

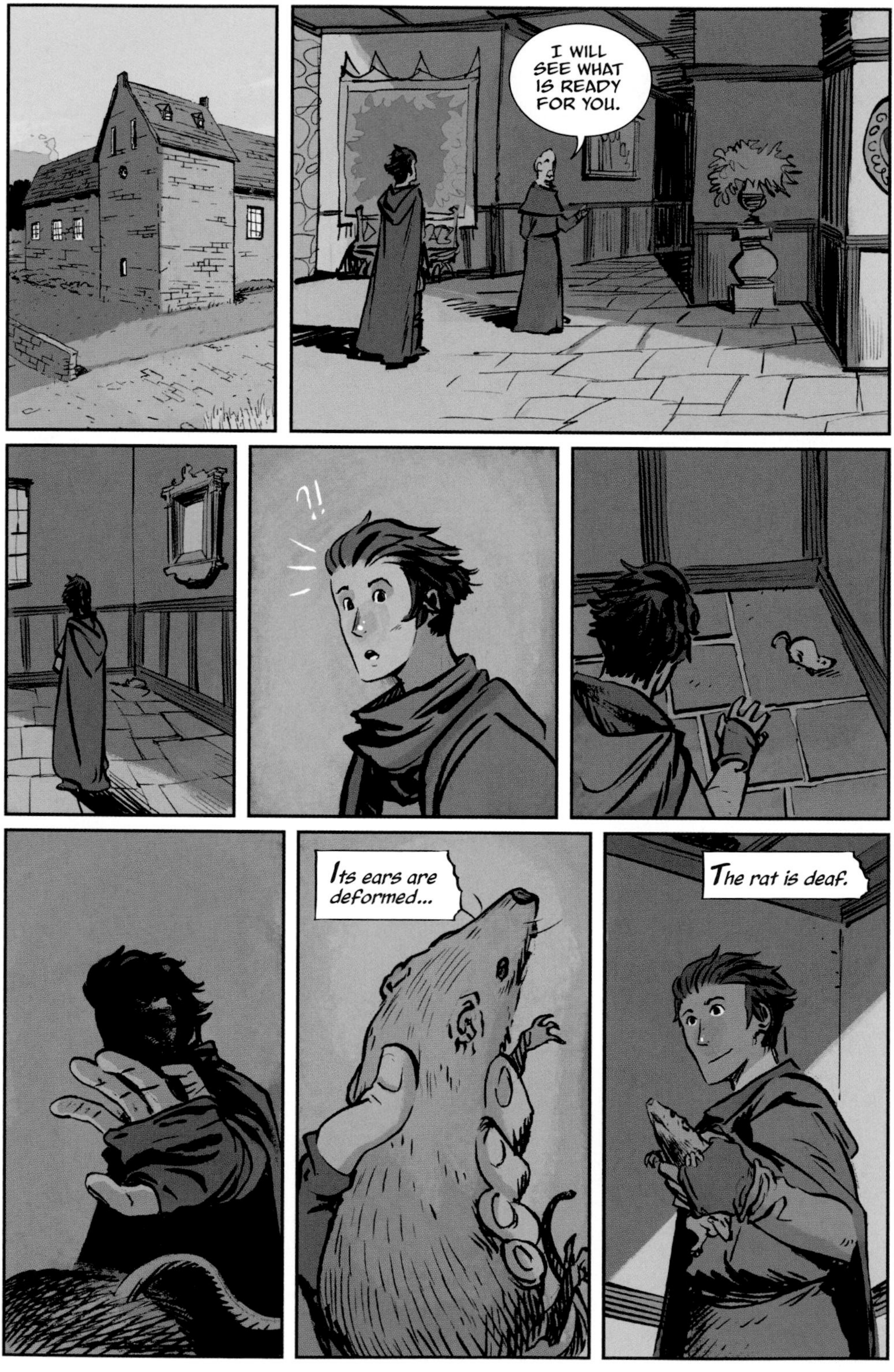
I WILL SEE WHAT IS READY FOR YOU.
?!
Its ears are deformed...
The rat is deaf.

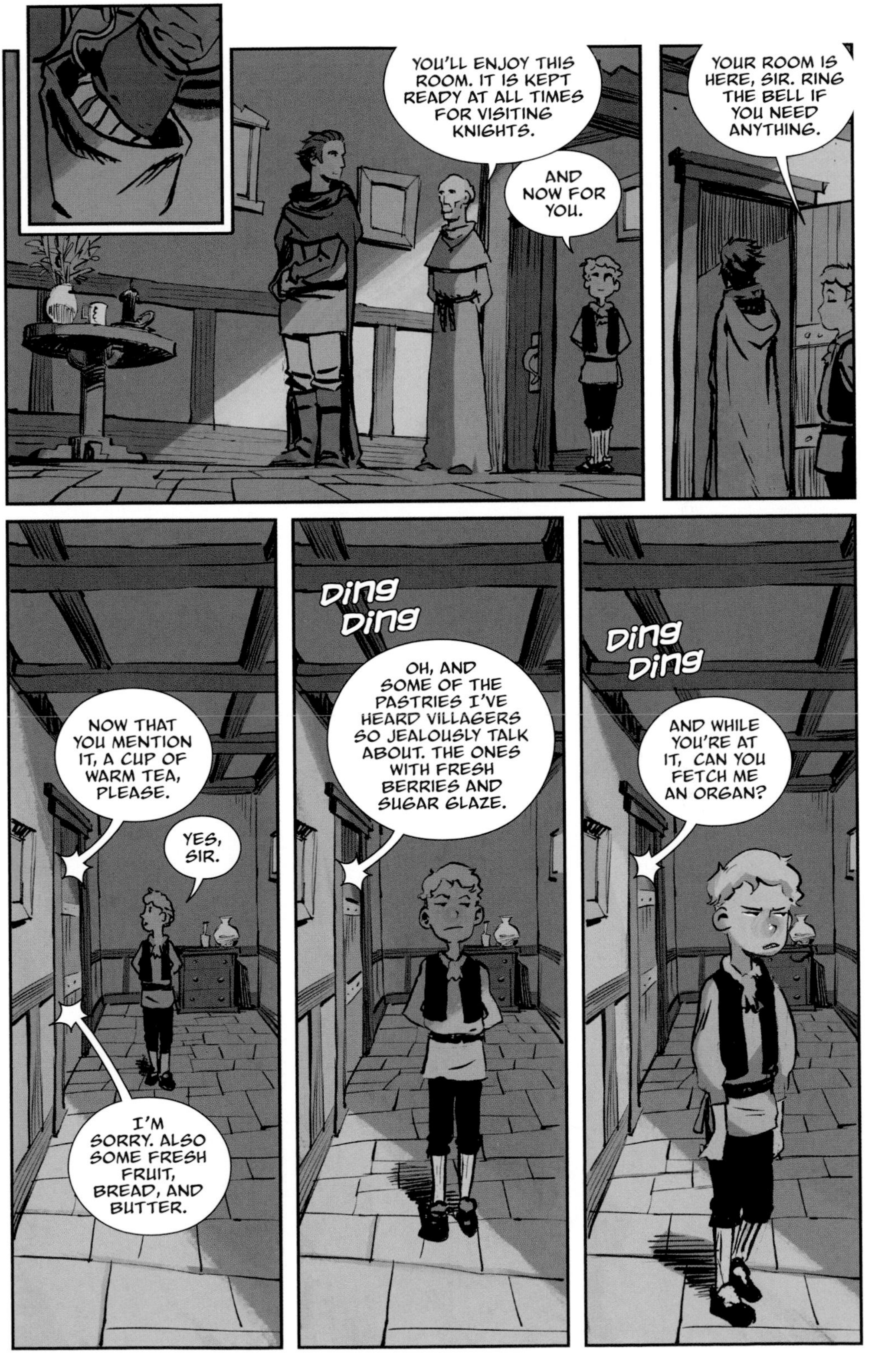
YOU'LL ENJOY THIS ROOM. IT IS KEPT READY AT ALL TIMES FOR VISITING KNIGHTS.
AND NOW FOR YOU.
YOUR ROOM IS HERE, SIR. RING THE BELL IF YOU NEED ANYTHING.
NOW THAT YOU MENTION IT, A CUP OF WARM TEA, PLEASE.
YES, SIR.
I'M SORRY. ALSO SOME FRESH FRUIT, BREAD, AND BUTTER.
Ding Ding
OH, AND SOME OF THE PASTRIES I'VE HEARD VILLAGERS SO JEALOUSLY TALK ABOUT. THE ONES WITH FRESH BERRIES AND SUGAR GLAZE.
Ding Ding
AND WHILE YOU'RE AT IT, CAN YOU FETCH ME AN ORGAN?

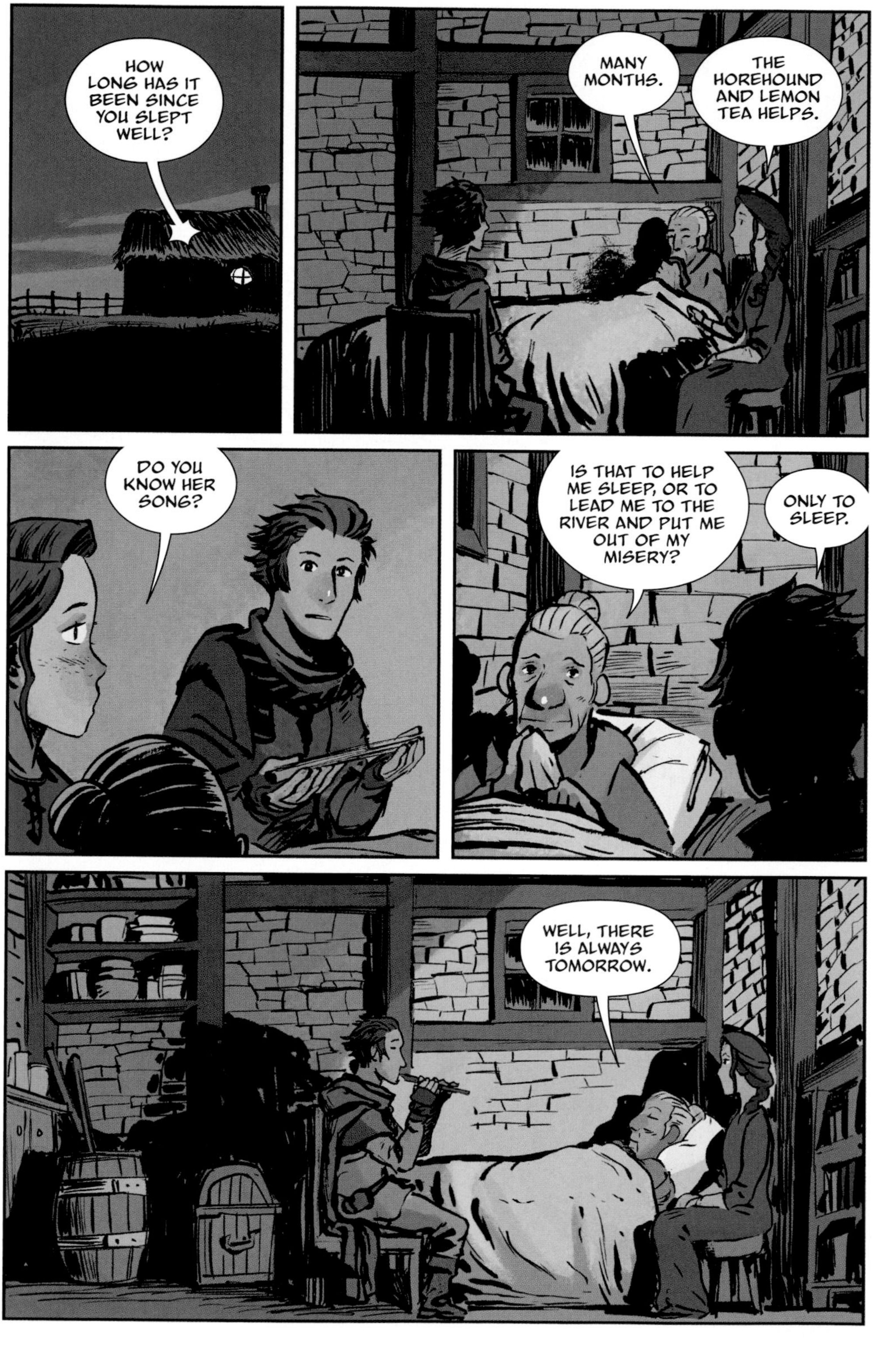
HOW LONG HAS IT BEEN SINCE YOU SLEPT WELL?
MANY MONTHS.
THE HOREHOUND AND LEMON TEA HELPS.
DO YOU KNOW HER SONG?
IS THAT TO HELP ME SLEEP, OR TO LEAD ME TO THE RIVER AND PUT ME OUT OF MY MISERY?
ONLY TO SLEEP.
WELL, THERE IS ALWAYS TOMORROW.

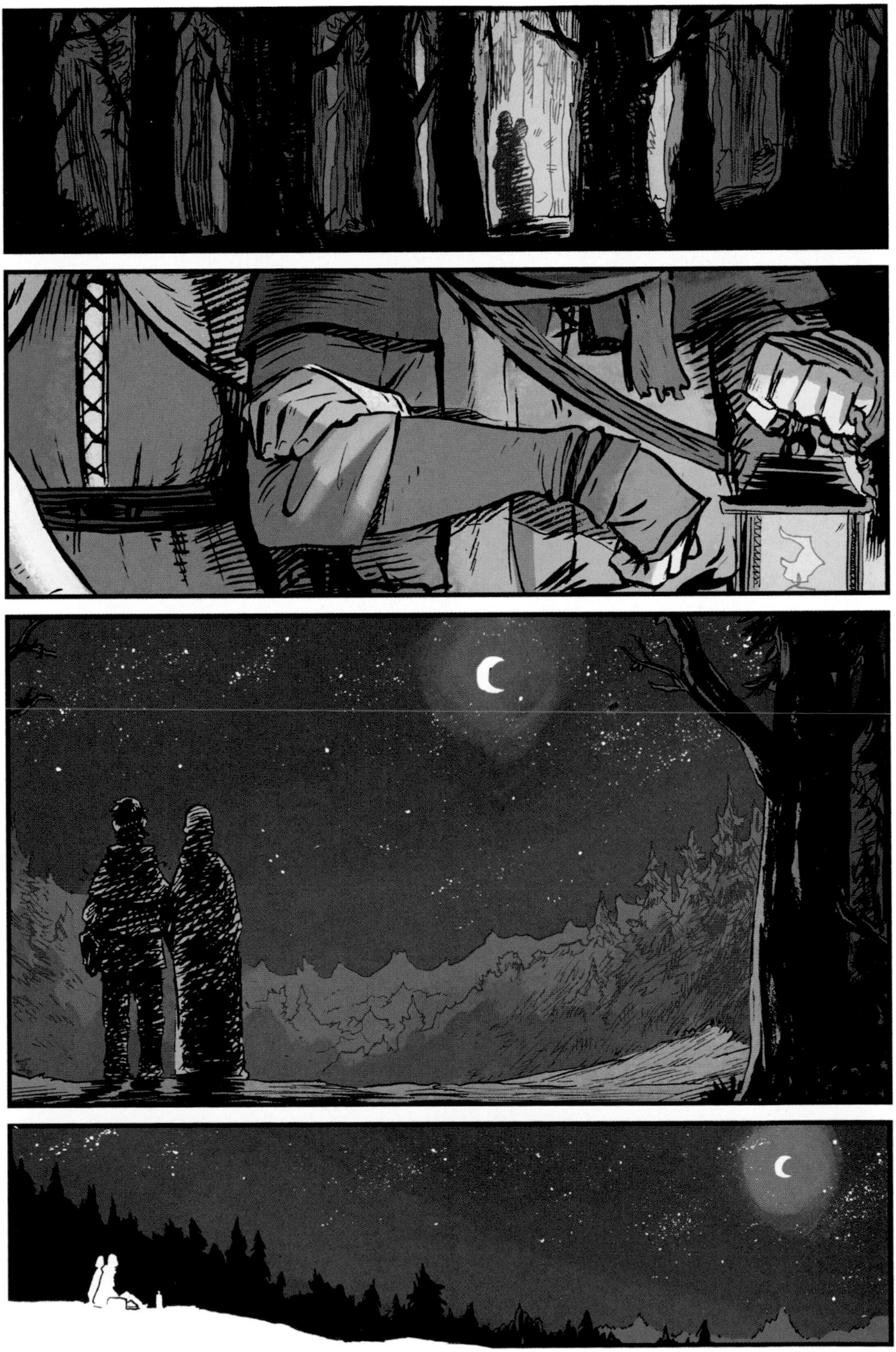

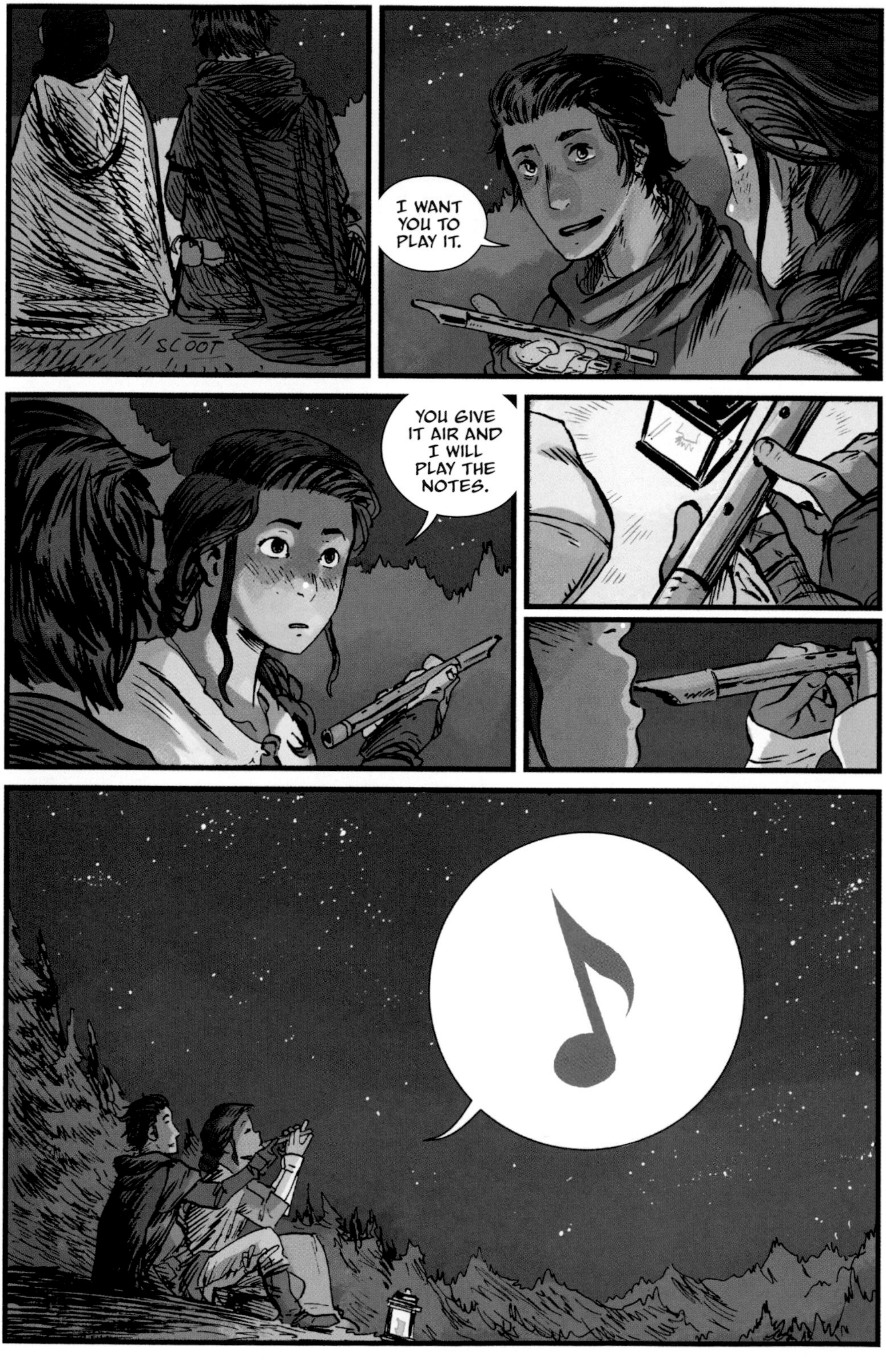
SCOOT
I WANT YOU TO PLAY IT.
YOU GIVE IT AIR AND I WILL PLAY THE NOTES.

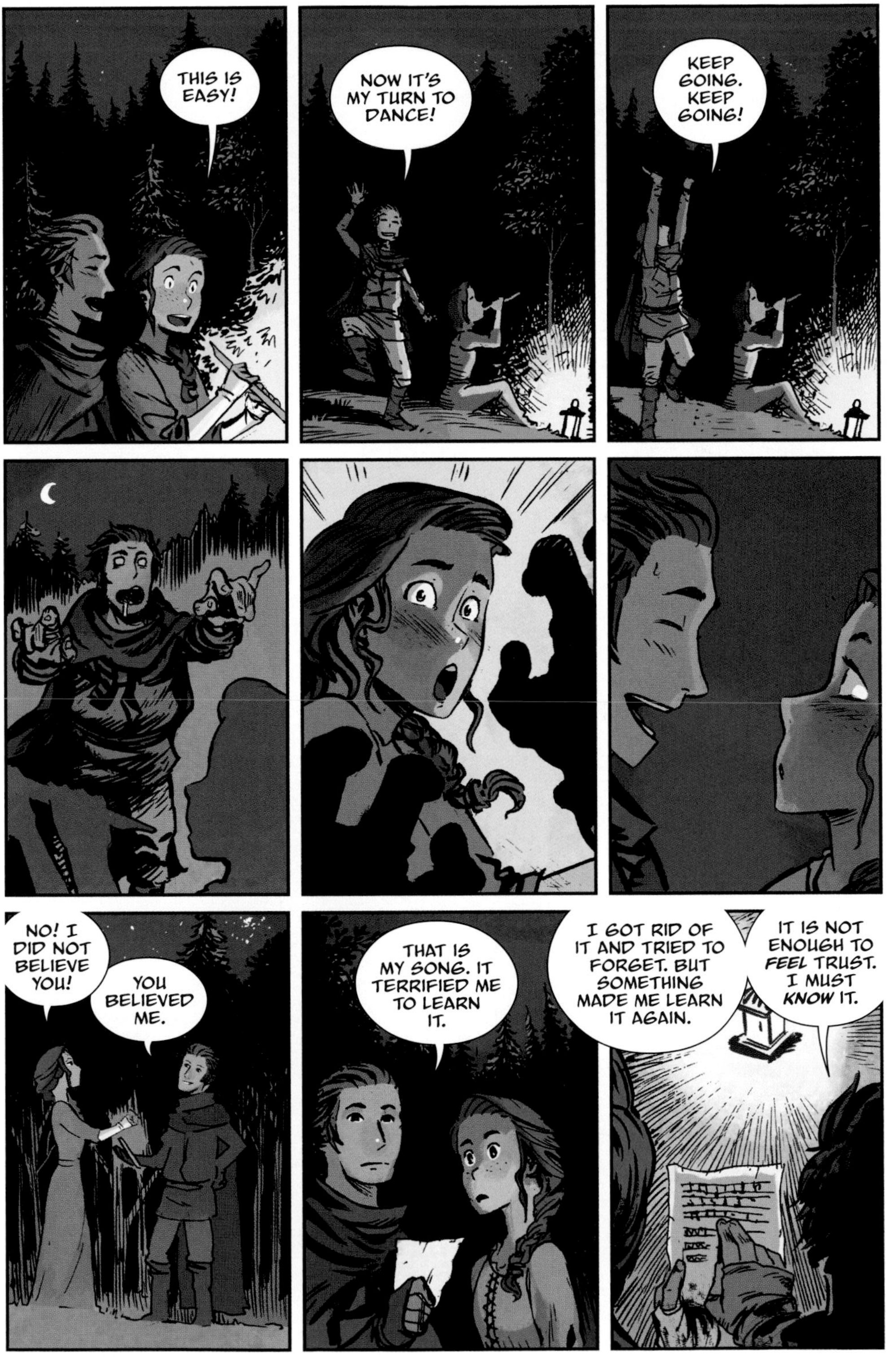
THIS IS EASY!
NOW IT'S MY TURN TO DANCE!
KEEP GOING. KEEP GOING!
NO! I DID NOT BELIEVE YOU!
YOU BELIEVED ME.
THAT IS MY SONG. IT TERRIFIED ME TO LEARN IT.
I GOT RID OF IT AND TRIED TO FORGET. BUT SOMETHING MADE ME LEARN IT AGAIN.
IT IS NOT ENOUGH TO *FEEL* TRUST. I MUST *KNOW* IT.

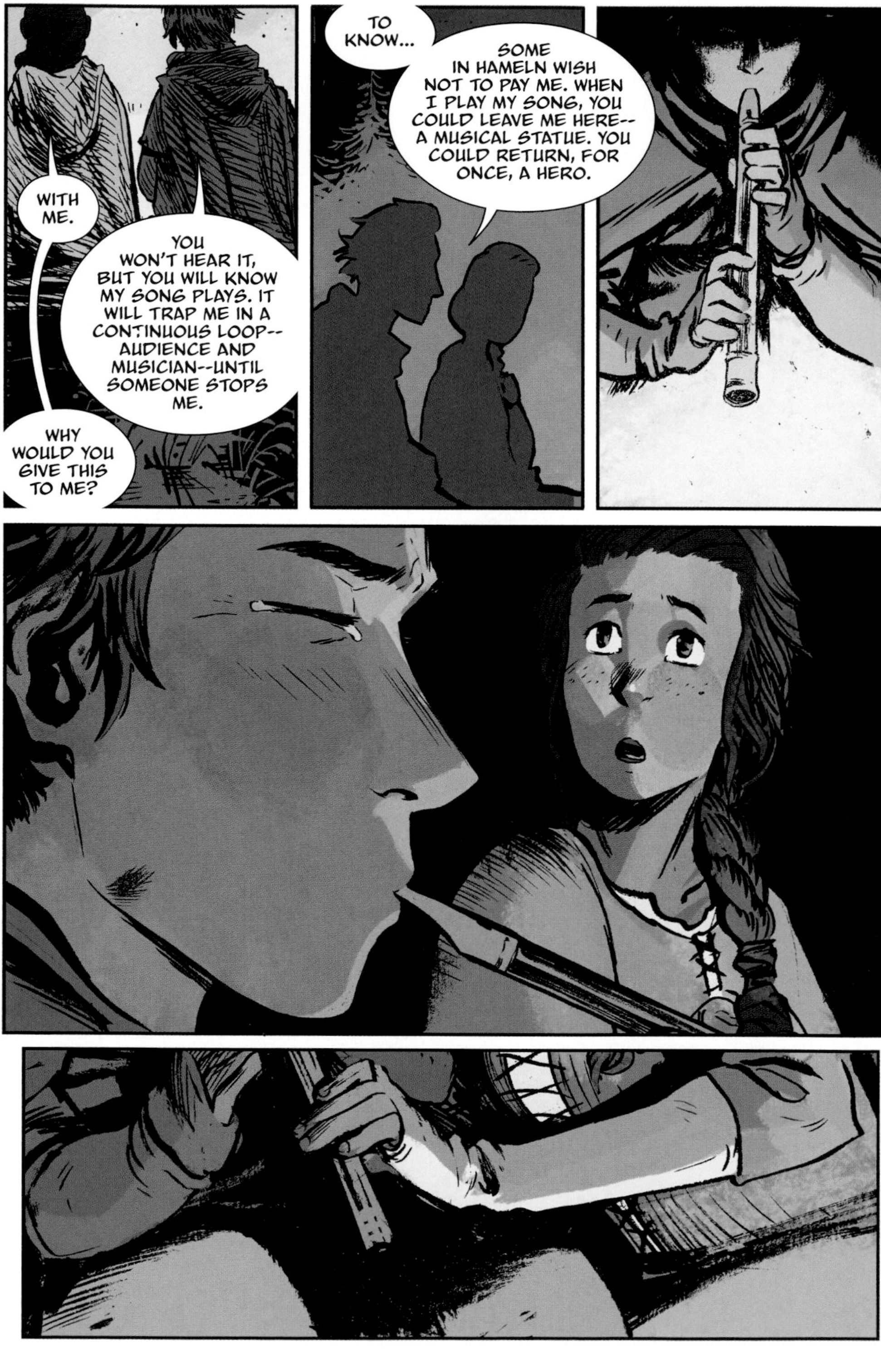
WITH ME.
YOU WON'T HEAR IT, BUT YOU WILL KNOW MY SONG PLAYS. IT WILL TRAP ME IN A CONTINUOUS LOOP--AUDIENCE AND MUSICIAN--UNTIL SOMEONE STOPS ME.
WHY WOULD YOU GIVE THIS TO ME?
TO KNOW...
SOME IN HAMELN WISH NOT TO PAY ME. WHEN I PLAY MY SONG, YOU COULD LEAVE ME HERE--A MUSICAL STATUE. YOU COULD RETURN, FOR ONCE, A HERO.

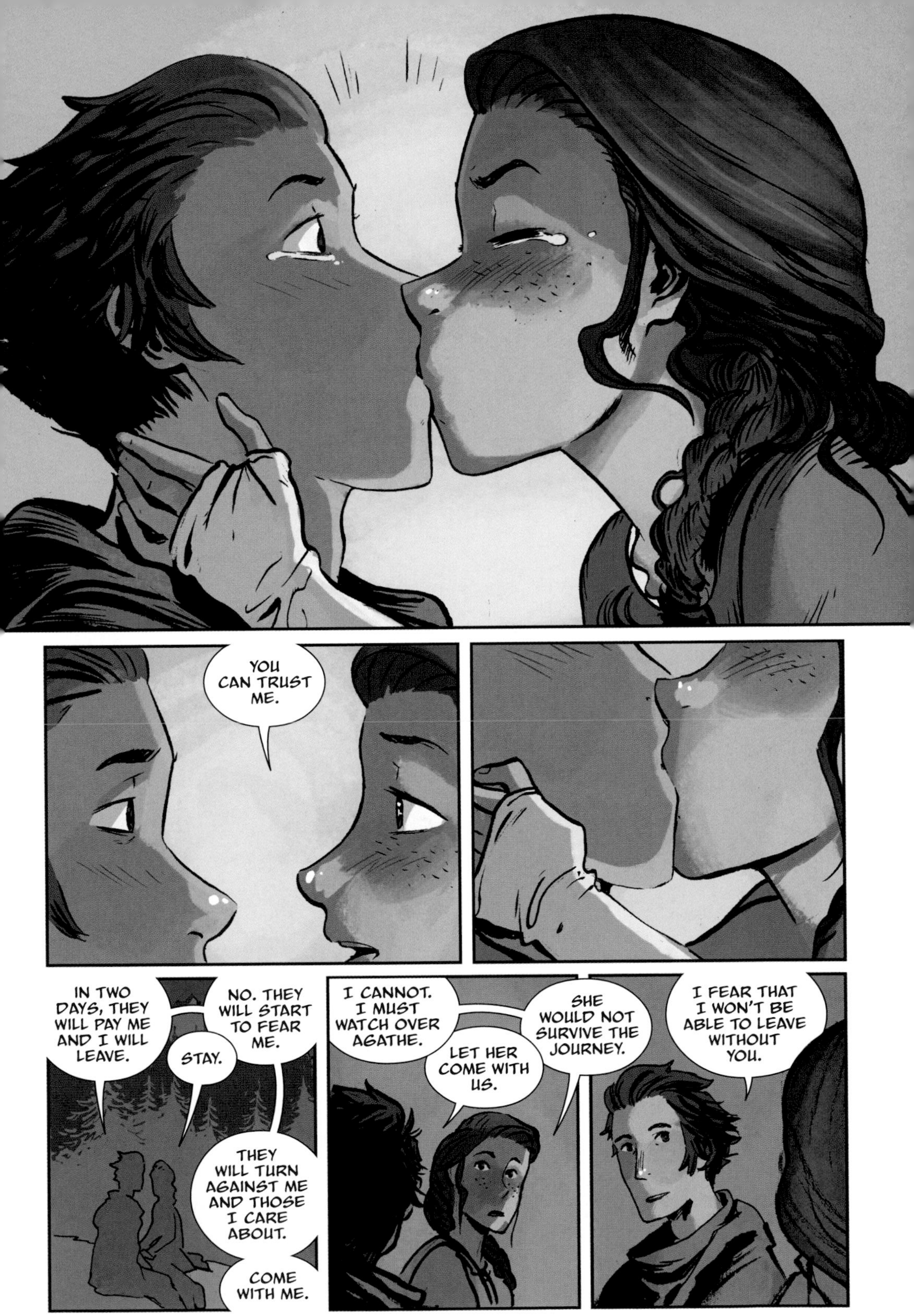
YOU CAN TRUST ME.
IN TWO DAYS, THEY WILL PAY ME AND I WILL LEAVE.
STAY.
NO. THEY WILL START TO FEAR ME.
THEY WILL TURN AGAINST ME AND THOSE I CARE ABOUT.
COME WITH ME.
I CANNOT. I MUST WATCH OVER AGATHE.
LET HER COME WITH US.
SHE WOULD NOT SURVIVE THE JOURNEY.
I FEAR THAT I WON'T BE ABLE TO LEAVE WITHOUT YOU.

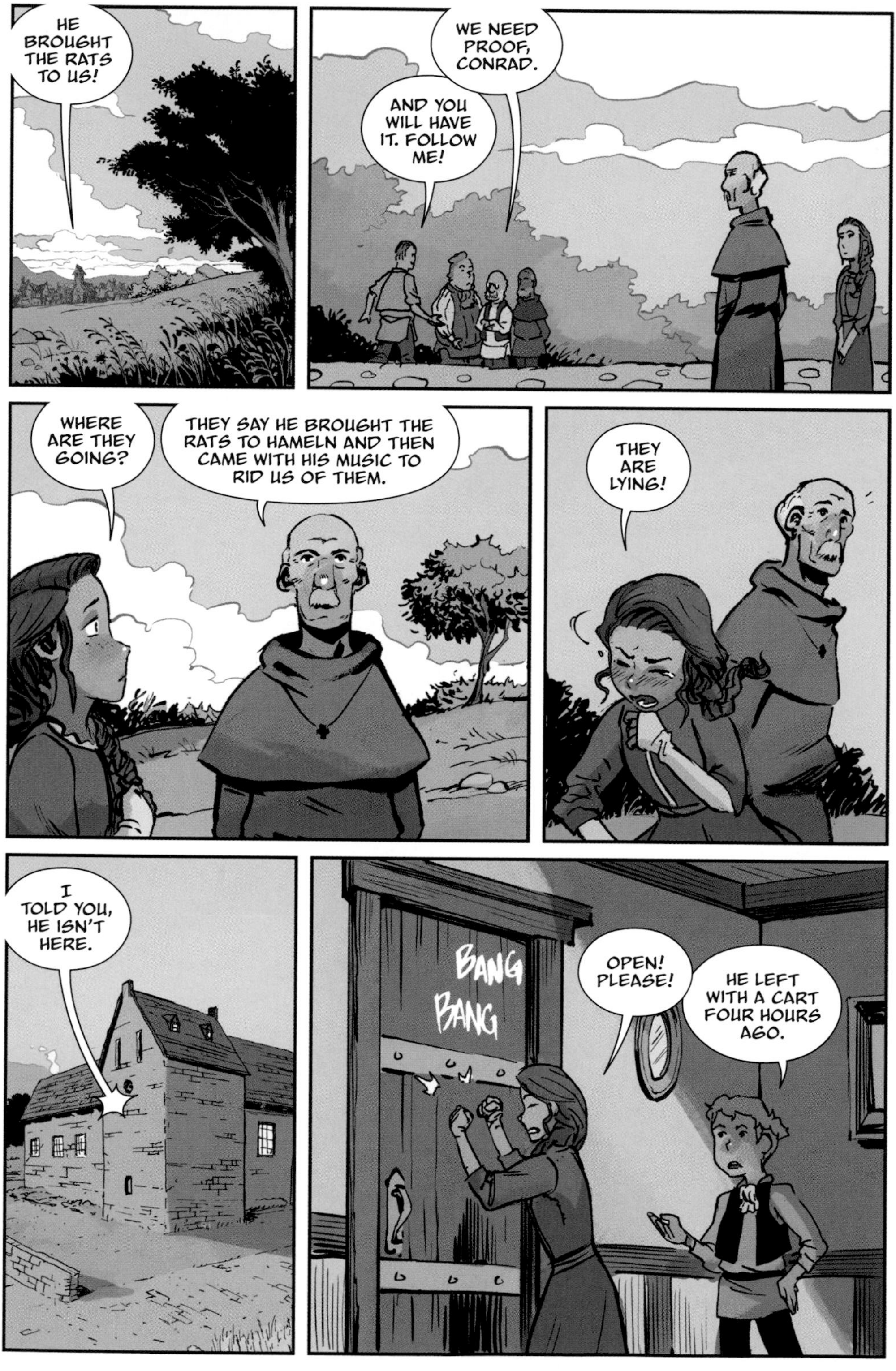
HE BROUGHT THE RATS TO US!
WE NEED PROOF, CONRAD.
AND YOU WILL HAVE IT. FOLLOW ME!
WHERE ARE THEY GOING?
THEY SAY HE BROUGHT THE RATS TO HAMELN AND THEN CAME WITH HIS MUSIC TO RID US OF THEM.
THEY ARE LYING!
I TOLD YOU, HE ISN'T HERE.
BANG
BANG
OPEN! PLEASE!
HE LEFT WITH A CART FOUR HOURS AGO.

SEE?

WHAT ARE WE SUPPOSED TO SEE?

WHAT DO...? THEY'RE CAGES!

THEY LOOK LIKE TRAPS.

YET HE DID NOT TRAP THE RATS. HE DROWNED THEM!

WHEN YOUR POISON DIDN'T WORK, WEREN'T YOU BUILDING TRAPS?

THERE WAS NO TIME. REMEMBER?

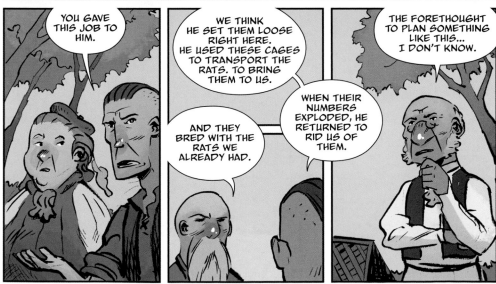

YOU GAVE THIS JOB TO HIM.

WE THINK HE SET THEM LOOSE RIGHT HERE. HE USED THESE CAGES TO TRANSPORT THE RATS. TO BRING THEM TO US.

AND THEY BRED WITH THE RATS WE ALREADY HAD.

WHEN THEIR NUMBERS EXPLODED, HE RETURNED TO RID US OF THEM.

THE FORETHOUGHT TO PLAN SOMETHING LIKE THIS... I DON'T KNOW.

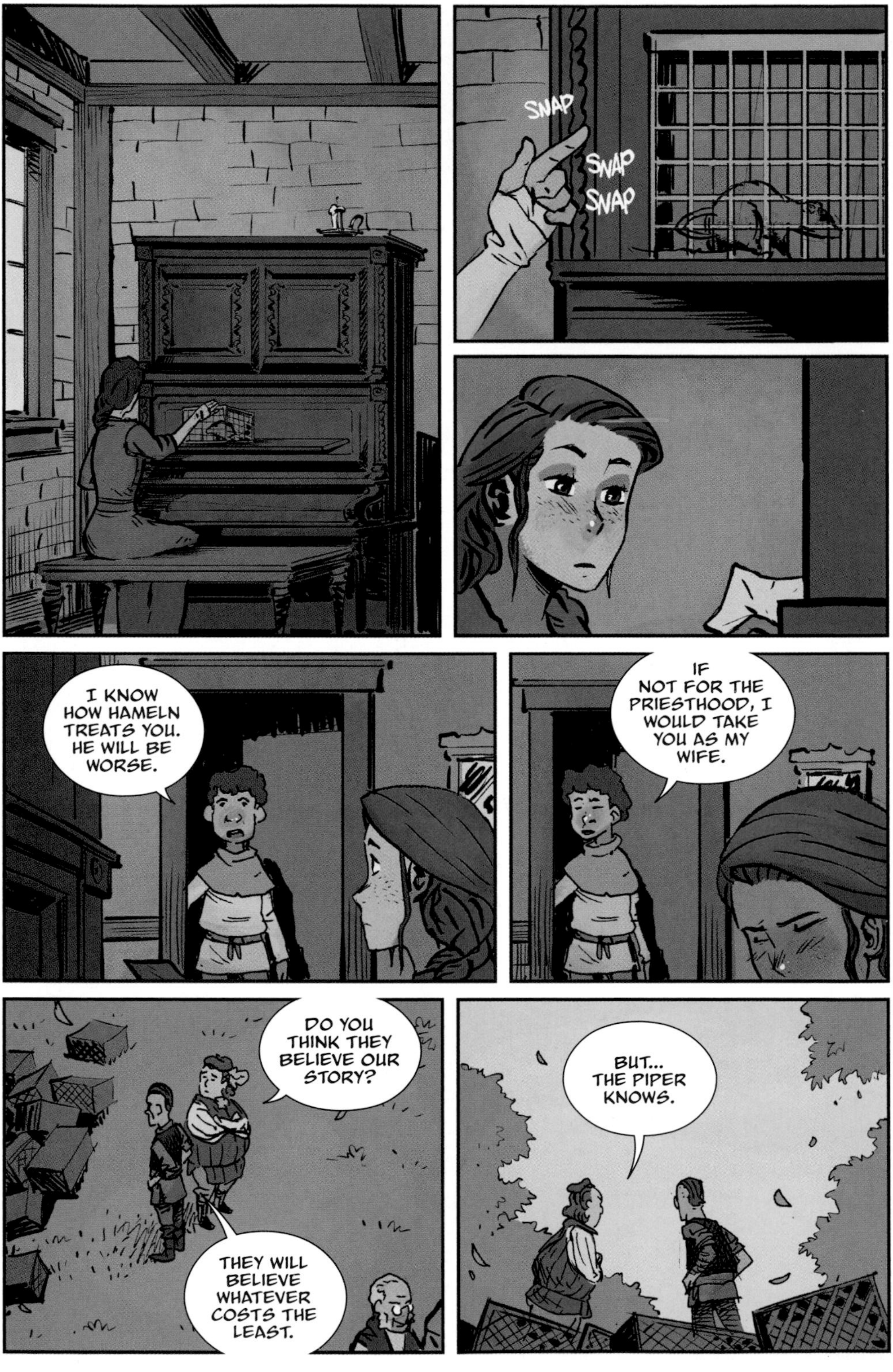
SNAP
SNAP
SNAP
I KNOW HOW HAMELN TREATS YOU. HE WILL BE WORSE.
IF NOT FOR THE PRIESTHOOD, I WOULD TAKE YOU AS MY WIFE.
DO YOU THINK THEY BELIEVE OUR STORY?
THEY WILL BELIEVE WHATEVER COSTS THE LEAST.
BUT... THE PIPER KNOWS.

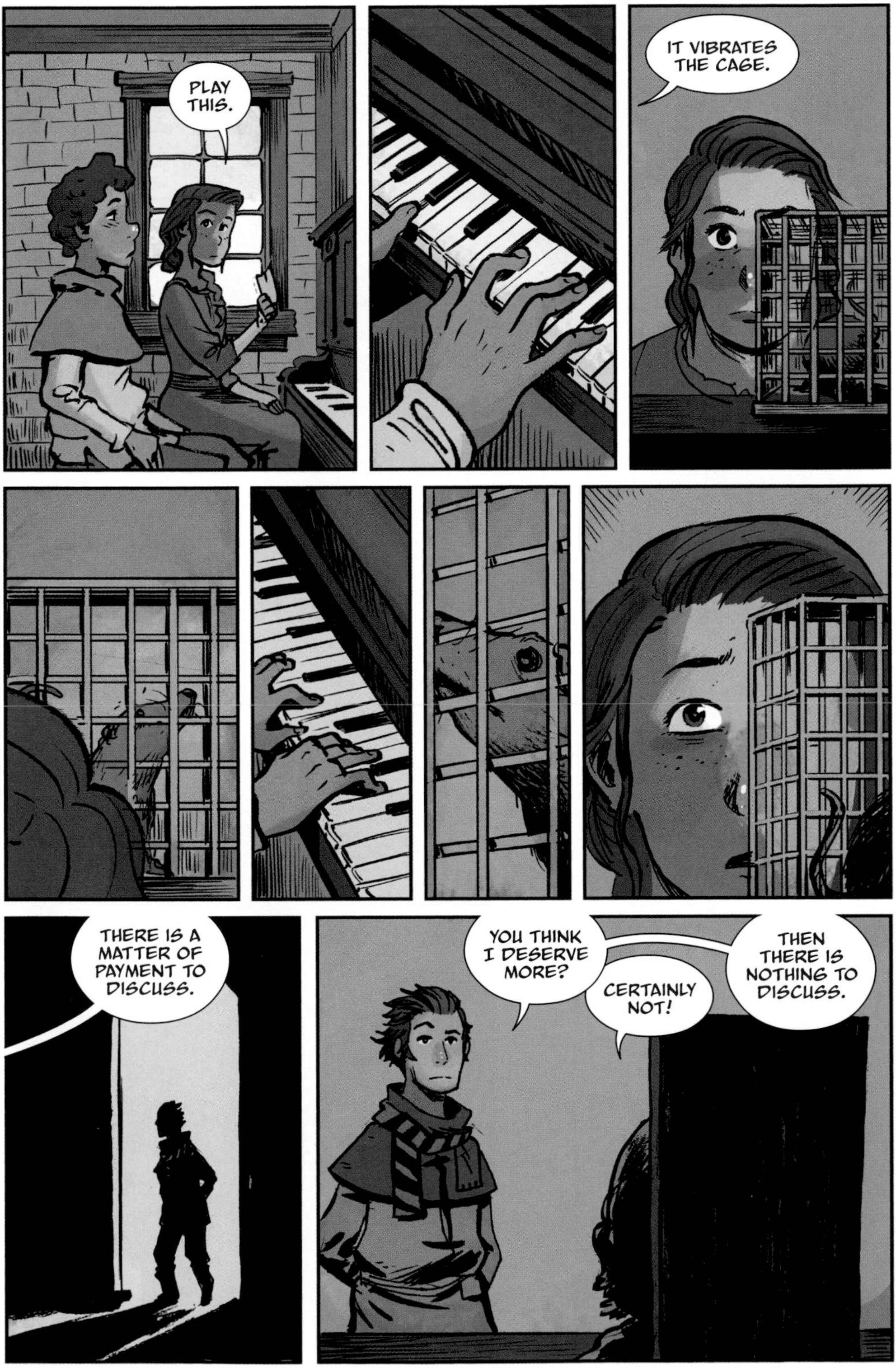
PLAY THIS.
IT VIBRATES THE CAGE.
THERE IS A MATTER OF PAYMENT TO DISCUSS.
YOU THINK I DESERVE MORE?
CERTAINLY NOT!
THEN THERE IS NOTHING TO DISCUSS.

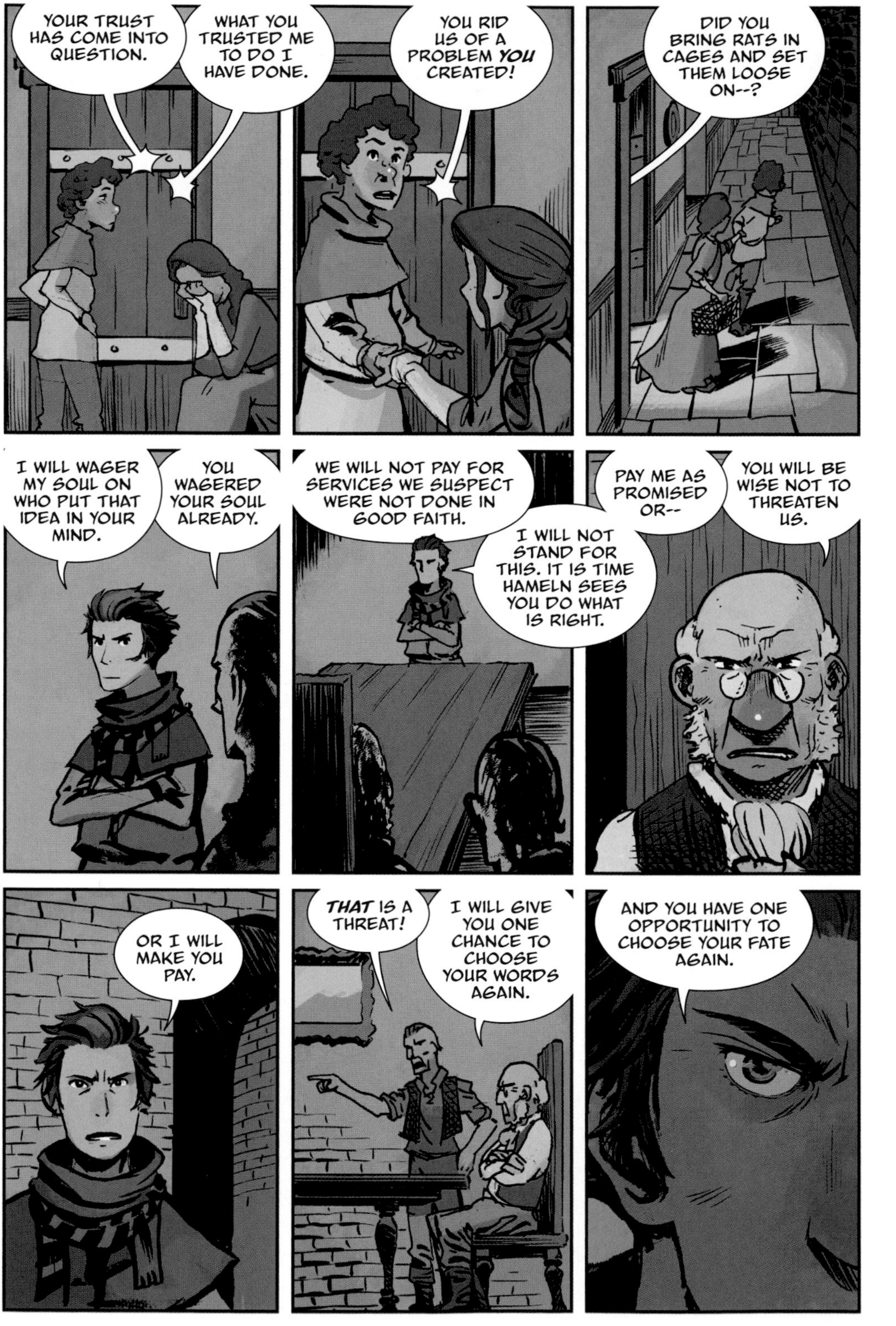
YOUR TRUST HAS COME INTO QUESTION.
WHAT YOU TRUSTED ME TO DO I HAVE DONE.
YOU RID US OF A PROBLEM *YOU* CREATED!
DID YOU BRING RATS IN CAGES AND SET THEM LOOSE ON--?
I WILL WAGER MY SOUL ON WHO PUT THAT IDEA IN YOUR MIND.
YOU WAGERED YOUR SOUL ALREADY.
WE WILL NOT PAY FOR SERVICES WE SUSPECT WERE NOT DONE IN GOOD FAITH.
I WILL NOT STAND FOR THIS. IT IS TIME HAMELN SEES YOU DO WHAT IS RIGHT.
PAY ME AS PROMISED OR--
YOU WILL BE WISE NOT TO THREATEN US.
OR I WILL MAKE YOU PAY.
THAT IS A THREAT!
I WILL GIVE YOU ONE CHANCE TO CHOOSE YOUR WORDS AGAIN.
AND YOU HAVE ONE OPPORTUNITY TO CHOOSE YOUR FATE AGAIN.

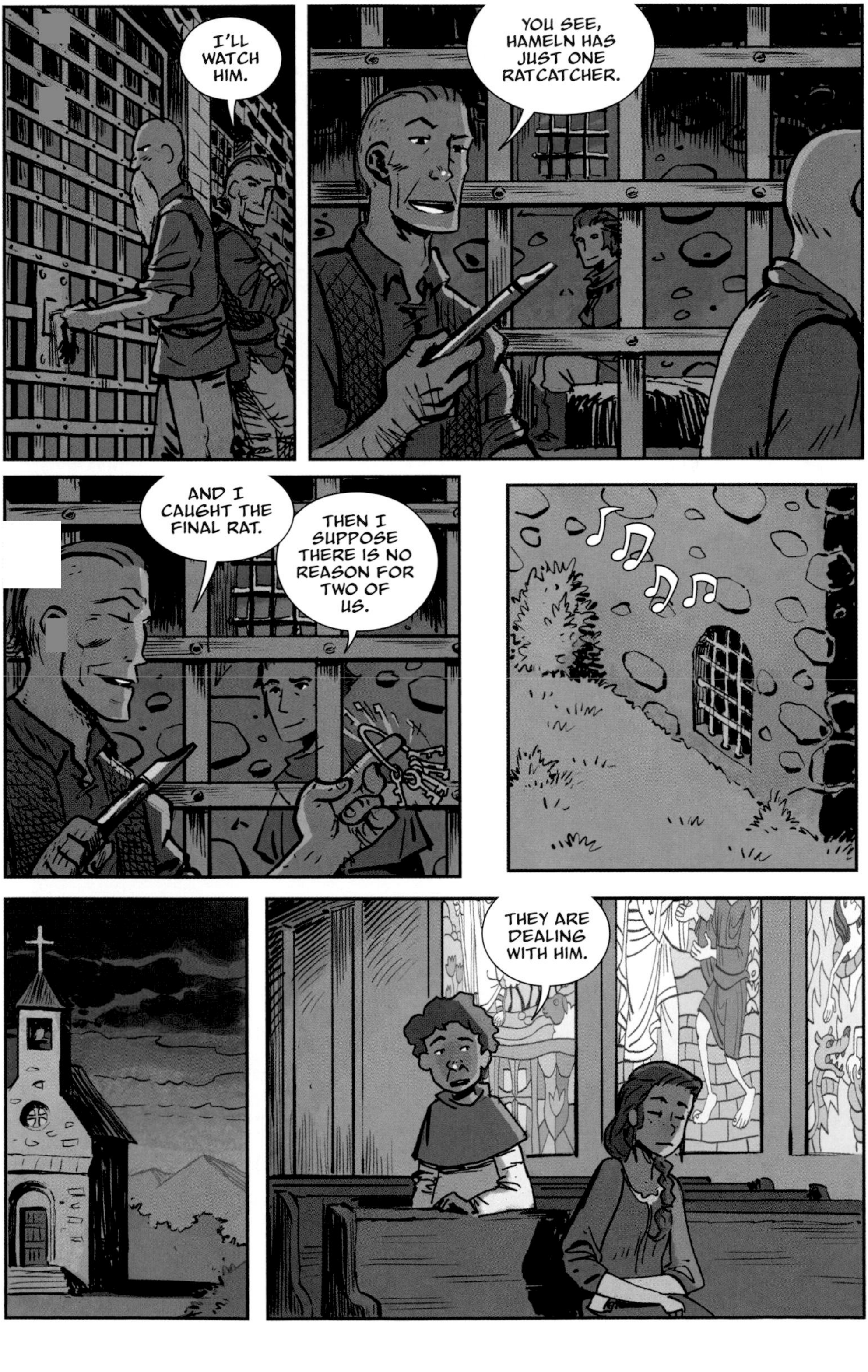
I'LL WATCH HIM.
YOU SEE, HAMELN HAS JUST ONE RATCATCHER.
AND I CAUGHT THE FINAL RAT.
THEN I SUPPOSE THERE IS NO REASON FOR TWO OF US.
THEY ARE DEALING WITH HIM.

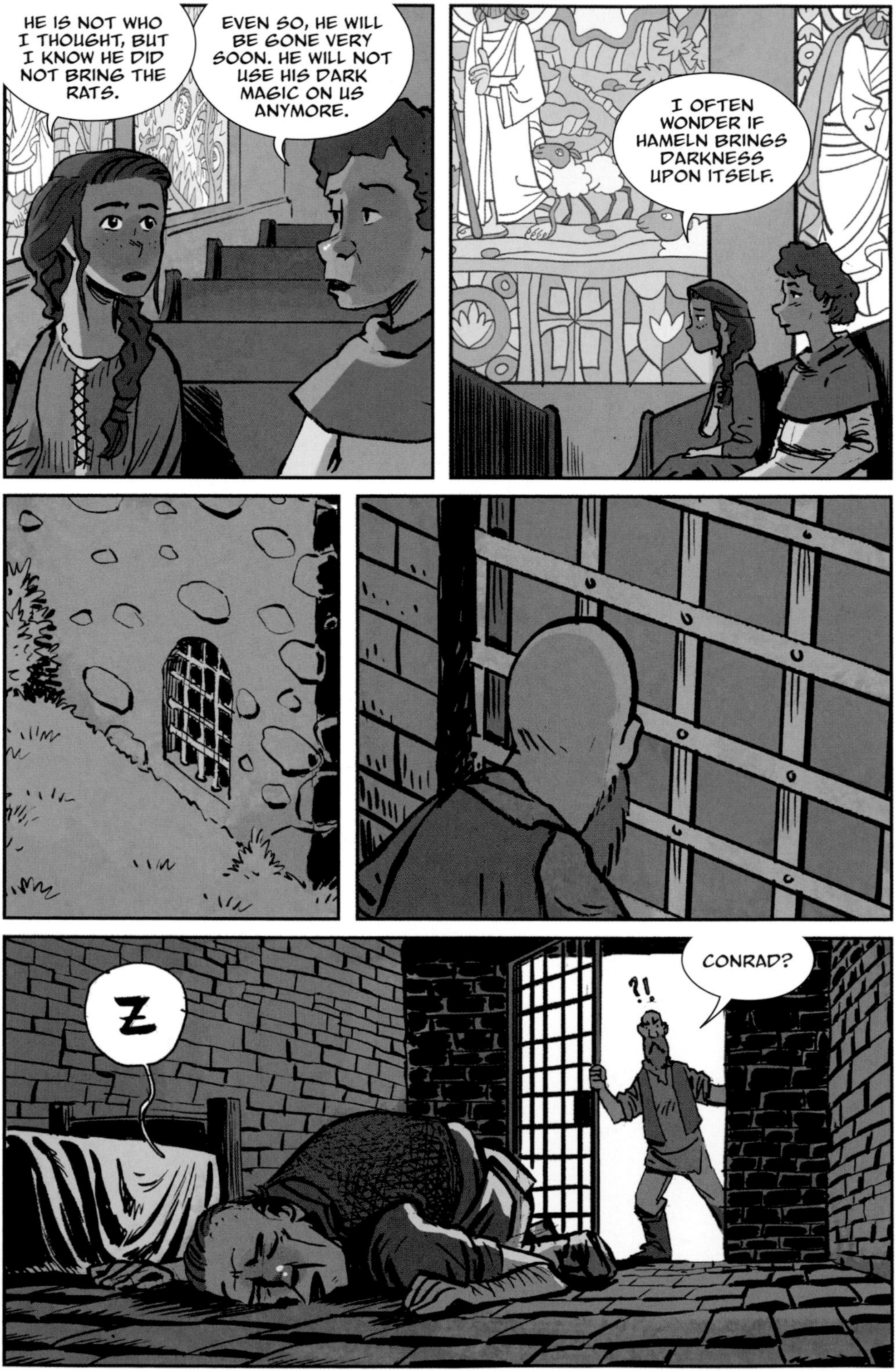
HE IS NOT WHO I THOUGHT, BUT I KNOW HE DID NOT BRING THE RATS.
EVEN SO, HE WILL BE GONE VERY SOON. HE WILL NOT USE HIS DARK MAGIC ON US ANYMORE.
I OFTEN WONDER IF HAMELN BRINGS DARKNESS UPON ITSELF.
Z
?!
CONRAD?

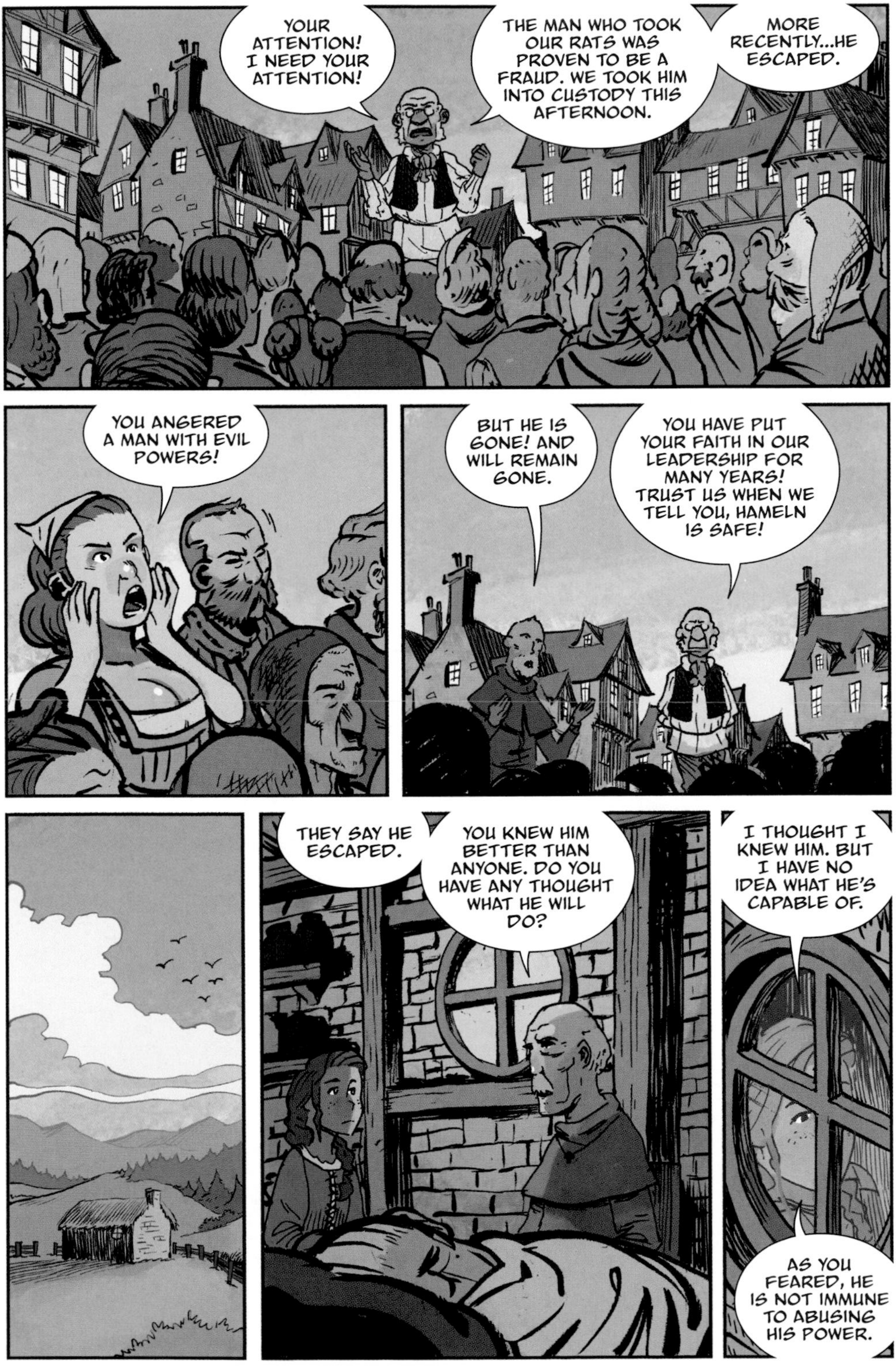
YOUR ATTENTION! I NEED YOUR ATTENTION!
THE MAN WHO TOOK OUR RATS WAS PROVEN TO BE A FRAUD. WE TOOK HIM INTO CUSTODY THIS AFTERNOON.
MORE RECENTLY...HE ESCAPED.
YOU ANGERED A MAN WITH EVIL POWERS!
BUT HE IS GONE! AND WILL REMAIN GONE.
YOU HAVE PUT YOUR FAITH IN OUR LEADERSHIP FOR MANY YEARS! TRUST US WHEN WE TELL YOU, HAMELN IS SAFE!
THEY SAY HE ESCAPED.
YOU KNEW HIM BETTER THAN ANYONE. DO YOU HAVE ANY THOUGHT WHAT HE WILL DO?
I THOUGHT I KNEW HIM. BUT I HAVE NO IDEA WHAT HE'S CAPABLE OF.
AS YOU FEARED, HE IS NOT IMMUNE TO ABUSING HIS POWER.

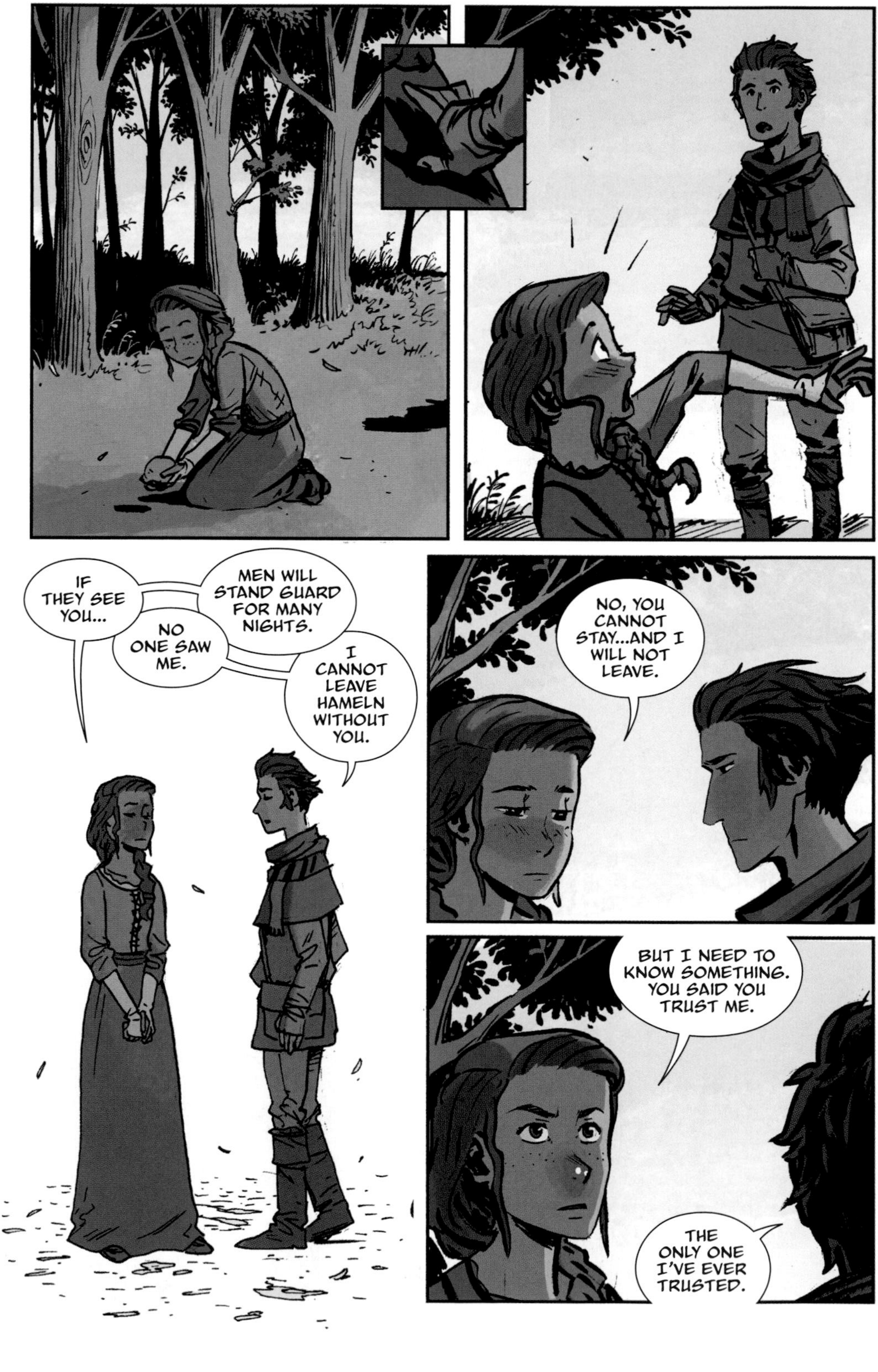
IF THEY SEE YOU...
MEN WILL STAND GUARD FOR MANY NIGHTS.
NO ONE SAW ME.
I CANNOT LEAVE HAMELN WITHOUT YOU.
NO, YOU CANNOT STAY...AND I WILL NOT LEAVE.
BUT I NEED TO KNOW SOMETHING. YOU SAID YOU TRUST ME.
THE ONLY ONE I'VE EVER TRUSTED.

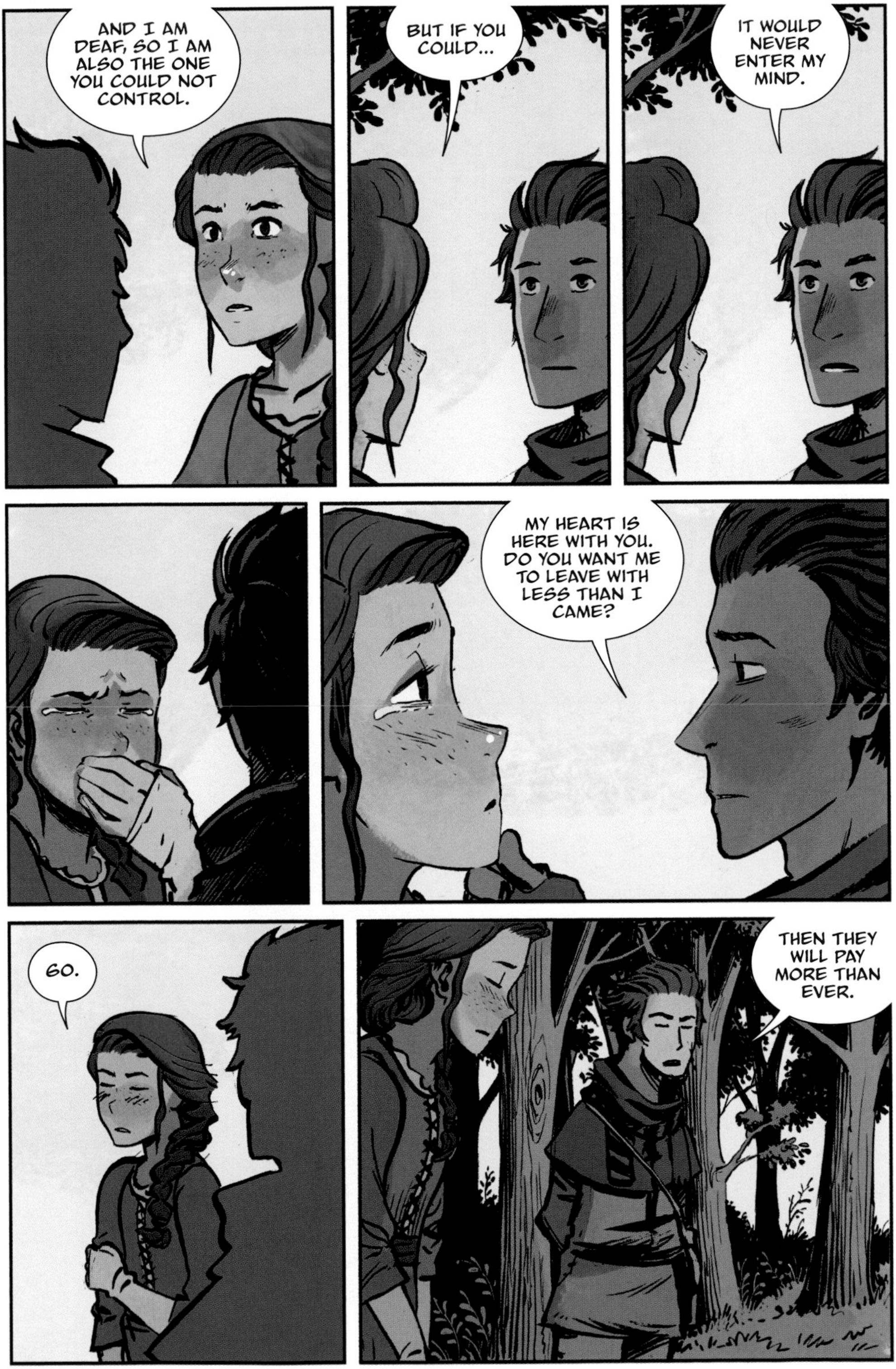
AND I AM DEAF, SO I AM ALSO THE ONE YOU COULD NOT CONTROL.
BUT IF YOU COULD...
IT WOULD NEVER ENTER MY MIND.
MY HEART IS HERE WITH YOU. DO YOU WANT ME TO LEAVE WITH LESS THAN I CAME?
GO.
THEN THEY WILL PAY MORE THAN EVER.

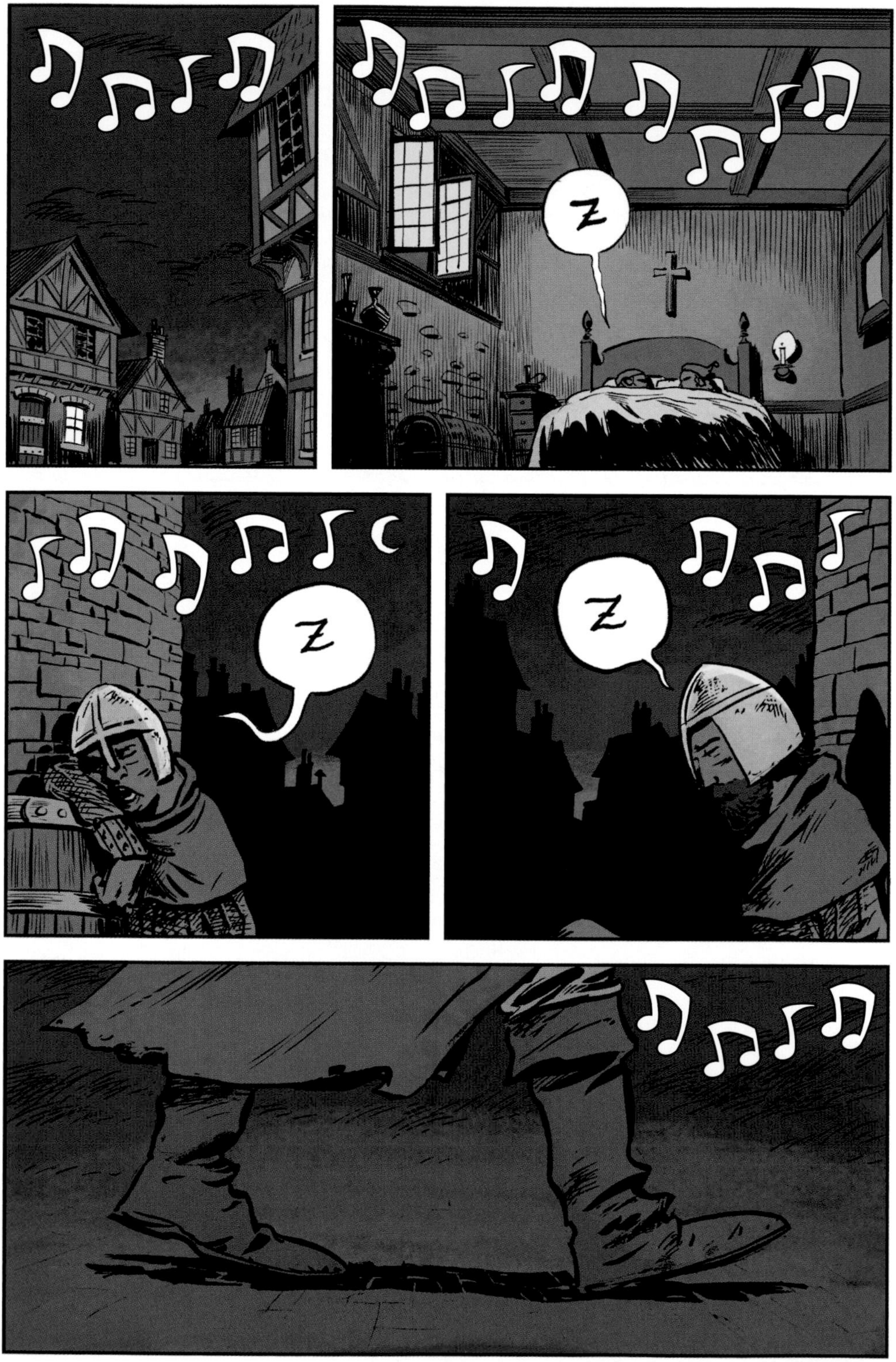
Z
Z
Z

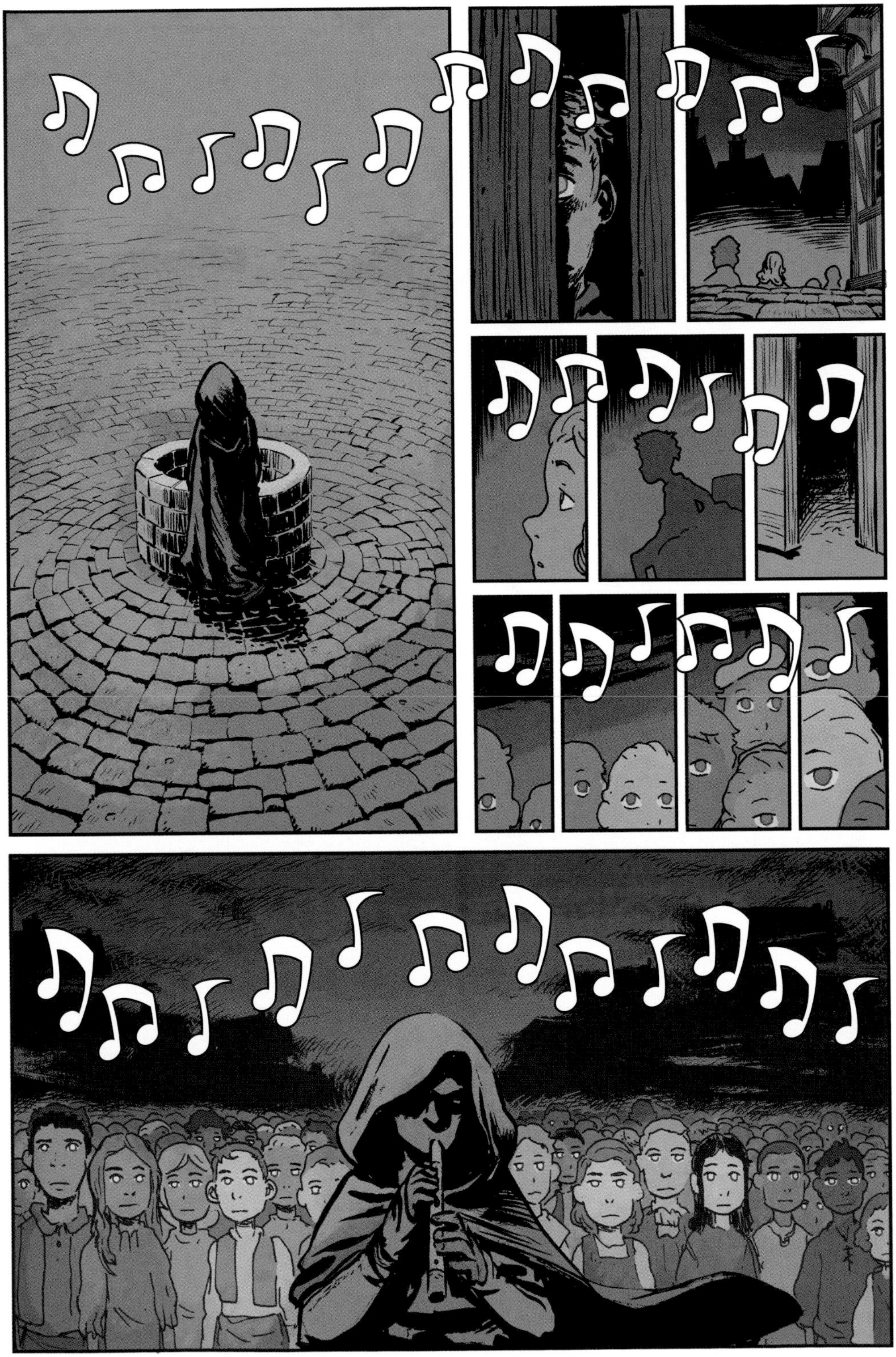

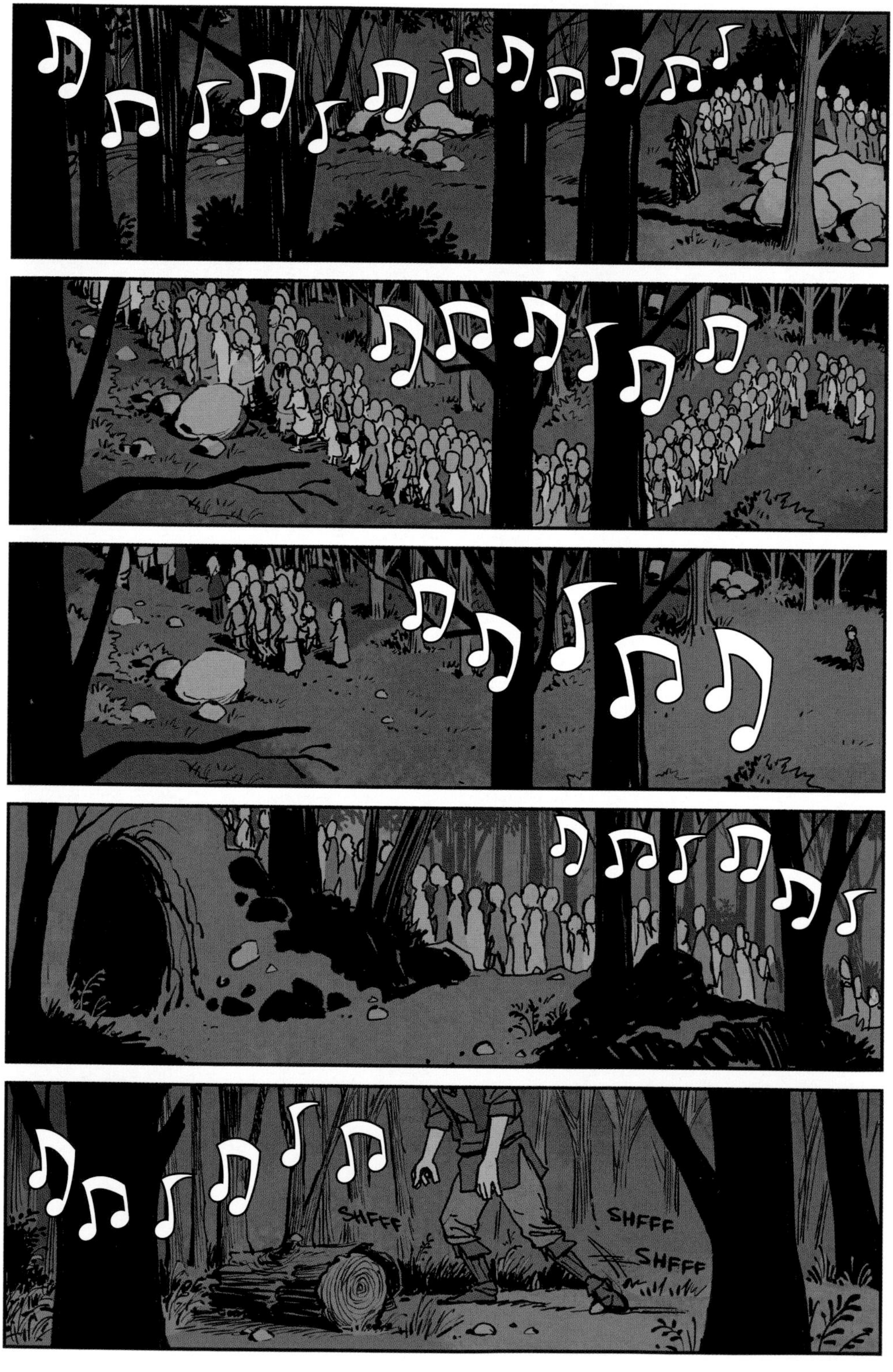
SHFFF
SHFFF
SHFFF

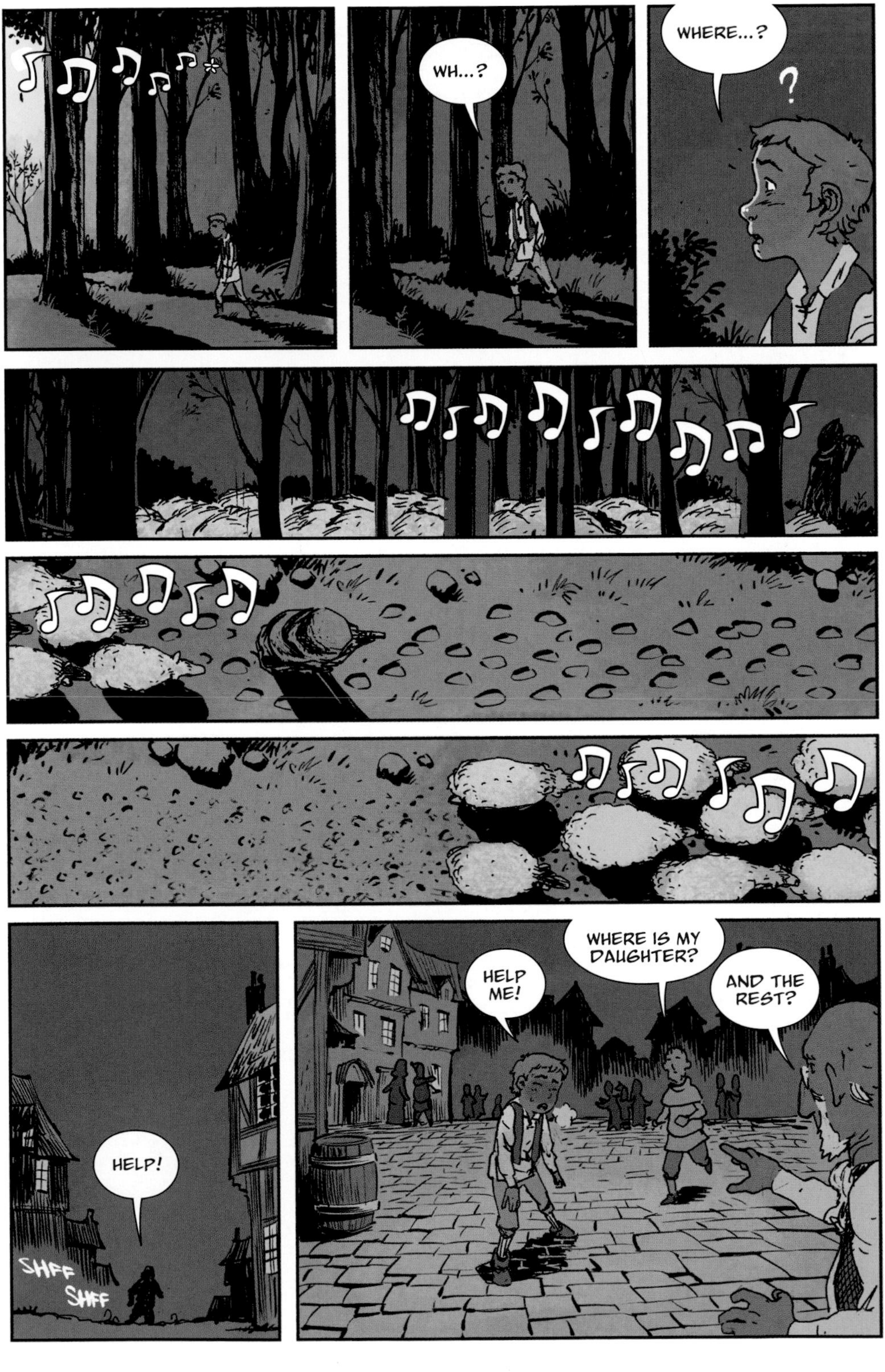
SHFF
WH...?
WHERE...?
?
HELP!
SHFF
SHFF
HELP ME!
WHERE IS MY DAUGHTER?
AND THE REST?

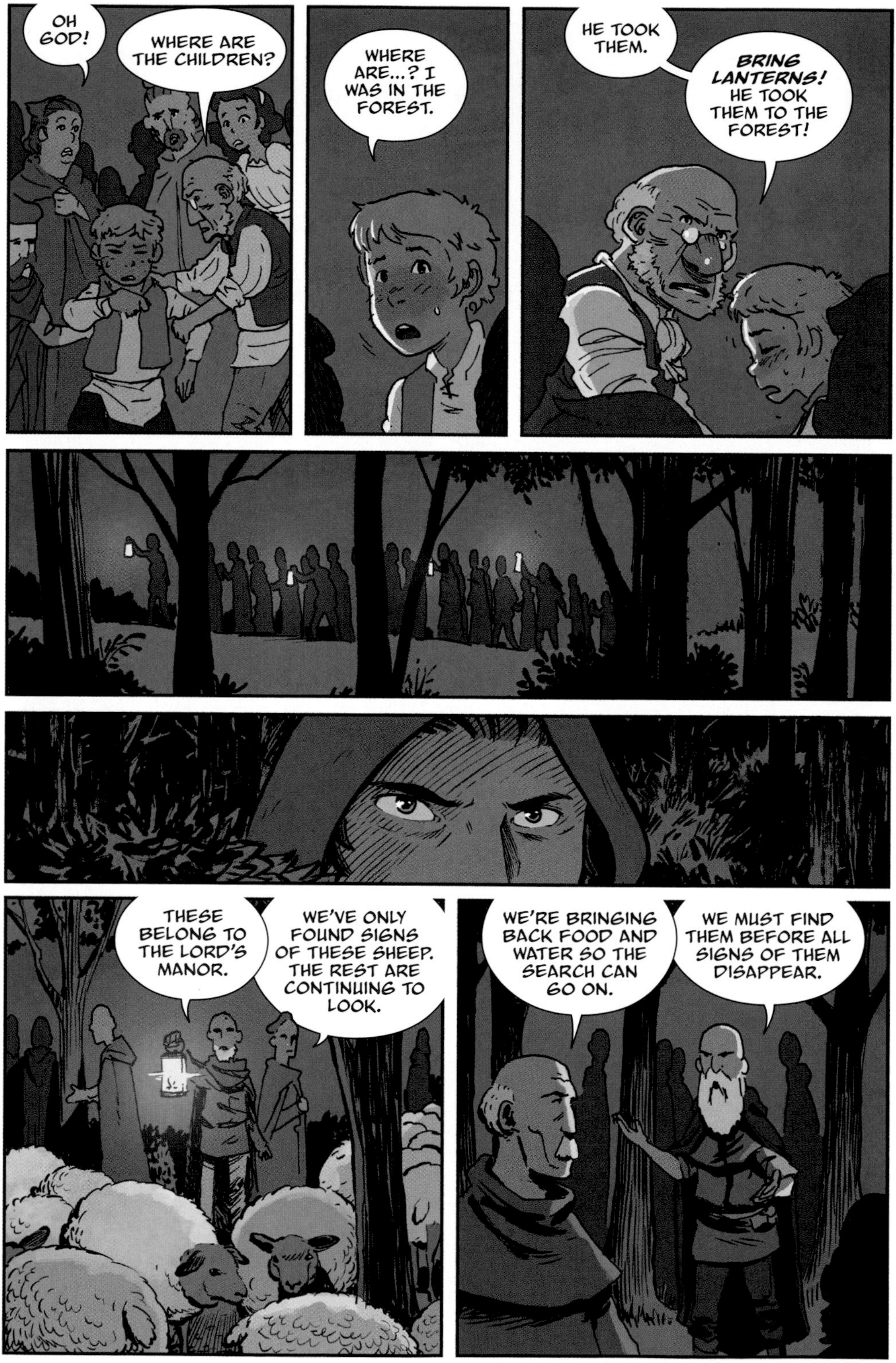
OH GOD!
WHERE ARE THE CHILDREN?
WHERE ARE...? I WAS IN THE FOREST.
HE TOOK THEM.
BRING LANTERNS! HE TOOK THEM TO THE FOREST!
THESE BELONG TO THE LORD'S MANOR.
WE'VE ONLY FOUND SIGNS OF THESE SHEEP. THE REST ARE CONTINUING TO LOOK.
WE'RE BRINGING BACK FOOD AND WATER SO THE SEARCH CAN GO ON.
WE MUST FIND THEM BEFORE ALL SIGNS OF THEM DISAPPEAR.

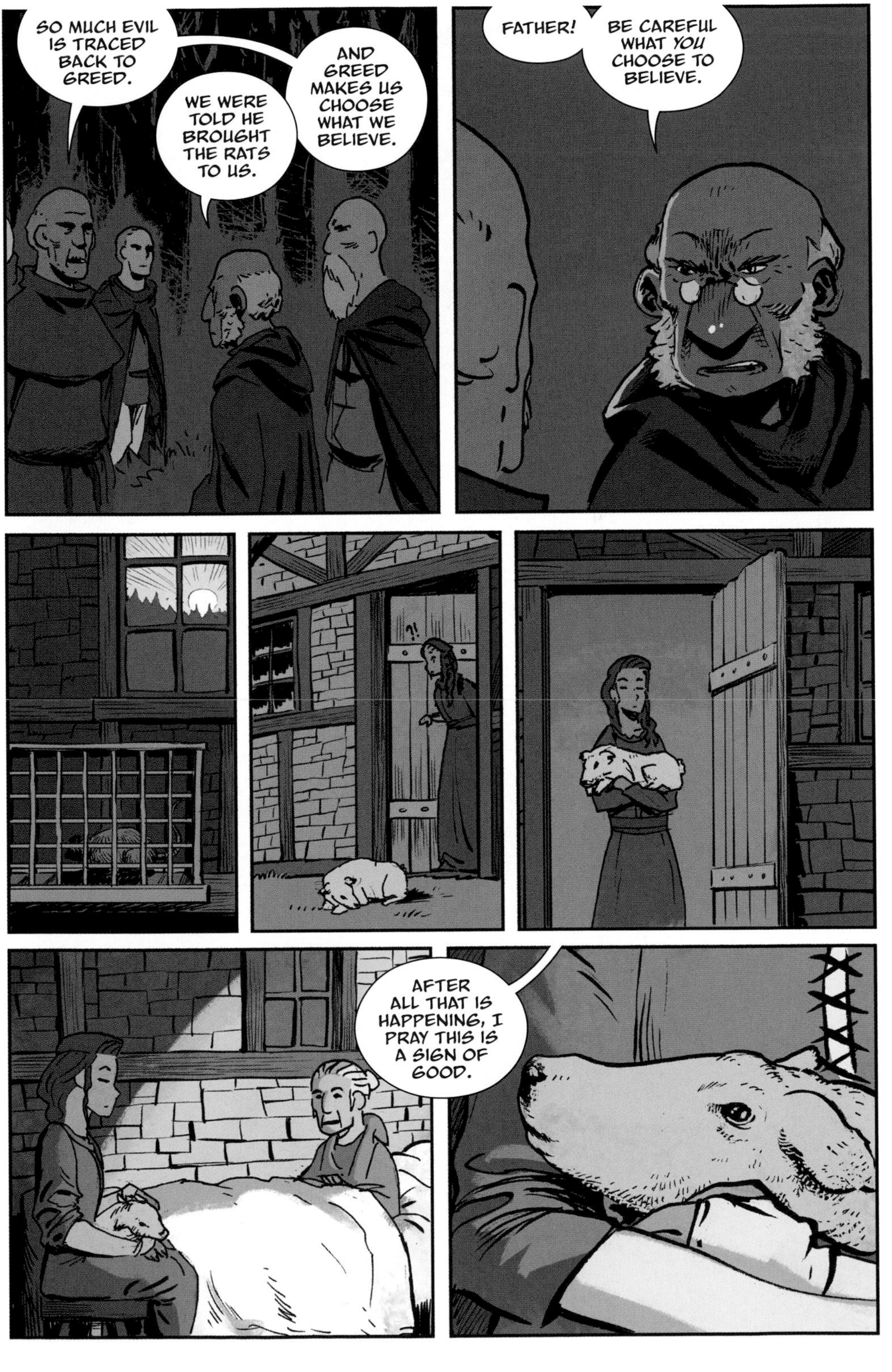
SO MUCH EVIL IS TRACED BACK TO GREED.
AND GREED MAKES US CHOOSE WHAT WE BELIEVE.
WE WERE TOLD HE BROUGHT THE RATS TO US.
FATHER!
BE CAREFUL WHAT YOU CHOOSE TO BELIEVE.
?!
AFTER ALL THAT IS HAPPENING, I PRAY THIS IS A SIGN OF GOOD.

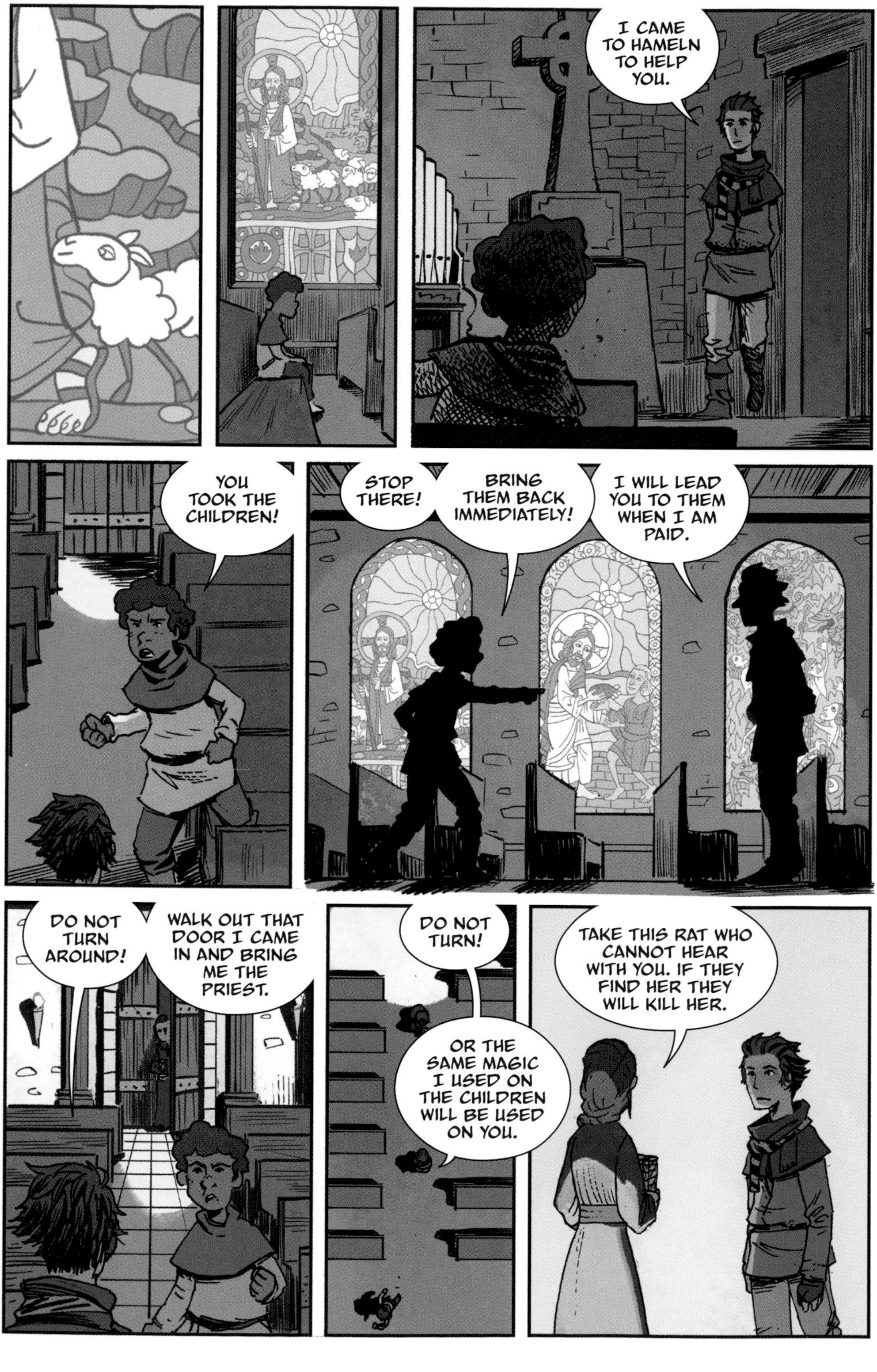
I CAME TO HAMELN TO HELP YOU.
YOU TOOK THE CHILDREN!
STOP THERE!
BRING THEM BACK IMMEDIATELY!
I WILL LEAD YOU TO THEM WHEN I AM PAID.
DO NOT TURN AROUND!
WALK OUT THAT DOOR I CAME IN AND BRING ME THE PRIEST.
DO NOT TURN!
OR THE SAME MAGIC I USED ON THE CHILDREN WILL BE USED ON YOU.
TAKE THIS RAT WHO CANNOT HEAR WITH YOU. IF THEY FIND HER THEY WILL KILL HER.

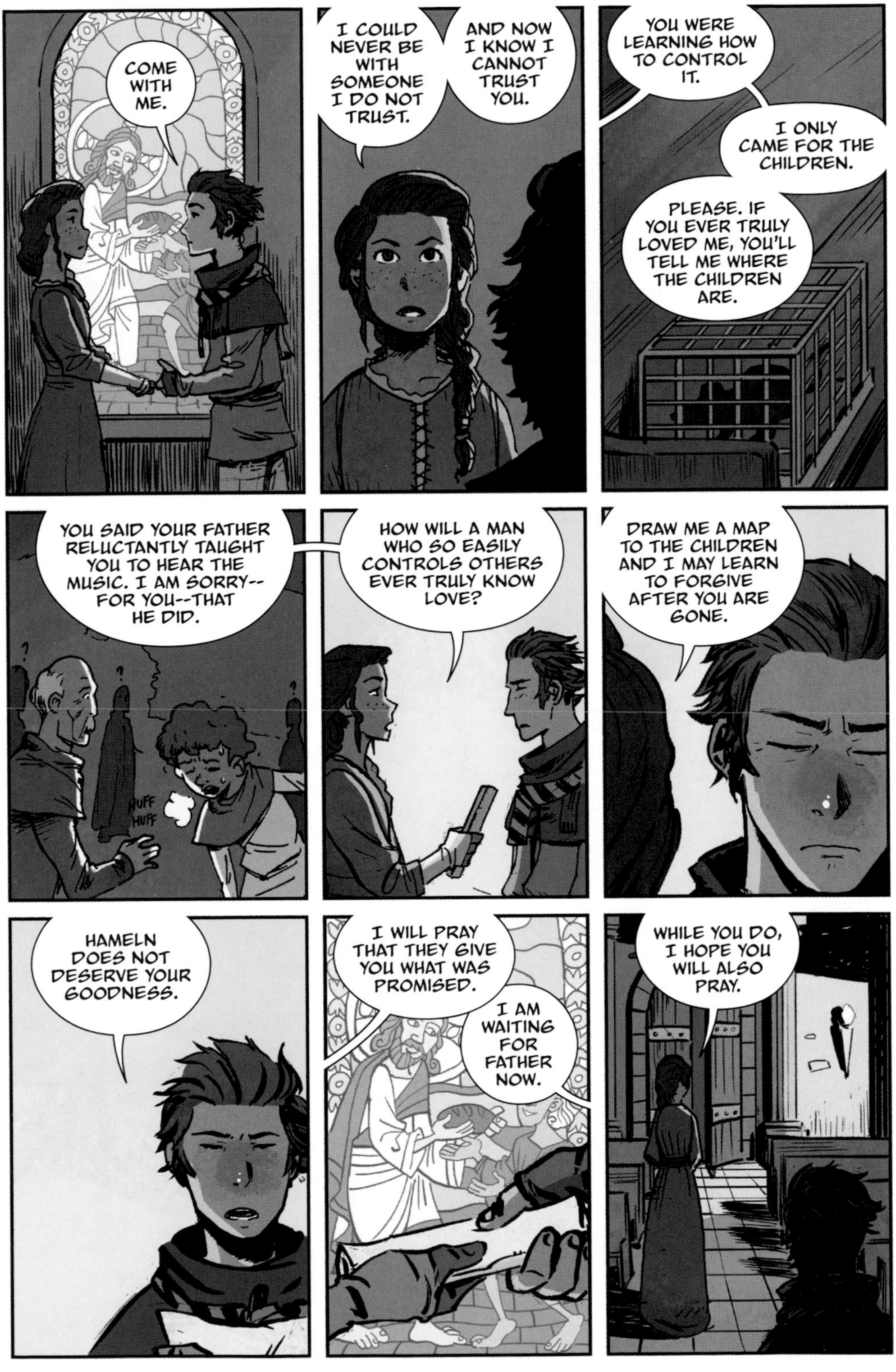
COME WITH ME.
I COULD NEVER BE WITH SOMEONE I DO NOT TRUST.
AND NOW I KNOW I CANNOT TRUST YOU.
YOU WERE LEARNING HOW TO CONTROL IT.
I ONLY CAME FOR THE CHILDREN.
PLEASE. IF YOU EVER TRULY LOVED ME, YOU'LL TELL ME WHERE THE CHILDREN ARE.
YOU SAID YOUR FATHER RELUCTANTLY TAUGHT YOU TO HEAR THE MUSIC. I AM SORRY--FOR YOU--THAT HE DID.
HUFF HUFF
HOW WILL A MAN WHO SO EASILY CONTROLS OTHERS EVER TRULY KNOW LOVE?
DRAW ME A MAP TO THE CHILDREN AND I MAY LEARN TO FORGIVE AFTER YOU ARE GONE.
HAMELN DOES NOT DESERVE YOUR GOODNESS.
I WILL PRAY THAT THEY GIVE YOU WHAT WAS PROMISED.
I AM WAITING FOR FATHER NOW.
WHILE YOU DO, I HOPE YOU WILL ALSO PRAY.

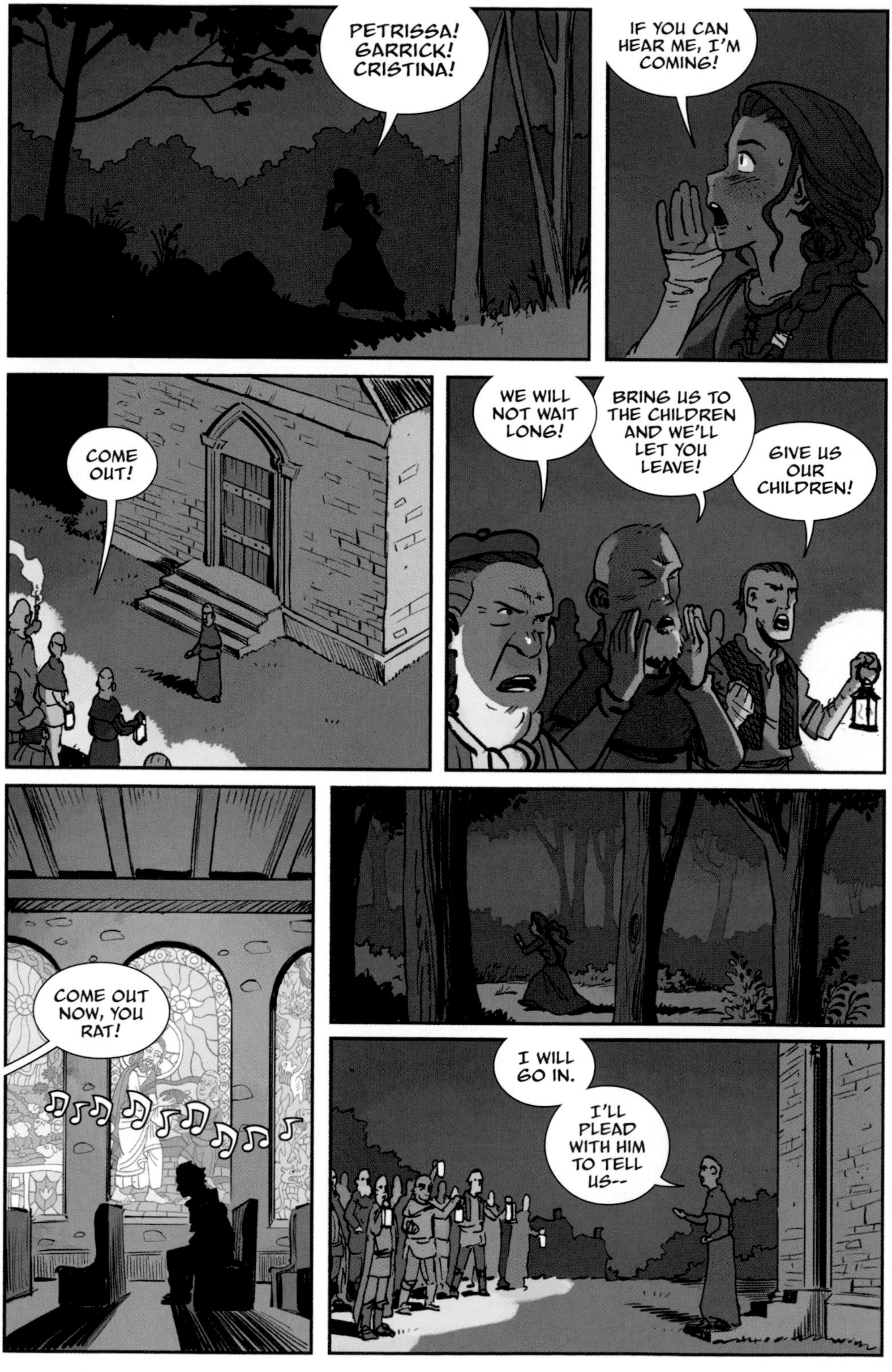
PETRISSA! GARRICK! CRISTINA!
IF YOU CAN HEAR ME, I'M COMING!
COME OUT!
WE WILL NOT WAIT LONG!
BRING US TO THE CHILDREN AND WE'LL LET YOU LEAVE!
GIVE US OUR CHILDREN!
COME OUT NOW, YOU RAT!
I WILL GO IN.
I'LL PLEAD WITH HIM TO TELL US--

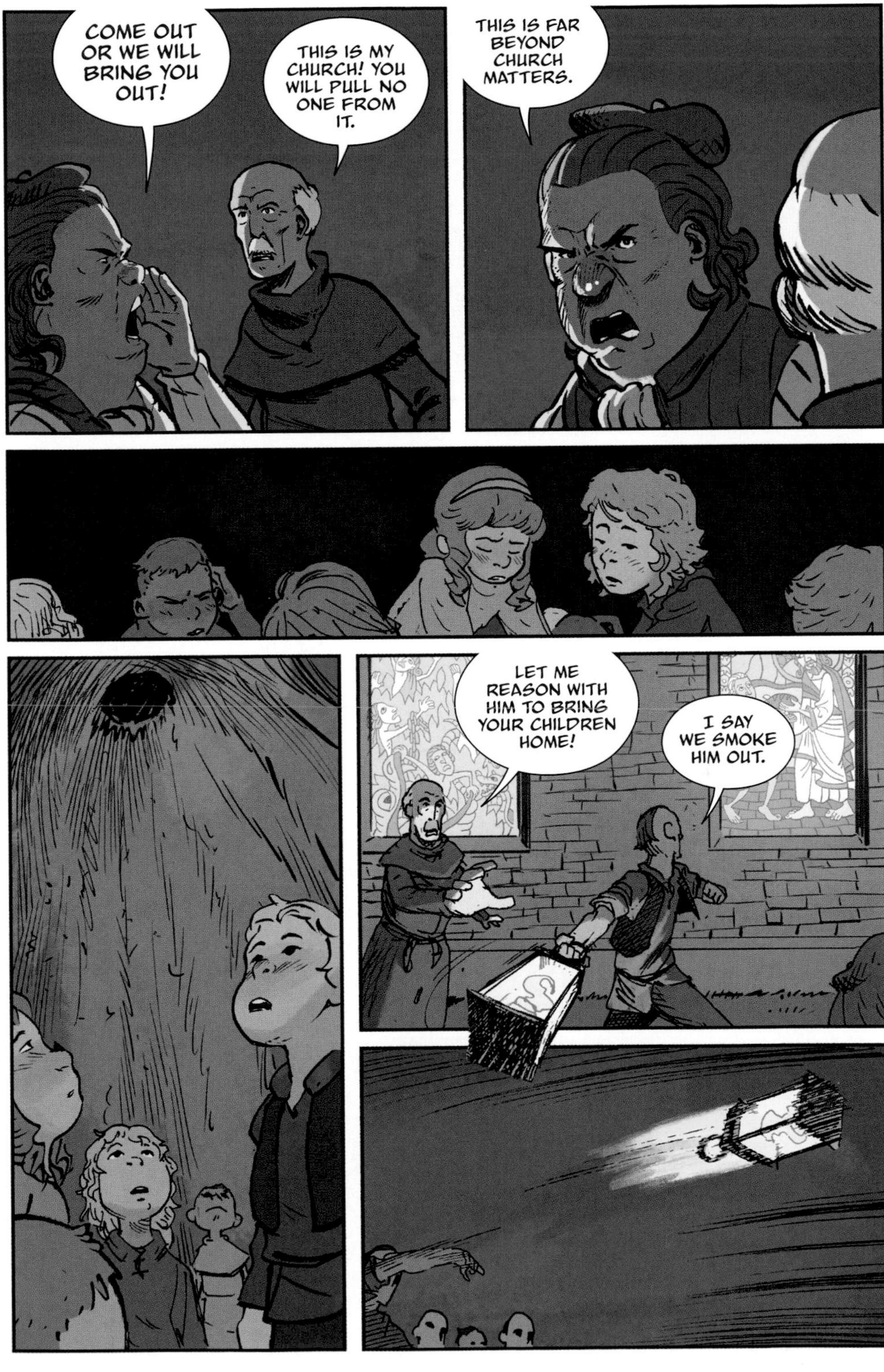
COME OUT OR WE WILL BRING YOU OUT!
THIS IS MY CHURCH! YOU WILL PULL NO ONE FROM IT.
THIS IS FAR BEYOND CHURCH MATTERS.
LET ME REASON WITH HIM TO BRING YOUR CHILDREN HOME!
I SAY WE SMOKE HIM OUT.

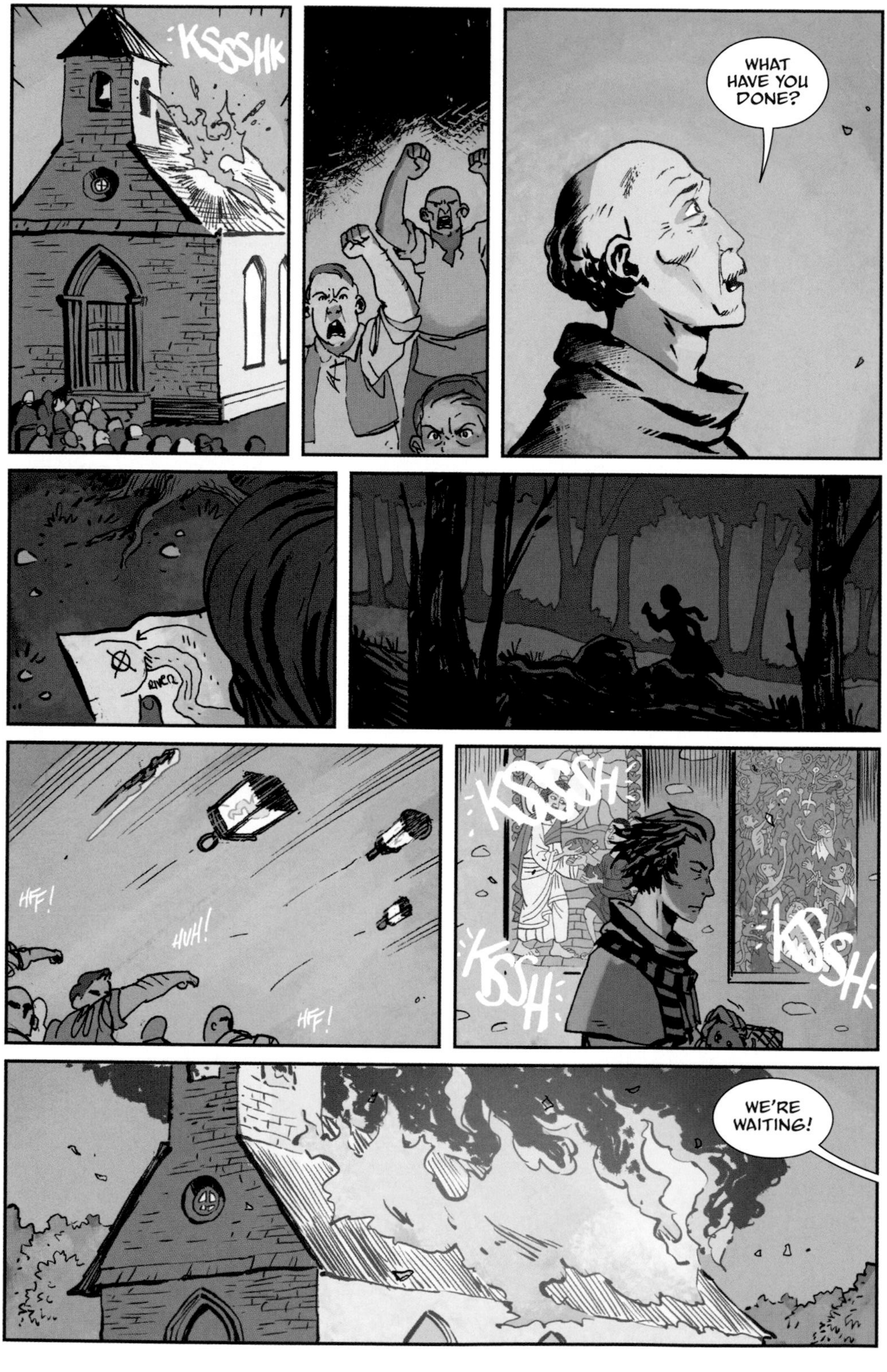
KSSSHK
WHAT HAVE YOU DONE?
river
HFF!
HUH!
HFF!
KSSSH
KSSH
KSSH
WE'RE WAITING!

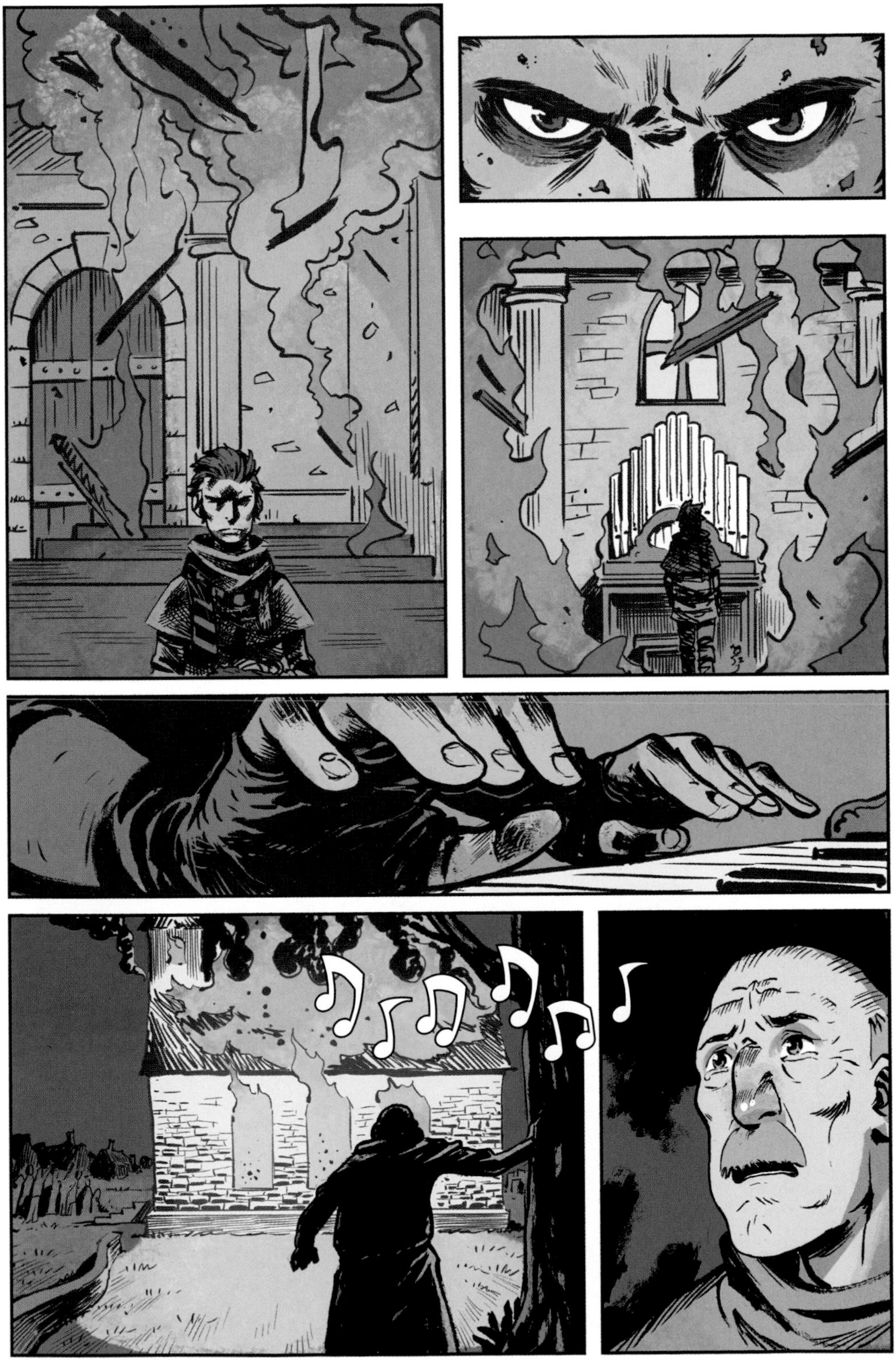

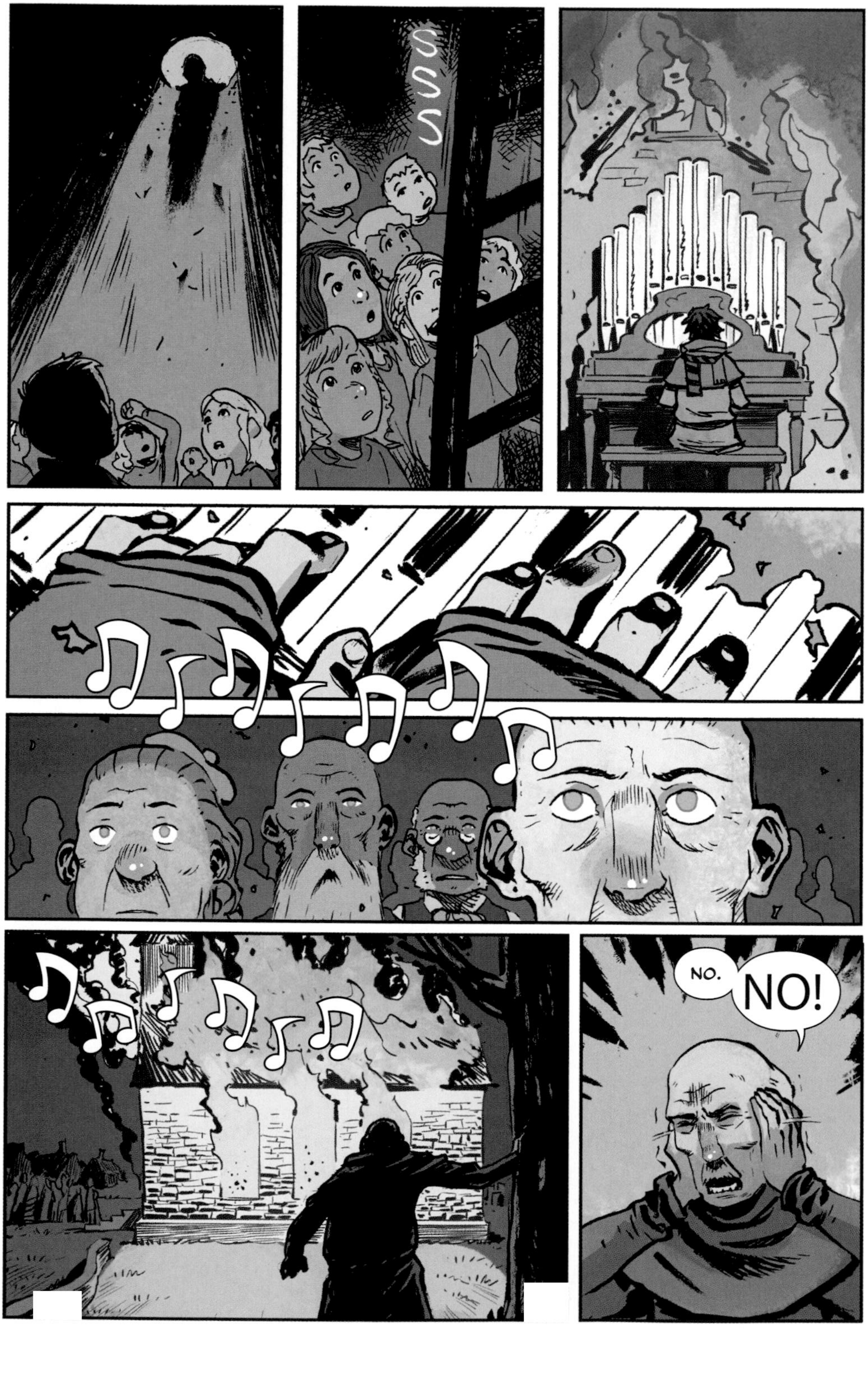
SSS
NO.
NO!

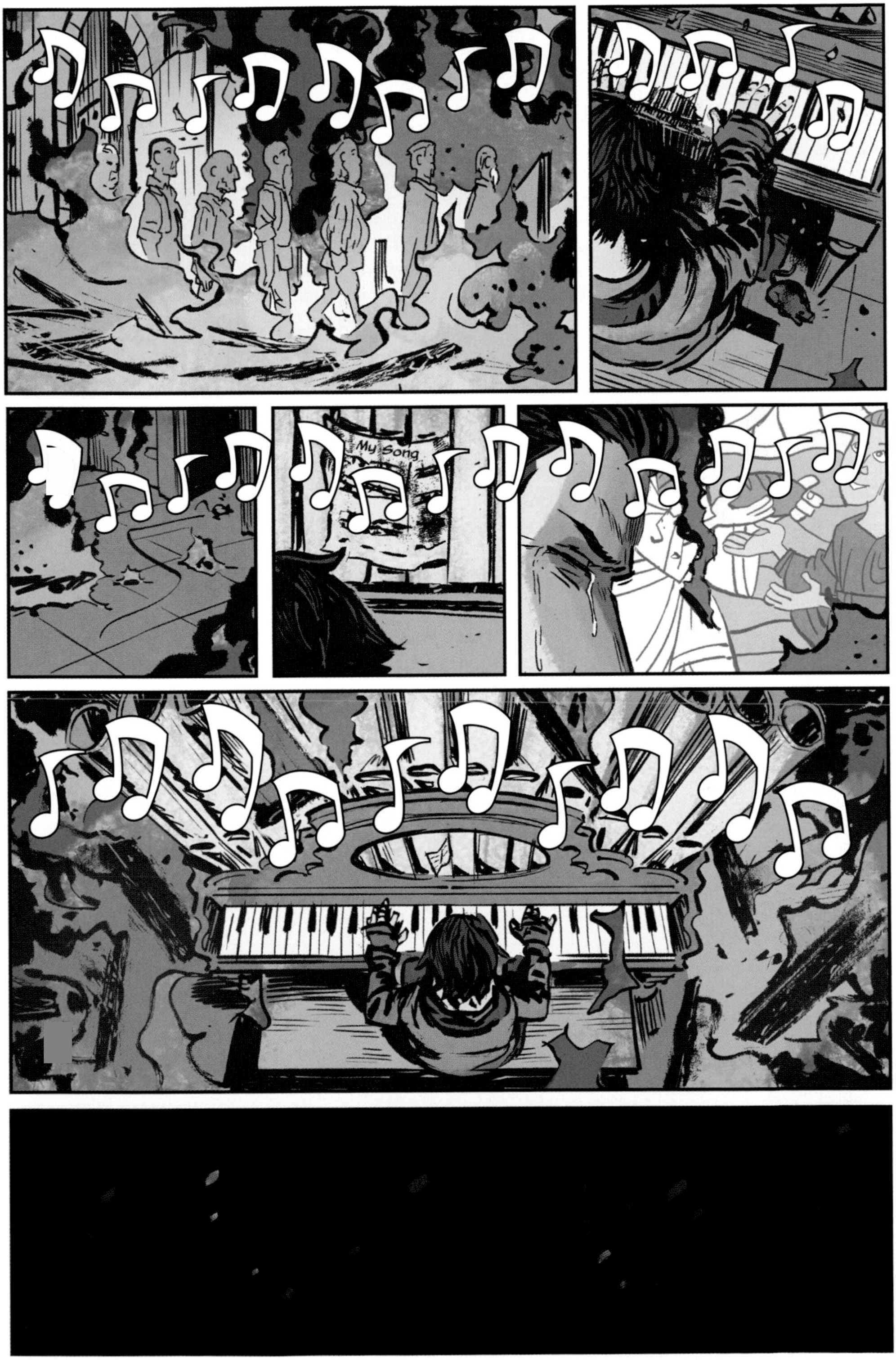
My Song

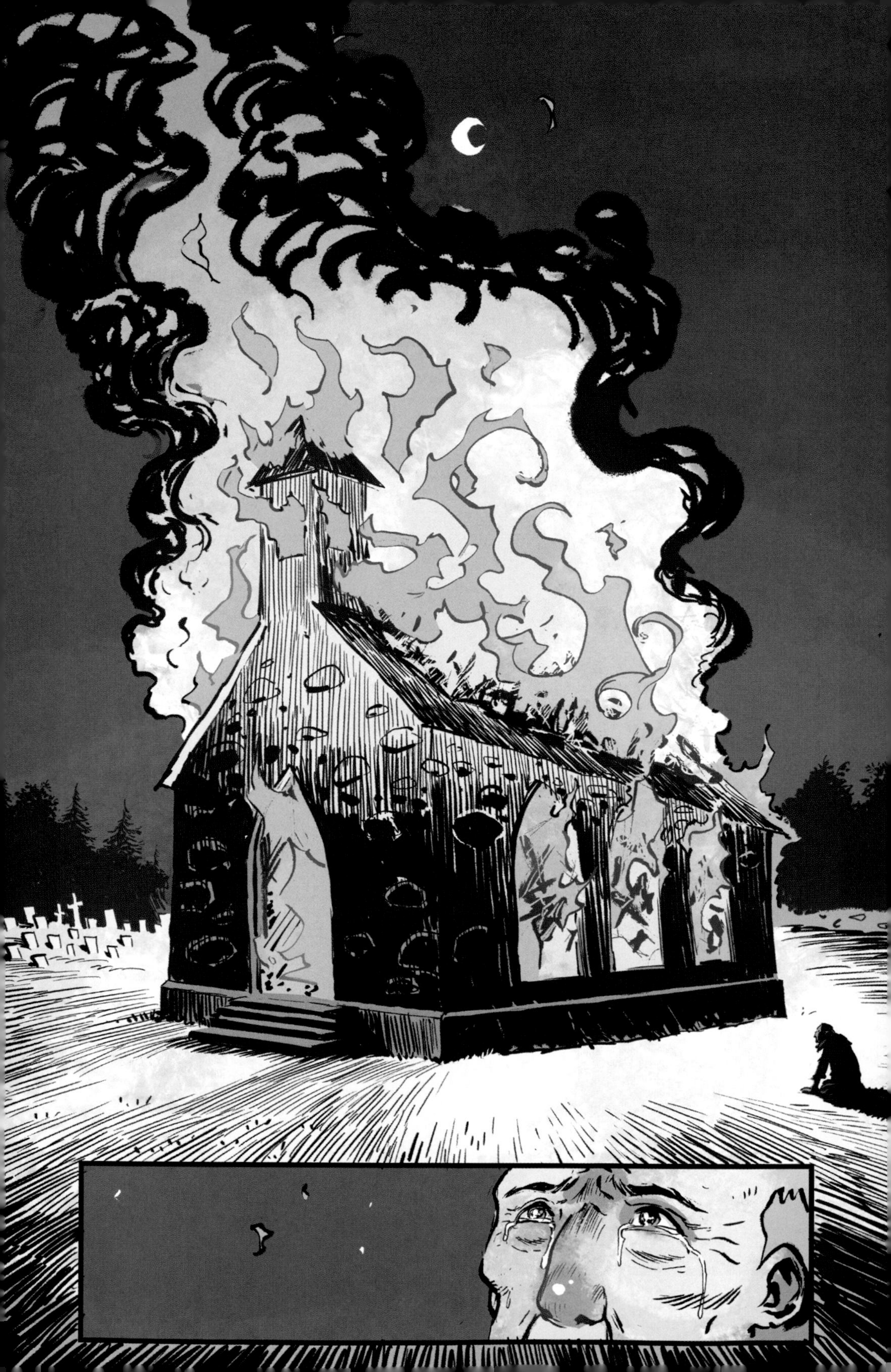

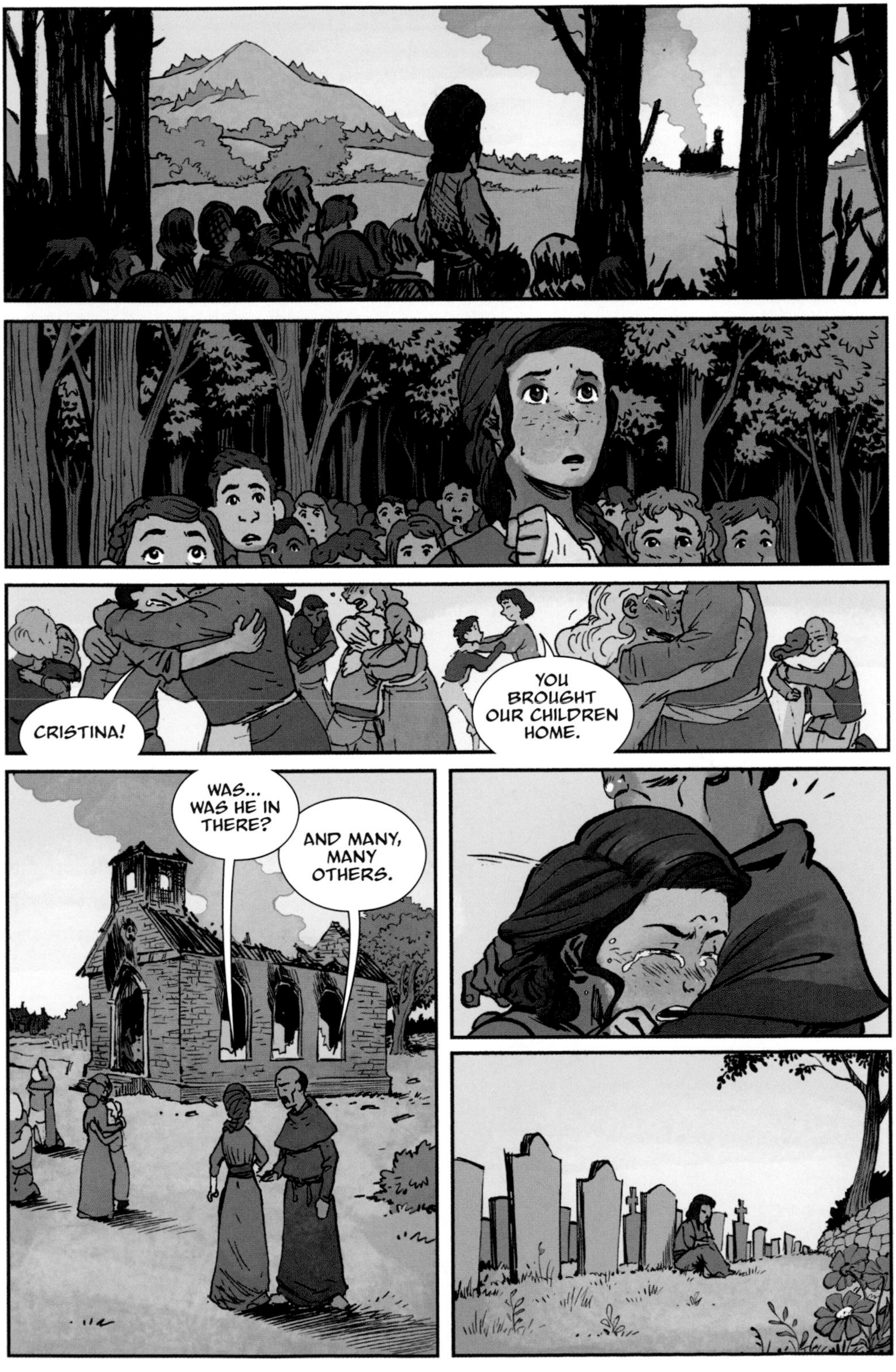
CRISTINA!
YOU BROUGHT OUR CHILDREN HOME.
WAS... WAS HE IN THERE?
AND MANY, MANY OTHERS.

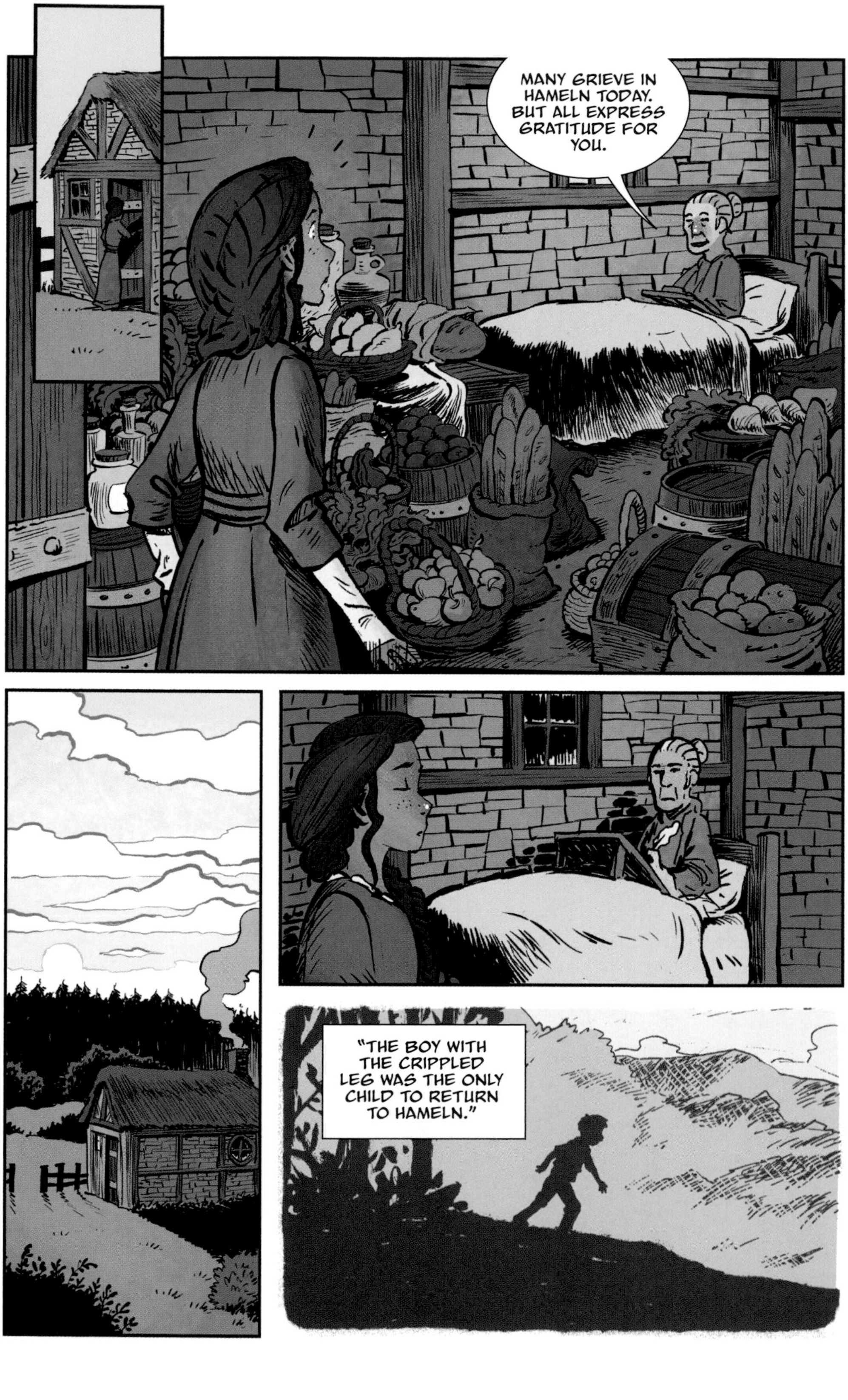
MANY GRIEVE IN HAMELN TODAY. BUT ALL EXPRESS GRATITUDE FOR YOU.
"THE BOY WITH THE CRIPPLED LEG WAS THE ONLY CHILD TO RETURN TO HAMELN."

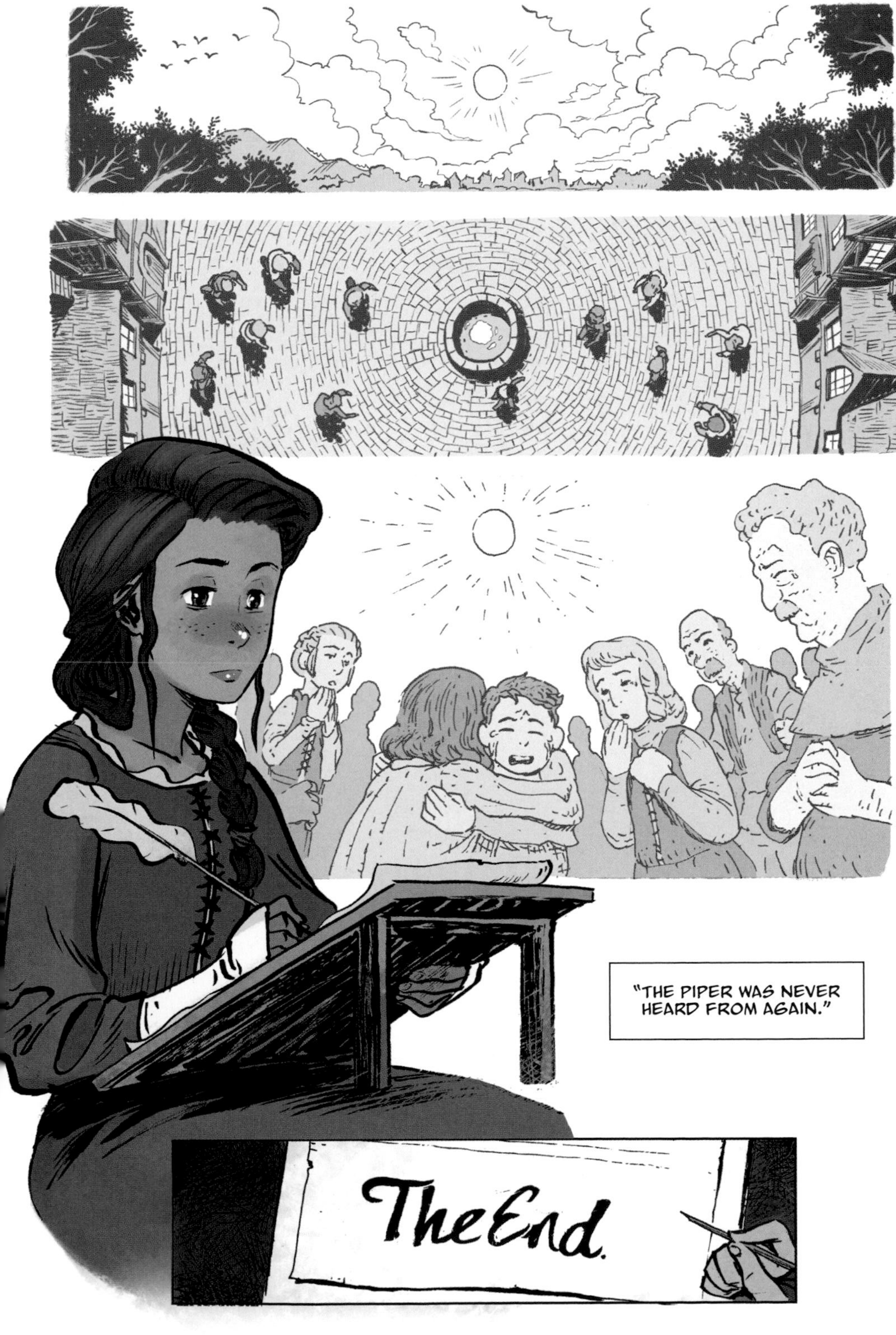
"THE PIPER WAS NEVER HEARD FROM AGAIN."
The End.

ACKNOWLEDGMENTS

NOTHING BUT HAPPY MUSIC NOTES TO

Jeff Stokely!

Ben Schrank, Jessica Almon, Tiffany Liao, and Deborah Kaplan

Triona Farrell, Gideon Kendall, and Ed Dukeshire

Laura Rennert

Quinette Cook
and the Minnesota chapter of
Society of Children's Book Writers and Illustrators

Stephen Chbosky
for the encouraging push to publish

Anthony Breznican
for the push toward a graphic novel

Reid Cain
of Dr. Cain's Comics and Games
for leading us to the perfect illustrator

Rene Kissien
our researcher and translator in Germany

Hameln City Council
much more helpful and honest than their
medieval forbearers are rumored to have been

Herzog August Library
Wolfenbüttel, Germany

The Brothers Grimm, Robert Browning
and all the other legend writers
who passed this story down to us

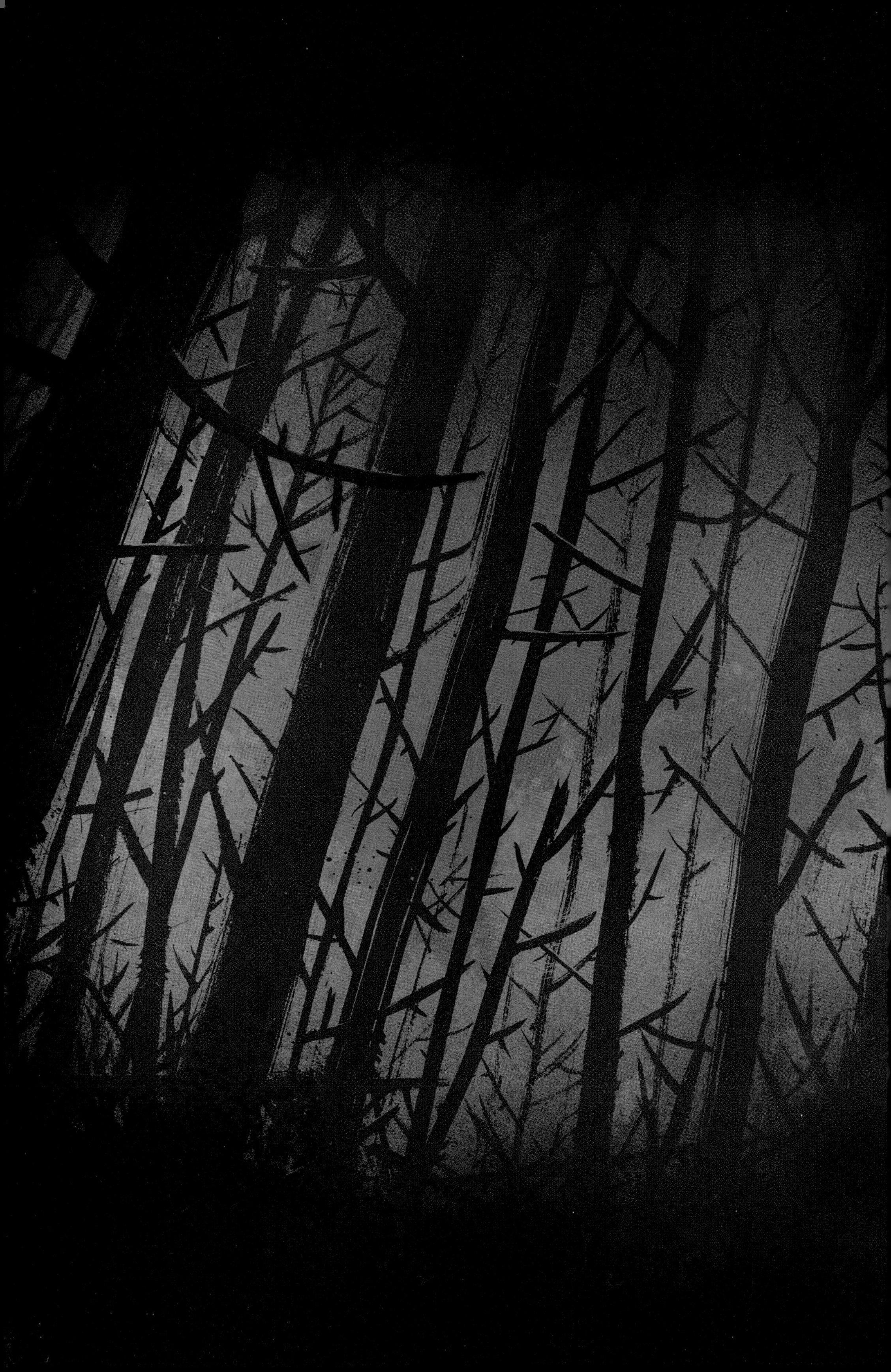

ALSO BY JAY ASHER:

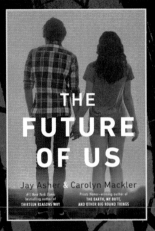

"Enough heart to make you weep."
—*The New York Times Book Review*

NOW A ORIGINAL SERIES!

"Without question a page-turner."
—*Kirkus Reviews*

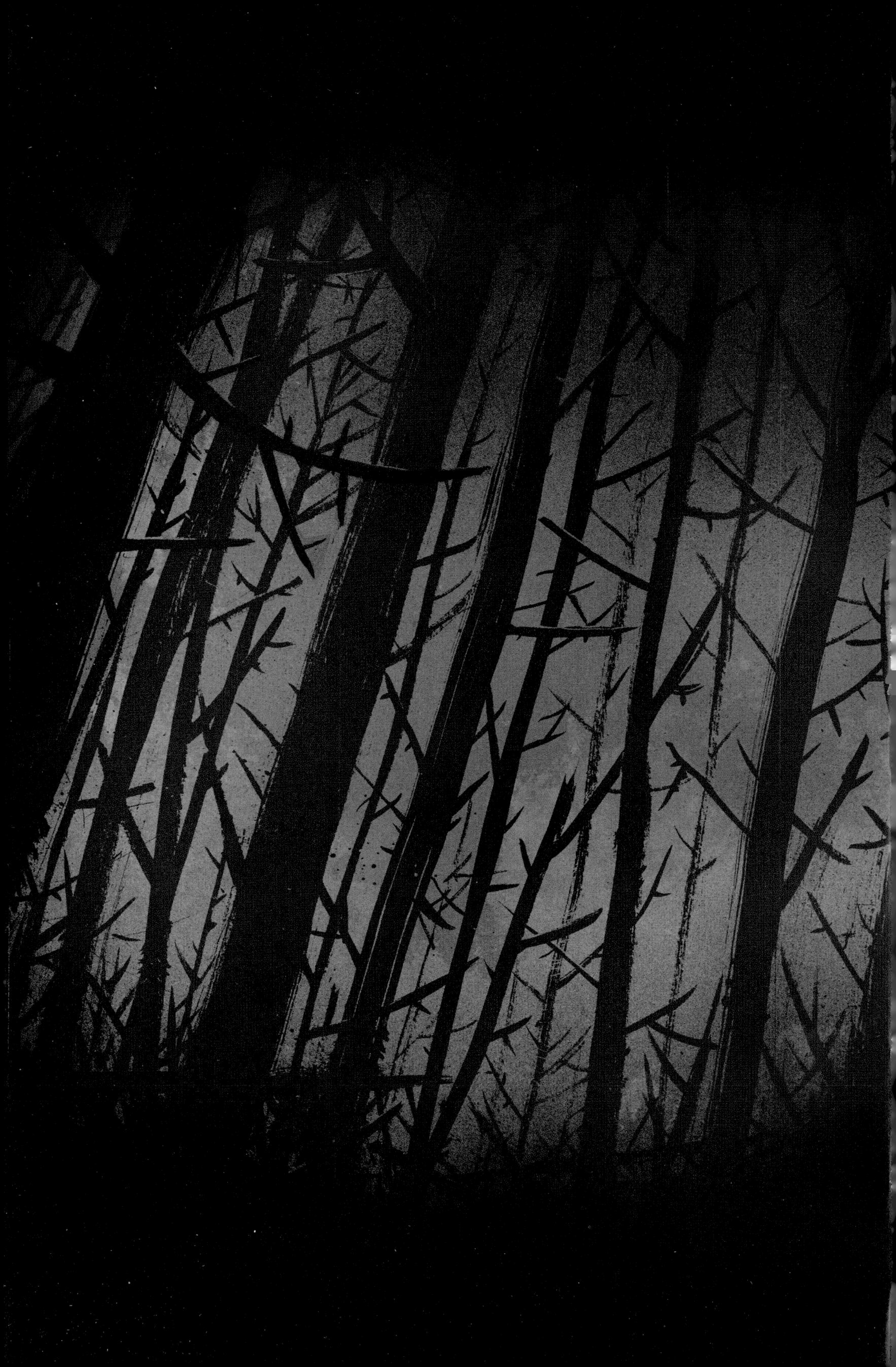